I0761899

WHERE SHADOWS WHISPER

BY

AMARA PHOENIX

By Amara Phoenix

THE SHADOWED WHISPERS DUET

Where Shadows Whisper — Book 1

Where Darkness Echoes — Book 2 (releasing 2026)

BY

AMARA PHOENIX

Book 1 in the
Shadowed Whispers Duet

Axiom Arcana Publishing

First published in 2025 by Axiom Arcana Publishing.

ISBN (ebook): 978-1-7642180-0-9
ISBN (paperback): 978-1-7642180-1-6
ISBN (hardcover): 978-1-7642180-2-3

Edited by Spineless Pages.
Cover design by B.B. Illustrations.
Interior design and formatting by Amara Phoenix.

CONTENT WARNINGS

Where Shadows Whisper is a romantic suspense novel that explores themes of danger, trauma, and healing. While darker elements are present, this novel is not intended to glorify trauma, and the focus remains on survival, choice, and the slow rebuilding of trust and connection

Where Shadows Whisper contains subject matter that may be difficult for some readers, including (without limitation) graphic violence, sexual assault, rape, coercion, emotional manipulation, and mature language. This book also contains explicit sexual content.

It is not intended for readers under the age of 18. Reader discretion is advised.

For a complete list of content warnings, please visit www.amaraphoenixauthor.com.

DEDICATION

To my younger self, who believed in magic between the pages and fell headlong into every story.

To the kid who read by torchlight and dreamed bigger than the page — the girl who kept every story she imagined tucked safely in her heart and never stopped believing in 'what if...?' moments.

This one's for you.

Chapter One

Du-dum. Du-dum. Du-dum.

The uncontrollable beat of my heart thrums wildly in my chest, suffocating in its desperate attempt to escape the tight confines of my rib cage.

Splash. Splash. Splash.

Feet slamming against wet pavement provides a steady rhythm to the deafening pulse pounding in my ears, driving my numb legs forward, step by agonising step. I barely notice the rain as it pummels down in persistent streaks, soaking through the torn rags that, only minutes ago, resembled a gorgeous, form-fitting dress, but which are now barely clinging to my shaking limbs in tattered pieces—like exquisite paper crudely torn from a once-beautifully wrapped present.

I chance a quick glance over my shoulder, peering into the engulfing darkness, anticipating shadowed figures to emerge at any moment.

I force my wobbly legs to keep moving, ignoring the relentless pounding in my head and the mounting ache in my limbs as my muscles scream at me to stop—to give in and collapse in a beaten, dejected heap on the cold, soggy ground. I push away the fear that's itching to engulf me, threatening to ice my veins and immobilise my feet. In its place, adrenaline seeps into every depleted fragment of my body, urging me to keep going.

If I don't, I know what awaits me. I wouldn't even make it through the night.

I have no choice. I have to run.

Escape.

Disappear.

A streak of muddy water trickles down my forehead and into my eye, blurring my vision. My foot catches on an uneven patch in the road, and I barely manage to regain my balance, narrowly avoiding a face-first collision with the wet pavement. My bag isn't nearly as lucky. It slips from my grasp, landing with a heavy splash in a pool of water.

Crap.

I rush forward and drag the soaked duffel back into my arms, wincing as the dark stain spreads rapidly across the rough fabric. It already feels several kilos heavier than before.

Thank you very much, Karma, my old friend. Always a blessing to know I can count on you in my most desperate time of need.

Fumbling with trembling fingers, I pull on the zipper and hurriedly scan the contents, exhaling in relief as my eyes land on the rolls of paper unceremoniously stuffed into the inner pocket. Miraculously, they appear unaffected by the bag's involuntary dive into the murky rainwater puddle.

A door slams somewhere in the distance, a sharp reminder that there's no time to waste. If I'm going to survive this seemingly endless night, I need to keep moving.

Hauling the bag over my shoulder, I force my protesting legs into motion once more. I swipe the back of my hand across my eyelid, wiping away the grimy water to ease the burning sting building in my eye. A faint metallic scent reaches my nostrils, and I glance down to find dark maroon droplets smearing across my skin, quickly diluted by the incessant raindrops falling heavily from the sky.

Blood.

I shouldn't be surprised. From the throbbing pain radiating from my forehead and the force of the blow that caused it, it's a miracle the rest of my face isn't splattered in blood as well. But there's no time to stop and examine the wound. If I'm lucky enough to escape this hellish nightmare with all my limbs intact, there will hopefully be time for all of that later.

Right now, all my energy must stay focused on keeping my body moving.

My muscles scream under the weight of the duffel bag, my breath puffing out in hard, fast pants as I drag one foot in front of the other. It'd be a lot easier to run if I could just abandon the bag, but there's no way I'm leaving without it. My entire life—my entire future—is dependent on the contents of that bag.

If I lose it, I'll have nothing.

No clothes.

No money.

No options.

The rain hammers against the pavement in a deafening symphony, barely masking the wind's angry howls as it tears through the vacant streets. I shiver as a cold gust of wind engulfs me in a tumultuous swoop, the icy blast diving into the very marrow of my frozen bones. The biting flow of frigid air is as ignorant of my shivering limbs as it is of the surrounding vegetation's valiant effort to bud its way to full bloom, ready to embrace a long-awaited summer despite this unseasonal, eleventh-hour bout of cold.

Summer.

The word drifts mournfully through my mind as another flurry of raindrops take flight in the hustling wind to slap against my frozen cheeks.

Where is this 'perfect summer' we've been promised for the past month?

The persistent rumbling of thunder roars in the distance, rolling through the sky like an ominous war drum. The brooding storm clouds create an eerie backdrop to the smothering darkness that swallows the late evening sky, suffocating any trace of moonlight. On any other night, the moon may have provided a glimmer of light and comfort, but the ominous black ceiling above makes the air both darker and gloomier than any summer night has the right to feel.

I finally reach the end of the street, where the road curves into a gradual bend. Relief nearly brings me to my knees when I spot the small, white-painted house peeking out from behind a large oak tree.

Smoke curls from the brick chimney, and a lone flame inside an ornate lantern sways gently beside the red-painted door, casting a wavering beacon of light against the pressing darkness.

I rush forward, halting when I reach the small gate. My fingers fumble with the latch, the task made all the more difficult by the relentless tremor in my numb hands.

The gate finally creaks open, and I stumble up the pebbled path, dodging water-logged patches soaking through the grass. Using what feels like the last of my strength, I climb the stone steps and collapse against the front door, my bruised knuckles rasping weakly against the weathered wood.

Five seconds pass.

Ten.

Fifteen.

I'm moments away from giving up, resigned to crumple onto the cold granite steps in a defeated heap, when the sound of a lock turning catches my ear.

The door creaks open a fraction, the narrow gap revealing an elderly woman wrapped in a violet wool dress draping her thin frame. Her grey hair is pinned in a loose bun atop her head, and shrewd but weary eyes peer out from behind large reading glasses perched slightly askew on her nose.

"My dear girl," she exclaims, opening the door wider as she takes in my drenched, tattered form. "Oh, heavens... I knew this day would come."

She reaches out with a huff, her frail arm steady as she clasps my shoulder in a surprisingly firm grip, ushering my trembling body inside as the door clicks shut behind us.

I immediately feel a soothing gust of warmth, and the familiar smell of scented candles and freshly baked bread wafts from the kitchen, filling the air with homely comfort. Under different circumstances, it would've made my mouth water. Right now, it takes all my willpower to quell the persistent urge to double over and rid my stomach of the few scraps of food I forced down earlier in the day.

Breathing heavily, I cling to my resolve, grappling with the unbridled emotions coursing through me as they threaten to consume me—to make me crumble into shattered, unsalvageable pieces as my shaking limbs rattle my bones.

"Let's get you into the living room, dear," the woman says, guiding me down a short hallway. "It's freezing out there tonight, and you've barely got any clothes left on you, silly girl."

She leads me into a small but quaint living room and ease me into a stuffy armchair in front of the brick fireplace, where a smouldering fire dances merrily, its flickering flames casting soft shadows across the faded, light-yellow wallpaper.

"Wait here, dear," she says, voice gentle. "I'll fetch you something dry to wear."

I glance up just in time to see her scurry out of the room, the shuffle of her wool slippers fading as she disappears into the hallway. Moments later, the old staircase creaks as she climbs to the second floor.

My gaze drifts back to the fire, watching as the swaying flames lick hungrily at the charred logs stacked against the sooted back plate.

For the first time tonight, I allow a fragile sense of calm to wash over me. I use the rare moment to inhale slowly, trying to steady my racing heart.

I know I'm running out of time.

If I had any sense at all, I'd already be out the door, running as far from here as possible.

But even as the thought forms, I'm utterly incapable of fighting the soothing embrace of the seductive fire.

Because the moment I leave this house, I know it's over.

The small fragments of stability I've clung to these past few years—those tiny fractions of constancy I've painstakingly assimilated—will disappear, leaving me with nothing and no one by my side. And as much as I've detested nearly every aspect of the life I've lived for the past six years, it has at least brought some resemblance of permanency into my existence. A sense of consistency that was sorely absent in the years before.

You can do this, Elaina, I chant under my breath as I gulp down another deep lungful of air. *Just hold on a little longer.*

As my heartbeat gradually drops from a skittering gallop to a twitchy canter, I take a moment to observe the antique furniture scattered around the small room. A tiny smile tugs at the corners of my lips as I spot a woven rug thrown haphazardly over the armrest of a worn, cream-coloured couch.

I've visited this house countless times in the years since my arrival in this seemingly inconspicuous neighbourhood. I'd come over as often as I could, whenever I managed to sneak out of the house unnoticed—a feat that became harder and harder as time went by. Each visit, without fail, the old, kind-hearted woman would pull out her knitting needles, her hands flying across fuzzy woollen threads as she worked on yet another intricately patterned creation.

The thought saddens me, knowing this will likely be the last time I ever lay eyes on one of her colourful designs. I'm going to miss the sight of her sitting on her porch in one of her flowery dresses, always greeting me with a bright smile as I made my way up her stone-paved path.

My sporadic visits here have been one of the few things I've truly treasured over these past few years.

Now, that will be taken from me too.

Or maybe, in the end, I'm the one to blame for everything good in my life always seeming to slip through my grasp, like threads unravelling from a fraying seam.

Maybe I'm the one to blame for everything.

As my mind veers into unwelcome territory, I sense movement in the hallway and turn to find the elderly woman shuffling back into the room with a pile of dry clothes in her arms.

"Here you go," she huffs, holding out a pair of worn but comfortable-looking sweatpants, some thick woollen socks, and an enormous sweatshirt with *Berkeley California* printed in large, capital letters across the front.

I peer into her soft, worried eyes as I reach for the clothes.

"Thank you, Iris," I whisper shakily, hoping she hears the sincerity in my words despite the tremor in my voice. Whether it quivers from the cold or from fear, I can't be certain.

"It's no trouble at all, dear," Iris responds gently, lingering on my shivering frame as she carefully inspects my ragged appearance, before drifting to what I can only assume is a pretty nasty cut on my forehead. She trails the crimson streak seeping from the wound to my right eye.

"Did you want to take a shower first?" Iris asks carefully, likely sensing my discomfort as her discerning gaze sweeps over my dishevelled state.

"No, that's okay. Just these clothes are fine," I say hurriedly, pulling my stiff facial muscles into a small but genuine smile that I hope conveys both gratitude and a silent plea for her not to ask any more questions. I can practically hear the unspoken interrogation resting on the tip of her tongue, threatening to spill out.

To her credit, she merely nods before letting out a deep sigh.

"I'll give you some privacy to change then, dear," she declares, heading for the hallway. "How about I make us both a nice cup of tea, and then I can whip us up a meal? I have some leftover meatloaf in the fridge that I was going to save for tomorrow, but now I've suddenly got a hankering for it."

"Iris," I call softly. She turns to me, her face filled with compassion and unspoken questions. "I—I can't stay."

"Nonsense," Iris huffs, waving my words away with a flick of her wrinkly hand. "You're not going anywhere tonight, young lady."

"I have to," I say more forcefully, willing a trace of urgency into my voice. I don't have the time or the strength to explain, and I'm praying Iris will understand—or at least let it go without forcing me to elaborate.

"I'm not letting you run off back to that house," Iris clips in a much harsher tone than I've ever heard her use. "There's absolutely no way I'm letting you slink back into that prison, tail between your legs, only for people like... people like *them* to take advantage of you! Not after—"

Her hands swipe through the air, motioning toward my tattered frame. "Well, one only has to take one look at you to know what kind of plans they had in mind for you tonight." Her voice has turned glacial, and there's a hint of ferocity in her expression I've never seen before. "You're not going anywhere, and that's final. And don't you dare try to change my mind."

Her arms fold against her frail hips with unwavering resolve.

I sigh wearily. "Iris, I'm not going back there, I promise. But I can't stay." My eyes plead with her to understand.

"And why in the world not?" she snaps, frustration evident in her rising pitch, though the worry swirling in her gentle gaze remains.

I look down at my shaking hands clasped tightly in my lap, unable to meet the weight of her watchful scrutiny. Fumbling for words, my feeble explanation is cut off by the roar of an engine thundering in the distance. The raucous sound instantly causes my heart rate to double. Not five seconds later, a car screeches past Iris's house, its headlights flashing sharp streaks of light across the paintings framing the living room walls.

It's all I need to snap out of my temporary paralysis.

"I—I don't have time to explain," I rush out, swiftly getting to my feet and nearly tumbling over from the numbness in my legs.

I catch myself on the armrest of the puffy chair, regaining my balance before yanking at the soaked fragments of fabric still clinging to my body. "I—I can't explain. I have to get out of here. I have to get away from him, Iris. From them. I just—I can't go back, and I can't stay here. They'll come for me, and I won't ever be able to escape again, a-a-and—t-they'll punish me, Iris. They'll kill me. I—I..."

My panicked words catch in my throat as the burn of tears spills down my cheeks. A tidal wave of terror rises inside me, threatening to pull me under, and I yank harder at the ruined strands of silk draped across my chest, the constricting fabric suddenly feeling too tight around my fragile limbs.

"*Shhh*, it's okay, my dear." Iris's murmur is soft and soothing. "Just breathe. We'll take this one step at a time. Now, let's get you out of those sodden rags. It won't do you any good if you end up suffering from pneumonia on top of everything else."

I nod, forcing myself to suck in a deep lungful of air.

Iris is right. I can't afford to fall apart right now.

I slowly regain a modicum of control, even as my heart rate pitter-patters in sharp bursts inside my chest. Using the small ounce of strength it gives me, I pull the torn dress above my head, focusing on the simple physical task as I ignore the splinters of pain ricocheting through my bruised body.

As the ragged material falls to the floor in a wet heap, I glance up—and instantly wish I'd left more than my soaked underwear on.

Iris's eyes widen in horror as they take in the cuts and bruises mottling my thin frame, trailing along my chest and arms, across my hollow abdomen and down my thighs.

Unable to withstand the raw sadness gathering in the weathered lines of her face, I glance down to the dark wooden floorboards and blindly grab for the jumper, quickly pulling it over my head and past my stomach to hide my bruised ribs.

I feign unawareness as I ask in a forced, calm tone, "Iris, do you still have your daughter's old costumes? From back when she did theatre?"

Iris's astute eyes snap to mine, dark irises swirling with surprise and curiosity. "I do. I keep it all upstairs in her room," she answers hesitantly. "Why?"

Shrugging on the sweatpants, I silently thank the creator of this cold and unforgiving world for having the foresight to make Iris the type of person who never throws anything away.

"Could you bring me one of the wigs she used to wear for her plays? Any wig will do, but if you have one that looks nothing like my own hair, even better."

A moment of silence follows my request. Iris's urge to question me is palpable, but as if sensing my reluctance to reveal more than I already have, she merely nods, turns around, and heads back into the hallway.

I pull on the rugged woollen socks Iris brought me with stiff movements, then toss the ruined remains of the silk dress into a plastic bag I find resting on top of a wooden bowl filled to the brim with knitting gear.

Walking over to the fireplace, I crouch down on my knees to soak up the last remnants of heat from the withering flames. I know I only have minutes before I'll have to head back into the ruthless storm, and I need every ounce of warmth my exhausted body can cling to.

As the gentle heat licks its way across my skin, I finally feel my muscles relaxing as the soothing warmth seeps into my bones.

I don't know how long I sit there for—I think I might even drift off for a minute—but it feels like mere seconds later when my ears catch the sound of Iris's feet shuffling down the stairs. I expect her to come straight back into the living room until I hear a range of clanks from the small kitchen at the opposite end of the hallway.

Another minute goes by, quiet and peaceful but for the roar of the raging storm outside. Even as my muscles gradually loosen and the coldness seeps from my stiff limbs, anxiousness slowly creeps in to take its place.

I'm running out of time with every second that ticks by.

I'm convincing myself to get up when Iris appears in the doorway, carrying a wig in one hand and a large carry-bag in the other.

She hands me the tuft of hair, and I bring it closer to the wavering firelight to examine it.

It falls to about shoulder length, with a thick, blunt fringe that should do well to cover the gaping wound on my forehead. The synthetic strands are coloured a glossy black, the complete opposite of my own, long, light blonde tresses.

Perfect.

"I packed some clothes for you that Sophie left behind when she moved out. It should all fit you nicely, I'd say." Iris hands over the carry-bag. "There's a bottle of water in there for you, and some sandwiches. It's nothing fancy, mind you, but it should give you some sustenance for the road."

Her worried eyes peer intently into mine, and a wave of fondness for this caring, kind-hearted woman washes over me. I refuse to believe this might be the last time I see her, even as I know, deep down, that it probably is.

I swallow down the lump lodged in my throat. "I don't know how to thank you, Iris," I croak, blinking back the tears threatening to break free. "You've been... Oh, Iris, you've been so kind to me. All these years, you've always been a welcome face in a bleak crowd. I truly don't know what I would've done without you."

"Oh, nonsense, dear." Iris brushes away my words, but I see the emotion stirring behind her wide-rimmed glasses all the same. "I'm the lucky one, to have had such a lovely young lady stopping by to keep an old woman company."

She follows me to the front door, where my duffel bag sits waiting. A small pool of water has gathered around it, seeping into the old floorboards.

"Will you be safe getting back to the house to get your car?" Iris asks as she clutches the door handle, ignoring the way the door rattles as the wind throws itself against it with gusto.

"I won't be taking my car," I answer absentmindedly, pulling my wet, tangled hair into a tight bun on top of my head before slipping on the wig. I ruffle the thick fringe until it falls just above my lashes, concealing as much of my face as possible.

"What on earth do you mean, girl?"

Not for the first time this evening, Iris's sharp tone crackles through the small house. "It's pouring out there! How are you supposed to get anywhere in weather like this, if not in a car?"

She keeps the front door firmly shut, her hand resting lightly on the brass handle as she waits for my response.

I sigh, wondering once again how much to tell her. One part of me—the frantic, desperate part—wants to push her aside, tear the door open, and hurl myself into the stormy night, running as far away from this life as I possibly can. But as I look into Iris's intelligent eyes, I know I owe her an explanation, fractured and disjointed as it may be.

After all, I risked a lot by coming here tonight, both for her and for me, and Iris helped me without reservations.

I know it probably wasn't wise to delay my escape by coming here.

I just couldn't stand leaving without saying goodbye.

"I'll run to the bus station," I finally say, ignoring the twitch of pain in my legs at the very thought of straining them again so soon. "It's only thirty minutes from here at a fast run. From there, I'll board a bus out of town."

"Don't be senseless," Iris scoffs as she glares at me with disbelief. "Look at the state of you. You're in no shape to walk that far, let alone run, silly girl."

She gestures to my forehead, which must be covered in blood by now, before lowering her scowl to my shoeless feet. I battle the trembling in my thighs and calves, willing my exhaustion to remain hidden. If she sees how depleted my body truly is, she'll never let me leave.

I sigh and look her straight in the eye, hoping she can read the sincerity on my weary face.

"I don't have a choice, Iris. I can't go back to the house. Not now, not ever. I won't be able to get away again. This—this is the only chance I've got."

Silence stretches between us as my words settle in the air. I can tell Iris's mind is working fast, likely running through all the ways she thinks I might be able to reach my car without Viktor's men catching me.

It won't make a difference, though. Even if I wanted to risk it, I already know there's no possible way I'll be able to sneak past the security cameras lining the front entryway, slip past Viktor's guards to collect the car keys from the table next to his study, creep back across the vast foyer to key in the code to the enormous garage, and drive my cherry-red Mazda MX-5 out of the driveway unnoticed.

Even on the best of days, that would be nothing short of an impossible feat.

Tonight? There isn't even a sliver of hope in the deepest, darkest corners of hell.

I'm snapped out of my futile mental escape plan as Iris lets out a small gasp, clasping my arm tightly in her wrinkled hands. Her face lights up with inspiration, her lips curving into a triumphant grin as she presses a hand to her forehead.

"But, of course," she exclaims, spinning around and tugging me back down the hallway. "I'm such an old fool, goodness me. I should've thought of it earlier."

Confused, I grab my duffel and follow after her to the back of the house. I'm mostly humouring her as an excuse to delay my imminent departure into the frigid night, but a twitch of curiosity still stirs within me.

Iris continues at a fast pace, only stopping when she reaches a narrow door at the other end of the corridor. Opening it, she leads us into a small laundry room. An old washing machine sits idly in the corner, with boxes of laundry powder and dryer sheets stacked on a small shelf above it.

I expect Iris to usher me out the back door leading into the backyard, but she pulls me past rows of damp clothes hanging neatly on foldable racks, her thin legs nearly tripping over a laundry basket partially buried beneath a pile of bed sheets.

She huffs in annoyance, shuffling forward as she shoves the basket aside with her foot. She halts when she reaches a large ironing board leaning against the back wall, cluttered with garment bags and other items hanging from rusty nails hammered into the old wood panel.

Her frail arms shake as she reaches for the ironing board, carefully shifting it aside. It's only then that I realise the wall behind it isn't a wall at all, but yet another door.

"You'll have to excuse the mess," Iris mutters, panting slightly from exertion. "I barely use this entrance anymore, so things have a tendency to pile up in front of it. Ah, here we go."

She clasps the rounded door handle, but as she twists, the door refuses to budge.

"Darn this old thing," Iris sighs exasperatedly. "It... always... tends... to... stick!"

With each muttered word, she pushes against the frame, but it doesn't shift an inch.

I step forward and gently place my hand over hers. "Please, Iris. Let me."

She steps aside, and I brace myself before throwing my weight against the door.

It takes several shoves, but with a final groan of wood against wood, it flies open.

At first, I'm greeting by nothing but dense darkness. I take a cautious step inside, halting when a strange scent reaches my nostrils—a not unpleasant mixture of dust, soil, and grass, blended with a faint whiff of gasoline.

Iris rustles behind me. A moment later, a lone light bulb flickers to life, illuminating the space in a dull, amber glow.

Rows of shelves line the walls, stacked from floor to ceiling with old cardboard boxes filled with rusty tools. A large lawn mower covered in limp, lifeless grass lingers in the corner, explaining the residual scent of decomposing vegetation.

But my attention is immediately drawn to the dark green Volkswagen Beetle parked idly in the middle of the room.

I take a few cautious steps closer, peering inside the dust-covered windows, careful not to trip over a pile of timber logs haphazardly stacked atop the dusty cement floor.

The car is clearly an older model, with round, sweeping curves and clean lines. Likely an early 2000s model, judging by the unassuming steering wheel and the vintage-styled centre console, complete with a cassette slot and a kick-ass retro radio system.

I give the exterior another quick sweep, spotting a few traces of rust along the wheelbase. It definitely needs a good clean, but otherwise, it's in decent condition.

"Iris, I had no idea you were hiding this old beauty in here," I murmur, running my fingers along the smooth, green bonnet. Despite the layer of dust, the paint beneath is glossy and vibrant, with barely a scratch in the mirror-like surface.

"It was George's," Iris says tenderly, a smile tugging at her lips. "He was very fond of it. Loved taking her out for a spin on warm summer days. He would always try to drag me along with him, always pushing for me to learn how to drive. '*My greatest failure in life will be that I never taught my wife how to drive a car*,' he often used to say."

She chuckles, though her face betrays a lingering sadness, as it always does whenever she speaks of her late husband.

"The poor old girl has barely seen the road these past eight years—not since George passed away. But my grandson comes over now and again to tinker with it, making sure she stays in good condition."

Hope rises in my chest as I tentatively ask, "So, it runs?"

"Oh, I should think so," Iris replies as she picks up a small, metallic box with a classic car depicted on the lid from a rickety old table in the corner.

Popping off the rusty clasp, she opens the lid to reveal a set of old car keys attached to a kitschy Volkswagen key chain. "Why don't you jump in and give the engine a crank?" she chirps, holding the keys out to me.

Despite my momentary burst of excitement, reality washes over me as familiar doubt creeps back in.

"Iris," I say cautiously, my short-lived hope quickly fading. "If you don't know how to drive, how do you plan on getting the car out of here unnoticed?"

"You will be driving, of course."

I frown. "But... how will you get the car back here?"

"Oh, I won't need it back, dear," Iris says matter-of-factly. "It's yours."

My jaw drops.

The howling wind crashes violently against the exterior walls, and the persistent drum of rain hammering against the tin roof is the only sound to break the deafening stillness engulfing us as I'm rendered speechless.

Iris just smiles at me, the glint in her eye telling me she's enjoying my open-mouthed disbelief.

"Iris," I exclaim hoarsely. "You can't just—just... Cheese on a cracker, Iris, you can't just *give me* your car!"

"Why not?" Iris replies calmly, as if only mildly interested in my response.

"Because—because..." My mind scrambles, unable to find the right words. "Iris—you're offering me a car. A *car*!"

I pace back and forth, arms flailing as I attempt to gather my jumbled thoughts.

"People don't just offer their car to someone on a whim, Iris. And not just any car. You're offering to give me your late husband's car. *George's* car, Iris. I can't take *George's* car! I just can't. It's probably really valuable, a-a-and... and it clearly means a lot to you, a-and... I just can't!"

Iris watches me with a composed smile, patiently waiting for a pause in my frenzied rambling.

"You're taking the car, and that's final." Iris's tone is kind but firm. "She's been sitting in here for nearly a decade, and I can count on one hand the number of times this girl has seen daylight in that time. I have no use for it, and I never will. I have no need for whatever money it might fetch should I sell it, and to be honest, I wouldn't feel right about selling it anyway. If I did, I would have done it years ago."

Catching my parted lips, she raises her palm, leaving no room to interrupt. "The car won't do anyone any good sitting in this old garage until I take my dying breath. All it does is make me sad that something once so beloved by my dear George is all but fading away with time, covered in dust and hidden amongst old paint tins and broken tools. She deserves a better fate than that, don't you think?"

Iris stretches out her hand once more, the key rattling noisily as she dangles it in the air.

"Knowing that giving this car to you may help you get a second chance in life, help you start fresh... Now, I can't think of a better reason for her to finally stretch her legs again. Nothing would bring me more joy than seeing my George's precious old girl become part of your new chapter, my dear. So, if not for yourself, then please—take her for me.“

Iris finishes her well-aimed speech with a firm nod, and I'm left speechless for the second time in as many minutes. I open my mouth hesitantly, but the stern, resolute glare she levels me with makes me clamp it shut.

Jangling the keys, she nods her head toward the Beetle.

I stare at her for several long seconds, my mind warring with itself. Iris's face shows nothing but kindness, sincerity, and firm determination.

Sensing I need one final push, she softens her expression and speaks in a low, gentle voice.

"My George always said this car brings good luck to its owner. It always did for us, and she never led us astray. I have a feeling you could do with a bit of luck for once, my dear. Take her."

I lower my head, gaze fixed on my sock-covered feet as a small lump forms in my throat

I know she's right. Deep down, I know I don't stand a chance if I leave this place on foot.

With a resigned sigh and a shake of my head, I grab the keys and walk around to the driver's side, carefully stepping over loose screws and dilapidated cardboard boxes filled with old trinkets. Pulling on the chrome handle, I find the door already unlocked.

The inside smells of leather and dust, and despite the stale air, the interior isn't in bad shape.

Opening the door fully, I sink onto the beige leather seat. It feels comfortable and lived in, yet I can tell the material has been well cared for, with minimal cracks and creases for its age.

I may have been driving around in a sleek, brand-new sports car for the past two years, and I'm not going to pretend I didn't enjoy cruising around in the zippy little coupe whenever I was permitted to leave the house, but there's something comforting about this charming, understated beauty.

She's got personality. Character.

I already love her.

I fumble around with the key for a moment before finally locating the keyhole. Taking a deep breath, I mutter a small prayer to the universe as I turn the ignition.

The car exudes a series of alarming splutters, making my heart lodge in my throat. For a few, terrifying seconds, I'm convinced it won't start. But then, with a loud, gurgling cough and a final, choked grunt, the engine roars to life.

Relief floods through my body, and I can't contain my jubilant excitement as I let out a loud whoop. I beam over at Iris, who's wearing a matching grin as she gives me a thumbs-up.

I press down on the accelerator, keeping the rhythmic hum of the engine steady to charge the battery. The motor revs happily, transitioning into a satisfied thrum whenever I ease off the throttle.

Once I'm confident she won't die on me, I pull the handbrake and climb out of the car.

By the time I reach Iris's side, she's already placed the carry-bag in the passenger seat. She slams the door shut with one hand, clutching a pair of black sneakers in the other.

"Put these on before you go off and get your feet wet again. We can't have you running around barefoot now, can we? You're already brewing a nasty cold, I reckon, and I see no reason to add hypothermia to your growing list of worries."

I gratefully accept the shoes and slide them on. They're slightly too large for my small feet, but in this moment, I'd be grateful for a pair of clown shoes if it meant keeping my feet warm and dry.

With my new sneakers firmly in place, I walk to the front of the car and chuck the waterlogged duffel into the front boot, moving it around the small compartment to buy myself time to school my expression.

As close as I was to high-tailing it out of this house mere minutes ago, I don't feel ready to say goodbye yet.

A few silent seconds pass until I know I can't afford to delay any longer. Straightening, I shut the bonnet as I fight to get a handle on my emotions.

"Iris, I—I..." My voice breaks, but Iris speaks before I can clear the lump from my throat.

"I know, dear," she says softly as she grabs my hand. Her wrinkled fingers brush a few strands of silky, ink-black hair behind my ear as I keep my chin tilted toward the grimy concrete floor, unwilling to show the unshed tears pooling in my eyes.

"You take care of yourself now, you hear?" Iris orders, her voice gentle as her frail arms wrap around me in a surprisingly tight hug. A lone tear escapes, trailing down my cheek as I hug her back.

"Thank you, Iris," I whisper. "For everything."

"Oh, you're welcome, my dear girl," Iris responds gruffly, giving me a final squeeze before pulling away. I catch a shimmer of wetness glazing her pupils as she nods to the Beetle.

"Now, off you go. There's no time to waste. The sooner we get you on the road, the better."

I nod stiffly, and before I can change my mind, I scuttle around the car and slide into the driver's seat.

As I adjust the mirrors, a low rumble carries through the air, the roar of thunder still wreaking havoc outside. I glance in the rear-view mirror to find the garage door slowly opening, revealing a torrent of water crashing down from the sky. My hands tremble violently as I clasp the gear stick and shift the car into reverse.

Gently lifting the clutch, the car creeps backwards. My heart flutters wildly as a waterfall of rain rattles noisily against the steel roof, drowning out all other sounds.

I tenderly make my way down the driveway, struggling to make out the road through the torrential downpour obscuring everything around me. When the rear tyres slide across the curb marking the end of the driveway, I delicately ease onto the road, pulling on the steering wheel to straighten the car as I glance up at the house one last time.

I can just make out the faint outline of Iris as she lingers in the garage doorway, watching me pull away. Her hand lifts in a small wave, and I lift my own in return, though I doubt she can see it through the persistent rain hammering against the windows.

"Goodbye, Iris," I whisper quietly, letting my hand fall.

Closing my eyes, I allow one silent, frozen moment in time to steady my racing heart. When my eyes reopen, my heart steels with renewed determination.

It's now or never, Elaina.

I shift the car into gear, lift my foot off the clutch, and take off into the stormy night.

Chapter Two

"That will be one thousand babki for night, little doll," the foul-smelling man in front of me wheezes, his stare roaming shamelessly over my body as he scratches at his patchy, week-old stubble.

I pretend to ignore his blatant stare, keeping my face carefully blank as I take in his beady eyes and mousy brown hair hanging in greasy clumps across his forehead. It takes everything in me not to gag from the overwhelming scent of dried sweat and whisky wafting off him, the revolting stench having assaulted my nostrils the moment I walked through the door.

I glance down at his wrinkled shirt, where a badge displaying the name Sergei sits crookedly across his chest, the letters so faded they're barely readable. My eyes trail further down his shirt, where a hairy belly protrudes from beneath the once-white fabric. His too-tight brown corduroy pants leave the excess flesh no choice but to spill over his beltline, on unsolicited display.

I would feel bad about my less-than-flattering assessment of this man if it weren't for the fact that his focus has been glued to my chest ever since I walked into this run-down motel. I have no idea what's caught his eager interest as I'm still wearing Iris's daughter's old sweatshirt, which does a decent job of swallowing my curves.

That doesn't seem to deter dear old Sergei, though. The man is too busy willing his eyes to develop X-ray vision.

I suppose I should be grateful. As long as he's busy ogling my breasts, he's less likely to pay close attention to my face—which, after a quick glance in the Beetle's rear-view mirror before I came in here, I already know is a disaster.

"Uhm, right," I mumble, rummaging through my bag until I fish out a crinkled thousand-ruble note from the side pocket. I place it on the counter and tentatively slide it toward Sergei, avoiding both the grease-slicked surface and his clammy palm as I hand it over.

It takes him a few seconds to notice the crumpled bill before he finally snatches it up with stubby, unkempt fingers. I barely stop myself from flinching when I spot several days' worth of grime and dirt lodged beneath his chipped fingernails.

"You sure you only want one night, little doll?" he breathes huskily, reaching down to adjust the front of his food-stained pants, where an undeniable bulge is starting to form. "I give you good discount if you stay more couple nights, yes?"

It's all I can do not to outwardly retch and bolt for the door.

It took roughly three seconds after walking into this shabby lobby to realise this place is far from any high-class establishment. The purple, stain-splattered fabric covering the lumpy chairs scattered around the room is full of tears, and the small windows lining the bleak, white walls are covered in so much dirt and grease that the dim, early morning light barely penetrates through the thick glass.

Behind the reception desk, a row of wobbly shelves holds everything from overflowing paper folders to a basket containing a set of broken table tennis paddles and a deflated soccer ball. In the corner of my eye, I spot at least four dead cockroaches scattered along the smudged skirtings.

It looks like the place hasn't been properly cleaned in months.

What the hell am I doing here again?

I bottle up my disgust, ignoring the hundred-and-one voices in my head screaming at me to get the hell out of this shithole. Sadly, this is all I can afford right now.

It's the only reasonably priced motel I've driven past in over two hundred kilometres, and after driving through the entire night, I'm minutes away from keeling over from pure exhaustion.

I silently remind myself that I only need to catch a few, short hours of sleep before I can get back on the road. The most important thing is to not leave a trail, and the best way to accomplish that is to stay in godforsaken places like this.

"Uhm, no, that's okay," I say cautiously, stealing a brief glance at Sergei's pudgy cheeks. "I'm just passing through. Thanks, though."

I stare pointedly at the money clasped in his meaty hand, which he has yet to do anything with. He's too busy staring intently at me, a hungry glint in his lewd gaze.

"Eh, well... That is real shame, *da*?" he finally grumbles, his protruding eyes raking over my body from head to toe, once again halting on my covered cleavage.

When several seconds pass without him making another move, I surreptitiously clear my throat.

"So..." I drag out the word, waiting until his hazy stare meets mine before continuing. "Did you have that room? If not, I should probably get back on the road, see if I can't find another place nearby..." I let the words trail off, hoping the not-so-subtle hint's enough to nudge him into action.

To my relief, he finally seems to snap out of his lustful trance.

"*Da*," he grunts, then turns to pick up an old, leather-bound logbook from the shelf behind him.

"I need details," he mutters as he flicks through the yellowed pages, locating a half-empty section somewhere near the middle of the book, where a long list of names has been scribbled in a choppy, barely legible scrawl. "Name, contact number, and ID."

My heart rate picks up speed as my mind rapidly flicks through my options.

I could show him the brand-new passport and driver's licence currently hidden in the side pocket of my bag, still tucked away inside the brown envelope I procured around eight months ago under the guise of going to the gynaecologist. It was the only excuse I could think of that would buy me more than five minutes alone, without Viktor's goons incessantly checking on me.

I still remember the way my heart nearly beat out of my rib cage as I snuck out the back door of the hospital and jumped into a cab, rushing across town to a less-than-flattering suburb on the outskirts of the city to collect my new identity documents from a dilapidated, unassuming office building.

If Viktor had gotten a whiff of my plans that day, he would've never let me out of his sight again. He barely did as it was, despite his arrogant belief that I'd never be reckless enough to attempt to run from him.

In his world, I'd be a fool not to have learnt my lesson the first time I tried.

Maybe I am. But there's no looking back now.

The most inconspicuous thing to do would be to hand the documents over to Sergei as if I have nothing to hide. The biggest problem with that plan is that I still have long, light blonde hair in the passport photo. Even a simple man like Sergei would have to be excessively daft not to question the difference between that photo and the sharp black bob currently framing my bruised face.

That said, he would also have to be particularly dim-witted not to question a person who refuses to hand over ID when checking into an establishment—even one as shady as this.

I'm already struggling to hide the traces of dried blood running down my forehead, and I'd rather not draw any more notice than I already have. Standing out means there's an even greater chance my presence here could be traced.

But the last thing I need is for dear old Sergei to give Viktor's men the new name listed in my passport if they find out I stayed here.

As much as I hate to give Sergei a perfectly good reason to jot an asterisk next to my name in his logbook, it's better if all he has to go by is a fake name I only intend to use this once.

It's okay, Elaina. You were expecting this. You know what to do.

I brace myself, making sure my voice is even and firm. "The name's Sara Smith. No contact number, and no ID, I'm afraid. I was *terribly* unlucky, you see. Had someone steal my purse on the train the other day."

Sergei's already shaking his head. "*Nyet*, little doll." A trace of suspicion narrows his eyes. "Protocols, *da*? Cannot risk motel for pretty little thing. Even one who look like you."

"Oh, of course, I completely understand," I say at once, coating my words in as much candour as I can muster as I surreptitiously slide another two-hundred ruble note across the desk.

Sergei glances down at it, a glint of interest betraying his hesitation. I can practically see the tiny wheels churning inside his head.

"It's just... I'm awfully tired, and I would just *hate* to spend the night sleeping in my car somewhere on the side of the road, all because of a ghastly bout of terrible luck caused by a good-for-nothing thief. I know it's a lot to ask, but do you think there's any way at all we might be able to get around those pesky little protocols?"

I blink innocently, holding my breath as I peer at Sergei through fluttering lashes.

Sergei studies the note again. When he looks back up at me, his expression is conflicted. I force myself to meet his assessing scowl, ignoring the overwhelming urge to look away.

He glances at the note one more time.

After what feels like an eternity, he finally snatches it up and stuffs it into his back pocket.

"Sara Smith, *da*?" he grumbles, closing the logbook without noting anything down. I guess this will be one of those overnight stays the tax office won't find out about.

Suits me just fine.

"Yes. Sara Smith," I reply confidently.

With a small shake of his head, Sergei turns to grab a key from an old cork board hanging on the wall behind him. Bizarrely, each key is attached to a matching cork ball dangling from rusted key chains.

"What's with the maritime theme?" I ask, aiming to divert Sergei from stewing too long on my less-than-convincing story. When his eyebrows bunch together in confusion, I nod toward the row of keys.

"Ah. I buy from old boat accessory warehouse that close doors years ago. Got many balls for very cheap. Like dirt price, *da?*" Sergei shrugs as he puts the logbook back on the shelf.

"Right." I struggle to think of a follow-up comment, but luckily, the conversation ends there as Sergei walks around the counter and shuffles his large frame across the lobby floor.

"Take stuff and follow."

I reach for my two bags as Sergei swipes a card across an ancient scanner hanging low on the wall next to a scratched-up metal door. It opens with a loud squeak, and I follow him into a large courtyard enclosed by a tall, dilapidated fence.

I briefly think back to the road sign I spotted as I drove past this place. '*Comfort Inn—your rustic roadside getaway*'. Even if the grimy reception area and dirt-cheap nightly rates didn't already give it away, it's becoming clearer by the minute that I've definitely not stumbled upon some quaint, hidden gem. Not by any stretch of the imagination.

The door we just walked through is located at the south end of a long, L-shaped, two-storey brick building. One glance at the faded orange bricks tells me the place is at least a few decades old.

The lower level is sparsely decorated, with plain green doors lining the length of the structure. There's barely a spot where the olive-coloured paint isn't peeling off the metal, giving each entrance an unwelcoming, eerie feel.

The doors are marked with plain brass numbers, separating each guest room from the next. Unflattering metal stairs situated on both ends of the building lead to a rickety second-storey balustrade, painted a rusty red.

As for the courtyard, it's bleak and uninviting, with tufts of weed-riddled grass scattered across a patchy lawn riddled with dirt and gravel. Two derelict wooden tables with splintered benches loosely attached to the frame stand atop two of the more prominent patches of grass—a haphazard attempt at providing guests with an outdoor seating area.

I can't imagine anyone voluntarily sitting out here. The desolate feel of the place sends a chill down my spine.

"This way," Sergei grunts as he lumbers over to the metal stairs leading to the upper floor.

Wheezing from the effort of climbing the short steps, he leads me along the row of doors before halting in front of a bronze-coloured *17* hanging crookedly from a nail on the green-painted surface. The dull shimmer of the number reflects the dim light creeping across the horizon.

I watch as Sergei sticks the old key into the lock and twists, grunting when it doesn't budge. Leaning his considerable weight against the door, he rattles the handle vigorously up and down. He's seemingly unaware, or unbothered, that his fervent efforts has caused his t-shirt to creep up his stomach, exposing even more of his fleshy pudge. Every inch of skin is covered in sweaty streaks of curly, dark hair.

After a few seconds of struggle, he finally wrestles the lock into submission, and the door flies open with a rusty squeak.

Sergei wheezes loudly as he braces himself against the door frame. He sounds on the verge of collapse as he wipes away the sweat beading across his protruding forehead.

I step inside the room, mostly to escape his foul breath.

My attention immediately falls to the large metal bed frame taking up most of the left wall, decorated in a faded frill of pink-and-yellow floral-patterned bed sheets. The worn covers stand in stark contrast to the flimsy red curtains hanging limply from plastic rods, offering minimal shade from the rising sun. A deep-orange, lint-covered carpet stretches across the floor, leading to a half-closed door that's barely hanging onto its hinges.

I assume this means I have a private bathroom, at least.

Thank God for small mercies.

Along the right-hand wall, I spot an antique dining chair and a large tallboy in mismatching shades of brown, next to an old entertainment unit that looks barely strong enough to hold the ancient-looking TV resting on top. The thing must be at least two decades old.

The entire room smells of dust mites, stale air, and an overpowering waft of rose-scented air freshener.

But it's a place to sleep, and right now, having somewhere to rest my exhausted body for a few hours is all I care about.

"Thanks, this is—uhm... this is great," I mumble half-heartedly. Sergei grunts unintelligibly before spinning around, trudging back down the stairs.

"Charming," I mutter to myself as I drop my bags on the floor and walk across the room to lock the door. I don't know whether to feel better or worse when I spot the rusty hasp-and-staple lock above the handle, a gigantic padlock dangling loosely from the staple.

It probably isn't a great sign that this motel provides padlocks as a standard feature in its rooms, even if the added security is welcome right now.

My brain is quick to remind me that a measly padlock wouldn't stop Victor's men if they found me here.

I sigh, pushing the unwanted thoughts to the back of my mind.

I'm here, I'm free—*for now*—and more than anything, I'm desperate for a shower and a nap. Desperate enough to shove images of locks, unwelcome intruders, and lewd motel owners from my mind as I begin to undress, folding the clothes Iris gave me into a neat pile on top of the spindly chair.

I step barefoot across the carpet, immediately regretting the decision when several months' worth of grime and dust particles grate against my bare soles. I guess they're about as dedicated to vacuuming guest rooms here as they are to sweeping away dead cockroaches in the reception area.

Tiptoeing across the floor, I open the door to the bathroom, halting when I catch my reflection in the small mirror above the vanity.

My breath hitches, caught in a vacuum of dread as I stare at myself in horrified dismay.

Large bruises scatter the entire left side of my torso, trailing up to my shoulder and down my upper arm. A small cut across my collarbone has left a dried trickle of blood running down my chest, stopping just above the dip of my right breast, where the skin is slowly turning a patchy shade of yellow-grey. It matches the bruises blooming around my left breast.

My eyes drift downward, landing on the large purple welts spreading across both thighs. Luckily, the bottom part of my left leg seems to have escaped relatively unscathed, with only a few minor cuts and bruises scattered across the pale flesh.

That's about the only part of me not covered in shades of blue, yellow, or purple.

Lifting my gaze to my face, I find haunted, hazel eyes staring back at me. The usually vibrant mix of blue, amber, and golden brown I inherited from my parents looks washed out and lifeless.

Come to think of it, there's barely anything left in my reflection that reminds me of my parents anymore. The rounded curves I inherited from my voluptuous Spanish mother are all but gone, replaced by gaunt angles and hollow dips. The wavy, honey-coloured hair I inherited from my Swedish father has long since been replaced by bottle-bleached, pin-straight strands.

As much as I've always despised the platinum blonde look, at least it somewhat resembled my natural hair. I barely recognise myself with this short, dark hairdo. The sleek, elegant wig looks completely at odds with my otherwise dishevelled appearance, and the way the silky black strands fall across my forehead feels foreign and unnatural.

I pull off the wig and undo the hair tie, letting my matted hair cascade down my aching back in tangled knots.

The deep cut slicing across my forehead stands out like a bloodstained warning label. The wig did a decent job of covering the unsightly gash, but without the benefit of the chunky fringe, the torn skin is clearly visible and impossible to hide.

I let my hand trail along my battered ribs, rounding the tender curve of my bruised breast before clasping the small, key-shaped pendant hanging from a delicate silver chain around my neck.

Even with the overwhelming stabs of pain ricocheting through my body with each small movement, the sight of the familiar necklace brings me a small sense of comfort.

It's the only token I have left from a life that once felt safe and happy. A life that seems impossibly distant now, like it belonged to someone else entirely.

With panic sprouting roots in my chest, I tear my gaze away from the mirror and grab one of the well-worn, stiff towels hanging off the bathroom vanity. Throwing it over the curtain rod, I step into the tiny shower, twisting the knob as I wait for the pipes to cough to life.

The water spits and sputters before settling into a trickling flow.

I sigh as the scalding streams over me, washing away the dirt and blood coating my defeated body.

After an hour of repeatedly dunking my hair in watery, cheap-smelling motel conditioner to work out the knots, I finally step out of the shower and wrap myself in the frayed towel.

With aching arms, I make my way over to my duffel bag, glancing at the pile of dirty clothes neatly folded on the chair. I'll have to find a laundromat at some point. The few pieces of clothing I managed to bring won't last me long.

I throw the bag on the bed and rummage through it in search of a dry set. Most of the items inside are still slightly damp, but the water-repellent material has at least kept some of the moisture away from the meagre belongings tucked inside.

I seize a pair of sweatpants that escaped with no more than a few damp spots and pair them with an oversized t-shirt. My whole body trembles from exhaustion and depleted adrenaline as I drape the shirt over my head before tucking the bag away.

Sitting down on the threadbare bed sheets, I run my fingers reflexively over the time-worn floral pattern. My eyes catch on a particularly washed-out pink-and-white lily. The delicate flower's pointed petals look as frayed as the sheets themselves, the once-vibrant leaves faded to a dull, greyish green.

I'm looking at a visual representation of myself. Like *I am* that faded, washed-out flower. Once elegant, vibrant, and full of life, but now merely a listless shell of my former self, my vigour and vivaciousness worn away by life's bitterness.

A small yelp escapes my lips as a loud crack reverberates through the room, followed by a flash of blinding light flaring across the pale walls through the small window. A moment later, thunder rumbles across the sky, triggering a tidal wave of rain hammering against the thin roof.

That's all it takes for my own river of tears to break free.

Curling into a fetal position on the cold, rigid mattress, I submerge myself in the storm tearing the night apart as I finally allow the sobs to tear through my body while an avalanche of sorrow drowns my heart.

Chapter Three

THE NEXT FEW DAYS pass in a blur.

After crying myself to sleep that first night, curled on top of tattered bed sheets in the gloomy, dejected motel room, I haven't allowed myself another moment of weakness. Whenever the anguish threatens to creep back in, I force it down, clinging to the only objective that truly matters: getting as far away as possible from the place I left behind.

This is my only chance to escape. If I mess it up, there will be no second chances.

The days crawl by, each one blending into the next. I wake to the staggering torrent of my own heartbeat hammering wildly in my chest, the remnants of another bad dream leaving every muscle in my body taut with tension. Once I manage to slow my frantic pulse, my eyes inevitably fall on yet another cracked ceiling in yet another dingy, uninviting motel room. A quick shower later, with my wig firmly in place, I'm out the door and back in the Beetle, making sure to leave behind as little evidence of my short stay in each location as possible.

After a swift stop at the first coffee shop I can find, I'm back on the road, speeding further and further away from where I came.

I only stop for necessities: fuel, toilet breaks, and the occasional meal.

By the time the sun inevitably dips behind distant hills, I'll have found my way to yet another dirt-cheap roadside motel, where I'll predictably be greeted by yet another indifferent, overworked staff member working the graveyard shift who'll be more than willing to turn the other cheek the moment I flash some cash beneath their underpaid nose.

I've only had to vacate three motels where the receptionists asked one too many questions and refused to rent me a room without proof of identification. Two of those times, I was able to find more... *accommodating* motels nearby. The third time, I spent two exhausting hours driving without a single vacancy in sight, eventually forced to stop on an abandoned road in the middle of nowhere.

I spent that night curled up in the backseat of the Beetle, layered in as many clothes as I could fit on my shivering frame, futilely attempting to fight off the frigid night air.

I didn't sleep at all that night.

Every sound had me on edge, convinced that at any moment, someone would appear outside the car window to drag me, kicking and screaming, back to my prison to face Viktor's wrath.

Nearly three weeks and nine country borders later, I still feel as exposed and unsafe as I did the night I left Iris's house.

Some days, I wonder if I'll ever feel safe again.

Chapter Four

I manually roll down the driver's side window as I speed along a narrow motorway, just as the sun peeks out from behind puffy white clouds.

I crossed the border into Spain several hours ago and have been driving aimlessly ever since, intent solely on putting as much distance as I can between me and Viktor's horde of brainwashed brutes.

Undoubtedly, they're out there somewhere, scouring the countryside for me, each one hoping to be the loyal soldier fortunate enough to wrench me back into Viktor's vice-like grip—praying they will be the one rewarded for their blind loyalty to their cruel boss, while I suffer the price for their heedless ambition.

Even with that miserable prospect never straying far from my mind, I can't help but admire my surroundings. The vast rolling hills interspersed by rocky cliffs and quaint cottages truly are breathtaking.

As I turn a sharp bend in the road, I spot an old, inconspicuous sign pointing toward a weathered path that disappears into the forest. The words *Bahía De Acantilado* are painted in bold capital letters across the worn surface.

Somewhere deep in my memory, that name rings a faint bell.

After weeks of blindly following monotonous road signs leading through one big town after another, I wonder why this name feels more familiar than any other place I've passed.

On a whim, I make a sharp turn, almost sliding off my seat as I veer onto the rough-textured road. As I continue down the winding drive, I scour my mind, trying to recall where I've heard the words Bahía De Acantilado before. I can practically taste the blurred edges of a memory, stored somewhere deep within the long-forgotten recesses of my mind. But no matter how hard I try, I can't for the life of me bring it to the surface.

Sighing in defeat, I shift my focus to the words themselves. From what I remember of my fairly mediocre Spanish—much to my mum's dismay—I'm almost certain *Bahía De Acantilado* translates to *Cliff Bay*, or *The Bay of Cliffs*. Unfortunately, understanding the meaning does nothing to jog my memory.

Frustrated, I let the thought go. After weeks of driving along dreary highways, I'm grateful for a change of scenery at the very least. The terrain is already shifting, the raw and untamed movements of the land so different from the gentle slopes and flat plains I left behind in Russia.

As I carefully navigate a particularly twisty section of the road, dense forestry rises on one side while a steep cliff drops off on the other. Overhanging branches stretch out to form a stunning canopy above, their denseness blocking each ray of sunlight attempting to pierce the thick vegetation.

Driving through the dreamlike archway, I envision travelling through a passageway to another world, eager to discover whether there's light at the end of the tunnel.

Another bend in the road, and the canopy overhead fades away. Moments later, the forest gives way to wide, open wheat fields stretching endlessly on either side of the narrow road.

Battling with the gear stick, I wrestle the car into a higher gear as I dive into the sea of golden stalks, manoeuvring the Beetle through the thick crop.

The wheat sways lazily in the mild breeze, each strand tall enough to graze the car's roof. If not for the modest road guiding my path, I would quickly lose myself in this yellow maze. The entire car is practically swallowed whole, limiting visibility to nothing but a thin strip of concrete and a sliver of golden-blue sky.

A few wheat strands tickle my cheek as they reach through the open car window, releasing a sweet, grainy aroma. My stomach gives a low grumble, and I stretch across to the passenger seat for a protein bar I picked up at a gas station several hours ago.

I briefly glance at the fuel gauge, noticing the needle dipping closer to the quarter-full mark. If nothing else, I pray this town has a petrol station. Otherwise, I may find myself stranded out here.

An outline of trees appears in the distance, and before long, I reach the base of a steep road leading into the rocky hillside.

"No way but up, I suppose," I murmur, stepping on the gas as I launch the Beetle forward.

The rapidly climbing path leads me into the heart of the mountain range, the gradual dips and curves of the pebbled track steering the car deeper into the rocky terrain. With each turn and bend, I'm rewarded with a new breathtaking view of the ever-changing landscape. Who knew a small, inconspicuous side road would lead me past some of the most beautiful scenery I've ever witnessed?

Five points for gut feelings.

As the road gradually slopes downward, fresh, salty air drifts through the open window. The unmistakable saline scent lingers on the warm summer breeze, telling me I'm close to the ocean.

The road finally opens up, revealing an uninterrupted expanse of blue sky. The blazing sunshine floods through the front windshield, forcing me to lower the sun visor. That's when my gaze falls on the outline of a rooftop ahead, closely followed by another, then another.

A large wooden sign comes into view, the words *Bienvenido a Bahía De Acantilado* painted in elegant cursive letters across the timber plate. Below it, in slightly smaller font, it reads: *Welcome to Cliff Bay.*

Excitement flutters in my chest as I follow the gradually widening road onto the main street of a small town.

The street is lined with quaint houses in a range of vibrant colours, interspersed with boutique stores and shops of all shapes and sizes. A tiny smile tugs at my lips as I take in the eclectic mix of terracotta tiles, white-painted stucco walls, and wide stone arches.

Despite the historic feel of the place, I spot various modern stores in trendy colours. Their floor-to-ceiling windows and sleek sliding doors blend effortlessly with the vintage-styled shops on either side, identified by their rustic facades and wrought-iron signs swaying gently in the breeze.

The town is alive with movement. Hordes of people mill up and down the paved pathways, chatting leisurely, wide smiles on their faces as they soak in the beautiful summer day.

The road eventually tapers off as I reach the end of a broad cobblestone street, blocked off to allow pedestrians a traffic-free path through the scenic courtyard marking the town centre.

I follow a smaller side road, passing a number of streets veering off in different directions until I finally spot the sign I've been searching for.

Playa. The Spanish word for beach.

That can only mean one thing.

Ocean.

Turning the car in that direction, I head past beautiful sandstone buildings and impeccably maintained flowerbeds, the pungent scent of salt and brine intensifying with every bend in the road.

The narrow footpath soon merges into a wide, cobble-stoned sidewalk lined with rows of palm trees swaying gently in the warm breeze. A moment later, I spot the outline of masts ahead and catch my first glimpse of the ocean.

The glittering water stretches out toward the horizon, a breathtaking backdrop to the picturesque seaside town. A gorgeous sandy beach hugs the water's edge, its continuous expanse of golden-white sand broken only by a small harbour filled with boats of all shapes and sizes—luxurious yachts bobbing next to rusty fishing vessels, docked beside brightly coloured sightseeing boats.

A paved walkway separates the sloping sand from the bustling seaside esplanade, lined with restaurants and ice cream parlours.

Framed by imposing rocky cliffs on one side and smooth, rock-clad slopes on the other, this town could've been plucked straight from the pages of a picture book.

I ease the car forward, pausing every few seconds to allow people milling between the beach and the esplanade to cross the road. I finally spot a vacant parking space outside a busy seafood restaurant and manoeuvre the Beetle into the tight spot before anyone else can snag it.

As I open the door, I'm hit with the hum of chatter and laughter drifting from the people crowding the tables along the crooked walkway. Huge white-and-blue-striped parasols shield from the blazing sun as they tuck into woven baskets of fish and chips, neatly wrapped in red-checked paper.

I climb out of the car, the back of my thighs sticky with perspiration. Thankfully, most of my bruises have faded enough that I can comfortably wear shorts and a t-shirt without worrying that anyone will notice the fading remnants of welts and cuts. I'm not sure I would've survived this heat if I were still forced to wear long pants and sweaters.

Movement catches the corner of my eye. Glancing toward the restaurant, my attention falls on a fair-skinned woman sitting at a table next to a red-haired man. Across from them, two young children bicker over what looks like a Scrabble board. The older boy snatches one of his younger brother's tiles and holds it above his head, just out of reach. His red curls bounce as he laughs, taunting his frustrated sibling.

I glance back to their mother, and my breath hitches when I find her looking directly at me. Her lips curve into a kind smile, the corners of her eyes crinkling. Sunburn marks her forehead and nose, her fair skin reddened from a long day spent in the sun.

She gives me a small wave.

Something in my chest tightens.

I sigh happily, letting the breeze brush against my skin as I take a sip of coffee. My eyes drift lazily across the scattered tables outside the cafe, settling on a small chalkboard sign a few tables over.

Beachside Bookworms – Join Us, *written in pink chalk, the dots over the 'i's replaced with tiny hearts.*

A group of women are gathered around the table. They lean in close as they talk, their laughter relaxed and unguarded. One of them pulls a paperback from her tote bag, and I recognise the cover instantly.

I read the same book several months ago in secret, after I snatched it from a second-hand shop. Viktor was too busy charming the owner to notice me slipping it into my bag, leaving a crumpled fifty-ruble note behind.

The girl flips open a page and points animatedly to a passage somewhere halfway through, setting off a chorus of excited chatter.

My gaze lingers on the book, then the girl.

She suddenly glances up and catches me watching. Before I can look away, she smiles and lifts her arm in an easy wave, nodding toward the sign, as if to say, Why don't you join us?

A faint whisper of hope stirs in my chest as my fingers twitch in my lap, itching to wave back.

A hand closes firmly around my wrist.

"Now, now, lapochka. Let us not draw attention to ourselves."

Viktor's grip tightens, measured just enough to avoid bruising. I fight not to flinch, knowing resistance will only make it worse.

He looks perfectly at ease as he watches a waiter refill a water glass at another table. I stiffen when he speaks again, his voice deceptively soft, rich Russian accent threading through every word.

"You seem distracted, lapochka. One could almost be fooled into thinking you do not want to be here with me. Is there something you would like to share? Perhaps you would prefer to sit over there, with those silly little girls?"

My throat tightens. I give a small shake of my head.

He hums low in his throat. "I should hope not. You do know how much I love taking care of you, do you not? How much I cherish the fact that you are mine, and only mine. You will let me continue to take care of you, won't you, lapochka?"

His thumb presses against the pulse point inside my wrist, slow and deliberate.

Out of the corner of my eye, I notice the girl still watching us. A faint crease mars her forehead as she studies me, and I do everything I can to keep my features steady.

Viktor turns to her. With practised ease, he flashes her a devastatingly handsome smile.

She bows her head, cheeks flushing as a shy grin splits her face.

Viktor leans into me, his lips grazing the shell of my ear.

"Is it not funny," he murmurs, "how some girls find it so easy to trust strangers?"

I spin on my heel and sprint in the direction of the beach, my pulse racing with each hurried step.

Only when I reach the sandy dunes do I allow myself to slow down, chancing a quick glance over my shoulder.

The woman by the seaside restaurant is no longer watching me. Her attention is back on her children, eyes alight with amusement as one of the boys gestures wildly, his face animated as he tells her something. She throws her head back with a bright laugh. The sound carries over the gentle ocean breeze.

I suddenly feel ridiculous.

I spent weeks running from dodgy motel to dodgy motel, doing everything I could to remain inconspicuous, yet the moment a perfectly normal-looking woman offers me a polite smile and a friendly wave, I act like a complete fruit loop.

Way to draw attention to yourself, Elaina.

Shaking my head, I continue down the beach toward the water's edge, forcing myself to shake off the lingering unease.

The soft coastal wind provides a soothing contrast to the sweltering heat, though the blazing sun quickly warms my pale skin as I take in the people scattered about the beach, basking in the lazy afternoon rays.

An elderly couple lounges in foldable chairs beneath an orange-and-white parasol, each engrossed in a thick paperback. Behind them, a small boy of no more than three or four is giggling loudly, his chubby hands gripping a bright red shovel as he eagerly fills a plastic bucket with golden sand. Further down the beach, a volleyball game is in full swing, the ball soaring over the net as players dive left and right, their laughter and playful taunts ringing through the air.

A group of girls have spread out on towels next to the court, sunbathing as they watch the match unfold. One of the players throws himself onto the sand, sending a spray of golden grains showering over them. Their high-pitched shrieks pierce the gentle buzz of nearby beachgoers.

They all look about my age, yet I feel as distant from them as if we were born on different planets.

I can't recall a single time in my life when I was able to lounge on the beach with friends, worrying about nothing more than whether my tan lines might show when I don a new summer dress later that evening.

These people seem so untroubled. So happy. Like they don't have a care in the world.

A knot forms in my chest as I watch their light-hearted banter. I avoid my gaze and turn to face the towering cliffside beyond the volleyball field, shaking off the unwelcome emotions.

The impressive rock face rises high above the town, at least a thousand feet into the sky, its jagged edges sharp and formidable. At the base of the cliff, rolling waves hurl against the pointed rocks jutting from the bubbling surface, sending powerful sprays of sea foam cascading against the rugged facade.

I watch the rhythmic motion as the waves ebb and flow, mesmerised by the ocean's effortless grace and unrelenting power.

It has always had this effect on me, ever since I was a little girl. Some of my fondest childhood memories are of those rare days spent at the beach, splashing in the shallows near the water's edge, feeling utterly content and carefree.

The ocean has always filled me with an inexplicable sense of exhilaration and vitality, unlike anything else. The way millions of tiny water droplets unite to create something so graceful, yet so profoundly powerful, has always made me feel as if every person, no matter how small or insignificant they might feel, has the potential to be part of something extraordinary.

I follow the rugged contours of the cliffside, taking in the deep grooves where time and elements have carved out jagged layers over the centuries. My eyes travel all the way to the crest, expecting nothing more than untouched nature and open sky.

My jaw drops.

Six conical spires rise into view, stretching high into the cloudless sky, their pointed peaks stark against the brilliant blue. The spires sit atop sand-coloured towers of varying heights and widths, the structure exuding an arresting medieval grandeur.

From my position near the foot of the cliff, I can't take in the full extent of the building, but as I squint against the glaring sun, I can just make out the outline of a battlement stretching between two towers, the alternating crenellations and merlons unmistakable.

"No way... They have an actual *castle* here?" I murmur in awe. How had I not noticed it the moment I stepped onto the beach?

I've always wanted to visit a castle, and I wonder what kind of shape it's in. *Perhaps they allow day tours?*

But staying long enough to visit would mean extending my time here.

I stand quietly, the sun high above me, the warm breeze whipping loose strands of hair around my face. The whoosh of waves, the distant cries of seagulls, the hum of laughter drifting on the wind—it all feels so... alive.

And in that moment, I realise that's exactly what I want.

To stay.

To linger in this vibrant, charming, sun-drenched town for just a while longer.

A stray lock of hair catches in my eyelashes, and I reach up to tuck it behind my ear. As the sunlight glints off the golden strands, icy realisation slams into me, knocking the breath from my lungs.

I forgot to put on my wig.

Panic seizes my chest.

I've been so careful. So vigilant.

Every time I've stepped out of the car, I've made sure to always stay in disguise. I've even worn the wig while driving, just to be safe.

But these past few days have been unbearably hot, and my scalp was getting uncomfortably itchy, so I foolishly allowed myself a brief reprieve.

Damn it!

For a split second, I consider running back to the car to retrieve it. But even as the thought flits through my mind, I know it's pointless.

Though no one seems to be paying any particular attention to me, some of these beach goers will already have seen me without the wig. Reappearing with an entirely different hair colour and style would only draw more notice.

The damage is already done. Might as well take advantage of it.

I inhale a slow, steadying breath, filling my lungs with the salty sea air as I will the tension to seep from my shoulders.

And for the first time in over a decade, I feel like I can finally breathe freely again.

Chapter Five

By the time I make my way back to the car, I feel strangely rejuvenated.

A stroll along the beach is by no means a miracle cure—I'm still sleep-deprived, tense, and undeniably uneasy—but an hour spent gazing at the ocean and breathing in the salty air has worked wonders for my mood.

Most of the restaurants along the boulevard have closed for the afternoon, likely preparing for the dinner rush later in the evening. The many ice cream parlours and cafés remain busy, however. People mill in and out of open shop doors, perched on rickety chairs and leaning against wobbly tables as they devour savoury pastries and rapidly melting scoops of gelato under the scorching sun.

I climb into the Beetle and ease back onto the road, following the wharf past the wide timber pier that stretches into the harbour, forming a narrow pathway for the steady stream of charter boats and fishing vessels returning to the marina after a long day at sea.

Beyond the harbour, the town stretches along the sandy shore, sprawling into a maze of small streets and buildings. The rocky landscape allows for more space between houses the further I drive from the bustling centre.

I'm about to make a U-turn when I spot a white-painted arrow pointing to a quiet side street framed by oak trees and rustic, wood-panelled houses. *May's Bed & Breakfast* is hand-painted in an elegant, swirling script along the base of the arrow.

Curious, I turn onto the small road and find my destination less than a minute later.

Letting the Beetle idle, I admire the beautiful front garden. The lush green lawn is immaculately maintained, with old leafy trees casting broad shadows over wooden benches and rickety tables scattered throughout the yard.

Two neat rows of blooming flowers frame a pretty limestone path leading from the front gate to the large, two-storey house about a stone's throw away. The white-painted structure has an old-fashioned charm, with dark-blue panelled shutters and a large front porch, where a wide pergola offers much-needed shade from the afternoon sun.

I switch off the engine and climb out of the car. When I don't spot anyone outside, I unhook the latch of the curved gate in the white picket fence enclosing the property and tentatively cross through the garden. Climbing the porch steps, I stop in front of the wide Venetian double doors. I'm about to press the brass doorbell when I notice one of the doors has been left slightly ajar.

I push until it glides open with a soft creak and step into a bright, airy foyer with high ceilings and dark, polished floorboards.

"Hello?" I call out hesitantly, my voice carrying through the quiet house.

I'm met with nothing but silence.

Glancing around the entrance hall, I'm about to call out again when the sound of faint footsteps reaches my ears from somewhere deep inside the house. A moment later, a woman appears at the other end of the hallway.

"Well, hello there," she greets brightly as she crosses the foyer.

"H-hello." I return her warm smile with a tentative smile of my own.

At a guess, I'd place her in her mid-to-late forties, the faint laugh lines around her rounded eyes lending her a kind and inviting presence. Streaks of grey thread through her honey-blonde hair, cut into a shoulder-length, feminine style that flatters her diamond-shaped face.

"How can I help you, love?" she asks, brushing her hands against the front of her apron, releasing small tufts of flour into the air. Her accent's unmistakably British.

"I was hoping you might have a room available?" I ask gingerly.

Her smile broadens. "We certainly do. We had a few people leave yesterday, and I just tidied up their rooms this morning. We have a big group arriving in a couple of days, but even so, we should still have plenty of space. How long were you looking to stay?"

"Only a day or two."

"No problem at all, love. Did you drive here?"

I nod.

"I'll open the gate so you can park out back while I fetch what we need to get you checked in. Any of the parking spots marked for guests will do. They should be easy enough to spot once you round the house."

With that, she shuffles away down the hall and disappears through a back door.

I hurry back out to the Beetle, and by the time I've coaxed the engine back to life, the front gate is already opening, allowing me to ease onto the wide gravel road leading around the house.

The back of the property opens into a sizeable parking area with around ten spaces, four of which are already occupied. I slowly pull into one of the vacant spots beside a sleek BMW, grab my bags from the boot, and make my way toward the back patio, where the woman is already waiting for me.

"I see you found a spot?" she smiles, peering over at my Beetle.

"I did. Thank you."

"Wonderful. Let's get you checked in, then, love. I'm sure you wouldn't mind a nice, cool shower, what with all this heat we've been having."

She leads me through the back door, veering left through a cased opening into a spacious living room. Antique bureaus and whitewashed cabinets line the walls, filled to the brim with crystal glasses and floral porcelain plates. A giant coffee table sits atop a plush carpet in the middle of the room, flanked by an old-fashioned three-seater couch and four stuffy armchairs.

"Here we are," the woman says, gesturing for me to sit as she plonks down on the couch. She's clutching a large, leather-bound book, which she places on the coffee table beside a set of keys.

"Alright, love. I just need some details for our booking system, and then I'll take you upstairs to show you to your room," she says, rummaging in her apron for a pen. "My husband, Marvin, has told me more times than I can count to get myself one of those—oh, what are they called again? *iTab*, is it? No—*iPen?*"

"iPad?" I suggest gently, masking the twitch of my lips as the contemplative crease on her forehead dissolves.

"Ah, yes! Exactly," she exclaims. "One of those iPads, that's it. Marv insists it'll make guest registration much easier, but I still prefer doing things the traditional way. I suppose I'm old-fashioned like that." She laughs self-deprecatingly as she shakes her head.

"I usually get Sally's daughter, Stella—that's our lovely neighbours across the road—to come over a couple of times a week to help me enter everything into the computer system. I've got one of those stationary monstrosities in my office, but Stella keeps telling me it's ancient and insists I need a new one."

She continues chattering as she flips open the leather-bound book to a fresh page, scribbling down the date. "I'll give you one of our cosier rooms overlooking the front garden," she chirps happily. "It just became available yesterday, and it's one of my favourites. I just know you'll love it. It has its own bathroom too, which is always a nice bonus, don't you think?"

She jots down a few more details, then looks up at me expectantly.

"What did you say your name was again, love?"

"Uhm, I didn't."

"Oh, my word! You're right." The woman gasps, looking mildly horrified. "I haven't even introduced myself, have I now? Heavens, what a host I'm being today."

She huffs, her blonde strands bobbing as she shakes her head before stretching out her hand. "My name is May. I'm the owner of this place, and I'm so happy to have you here. If you need anything at all during your stay, you're welcome to come see me anytime. I'm usually found pottering about the house or out in the garden tending to the flowerbeds. I don't usually stray too far from the property unless I'm out buying ingredients for supper. But on the off chance you can't find me, you can always seek out my husband, Marvin. He's just out for the moment grabbing some light bulbs for the back patio—the outdoor light stopped working last night, and so I told him, *Marv, we need to get it fixed right away*—but as soon as he's back, I'll introduce you so you'll know who to look for."

She rattles this off while hardly pausing for breath. Excessive chattiness normally makes me nervous, but something about May's warmth puts me at ease.

"I'm Elaina," I say, shaking her hand and offering a more genuine smile than I've given her so far.

"Hello, Elaina. Welcome to my humble Bed & Breakfast." May's wide grin enhances the soft creases framing her features. "I'll just finish noting down your details, and then we'll get you settled upstairs. Did you have an ID I could grab off you there, love? Might speed up the process a bit."

"Uhm, yes, of course," I mumble as I drop to the floor and reach for my bag, turning my back slightly to block May's line of sight.

I rummage through the side pocket until my fingers brush against the brown envelope. Pulling open the flap, I slide out the brand-new passport and driver's licence, leaving the credit card tucked inside. It's linked to a hidden Swiss account with a single dollar to its name, which won't do me any good here.

My eyes flick to the photograph on the licence, where my own face stares back at me, next to the name printed on the glossy surface. *Elaina Adelita Delano.*

It still feels strange, seeing that combination of familiar names paired with my picture.

My gaze sweeps over the details, landing on the fabricated date of birth declaring I'm twenty-four—one year older than I actually am.

Pushing down the ripple of nerves, I tuck the envelope safely back into my bag before handing the documents over to May.

"Elaina Adelita Delano," she reads aloud, scribbling the details into the registration book in her neat, loopy handwriting. "What a lovely name. And such an unusual middle name."

"Thank you," I reply quietly, the words *it was my mother's* teetering on the tip of my tongue before I bite them back. The less May knows about me, the better. Distance and anonymity are the only forms of protection I have left.

And yet, I'm tired of driving endless miles without a destination. Tired of waking up in grimy roadside inns with about as much character and warmth as the weary undersoles of a pair of worn-out shoes.

For once, I just want to stay somewhere nice. Somewhere comfortable. Even if it's only for a night. A place where I can take a deep breath without the overwhelming stench of mould and mildew clogging my lungs.

"Who would you like me to list as your next of kin, love?" May's voice pulls me from my thoughts.

"Oh. I—" I falter, caught off guard. "I-I don't... Well, I don't actually have any next of kin," I mumble, my voice small as I drop my chin to avoid her gentle gaze.

"Oh, love," May murmurs, her words laced with gentle sympathy. "You know what, let's not worry about it. I'll just leave that one blank, shall I?"

I exhale a silent breath of relief as she hums to herself, filling in the remaining columns before slamming the book shut and placing it back on the coffee table.

"Alright, then." She claps her hands together. "Now that's all sorted, let's get you to your room."

She scoops up the set of keys as she stands, and I grab my bag, following her into the foyer.

"This place is gorgeous, by the way," I remark as we climb the curving staircase, the wood squeaking softly beneath our steps.

"Thank you, love," May says proudly as we reach the second floor, where a large round window has been left open to let the summer air flow through the upper landing. As she rounds the railing, the floral fabric of her dress flutters lightly in the breeze. She gestures around the open space.

"This house has been in my family for generations. When my grandmother passed away some years ago—this used to be her home, you see—I just knew it would make a wonderful B&B."

She stops in front of a blue door and pushes down the brass handle. As it swings open, I notice a sign on the wooden surface that reads *The Summer Room*, a delicate wreath of magnolia-blue forget-me-nots framing the hand-painted letters.

I follow after May as I step over the threshold.

The space is small but quaint, with large windows overlooking the front yard, allowing ample sunlight to flood through. A cast-iron bed with soft cream-coloured sheets sits near a doorway leading into a compact bathroom, flanked on either side by framed pictures of brightly coloured wildflowers and pink tulips.

The rest of the room is modestly furnished, with a pair of antique bedside tables, a matching wooden tallboy, and a small chair nestled beside the open window.

"I hope you'll find it to your liking," May says, gesturing around us. "Fresh towels are on the bed, and you'll find a spare toothbrush and toiletries in the bathroom if you need them. Irons and ironing boards are located in the cupboard in the hallway, and we have plenty of spare towels should you need more of those as well."

I walk over to the window, dropping my bag onto the chair as I look out onto the street. A couple strolls past hand in hand, smiling at each other as they head toward the beach, an overexcited border collie tugging impatiently at its leash to hurry them along.

"Breakfast's included, of course," May continues, her voice warm and inviting. "And I usually make a little extra for supper, just in case. Most visitors like to head into town for dinner—there are so many lovely restaurants, especially near the harbour—but if you ever feel like staying in one night, just let me know, and I'll be sure to make something extra tasty."

Turning from the window, I meet May's easy smile. "Thank you, May. You're very kind. And this room is wonderful."

"Oh, I'm so glad you like it," May trills happily. "I've got your keys here as well. The brass one is for your room, the small silver key is for the front door in case it's ever locked—and the clicker is for the front gate."

She hands me the set of keys, attached to a silver key chain with *May's Bed & Breakfast* elegantly displayed in cursive letters.

"Alright then, love. You get settled and have yourself a nice, cool shower while I whip us up some food."

"Oh, no, that's okay," I hurry to say as May moves into the hallway, my pulse picking up involuntarily. "You don't have to do that. I was just going to head into town and grab a sandwich."

May tuts. "Nonsense, love. A sliver of a thing like you needs proper sustenance, and it'd just be plain old silly for you to head all the way back to town when I've got plenty of food right here. Now, you just settle in up here, and I'll see you downstairs in a few."

With that, she spins around and disappears down the hallway, leaving me no room to argue.

Chapter Six

HALF AN HOUR LATER, I emerge from the bathroom freshly showered, my skin carrying the faint scent of jasmine from a luxurious body lotion I discovered tucked inside the vanity.

Dressed in clean clothes, I gather my damp hair into a loose bun atop my head, too drained and hungry to bother with a hairdryer.

As I step into the downstairs foyer, the mouth-watering aroma of home-cooked food lures me toward the back of the house. I follow it through an open doorway into a spacious kitchen, where a massive dining table takes centre stage. Twelve chairs encircle it, woven place mats neatly arranged in front of each seat.

A stunning bouquet of fresh flowers serves as the table's centrepiece, and I lock onto a carafe of iced lemonade perched on one end, accompanied by a tidy stack of upturned glasses. The sight alone scratches at my thirst.

Behind the island counter, May stands at the stove, the rich scent of simmering chicken broth and fresh herbs filling the air. I slide onto one of the four bar stools, claiming the end seat as she pulls out bowls and spoons.

"There you are," she says, giving me a warm smile over her shoulder. "I hope you like chicken soup, love. I know it's not exactly soup weather, but I had some homemade stock to use up, and Marv picked up some lovely chicken thighs from the farmer's market the other day. Seemed perfect for a hearty meal."

My stomach twists with hunger. "Chicken soup sounds wonderful," I assure her, inhaling deeply as the fragrant steam curls around me.

May gives the pot a final stir before ladling generous portions into two bowls. Slipping on a pair of oven mitts, she turns to the oven and pulls out a freshly baked loaf of bread. The rich, buttery aroma nearly makes my knees buckle. My stomach growls in open appreciation as I take in the golden, crusty perfection.

"Here we are." May slices up two wedges, spreading them with a thick layer of butter before handing me a plate. "Dig in, love."

I scoop up a spoonful of the creamy soup, blowing gently before letting the warm liquid coat my tongue. The depth of flavour is instant—warm, rich, and comforting. A deep moan of satisfaction rumbles up my throat.

"Oh my god. May, this is amazing," I gush, already lifting another steaming spoonful to my mouth. Dunking a slice of bread into the broth, I take a blissful bite. My taste buds all but burst into a happy dance. I don't think I've ever tasted anything so delicious.

"I didn't even realise how hungry I was until the scent of your cooking wafted up the stairs to lure me down here."

May chuckles "Nothing makes me happier than feeding people. Cooking's my favourite pastime. Marv swears I'm the reason he hasn't been able to button his pants properly in eight years."

An unexpected laugh escapes me as I shovel in another spoonful, too caught up in the delicious flavours to care when the scalding liquid burns my tongue.

"Goodness, you really were hungry, weren't you?" May muses, eyes twinkling.

I force myself to slow down, wiping my mouth with a serviette. "Sorry," I say sheepishly. "It's been a long time since I've had a home-cooked meal."

May nods in understanding, even as curiosity stirs in her expression. "Where did you say you were from again, love?"

I take a deliberate bite of bread, chewing slower than necessary as May pours us both a glass of lemonade. I don't want to veer into this line of questioning, but I also know avoiding it will only incite more questions.

Good thing I'm no stranger to white lies.

"Well," I say carefully, washing down my bite with a gulp of lemonade. "I was living in Moldova until recently, working in a flower shop."

That much is true—the part about the flower shop anyway. I haven't set foot in Moldova since I was sixteen. Not since Viktor found me.

"Oh, so you're Moldovan?" May's question is laced with intrigue as she studies my fair features.

I hesitate, weighing my answer. Too many details will tangle me in a web of lies. Too few will leave gaps.

"No," I answer eventually, stirring the spoon through the dwindling remains of my soup. "My family's originally from Scandinavia. Well, my dad is. My mum's from... Italy."

Spain, Italy—close enough. The fewer breadcrumbs I leave behind, the better. I can't risk making it too easy for anyone to connect the dots.

Not that May seems the type to dig too deeply.

"We moved to Moldova when I was six, after my dad got a job there."

May's face lights up. "Oh, how exciting! I've never been to Eastern Europe myself. After Marv and I moved here from England about twenty years ago now, we've only managed to travel a handful of times. The B&B keeps us so busy these days." She sighs wistfully. "I bet there's so much to see over there. Just think of the history, the culture."

"There's certainly a lot to take in," I say vaguely. I may be a decent liar by this point, but I have no desire to weave elaborate stories about a life I never actually got to live.

A life I *could* have lived, stolen from me before I could claim it.

"I can imagine you must miss it," May muses, sipping her lemonade. "As much as I love the idea of travelling, I'd miss Bahía De Acantilado entirely too much to ever leave."

She pauses, then asks casually, "Do your parents still live in Moldova?"

The question stops me cold, the spoon hovering above my bowl as I freeze mid-motion.

I slowly lower my hand. "My parents passed away in a car accident many years ago."

May inhales sharply, her hand flying to her mouth. "Oh, love," she whispers, sorrow etched into each faint groove of her face. "I'm so terribly sorry."

I offer a small nod.

May's lips part, but I steer the conversation before she can ask another question. Better to give her small slivers of the bad parts so she doesn't go looking for the worst ones.

"It was difficult at the time," I say evenly, keeping my tone detached—like I'm recounting someone else's story. It's the only way to stop my voice from shaking. "I was still young when it happened. I felt so lost. So alone. I missed them every day." I pause. "Especially after I got thrown into the foster system."

A shudder ripples through me at the memory. No matter what I've been through since escaping that life, I still catch myself thinking about what could've happened to me had I stayed. If I would've been better or worse off.

"I moved through a couple of different homes, like most foster kids do. The guardian I eventually ended up with..."

I hesitate, refusing to give him the title of *dad* or *parent*. "Let's just say he wasn't the hard-working type. We struggled for money. A lot."

And any money he *did* have certainly wasn't spent on me. Who needs food when there's beer to drink and cigarettes to smoke?

"When I turned fourteen, he seemed to care even less. Some nights there wasn't enough food in the house to keep me from starving. I guess by then, I wasn't bringing in as much money for him. Government payments diminished as I got older. To him, I became little more than an... occasional distraction."

My stomach tightens at the words, but I push past it. "Eventually, I had no choice but to find work, just to survive."

"Oh, love," May whispers again, her voice so soft I barely catch it. "I don't even have words."

"It's okay," I say with a practised smile. "It was a long time ago. It's not as painful to talk about anymore."

It's everything that's happened since then that still suffocates me. But, of course, I can't tell May that.

She exhales shakily, visibly unsettled.

Silence hangs between us, thick and heavy. I bite off another piece of bread, giving her a quiet beat to collect herself.

When she finally looks up, her eyes glisten with unshed emotion.

"It's just awful," she murmurs, "how life can turn upside down in the blink of an eye." She shakes her head woefully. "Life isn't always an easy road to traverse. We're often blind to the obstacles we're about to face until we're already turning the corner, staring them dead in the eye."

She's not wrong. I learned that lesson the hard way.

"But surely," she adds gently, "it couldn't have been easy to find work at that age?"

"It wasn't," I admit, scraping the last of my soup from the bowl. "But I figured it out eventually." I clear my throat, hoping the slight hitch in my voice goes unnoticed.

"And what brought you here, of all places?"

It's a fair question. I mull it over, carefully selecting my words.

"For the past couple of years, I worked in a flower shop." I keep my tone light. "It was a decent job. The pay was okay, and I liked the work. But it was time to move on." A watered-down version of the truth, but hopefully enough to keep her curiosity at bay.

"So I quit," I continue—no need to mention that I left without a word. "Packed a bag with most of my belongings and took off in Iri—" My breath snags as I catch the slip. "—uh, *my* Beetle."

I don't let the wince show on my face. "After a few days of aimless driving, I ended up here."

May absorbs my words in thoughtful silence. When she finally meets my gaze, her face is solemn.

"Sweet girl," she murmurs. "I can only imagine how difficult these past few years must've been for you. But you're strong, love. Many would have crumbled under the weight of what you've been through, but you... you kept going."

Even though my story is nothing more than a skewed rendition of the truth, seasoned with white lies and half-truths, her words still strike something deep within me.

It feels almost therapeutic to let a sliver of my hurt slip into the world, even for just a moment.

"Thanks, May," I whisper, soaking in her compassion. "That's kind of you to say. And... thank you for listening."

She clasps my hand, giving it a gentle squeeze before gathering my empty bowl. "More food?"

"Yes, please."

After weeks of tasteless meals wrapped in plastic, I watch with satisfaction as May fills my bowl to the brim with more rich, creamy soup.

"Will you be staying in Spain for a while?" she asks as she places it in front of me. "After you leave Bahía De Acantilado?"

I shrug. "I don't have any concrete plans. I suppose I'll keep driving, see where the road takes me. I have some money saved up, but it won't last long. I'll have to find work sooner or later."

Even to my own ears, my voice lacks enthusiasm. The though of continuing on as I have feels exhausting. Three weeks on the road, hiding in dingy motels and constantly looking over my shoulder has taken the shine off the idea of 'freedom', even if I'd choose this life over the one I left behind any day of the week.

May hums thoughtfully as she moves to the counter, slicing another piece of bread. "And while you're here? Any plans?"

"I'm not sure yet," I admit. "I haven't really had a chance to explore."

"Oh, there's so much to do," she trills, her excitement infectious. "You must do the lighthouse walk. It's stunning. And take a stroll through town square—there's always something happening around there, especially now that the tourists have started trickling in."

She continues rattling off suggestions—museum tours, water activities, botanical gardens. I'm only half listening when her mention of guided cliff walks pulls me back to my trip to the beach, and I tune back into the conversation.

"Hey, May," I interject as she pauses to catch her breath. "I drove past the beach earlier and noticed that old castle on top of the cliff."

"Ah, you mean *Castillo del Acantilado.*" The Spanish rolls effortlessly off her tongue.

"Is that what it's called?"

"Most of the emigrants here call it *Cliff Castle,*" she explains. "It was named so many centuries ago, and it's still the most famous landmark around these parts."

"Do they do day tours?" I ask eagerly.

May scratches under her chin. "They do, occasionally. But as far as I know, they limit them during high season, to give the guests privacy."

"Guests?"

"Well, yes." May frowns. "It's a hotel."

"A hotel?" I echo, scrambling to catch up.

She nods. "Hotel Acantilado. One of Cliff Bay's most famous attractions."

I lean forward, my interest piqued. "Have you ever been?"

"Never for a night," May admits with a wistful sigh. "I would've loved to though. They host a few balls up there every year, and sometimes they invite the townspeople. Marv and I went to one of their Christmas parties about... oh, five or six years ago now. The entire castle was draped in lights, and the ballroom had the most spectacular Christmas tree you've ever seen. Nearly touched the ceiling."

"Wow," I breathe. A vision forms in my mind of an ancient castle, glittering under the stars, guests peering over the cliff's edge at the town below, twinkling lights reflecting off the sea.

It sounds like something out of a dream.

"How old is the building?" I muse. "I can't imagine running a hotel in an old castle is cheap. The upkeep alone must be enormous."

"Oh, I'm sure it is," May agrees. "But they've put a lot of work into it over the years—not all of it voluntarily."

I tilt my head. "What do you mean?"

She sets down her glass. "The castle was originally built in the sixteenth century, during the Anglo-Spanish war, to help defend Northern Spain from British invasion. Over time, it saw several expansions, the biggest during the Peninsular War around 1810. After the Spanish Civil War, the family used it as a vacation home—until Cyclone Martin hit in 1999."

Her smile withers slightly at the mention of the storm.

"Castillo del Acantilado took a serious hit. Large sections of the roof collapsed, entire walls caved in. If the family had been there when it hit, it could've been disastrous. Thankfully, all the staff had already evacuated to town after warnings went out about the storm's devastation in Western France."

"What did the family do when the castle collapsed?"

"Not much at first. They secured what remained, made sure nothing else would fall. But otherwise, it sat empty for years. A real shame."

May pours me another glass of lemonade. "When Marv and I first moved here, it was still abandoned. We'd walk up the cliff now and then, peering through the gaps in the old boundary walls. Even in ruins, it was a breathtaking sight."

I picture it—an old, majestic fortress, battered by the remnants of weather and war, its stone walls crumbling, yet still standing defiantly against the sea.

"When did they finally decide to restore it?" I ask, trying to mask my growing intrigue.

"About eight years after the storm hit," May recalls. "One day, the owners showed back up in town, and suddenly, the harbour was swarming with ships unloading materials. Workers took up residence on the cliff, labouring day and night to restore the building to its former glory, and then some. It was quite the transformation."

"And then some?"

May nods. "The owners were determined to preserve the castle's history, of course. Anything less would've been a tragedy. But it soon became clear they had no intention of keeping it as a private home anymore. From what I hear, they own several estates around the world, and a place like that? It's too grand for a simple vacation retreat—even for a family as wealthy as theirs."

I lean forward to rest my elbows on the countertop, visualising long, empty corridors of stone, cold air whispering through cavernous halls.

"So they turned it into a hotel instead?"

"Exactly. There weren't many hotels in the area back then, and those that did exist were little more than motels. Summer always brought visitors—boats docking, hikers exploring the surrounding cliffs, tourists coming in from nearby ports. But even so, this was more of a quiet retreat than a true tourist hub. I suppose the family saw an opportunity."

"It really is a beautiful place," I muse, thinking of the town square, the endless golden beach, and the towering cliffs.

Nostalgia softens May's features. "Isn't it? I used to visit my grandmother here as a child. My summers in Cliff Bay were some of the best of my life."

She gazes out the window, momentarily lost in the past. I allow her a quiet moment before asking, "How long did the renovations take?"

May shakes her head slightly as she refocuses on me. "Not as long as you'd think. Construction started at the beginning of the summer season, and by May the following year, they were welcoming guests. I remember the grand opening party they threw. Celebrities, socialites, all the who's who of Europe—and even some from America. From

Milan to Manhattan, it seemed just about everyone descended on this place. Quite an event for a town like this."

Her eyes twinkle at the memory. "It was a novelty back then, seeing such illustrious guests wandering our streets. Now, it's almost expected. The owners are very well connected, and the hotel's reputation has only grown over the years. After all," she adds with a wink, "it's not every day you get to sleep in a castle, no matter how famous you are."

She leans back in her chair, swirling the last of the lemonade in her glass.

"For the first few years after the opening, the owners kept expanding the hotel. At the end of each summer season, they'd shut it down, bring in new teams of builders, and the renovations would continue. Over time, it's become quite the place. Incredible, really, how they've managed to modernise it while keeping the original structure and history largely intact."

"How so?"

May chuckles at my eagerness. "Well, I wouldn't know everything they did during those extensive renovations. As I told you, I've only been up there a couple of times, and I never got to see the castle before the storm hit. But Marv and I joined one of the tours that first summer when they opened, along with some of the other townsfolk."

Her eyes drift to the ceiling lamp above the kitchen table, narrowing slightly as she searches her memory.

"Let's see if I recall... Rather than restoring the original structure exactly as it was, the owners modernised it to appeal more to visitors. For instance, instead of the original shuttered windows typical of fortresses of that age, they installed floor-to-ceiling glass panes. They added balconies to many of the rooms and knocked down countless walls to create a more open feel. Of course, they also upgraded the kitchen, put in commercial laundry facilities, built a brand-new pool and gym area, and completely overhauled the plumbing and electrical wiring."

She waves a hand, as if brushing over the finer details. "I couldn't pretend to know all the improvements, but I *do* know it's a spectacular hotel—with a price tag to match."

"That, I believe," I sigh dreamily. "I'd love to see it. It sounds incredible. Too bad they don't offer summer tours."

"Well..." May taps a thoughtful finger against her upper lip. "I did notice some signs around town advertising vacancies. They always bring in extra staff for the summer season. Perhaps you could head up there and inquire?"

Dumbfounded, I blink at her. "Work there? *Me*?" I shake my head. "No, no. I—I've never worked in hospitality before. I don't have the right experience or qualifications. And in any case, I'm not staying here, remember? I'll be leaving in a couple of days."

"True, that *is* what you told me," May acknowledges. But something in her expression gives me pause.

"What?"

She exhales, giving me a long, knowing look. "It's just..." A beat passes before she shrugs. "You said you had no plans, no real destination in mind once you leave this place. And if I'm being honest, love, you didn't sound particularly excited about getting back on the road."

I don't respond right away, shifting uncomfortably under her gentle scrutiny.

"Of course," she continues, "it's your choice. I wouldn't dream of pushing you into something you wouldn't want to do. If you want to leave, then that's what you should do. I'm not going to assume I know what'll make you happy.

But if you'll allow me, I *will* say that I do think you might enjoy working up there, if only for a few weeks. You seem utterly enchanted by the place, and you did say you needed a job."

She smiles. "The pay's supposed to be quite good, and they provide accommodation for out-of-towners. My niece worked there one summer a few years back, and she had a wonderful time. In fact, she went on holiday to Mallorca last Christmas with one of the girls she befriended there."

I open my mouth to dismiss the idea again—but the protest dies on my tongue.

She's right.

I *don't* feel excited about leaving. The thought of getting back on the road so soon coils around my ribs like barbed wire.

This is the first place I've felt a spark of my old self in months—maybe even years. I can't keep running forever. At some point, I'll have to stay put, earn some money. Eat something other than instant noodles and oatmeal for the foreseeable future.

So why not here?

Spain is far from Viktor. Far from his men. I could keep moving, but to where? Unless I leave Europe altogether, I won't be much safer anywhere else. And while I trust my new identity documents, flying across an ocean is a much bigger risk than crossing open borders by car.

I glance up at May, my voice hesitant. "Wouldn't all the positions be filled by now?"

"Most of them, perhaps. But a hotel that size? I wouldn't be surprised if they still needed an extra hand or two."

She gathers my empty bowl and moves to the sink. The soft clanking of dishes fills the silence as I stare out the window, my mind racing.

Could I really do this?

"Okay," I say before I have a chance to talk myself out of it.

May spins around, excitement lighting up her face.

"I'll try," I add quickly. "I doubt they'll have anything left I'm even remotely qualified for. But, I'll give it a shot."

"Wonderful!" May claps her hands together. "I have a good feeling about this, Elaina. Bahía De Acantilado is a magical place—it brings good fortune to those who need it."

She walks over to me, clasping my hands tightly in hers.

"I don't know much about your past, love," she says softly, "but I can tell you've endured things no one your age should have to bear. I think it's time for some good fortune to come your way."

A warm smile curves her lips. "And I have a feeling it will. You just wait and see."

Something wedges itself behind my voice, and I swallow it down, offering her a small, grateful smile.

I haven't met many sincere people in my life. I can count on one hand the number of people who've shown me genuine kindness in the past decade.

But everything about May radiates warmth and compassion. And for once, I allow myself to absorb just a fraction of it.

Maybe, just maybe, she's right.

Taking a deep breath, I lift my chin.

"Alright, then. What does a girl have to do to land a job at a castle around here?"

Chapter Seven

The bell above the door jingles as I step out of *Tijeras de Oro*, the warm breeze lifting my freshly cut hair and sending it swirling around my shoulders.

The bustling walking street hums with life—street musicians strumming cheerful tunes, the scent of fresh pastries wafting from a nearby café, bursts of laughter and chatter filling the air.

Yesterday turned into a slow, sun-drenched afternoon. May and I spent the fading daylight hours in the garden, sipping fresh lemonade as she regaled me with stories of her childhood in England. When her husband returned home around seven, we gathered on the front patio for gazpacho and spicy tortillas as we watched the sun dip behind the trees.

By the time darkness seized the skies, exhaustion weighed heavy on me, and I barely managed to drag myself up the stairs before collapsing into bed.

This morning, I slept in later than usual, jolting awake to find the clock already ticking past nine. Wrapped in a towel, I spent the next thirty minutes battling my hair, knotted and tangled after a day spent twisted in a damp bun.

For as long as I can remember, my hair has reached past my waist, cascading in soft waves. My dad used to joke that my mother and I were mirror opposites, her straight, dark brown strands a stark contrast to my wavy blonde tresses.

Then I met Viktor.

He insisted I grow it even longer, and before long, it had surpassed my waist to rest along the back of my thighs. Soon after, he demanded I change my natural, ash-coloured blonde to a lighter, golden tone, and eventually, to a pearly platinum hue.

I never liked it. It never felt like me. It was the colour *he* wanted, the look *he* preferred.

It was never *my* choice.

But as I combed through the knots, it suddenly hit me that I don't have to follow Viktor's rules anymore. I don't have to be the woman he moulded me into. And if I truly wanted to disappear, shedding that old image would be the smartest thing I could do.

In a place like Spain, my pearly blonde hair already makes me stand out more than it ever did in Eastern Europe, and the last thing I need is to be more recognisable.

Easier to find.

So this morning, I asked May for directions to the best salon in town.

Three hours later, I barely recognise myself.

My hairdresser, Carlos—all expressive hands and dramatic gasps—took one look at me and declared, *"Dios mío! Such* gorgeous *locks, darling! But we simply* must *do something about this colour. And this length?* Stunning, *darling, but where is the movement? The life? You need* layers, *cariño! A touch of fringe, perhaps? Trust me, darling, you will be a* vision *when I'm done with you!"*

And as I stroll down the cobbled street, I can't help but cast furtive glances at my reflection in the shop windows, mesmerised by the way my new caramel-toned strands shimmer under the afternoon sun, streaked with swirls of honey and champagne.

The heavy length that once reached my thighs now falls to my lower back, cascading in soft, voluminous waves. Carlos may not realise it, but he gave me more than just a haircut today.

He gave me back a piece of myself. One I thought had been forever lost to tragedy and cruelty.

When I arrive back at the bed and breakfast, I find May at the kitchen island, expertly chopping onions and juicy, sun-ripened tomatoes.

"Hi, May."

"Hello there, love," she replies, focus fixed on her cutting board. "I'm making lasagne for supper tonight. Sally and Stella will be joining us. Would you like to as well?"

She glances up briefly, then stops short. The knife clatters onto the bench.

"Oh, my Lord," she gasps, her hands flying to her mouth. "You look *fabulous*!"

A flush creeps up my neck. "Thanks," I mumble awkwardly, tucking a curl behind my ear. "Carlos did a pretty good job, I guess."

"*Pretty good*?" May looks positively enchanted by my transformation. "Carlos is a magician! What a difference. You look fantastic, love. More like yourself somehow, if that's not too bold of me to say."

I smile, surprised by how right her words feel. "I do feel more like myself." More so than I have in a long time.

May beams. "I'm delighted for you, love. Now, all you have to do is land that job at Cliff Castle, and your summer will be off to a fantastic start."

I take a steadying breath, ignoring the nervous flutter in my stomach as I veer off Main Street and pass the familiar welcome sign to town as I head out of Bahía De Acantilado. The road stretches ahead, winding toward the rugged cliffs, and I keep my eyes peeled for the small turnoff May told me to look out for.

Sure enough, a large sign marks the fork in the road, its bold lettering confirming my destination: *Castillo del Acantilado.*

The paved road hugs the base of the hillside, curving gently toward the dense forest spilling across the rocky terrain. Trees close in on either side, the thick canopy filtering the golden sunlight as my Beetle grinds its way up the incline. The ascent is steep at first but soon levels out, the vegetation thinning as glimpses of the coastline appear through the foliage.

Ten minutes pass before I finally spot the outline of the castle's outer boundary wall looming ahead, a barrier of ancient stone blending seamlessly into the wild landscape. The wall stretches far in both directions, with a massive iron-clad gate standing guard at the centre. The towering double doors cast deep shadows over the entrance.

As I slow to a stop, a figure emerges from a small guardhouse built into the wall. The man steps forward, his crisp uniform sharp and pressed.

"*Hola, señorita,*" he calls out as I roll down my window. "*Bienvenida al Castillo del Acantilado. Va a registrarse con nosotros hoy?*"

I blink at him, my mind scrambling to piece together the rapid-fire Spanish. His words roll smoothly off his tongue, but I can't make sense of them fast enough.

"*Señorita?*" he prompts, brows pulling together. "*Está todo bien?*"

I quickly glance at his name tag. "*Disculpa, eh... Marco?*" I give him a sheepish smile. "I'm sorry to admit my Spanish is... not great."

His face breaks into a wide grin, revealing a set of startlingly white teeth.

"Ah! *Perdón,* señorita. I assumed you were one of the guests arriving from Costa Rica today. My mistake." His English is fluent, even as his accent thickens certain syllables. "Please accept my apologies."

"There's nothing to apologise for," I say, waving a dismissive hand. "I should be the one apologising for arriving in Spain with barely more than a handful of Spanish words in my vocabulary."

Marco chuckles, his chocolate-brown eyes twinkling. His easy confidence is infectious, and my shoulders relax a bit.

He really does have astonishingly white teeth, the row of pearly whites standing out against his deeply tanned skin. He's in his early twenties at most, his tightly coiled hair cropped short, framing a smooth, clean-shaven face with sharp cheekbones and a boyish charm. His slim, athletic frame accentuates his fitted security uniform.

"So," he says, casually leaning against my car door. "What brings you to our humble abode on this fine summer day, señorita?"

I glance past him at the looming gate as a muffled snort escapes. "Humble abode, huh?"

"Compared to the *Alhambra*, at least," he muses with a grin.

I smile back as I contemplate my words. Will he let me through the gate if I admit I'm just here on a whim, looking for a job well past the window for new hires?

"I—" I fumble, then blurt out, "I have a job interview."

I don't expect my fib to work, so Marco's easy nod catches me by surprise. "*Ah, sí. Por supuesto.* This is the busiest season we've had in years. Makes sense they're looking for extra staff."

He glances toward the guardhouse, then holds up a finger. "*Un segundo.* Let me grab you a visitor's badge."

He strides away, disappearing through the narrow doorway. He re-emerges seconds later with a small badge in hand.

"*Aquí tiene, señorita,*" he says, handing it over. "Just fasten it to the front of your shirt. That way the doorman will know you're a visitor. Have you been to the castle before?"

"Never," I admit as I carefully pin the badge to the rose-colored blouse May lent me when she realised I didn't have anything remotely suitable for a job interview in my duffel.

"*No problemo, señorita.* Just follow this road until you reach the main courtyard. Take the first exit on your right, and there will be signs directing you to the visitor parking. *Buena suerte.*" He winks as he pivots on his heel and strolls back to the guardhouse.

A moment later, the massive iron gate groans as it drifts open, revealing the grand property beyond.

With anticipation humming through me, I ease the Beetle into gear.

Chapter Eight

THE WORLD IS SUDDENLY awash in green.

A wide driveway stretches endlessly before me, flanked on both sides by towering palm trees. Their lush fronds form a majestic archway as I guide the Beetle up the gently curving path, swivelling my head left and right.

The rolling hills are blanketed in lush, emerald grass, cut to immaculate precision, lending the space a grand, almost regal feel. The entire property is a picture of manicured perfection.

Vibrant flower beds burst with rich hues of red, yellow, and violet. Narrow stone pathways zigzag through the terrain, winding between ornate fountains, where water trickles over carved ceramic sculptures. The soothing trickle adds to the dreamlike serenity of the estate.

In the distance, the outline of stone towers looms, spear-like peaks piercing the bright blue sky.

As the driveway ascends, the rolling hills level out, giving way to the dense forest embracing the estate before it surrenders to the rugged cliffs plunging into the sea far below. The untamed wildness of the raw landscape only adds to the cultivated splendour of the pristine grounds.

Reaching the end of the tree-lined avenue, I finally spot the courtyard Marco mentioned.

My jaw drops.

The driveway spills into a gigantic circular plaza, paved with pale grey stone. At its centre, a stunning marble fountain rises high, water cascading down four intricately sculpted tiers. Each level mimics jagged cliff sides, and at the very top, an eagle perches with its wings outstretched, its alabaster eyes locked in an eternal hunt for prey. The fountain is framed by a ring of meticulously arranged flowers, their colours bursting against the sandstone backdrop. The plaza must span over three hundred feet, adding to the regal ambience.

But it isn't the fountain that renders me speechless.

Castillo del Acantilado rises before me, grand and imposing. Wide stone steps lead to a breathtaking portico, its marble pillars supporting a dark-tiled roof that overhangs the massive double-gated entryway.

The sandstone walls stretch for hundreds of meters in either direction, seamlessly merging with the cliffs they stand upon. Large, wide-framed windows adorn every level, allowing natural light to spill into the interior. Some floors even boast floor-to-ceiling French doors, leading to elegant balconies that jut out over the grounds, offering what must be unparalleled views of the property.

And above it all, the castle's pointed towers rise into the sky, the weathered stone brushing against the thin veil of drifting clouds.

It's the most extraordinary structure I have ever seen—an architectural masterpiece effortlessly blending history with modern grandeur.

I edge onto the circular courtyard, following the signs guiding me toward the visitor parking until I pull into a spacious spot that could easily fit a car twice the size of Iris's old Beetle.

I take a steadying breath and check my reflection in the rear-view mirror. My new caramel-toned hair frames my cheekbones in soft waves, and my blouse is still crisp from this morning's hurried ironing session under May's watchful gaze.

You can do this, Elaina.

I step out of the car, my legs slightly unsteady as I make my way toward the entrance. A porter dressed immaculately in a tailored uniform stands stiff outside the grand doors. As I approach, he offers a polite bow.

"*Buenas tardes, señorita.* Welcome to Castillo del Acantilado." He straightens and reaches to open one of the heavy doors for me.

I nod my thanks as I slip past him into the foyer.

The soft heels of my boots—borrowed at May's insistence, after she saw the state of my old sneakers—click against the marble floor, the sound echoing through the cavernous space.

The lobby is a picture of understated luxury. Sleek, beige-coloured lounges are arranged in intimate clusters around glass-topped coffee tables. A few guests lounge in the seating areas, some with suitcases at their sides, others idly flipping through glossy magazines. Bellhops move deftly through the space, manoeuvring golden luggage carts toward the bank of elevators.

To my left, an imposing front desk made of polished timber and veined grey marble stretches along the length of the room. A tall woman stands behind it, typing furiously at her computer. Her focus is unwavering as her manicured nails clatter across the keyboard.

She looks as if she's been assembled with a ruler and a pair of tweezers. White shirt neatly tucked beneath a tailored blazer. Chic beige-and-black-striped scarf tied elegantly around her collar. Blonde hair pulled into a severe bun, tight enough to look painful.

Even with her rigid demeanour, she's striking. High cheekbones, full lips, impeccable style, immaculate makeup. Yet there's a sharpness to her beauty—an iciness that makes her seem more statuesque than approachable.

As I approach, her chin lifts ever so slightly.

"Welcome to Hotel Acantilado. How may I assist you today?" Her voice carries a practised melodic hum, but there's a clipped edge beneath the polish.

Her cool gaze sweeps over me in a quick but adept assessment. One perfectly arched brow rises ever so slightly.

I clear my throat. "Hi. I—my name is Elaina Delano, and I..." I falter. "May—" *No, wait. That's not what I meant to say.*

I take a deep breath. "I was told there might be some vacant summer positions still available?"

Her eyebrow ticks higher with each stuttered word.

Several agonising seconds pass in silence, stretching the moment until my palms feel clammy against my sides and my cheeks burn under the weight of her scrutiny.

With a perfectly rehearsed smile that fails to reach her eyes, she finally parts her painted lips. "I see. Well, I'm afraid we don't."

The words land like stones in my stomach.

"Oh."

That's it, then. I'm too late.

Of course, I'm too late. A place like this must've had applications pouring in for weeks. People with hospitality experience, polished resumes, and references from luxury hotels, all vying for a chance to work at this magical castle. What was I even thinking, coming here on a whim, hoping for a shot?

Swallowing my disappointment, I manage to ask, "Is there any chance something might open up?"

The woman offers another artificial smile. "I wouldn't hold my breath. I doubt any of our current openings would be right for you."

I frown. "So then... Does that mean there are still positions available?"

A flash of mild irritation crosses her face, as though I'm an insect refusing to be shooed away. "Some *limited* positions, yes—none of which are particularly relevant where you're concerned."

Despite my nerves, something in me bristles. "But you haven't even asked about my qualifications."

"That may be so." Her mouth presses into a flat line, her voice taut with condescension. "But I'm not convinced you would be a good fit here. I suggest you explore more... *suitable* options in town." With that, she turns back to her computer without another word.

Heat rushes to my cheeks, embarrassment mingling with irritation.

This woman doesn't know me. Doesn't know anything about me. And yet, she's dismissing me without a second thought, already writing me off?

I straighten my shoulders. "With all due respect, ma'am?"

The woman's murky blue irises snap back to mine at the change in my tone.

"Without asking me a single thing about my skillset or experience, how could you possibly determine whether or not I'm qualified for a position here?"

Her nostrils flare. "With all due respect, *Miss*," she echoes acerbically, leaning forward slightly, as though daring me to challenge her. "As *I'm* the one currently employed at this hotel, I think I'm more than capable of making such an assessment at my own discretion."

Folding her arms across her starched blazer, she gives me another unimpressed once-over. "And as I already said, we don't have anything available for you. The hiring process for summer positions closed weeks ago. You should've applied then."

The smug arch of her brow punctuates the statement, like a final, deliberate flick of a dagger.

I open my mouth to respond—though what I plan to say, I'm not entirely sure—when movement catches my eye.

A man appears at the woman's side, his expression one of barely concealed alarm, though it's swiftly masked by a polite smile. He's dressed just as impeccably as she is, his black suit crisp against his white shirt. But unlike her, he has opted for a glossy pink tie and a matching pocket square, a stylish contrast that somehow softens the formality of his appearance.

Despite his silver-tinted hair, styled in a modern faux-hawk with the sides tapered into a low fade, he can't be much older than she is. Early thirties, at most.

His angular features are undeniably attractive, but it's his honey-coloured eyes that stand out. They're warm and kind—a stark contrast to the frigidity emanating from his colleague.

"Is everything okay here?" he asks, casting furtive glances between us.

"Yes," the woman snaps before I can reply, her penetrating glare as icy as her tone. "Everything's fine, Ryan." The way she says his name is clipped and impatient. "I was just telling Miss Delano here that we don't have any available positions for her. She was just about to leave."

Ryan exhales softly, and his polite smile shifts to one of apology. "Ah, I see. And what position were you applying for, doll?"

"Well, we never actually got that far," I say, unable to stifle the hint of annoyance in my voice.

A frown creases Ryan's smooth forehead. "Come again?"

I force a breath through my nose. "We never discussed positions, because apparently, I'm not suitable for any role here—regardless of the experience I might have."

Before I can decipher the look on Ryan's face, he closes his eyes and exhales heavily. "Would you mind waiting here for a second, doll?"

Not giving me time to answer, he reaches for the woman's arm and pulls her aside.

"What the hell are you doing, Harriet?" His sharp hiss carries through the marble hall. "You're turning her away without even knowing what position she's applying for? What's the matter with you?"

"She's not the right fit," Harriet bites back, her voice brimming with contempt.

Ryan groans. "Oh my gosh, woman. What's gotten into you? Oh, what am I saying... When has something *not* gotten into you lately?" He lets out a frustrated laugh. "You don't even know the girl. How can you possibly take one measly look at her and decide she's not suited to work here? I don't even—"

He clamps his mouth shut when he notices the looks they're garnering from a few guests loitering about the lobby, peering over at them with vague curiosity. Lowering his voice, he takes another calming breath, and I have to strain my ears to hear what he says next.

"You heard what señor de Águila said at the staff meeting last week. We're busier than ever this summer. We need the extra help, in more departments than one. At least hear the girl out before you dismiss her."

"I've already said no." Harriet's voice is resolute.

"Oh, so this is about pride now?" Ryan's tone shifts from irritation to incredulity. "Come on, Harr. Give it a rest, will you? When are you going to stop this crap?" He sighs. "It's time to get off your high horse, doll. You're better than this."

Harriet draws a huffed breath, ready with another cutting reply—but her retort never comes. A loud bang echoes through the lobby as a side door flings open.

A short, plump woman appears in the doorway, her stylish brown bob bouncing as she rushes forward. Her bright red pantsuit matches the red of her flushed cheeks. High heels clack frantically across the marble floor as she barrels toward us, wide-eyed and breathless, exuding an air of frenzied panic.

"Ryan! Harriet! We have a problem."

I barely have time to register her words before she's at my side, her voice rising in urgency. "What the ever-loving fuck happened with the flowers?!"

Her voice booms through the grand lobby, loud enough to make several guests pause mid-conversation.

A surprised snort rises in my throat, but I quickly swallow it down, not wanting to draw attention to myself while this spectacle unfolds. Harriet, however, is visibly mortified, her mouth twisted in a horrified grimace.

"Cindy, lower your voice, for Christ's sake," she hisses, casting a frantic look at the elegantly dressed guests nearby. "For the love of common sense, woman, you can't just barge in here screeching like a banshee. We have standards to uphold."

Cindy waves off Harriet's outrage with a flick of her manicured hand, her dagger-like, red-painted nails cutting through the air like miniature swords. "Who cares about goddamn decorum right now?" she snaps, fanning her face in a futile attempt to banish the sweat glistening on her forehead. "I couldn't give two flying fucks about *standards* when there's been a massive cock-up with the fucking flowers, Harriet!"

"What flowers?" Ryan interjects smoothly, stepping in before Harriet can combust on the spot.

"The goddamn flowers for the goddamn engagement party tomorrow fucking night," Cindy bellows, each swear word hitting with dramatic emphasis.

Ryan frowns. "The Pérezo party? I thought Annabelle already sorted everything? The flowers were delivered this morning, weren't they?"

"Oh, they were delivered all right," Cindy snaps, throwing her arms in the air. "Each one individually wrapped in its own bloody cellophane parcel, that's how they were bloody delivered."

Ryan looks thoroughly baffled, but I'm already piecing together why Cindy's on the verge of a meltdown.

Harriet doesn't even try to mask her contempt. "Rather than screeching and squawking like a headless chicken until you've successfully chased all our guests away, perhaps you could explain, in *plain English*, why you're acting like a complete loon in the middle of the lobby?" she sneers.

Cindy doesn't even blink. "We ordered bouquets, Harriet. *Bouquets*, you hear? Do three hundred individually wrapped rose stems sound like *bouquets* to you?"

A visible vein in Cindy's temple pulses as she growls. "How in bloody hell are we supposed to pull together twenty table arrangements *and* several grand floral displays by tomorrow afternoon? You tell me that, and then you can tell me to calm down."

Harriet's lips purse so tightly they nearly vanish as an elderly couple hurries past, stealing wary glances over their shoulders.

Sensing disaster, Ryan steps in once again before Harriet can erupt. "Why haven't you phoned Annabelle to send some of her girls up here to help?"

Cindy lets out a maniacal laugh. "Of course I already bloody phoned Annabelle. That's the first goddamn thing I did. But, surprise, surprise—turns out her son is getting married tomorrow. I mean, why wouldn't it be tomorrow, of all bloody days of the whole bloody year? And her entire shop is closed for the rest of the week."

"Oh." Ryan grimaces. "That's... unfortunate."

Cindy flings herself onto the front desk, pressing her forehead against her folded arms. "I'm going to get fucking fired," she wails.

I hesitate.

Could I?

Should I?

"Excuse me?"

My voice is barely audible over Cindy's theatrical groaning, but the hesitant words are enough to make all three of them turn to face me in unison.

Cindy eyes me sceptically, much like Harriet did earlier, though without the same effortless disdain.

"And who are you, girl?"

I push past the sudden flutter in my chest. "My name's Elaina. And... I think I might be able to help."

Ryan and Cindy exchange curious glances, while Harriet looks like she's trying to will me out of existence.

"What do you mean, 'help'?" Cindy prods, but I don't miss the spark of hope in her brown eyes.

I take a steadying breath. "I couldn't help overhearing what you were saying just now. About the flowers?"

Harriet scoffs under her breath. "I don't think anyone from here to San Sebastián could help *overhearing*."

Choosing to ignore her biting remark, I soldier on. "I used to work in a flower shop and curated arrangements for big events all the time. If the party isn't until tomorrow night, there's still time to put everything together."

Harriet looks like she wants to smother the words coming out of my mouth. Cindy, however, seems poised to lunge over the desk to embrace me like her long-lost daughter.

"You better not be yanking my chain, girl," she warns, heels clicking an excited little dance across the marble. "Because if you can actually pull this off, you'll be saving my sweet, round hide. Hell, you'll be saving the whole event—and probably the wedding too, seeing as the bride will undoubtedly have a hernia if this engagement party doesn't go off without a hitch."

I offer her a modest smile. "I'd love to help."

Cindy turns to Ryan and Harriet with an exaggerated flourish of her hands. "And why, may I ask, did you not bring this *wunderkind* to me earlier?" Her finger waggles in a scolding motion. "Here we have a girl on deck with flower-arranging experience, and you people hide her from me? Tsk, tsk!"

Harriet looks like she just bit into a lemon. "That's because she's not 'on deck'," she hisses. "She's not a staff member. She doesn't work here."

Cindy blinks, then frowns, before a trace of horrified understanding crosses her features.

"Oh my... Are you a guest, girl? Did I just hijack a guest from their vacation to help me save another guest's party?"

Harriet scoffs. "Wouldn't that just be a fitting move for a woman of your class?"

"I'm not a guest," I say quickly. "So don't worry about that. And you didn't hijack me. I offered. I actually came here to enquire about summer vacancies. I was about to leave when I overheard your conversation." I shrug. "Figured I might as well help where I can. Make the trip worthwhile."

Cindy looks at me like I just handed her a lottery ticket. "Well, looks like you'll be starting work sooner than expected, girl. Come on, let's get you set up in the Ocean Room."

"Now, hang on just a minute—" Harriet snaps, blonde strands escaping her painstakingly slick bun. "She *didn't* get a position. She's *not* hired. She's not supposed to be starting *any* job here, period."

Cindy frowns. "Why the hell not?"

Harriet looks one syllable away from slapping Cindy across the cheek, but Ryan hurriedly steps between them, raising a calming hand.

"Look," he says, adopting a conciliatory tone. "How about we table the discussion of a permanent position for now? Right now, we have an engagement party to save."

He turns to Cindy. "Elaina has yet to be officially hired—" Harriet's scoff is loud, but Ryan keeps going like he didn't hear her, "—so while it's wonderful that she's offered to help, we'll need you both to return here afterwards to... discuss options."

He sneaks a quick glance over his shoulder before throwing me a discreet wink. "And no matter what happens after today, we can't have you working the entire afternoon for free, now can we?"

"That's sorted then," Cindy exclaims, clapping her hands. "Come on, girl. Let's save this engagement party before we're all jobless in the morn'."

Chapter Nine

By seven-thirty, I'm wiped. My arms feel like overcooked noodles, my feet ache, and every muscle in my back protests with each movement—but despite it all, there's a thrill buzzing beneath my skin.

I spent the entire day working alongside Cindy's event crew, draping delicate garlands of peach-coloured roses from the ceiling in graceful arcs and arranging towering floral centrepieces, each bouquet carefully matched to complement the elegantly set tables.

The work was demanding, but watching the sparsely decorated ballroom transform into something magical with every precise placement felt nothing short of exhilarating.

After leading me away from the reception area, Cindy took me through a maze of corridors before stepping into one of the most breathtaking rooms I have ever seen.

The northern wall of the gigantic ballroom is lined with floor-to-ceiling windows framing an uninterrupted view of the ocean stretching to the horizon. The wide Victorian terrace doors have been propped open all day to allow the summer breeze to drift in, carrying the scent of roses, lilies, and fresh eucalyptus. A small stage has been erected for the live band flying in from Madrid, and after some strategic planning with Emma and Keisha—the two decorators Cindy assigned to assist me—we decided to adorn it with cascading rose garlands and fairy lights, creating a dreamy, romantic backdrop to the opulent room.

When Cindy came to check on our progress an hour ago, she practically skipped through the hall in her impossibly high heels, clapping her hands in delight.

"You are a marvel, my girl," she exclaimed, brushing her fingers across a cream-coloured rose petal peeking out from one of the gigantic arrangements at the bridal table.

It'd been a long time since anyone genuinely appreciated my contribution.

Since anything I did felt like it mattered.

I couldn't stop beaming.

As we wrap up the final touches, Keisha plops down on the edge of the stage with a groan, taking a long gulp from her water bottle.

"Thanks so much for your help today, Elaina," she sighs, turning to me with a grateful smile. "I really don't know what we could've done it without you. Cindy probably would've fired half of us out of sheer frustration. Or if not her, then señor de Águila for sure. We would've been screwed."

Her pretty face contorts into a comical grimace.

"I'm sure you guys would've found a way," I giggle. "But I'm glad I was here to help."

Keisha's tone shifts, even as her smile lingers on her lips. "No, honestly." She leans forward, lowering her voice. "You saved us from a *lot* of stress and shouting over the next twenty-four hours. And trust me—when you cater to the kind of people we do up here, the last thing you want is more stress."

Before I can respond, Emma saunters over, rolling her shoulders stiffly.

"What're you girls gossiping about?"

"How Elaina totally saved our butts today," Keisha replies, tossing Emma a water bottle as she pulls a gigantic hair tie from the back of her head, releasing the thick braids to fall down her back.

Emma grins at me. "You definitely did. Lord knows what we would've done without you. All those flowers..."

I offer a modest smile, even as warmth spreads through my chest.

"Hopefully, the clients will be pleased," Emma murmurs around a yawn as she sinks onto the floor, leaning against a table leg. "And de Águila, too. Yikes, can you imagine his face if we'd screwed this up?"

Keisha lets out a loud guffaw. "Oh, he'd snap. Making the hotel look bad? Making the *de Águilas* look bad? None of us would survive that blow to his ego. I was just telling Elaina that he'd probably have Cindy fire us all on the spot."

That's the third time I've heard that name.

"De Águila..." I echo, testing the name on my tongue. "Is that the owner?"

Emma chokes on a sip of water, spluttering as it slides down the wrong pipe. Keisha simply gapes, as if I've just announced I've never heard of the Pope.

"You don't know who the de Águilas are?" Emma wheezes, swiping at the water dribbling down her chin.

I suddenly second-guess voicing my question. "I—no? Not really?"

Emma and Keisha exchange a look.

And now I really want to know what—or who—I've missed.

Keisha fans herself, eyes twinkling with mischief. "*Oooh*, girl, you're in for a treat when you finally get to lay eyes on señor de Águila junior. That man is *fii-ine*." She draws out the word in a slow, sing-song tone, tilting her head from side to side with each syllable.

"She's not lying," Emma chimes in, a dreamy look glazing her eyes. "What I wouldn't do for just one night with a man like that."

I arch an eyebrow. "Junior... So the son runs the hotel?"

Keisha nods. "Passed down from dad to son. Well... sort of."

"Sort of?"

She shrugs. "Technically, it's his mum's property. Mrs de Águila inherited it from her father. She was the sole heir to his fortune. But it was her husband, de Águila senior, who converted the castle into a hotel when Domenico—de Águila junior, that is—was only seventeen." Her eyes go round. "Imagine being groomed to run a hotel of this stature before you're even out of puberty."

She sweeps her arms around the grand room, gesturing to the chandeliers twinkling softly above us.

I let that sink in. *Seventeen?*

"At seventeen, I was too busy chasing boys and searching for the perfect mascara that would give me Lady Gaga vibes," Emma sighs.

Laughter spills between us, and I let myself get caught in it, even as a dull ache nudges at the edges of my mind. If only my worries at that age had been as simple as hunting for cheap mascara and gossiping about cute boys.

Keisha snorts, dragging me back to the present. "I bet good ol' Domenico still found plenty of time to chase skirts, despite his other... *less enjoyable* responsibilities." A sly grin tugs at her lips.

"Oh, you can put money on that, girlfriend." Emma nods emphatically.

The amused glance they exchange carries layers of meaning, but I'm too curious to find out more about the owners to ask them about it right now. "Is de Águila senior still involved in the operation of the hotel?"

Keisha shakes her head. "Not really. He ran things officially until Domenico turned twenty-seven, which is when he handed over the reins. Though, from what I've heard, Domenico was practically running the place on his own by the time he was twenty-three."

Emma smirks. "Daddy dearest went off to play with his real pride and joy—the family's shipping business."

My brows lift. "Shipping business? They're involved in the shipping industry too?"

"That's where the real money is," Keisha nods. "The de Águilas made their fortune in shipping. The hotel is just one of many golden eggs in their little empire."

She rolls her neck, stretching her arms above her head. "Domenico's mum never cared about the business side of things, so her husband got the honours. Jackpot for him, I suppose, marrying into all that wealth."

"I guess so," I murmur.

I know better than most how money can feel less like a privilege and more like a chain. How it pulls you down, each glittering coin an added weight, a link in a gilded cage. I silently wonder if de Águila senior ever felt the pull of that weight, or if he wore his newfound fortune like a crown.

I glance back at Keisha. "Does Domenico—de Águila junior, I mean—have anything to do with the shipping side of things?"

She shrugs. "I think he's partially involved. He's got stuff going on outside these castle walls, that's for sure. The guy practically lives on planes. Always flying in and out, off to

God-knows-where. But with the kind of wealth and influence he was born into, I suppose he can pick and choose what he wants to be involved in."

She lets out a low whistle. "All the money he could ever dream of and the world at his feet before he even had a full layer of hair dusting his balls." She shakes her head. "Can you imagine how much ass that must've gotten him?"

"As if he didn't get enough already," Emma snorts. "One look at the guy and you know he was practically born drop-dead gorgeous. Add a mountain of money and a body sculpted by the gods? Lethal combination."

"And rumour has it, more than a few dozen women have taken a sip of that lethal love juice over the years," Keisha adds playfully.

Their laughter intertwines, but I don't join in. "Sounds like a real charmer," I say dryly.

Keisha waggles her brows suggestively. "You know what they say—we girls love 'em bad."

"Oh, I've had enough bad for a lifetime," I mutter under my breath.

Keisha flops onto her back with a lazy stretch, yawning. "Trust me, chick. When de Águila junior walks into a room, your panties will be soaked in no time, whether you want them to be or not."

Before I can flat-out reject that statement, the double doors at the far end of the hall swing open.

Cindy scurries inside, heels clicking sharply against the floor as she makes her way toward us.

"All finished?" she asks, her voice bright with satisfaction.

"Yes, ma'am," Emma responds, pushing herself up to her feet.

Cindy waves a hand. "Oh, sit down, girl. God knows you all deserve it. You've been absolute troopers today, all of you."

She turns to me. "Elaina, you have no idea how grateful I am for your help. You're a true, last-minute, life-saving grace, you are."

A soft blush warms my cheeks. "I'm just glad I could help, Cindy."

"Now," she slaps her palms together, turning on her heel. "Come with me. We'll head over to Ms I've-Got-A-Stick-Up-My-Ass in reception so she can note down your bank details and make sure you get paid for all this hard work."

She nods at Keisha and Emma. "Girls, you're free to go. I'll see you both here tomorrow at nine am sharp."

With that, she marches out the door without waiting for me to catch up.

I scramble to my feet and scurry after her, throwing one last glance at Keisha and Emma—who are both smirking at me with knowing smiles, like I should know something they already do.

Something tells me... I will soon enough.

Harriet lifts her head as we approach the front desk. The second she sees me, her posture stiffens.

Fortunately, she's already assisting an elderly couple checking out, allowing us to bypass her straight to Ryan.

"How'd you go, doll?" Ryan asks, his smile warm as he glances between us.

"She's a marvel," Cindy exclaims, practically bursting with pride. "An absolute lifesaver. The Ocean Room looks fantastic, thanks to this trooper."

Ryan beams. "That's wonderful news. I had a feeling." He winks at me. "Wait here for just a second, doll. I'll be back in a flash."

He disappears through a back door, returning moments later with a neat stack of papers in his hands.

"I took the liberty of printing out a few employee forms earlier," he says, handing them to me. "The top one is for your bank details so we can pay you for today's work." He gestures to the rest. "The other documents include an employee application and some standard forms we require before employees can officially start."

My heart rate speeds up.

"Does... does that mean I have a job here?"

Ryan opens his mouth, but Harriet's voice slices through the air like a blade, cutting him off.

"Ryan, we talked about this."

She leans over the desk and snatches the papers from my hands. "We don't have any available positions for her in event planning. That team is already fully staffed."

Cindy lets out a disapproving huff. "This girl saved our asses today!"

Harriet lifts her chin defiantly. "That may be so, but that doesn't magically create a job opening."

"What about her flower decorating skills?" Cindy presses. "Having someone on my team who actually knows how to arrange flowers would be a huge asset. We could start buying individual flowers in bulk instead of pre-made bouquets, and the hotel could charge clients directly for the service. It would increase profitability."

Harriet's jaw tightens. "As helpful as that may be from time to time," she grits out, "putting together a few bouquets does not amount to a full-time job. We don't have enough regular events to justify hiring a dedicated florist."

I can already feel the opportunity slipping through my fingers.

"I have other skills too," I interject before Harriet can shut me down completely. "I'm not just good with flowers. I have experience in event planning and decorating, so I can support the team however they need. I've worked as a part-time administrative assistant for years. And I have experience in gardening and olericulture, so I'd love to help with the gardens and flowerbeds. I've even done some baking and cake decorating, if the kitchen ever needs a helping hand."

I search my mind for anything else that might sway her.

"Honestly," I add in a last-ditch effort, "I'm happy to work wherever I'm needed. Just give me a chance. I won't disappoint you."

A heavy silence falls over the desk as we all wait with baited breaths.

Harriet finally opens her mouth, but rapidly snaps it shut when she glances over my shoulder. For the first time today, something other than contempt crosses her face.

Apprehension.

A strange sense of foreboding trickles through me.

I turn slowly.

My eyes zero in on a pair of immaculately polished dress shoes, so pristine they practically gleam against the tiled floor—a glaring contrast to my own scuffed black pumps.

I slowly trace a set of tailored dark blue suit pants matching a perfectly fitted jacket, the smooth material neatly buttoned across a silken shirt stretching enticingly across a broad muscular chest.

As if of its own free will, my head tilts upward—and I'm met with a pair of familiar, steely blue eyes.

Chapter Ten

I gasp, stumbling backward until my back collides with the reception desk.

My heart slams against my ribcage as I stare, wide-eyed, into the depths of the lightning-blue irises gazing intently back at me.

My mind scrambles to place where I've seen those mesmerising eyes before, even as a sharp, inexplicable sense of dread curls in my stomach, preventing me from making the connection.

I force myself to look away from the dizzying intensity of his hooded stare to trail across his flawless features—past his perfectly symmetrical nose to a pair of full, sculpted lips, edged by a chiselled, neatly shaven jaw. His deep-olive skin stretches taut across sharp cheekbones, accentuating the striking angles of his face.

I track the clean line of his chin, sweeping over strong, prominent eyebrows and thick, jet-black hair, each strand styled to perfection in smooth, silky waves. The provocative lift of one of those impeccably groomed brows jolts me from my daze, and I snap back to the present, heart hammering.

Heat spreads across my cheeks as his gaze bores into me, seeming to undress my every movement and thought.

I have no idea how long I stand there, trapped by the magnetic energy radiating off him, until an awkward cough from somewhere behind me finally breaks the spell.

As the weight of his scrutiny drops from my shoulders, I realise I've been holding my breath.

"What's going on here?" His velvety smooth voice is potently masculine. Each word is pronounced with a distinct, molten accent, his rich baritone commanding the room.

I glance over my shoulder to find Harriet staring nervously at him, her fingers tugging at the edges of her tailored blazer.

"Everything's perfectly fine, señor de Águila. We were just clearing up a small... misunderstanding."

Ah. So this is the infamous Domenico de Águila.

Domenico locks Harriet in place with a long beat of stifling silence. "Misunderstanding?" A brooding edge laces his words.

Harriet hesitates, earning another sharp lift of his brow.

"It's—it's nothing of concern, sir," she rushes, attempting a casual smile. "Miss Delano arrived earlier this morning to enquire about available positions. Naturally, I informed her that most of the vacant roles had been filled weeks ago, and that I didn't think she—" Her words falter under his icy glare.

"If Miss Delano"—his cool tone slices through the air as he gestures to me with a slight nod—"stopped by early this morning, why is she still here at"—he flicks his wrist, glancing at his watch—"six o'clock in the afternoon?"

Harriet's eyes widen, her anxious tugging intensifying. "Well—" she falters, running the tip of her tongue over her dry lips.

"*Disculpe*, señor," Cindy interjects, drawing Domenico's attention to her curvy frame. "My apologies for interrupting. But Elaina here has been helping my team out all day with the Pérezo engagement party."

When Domenico's eyes narrow, she hurries to elaborate. "There was a slight misunderstanding with our flower order this morning. Elaina overheard me discussing it with Harriet and Ryan and volunteered to help. She's been a real lifesaver, señor. Saved us all a lot of headaches."

Domenico turns back to me, mild curiosity flickering across his face as he assesses me from head to toe, lingering briefly on my modestly exposed cleavage.

"I see," he murmurs, his tone eerily calm.

I force myself to hold his stare, steeling my nerves against the full weight of his scrutiny until he finally severs the connection, shifting without a word as his focus returns to Harriet.

"And?"

Her brows knit together. "Sir?"

His jaw ticks. "Her employment. Have we finalised the paperwork yet?"

"Well... no, sir," she admits. "As I was explaining to Miss Delano, we've already filled all the available positions in the events te—"

"So, what you're telling me is, that despite this being our busiest season yet, we somehow have no available positions for a young lady who so graciously volunteered her own valuable time to assist our events team with a vastly important event for one of our most prestigious guests"

His voice is controlled, but the underlying command behind his words is unmistakable. "The failure of which, dare I say, would've been catastrophic?"

For the first time since I met her, Harriet looks utterly lost for words.

"Sir, if I may?" Ryan steps in, keeping his back straight under the weight of Domenico's cold assessment. "With your permission, señor, we were discussing placing Miss Delano in an assistant position of sorts. Given the increased number of guests this season, it could be beneficial to have an extra person available to assist across departments on a rotational basis."

Ryan flicks a glance my way, shooting me a nearly imperceptible smile as we wait for Domenico's response.

He remains silent for a long moment, his demeanour contemplative.

When he finally speaks, his tone is matter-of-fact. "Make sure she receives all relevant employment forms before she leaves. She moves in on Sunday, with a Monday start. Make the appropriate arrangements."

For a split second, I'm sure I must've misheard him.

My heart pounds violently, but before I can process what just happened, Domenico's attention settles back on me.

"Welcome to Castillo del Acantilado, Miss Delano," he says smoothly, a dangerous gleam in his expression that I'm not sure I like. "I look forward to seeing you again soon."

With that, he spins on his heel and strides confidently across the entrance hall, pushing through the large double doors without so much as a backward glance.

The two brawny security guards fall into step behind him, silence trailing in their wake.

"I'm so thrilled for you," May exclaims as she glides effortlessly through the kitchen, her hips swaying to Billie Holiday crooning from an old CD player in the corner.

She was ecstatic when I revealed I'd landed the job, practically rushing over to throw her arms around me in an exuberant hug. The unexpected burst of affection caught me off guard, but surprisingly, I didn't mind it.

"Thanks, May," I say, beaming. "And thanks again for tipping me off. I wouldn't have even known to enquire about it if it hadn't been for you. I want you to know how grateful I am—not just for the job, but for all the kindness you've shown me since I arrived."

"Oh, stop it. It's been my pleasure." May waves off my gratitude with a dismissive flick of her hand. "It's been lovely having you around. Marv and I have enjoyed your company immensely. I'm glad you'll be sticking around these parts a while longer. Let some of the Bay's magic take hold of you." She winks playfully as she walks over to the stove, checking on the chicken-and-tomato casserole warming in the oven.

"Was it hard getting the job?" she asks over her shoulder.

"I wouldn't exactly say it was easy." I picture Harriet's perpetually tight-lipped look. "I don't think the main receptionist likes me much. If it had been up to her, I definitely wouldn't have ended up working there."

I'm still not sure what made the woman instantly dislike me so. You could've fried an egg on her forehead from the heat of her fury when Domenico de Águila walked away after offering me the position she so vehemently tried to deny me.

May tuts. "I cannot see anyone not liking you, honey. I'm sure she was just having a bad day. She'll come around. You'll see."

Some days, I wish I had even a smidge of May's relentless optimism.

"Here's hoping."

"Well, someone up there must've liked you," May chirps as she pulls the casserole from the oven. My stomach immediately rumbles, the heavenly aroma making my mouth water.

"The owner, it seems," I say absently, my hunger overriding my thoughts.

"Come again?"

I frown at May's sudden look of astonishment.

"The owner," I repeat, hopping off the bar stool to grab a dinner plate. "Domenico de Aguila appeared in the lobby just as I was about to leave. The head of the events team told him how much I'd helped out today, and... well, he told them to give me a job."

Sliding back onto the bar stool, I glance up to find May watching me, a contemplative look shading the crease of her brow.

"What?"

"How interesting," she muses. "From what I've heard, it's not like Domenico de Águila to do any favours for anyone. Not unless it directly benefits him, that is." She purses her lip before an amused smile reappears on her face. "I guess you must've made quite the impression. The important thing is that you got the job you wanted."

She moves to ladle steaming spoonfuls of casserole onto my plate. "I told you I had a feeling some good fortune was about to come your way."

"Perhaps," I murmur, even as a familiar sense of foreboding curls in my stomach.

Something about the way Domenico de Águila looked at me today unsettled me. Even now, picturing the way his sharp gaze bore into mine sends a tremor through my pulse.

There was something there, lurking beneath his cool exterior. Something unreadable. Something darker.

Whatever demons that man is hiding, I vow to stay far away from them—and him.

The last thing I need is more demons plaguing my life.

And yet, even with that resolution firmly in mind, a pair of endlessly dark, haunting eyes lingers behind my eyelids as my head hits the pillow an hour later, slipping into my dreams and making my skin prickle with unease.

Chapter Eleven

I smile as I spot Marco stepping out of the guardhouse, his cheery wave a welcome sight as I approach the wide timber gates.

"*Hola, señorita,*" he calls as I roll down the window. "Welcome back."

"Please, call me Elaina."

"Elaina," he echoes, my name wrapped in his smooth accent. "It's nice to see you again. I hear you've come to stay this time?"

I nod. "You heard right. You're officially looking at Hotel Acantilado's newest recruit."

His endearing smile widens. "Our gain," he says with a wink, sending a faint blush creeping across my cheeks. No wonder they keep Marco at the front gate—he's quite the charmer.

"So, do I still need a visitor's badge today, or does my newfound status grant me safe passage beyond enemy lines?" I quip, mostly to distract myself from the weight of his chocolate stare lingering on me.

Marco clicks his tongue. "No, no, missy. You're part of the in-crowd now. *A chosen one.* From this day on, you carry the honour of wearing the most coveted of insignias"—he slaps his thighs in a dramatic drum roll—"the Hotel Acantilado staff badge." His fingers spread wide, jazz hands fanning through the humid air. "Congratulations, *bella.* Wear it with pride."

Giggling, I fail to stifle my laughter. "Will I be receiving this badge of honour from you, good sir, or must I venture into the lion's den to claim it?"

Marco's grin becomes sombre with faux seriousness. "*Ay*, I regret to inform you that the privilege of handing out our cult crest has yet to be bestowed upon a soldier of my standing, milady." He places a hand over his heart, suitably desolate. "That honour remains with She-Who-Should-Never-Be-Interrupted in reception."

I burst out laughing. There's only one person he could be referring to.

Marco looks pleased with himself as he flashes a mischievous grin. "You see, the true test of your worthiness is not the job interview. *No.*" He leans in slightly and lowers his voice theatrically. "It's whether you can survive obtaining your badge and room key with your head still attached after facing the mighty blonde reception dragon."

I snort. It's impossible not to like Marco, with his playful personality and easy charm.

"She's like that with everyone, then?" I ask, oddly relieved. For a second, I thought it was just me. Well... me and Cindy.

Marco shrugs, his relaxed smile back in place. "You'll get used to her. She's not all bad, once she starts seeing you as part of the crew. No one's nominating her for Miss Congeniality anytime soon, but she usually softens once you've stuck around long enough."

"Here's hoping," I mumble, unconvinced.

A glance at the clock on the Beetle's dashboard makes my stomach lurch.

"Shit. I better head in before she really does separate my head from my body."

Marco guffaws, stepping back from my car. "We definitely can't have that." He casts me another quick glance before he spins around as he calls over his shoulder, "I'll open the gate for you."

A moment later, the wide doors rattle as they ease open. I edge forward, waving to Marco in thanks.

He salutes, mouthing, "Good luck," as I drive past.

"Thanks, Marco," I murmur to myself, the beat of my heart suddenly matching the rhythm of the engine. "I'll need all the luck I can get."

"There you are," Harriet snaps as I step into the lobby two minutes early.

"Here I am," I reply brightly, keeping my tone light and friendly.

Kill 'em with kindness, Elaina.

"Mornin', doll," Ryan greets as he appears behind Harriet, his wide smile brightening his handsome face. "Welcome back. Ready for your new adventure?"

"You bet," I smile back, feeling that same bubbling mix of nerves and excitement I've been navigating for the past two days.

"Enough chitchat," Harriet interjects before Ryan can respond. With her usual frigid glare, she slides a thick white envelope across the desk. I lunge forward , catching it before it tumbles to the floor.

I sneak a glance at Ryan, who twists his mouth into a comically chastised pout.

An involuntary snort escapes me, and I force a cough to cover it before Harriet catches on.

Even so, her eyes narrow suspiciously as they shift to Ryan. He's already turned back to his computer, typing away with a carefully blank expression.

Not wanting to become her next target, I tear open the envelope. Inside, I find a stack of documents, a black staff badge with my name in gold font, and a sleek key card embossed with the hotel's emblem: an eagle with its wings spread wide, a fortress-like building framed behind its golden feathers.

"The envelope contains everything you need to know about your role—general assignments, what days you'll be expected to work in which department, working hours, and shift locations," Harriet explains briskly as I inspect the papers. "You'll have a typical work schedule each week, but since you'll be assisting various departments, it will change as needed. Any updates will be delivered to your room. If urgent assistance is required, HR will send someone to inform you. You'll be expected to work whenever and wherever you're needed. Understood?"

I nod fervently.

"The envelope also contains your employment contract, payment details, tax forms, and other required documentation. Deliver the finalised paperwork to me by tomorrow morning. No excuses."

I nod again, studying the eagle emblem engraved on the front of the reception desk as Harriet rattles off instructions until her sudden silence draws my gaze. She's watching me closely.

"Your hiring was... unconventional." Her voice carries an unmistakable edge of disdain. "We typically conduct an extensive interview process, including comprehensive background and reference checks. You, however"—her lips curl as she looks me over—"we know almost nothing about."

I meet her stare head-on, maintaining an air of cool indifference.

"Señor de Águila may have approved your employment, but that does not mean I will allow further deviations from protocol," she continues, her voice dripping with disapproval.

The trepidation unfurling in my gut is impossible to ignore, but I force myself to respond calmly. "Of course."

Harriet's expression tightens, but she doesn't press. "You'll find a document requesting your employment history and references in your envelope. Fill it out and return it to me by the end of the week."

I swallow hard. "No problem."

Shit.

"Now, now. Enough with the iron fist," Ryan interjects, breaking the thickening tension.

Harriet shoots me a final, tight-lipped look before gesturing to the key card and badge in my hands. "Wear the staff badge on your uniform during work hours. Uniforms can be picked up from the administration department on level eight and must be worn at all times during your shifts. The key card grants access to your cabin. Don't lose it."

"Here, doll." Ryan waves me over to the counter, where a large map of the hotel grounds is spread out.

He points to a cluster of small buildings arranged in an asymmetrical half-circle at the edge of the forest that encloses nearly half of the impressive property.

"This is the staff village," he explains, tracing his index finger around the area. "It's where you'll be spending most of your time when you're not on shift."

His finger moves to rest on the largest building in the cluster.

"This is the main lodge. That's where meals are served and staff hang out between shifts. This building here"—he points to a smaller structure—"houses the communal showers. These other buildings you see are mostly staff cabins."

He taps one of the small squares positioned slightly northwest of the lodge.

"This is cabin fifteen. That's where you'll be staying. Each cabin has a number on the door, so it shouldn't be hard to find."

He folds the map and hands it to me. "We've arranged for one of your new roommates to show you around. She's finishing her shift now, so she'll meet you at your cabin. Think you'll be okay finding it on your own?"

I glance down at the folded map. "I'm sure I'll be fine," I say, relieved to have a few moments to myself. "My car's parked in the visitor area. Is there somewhere I can leave it long-term?"

Ryan holds out his hand for the map. "I'll show you the way to the staff park, doll."

Chapter Twelve

A few beads of sweat trickle down my forehead as I make my way along the path toward the line of trees edging the castle grounds, my bag slung over one shoulder and Iris's backpack secured on my back.

Ivy-clad stone walls tower above me, and impeccably trimmed hedges and neat rows of leafy trees line the paved walkways, lending the estate a peaceful calm.

Rounding a bend, I finally spot a robust, one-story log cabin nestled at the forest's perimeter. Thick timber beams frame the structure, with a stone-tiled roof jutting out over a spacious front porch, where laughter drifts through the open front door.

Clinging to my temporary pocket of solitude, I follow a narrow path that winds around the left side of the cabin.

The building is larger than I first assumed, the log walls extending several metres beyond the first row of trees. Though the square windows are positioned too high for me to peer through, the echo of laughter and the faint trill of music tells me the lodge is bustling with activity. The mingling sounds merge with the soft crunch of leaves beneath my feet as I cross the packed dirt.

Up ahead, a clearing opens between the trees, offering my first proper glimpse of the staff village.

A long row of identical wooden cabins stands a few metres apart in a loose half-circle, enclosing a larger building in the middle. The signs above each entrance confirm it's the communal showers Ryan mentioned. As I pass, the faint sound of running water filters through the small ventilation gaps beneath the soffit.

Several benches are scattered among the trees, the unkempt grass and wild shrubs a stark contrast to the immaculately manicured castle lawn.

Walking past the first set of cabins, it's immediately obvious they're all occupied. Nearly every porch is cluttered with an eclectic mix of sandals, flip-flops, and towels, with swimwear draped haphazardly over wood railings to dry.

I spot cabin fifteen about halfway up the path.

On one side of the small porch, a line of shoes is arranged in a perfect row against the wall, each pair meticulously placed beside the next. On the opposite side, a chaotic heap of footwear spills across the wooden planks in complete disarray.

More curious than ever to find out who I'll be sharing this little hut with over the next few weeks, I lift my hand to the door and knock softly.

Silence.

I knock again, harder this time. "Hello? Anyone in there?"

Still nothing.

Shrugging my duffel off my shoulder, I dig through the envelope Harriet handed me and fish out the key card, scanning it over the small reader above the brass door handle. A metallic click sounds, and the door swings open.

A small, panel-clad room greets me.

Two massive loft beds dominate either side of a narrow doorway directly across from the entrance. The bed on the left features a small ladder leading up to the top bunk, while the lower level has been converted into an open wardrobe, with shelves and drawers stacked neatly beneath a wide clothing rack crammed with brightly coloured clothes.

The bed on the right has a more traditional loft setup, though the top bunk is strewn with suitcases, purses, and spare clothes, making it look more like an extra storage shelf than a place to sleep.

The bottom bunk is carefully made, a light-pink duvet folded at a perfect angle, three tiny throw pillows carefully arranged op top with military precision. A small lamp, a book, and a pair of reading glasses rest on the bedside table, all positioned at perfectly symmetrical angles.

I continue my sweep across the modestly sized room. Two large tallboys and a white-painted vanity line the right-hand wall. On the left, an unmade double bed—littered with makeup, hair products, and discarded clothing—takes up most of the corner.

An overflowing shoe rack leans against the wall, next to a couple of wall hooks and a full-length mirror hanging beside the front door. A tiny fridge at the foot of the double bed rounds out the room's sparse furnishings.

Crossing the room, I drop my bags at the foot of the left bunk and ease open the only other door.

A cramped bathroom greets me—just enough space for a narrow vanity, a toilet squeezed into the corner, and a rickety shelving unit packed with spare toilet rolls, a few boxes of tampons, and a half-empty pack of condoms.

My gaze lifts to the small mirror above the sink, locking onto my own reflection.

Lifting a hand, I brush my fingertips over the thin scar that now mars my forehead. If only all my invisible scars could heal as swiftly as this one.

I'm yanked from my thoughts by the sudden sound of the front door slamming open. My heart jolts as it crashes against the wall with a resounding bang.

Eyes wide, I peer around the bathroom door, my brain scrambling to make sense of the tangled mess of limbs.

"Oh, Dean, yes," a female voice moans, her breathy pants merging with a series of deep, masculine grunts.

A wild mane of curly red hair tumbles down a toned, feminine back as the woman throws her head back, her legs wrapped tightly around the waist of a ridiculously muscular man. His bulging muscles ripple down his shoulders and arms, biceps flexing as he pulls away just long enough to tear her top off, revealing a lacy, scarlet red bra.

His glazed pupils linger on her ample cleavage before he dives back in, his mouth trailing hungrily down her chest, large hands palming her breasts. His squeeze earns him a loud, breathless moan.

As his lips move along the curve of her breasts, the woman paws at his shirt, mewling softly. He pauses to yank it over his head, tossing it aside impatiently. A moment later, her black skirt follows as it slides down her tanned legs, landing in a messy heap on the floor.

"Fuck, baby. I've been waiting for this all day," the man rasps, a low groan rumbling in his throat as the redhead slides her hand down in a seductively slow motion to cup the prominent bulge straining against his crotch.

As she fumbles with his zipper, I finally snap out of my stunned daze.

"Excuse me?" I blurt.

My voice is drowned out by their escalating moans.

I clear my throat and try again, louder this time. "Uhm... excuse me?"

A wet smack echoes through the room as the couple breaks their passionate kiss.

Two surprised faces turn to stare at me.

"*Ooh*, you must be the new girl," the woman exclaims.

Mortification barely has time to settle in before she bounces out of the man's arms and skips over to me, her voluminous curls swirling around her pretty, delicate face as she throws her arms around my neck in a firm hug.

"I'm Tiana," she chirps, practically radiating delight as she takes a step back. "It's so nice to meet you!"

I do my best not to stare at her nearly bare chest as I scramble to meet her exuberant energy head-on. If she notices my discomfort, she doesn't seem to care. She stands confidently in the middle of the room, as if having her curvaceous body on full display is the most natural thing in the world.

"Hi. Yes, I'm—I'm Elaina. Your new roommate. Uhm... hi."

Tiana claps her hands together. "Oh, I've been dying to meet you. Ryan and Harriet told me you were arriving today. So sorry I couldn't meet you in reception. I got... held up."

She winks as she gestures toward the shirtless giant behind her.

"Oh. Yes, I can—see that," I fumble. "I'm so sorry for interrupting you," I add hurriedly, risking a quick glance at the muscular man. "I just got here a few minutes ago and was checking out the cabin, and then you guys came in so suddenly, and you didn't seem to notice I was here, and obviously I wasn't trying to—I mean, I didn't want to interrupt, but there was no way for me to—You guys were right in front of the door, and..."

I trail off.

To my surprise, Tiana throws her head back and lets out a raucous laugh.

"Oh my god, that's gold," she cackles, resting her hands on her waist as she snorts. "Less than five minutes in this place, and you're already *this* close to witnessing your first sex show." She holds her thumb and index finger a centimetre apart, then lets out another peal of laughter. "Honestly, considering what normally goes on around here, I'm surprised it took you this long."

She grins at me, her eyes dancing with mirth. "What a welcome, huh? Sorry, hun. We'll be sure to work on our entrance for next time."

With a sassy wink, she prances back to the shirtless heap of muscle, her toned butt swaying enthusiastically.

"Alright, babe, off you go. We'll have to take a rain check on this afternoon's delights," she chirps, rising onto her toes to peck him on the nose before sauntering across the room to fetch his shirt, tossing it at him.

The guy catches it mid-air. "Ah, come on, T," he whines, his face a mix of frustration and exasperation as he rakes a large hand over his buzzed head. "You can't just leave me hanging like this." He gestures to the sizeable bulge still straining against his pants.

"Sorry, babe, no time," Tiana sings, sounding entirely unbothered. "I promised I'd show Elaina around before she starts her new gig tomorrow. Priorities, babes."

"I know what I'd fucking prioritise," Dean mutters under his breath.

Tiana snickers. "Aw, come on, big guy. I know you can think of at least a hundred other ways to rid yourself of those blue balls real quick." She gives him a playful shove toward the door. "Now, off you go, handsome."

"Jerking off in the shower wasn't exactly what I had in mind for this afternoon," Dean grumbles as he adjusts himself, wincing slightly.

Tiana just beams at him as she sashays to the door, giving him a light slap on the ass as he walks past.

"Later, babes," she calls after him before swinging the door shut in his face as he turns to glower at her, another complaint forming on his pouty lips.

She spins back to face me, slapping her palms together.

"Now then," she exclaims, twirling across the floor to scoop up her discarded skirt and tossing it onto her unmade bed. "Did you want to shower first, or should we just hightail it outta here?"

She looks at me expectantly, her violet-blue eyes almost too large for her petite face.

"I had a shower before I got here," I say, watching as she rummages through the pile of clothes strewn across her bed, eventually pulling out a pair of ripped denim shorts and a burnt-red top that perfectly complements her wild hair.

"Even better," she chirps. "Let me throw these on, and I'll give you the grand tour of your new home, sweet home."

Chapter Thirteen

"I'M SO SORRY FOR interrupting you and your boyfriend earlier," I apologise again as Tiana leads me up the dirt path to the staff lodge.

"Boyfriend?" Tiana echoes, chuckling as she glances at me. "Dean's not my boyfriend."

"He's not?"

She snorts. "Definitely not. He's my—hmm, how to best explain Dean?" She scrunches her nose in contemplation. "Dean's my... boy toy. How's that?"

My eyebrows lift. "Boy toy, huh?"

"Yep," Tiana chirps, unabashed. "I mean, did you *see* his muscles? And the size of his package?" She fans herself. "I couldn't let all that deliciousness go to waste, now, could I?"

I rein in my smile. "I guess not."

Tiana lifts a shoulder in a carefree shrug. "Dean's a sweetheart, really. But he's... a simple guy, you know?" She smacks her lips. "He's easy to read, knows what he wants, doesn't play games. And God knows he knows how to give a girl one hell of a good time. But I'm under no illusion that I'll ever be anything more to him than a good fuck."

I wince. "Does that bother you?"

"Not in the slightest," she says lightly, tone utterly sincere. "After all, that's all he is to me. How could I be mad at him for feeling the same way?"

Catching my surprise, she smirks. "Trust me, chick. Any girl would be a fool to fall for Dean. He's probably fucked his way through at least thirty of the female staff at this hotel since he started working here a couple of years ago."

I falter. I can't imagine sleeping with a guy who's already been with over thirty women I not only know but have to work with every day.

Tiana seems to read into my silence. "Look. Dean's a good friend, that's all. I don't care what he's done in the past, or even really what he does now. We know exactly where we stand with each other. And we both know the only thing we'll ever really want from one another is a damn good orgasm. Or multiple orgasms, I should say." She grins shamelessly. "As long as he makes sure to wrap up his delectable parcel every time he intends to use it, his business is his business."

I can't help but admire her blasé attitude. I don't know if I could ever be as carefree as Tiana seems to be when it comes to something as intimate as sex.

"So, you're not the relationship type, then?" I ask as we approach the communal showers.

"Now, where's the fun in that?" Tiana wriggles her eyebrows suggestively, coaxing a laugh from me.

"Honestly, though?" Her cheeky smile softens slightly. "I was born with two hormone-ridden X chromosomes too, so I can't deny that there's a teeny tiny, slightly sappy part of me that wouldn't mind finding someone I feel a deeper connection with. Someone who makes my heart beat just a little faster, who makes my stomach flutter just that little bit wilder when he looks at me a certain way."

She shrugs. "I simply haven't felt that way about anyone before. Don't get me wrong—I've had a couple of long-term boyfriends, and I definitely experienced my fair share of hormonal lust and jealousy throughout high school. But ever since I shook off those raging teenage growth hormones, the reality is that no one has managed to hold my interest for more than a few nights of fun ever since."

She does a little shoulder shimmy. "What can I say? I guess I like my men dark, naughty, and complicated, and most guys I've met... Let's just say it doesn't take a brain surgeon to figure out what makes 'em tick."

She clicks her tongue. "But enough of that. Let the tour begin! This here is the shower house, open twenty-four-seven. Girls to the right, boys to the left—and if you identify as neither, or you're otherwise uncomfortable with communal showers, have a chat to Ryan and he'll be able to sort you out. Now, don't be alarmed if you hear loud screams mixing with the sound of running water at any odd time of the day. This place is by far one of the most popular spots for getting your rocks off around here."

She gives me a knowing look before twirling her finger in a circle. "The cabins around us are mostly accommodations for seasonal staff. Twenty in total, each one holding up to four people. Every cabin is occupied, most of them full."

Gesturing for me to follow, she adds, "We had another girl in our cabin for about three days, but her grandfather got sick or something, so she left. That's how a spot opened up for you." She beams.

"Who's the other girl staying in our cabin?"

"Oh, that's right. You haven't met Bethy yet."

"Bethy?"

Tiana laughs. "Her name's actually Bethany. She's a hoot 'n a half that one, I'll tell you." She rolls her eyes. "Let's just say she's about as different from me as you could possibly get."

My mouth rounds in a silent "oh".

"So, not best friends then?" I venture, unsure what kind of mess I've just stepped into.

"Now, that's the understatement of the decade," Tiana scoffs, wry amusement lacing her voice.

I bite my lip. The last thing I need is to enter the roommate edition of World War III.

"I suppose it's more accurate to say *I'm* not *her* best friend," Tiana continues as we head toward the staff lodge. "Bethy's alright, really. She's super tidy and clean—you probably picked up on that already. And she works a lot, so she's barely ever around. She's just a tad... uptight, you know? She despises people who don't follow every rule under the sun to a T. She's practically ready to write you down in her little black book of sin the moment you even hint at crossing half a toe over some invisible line."

Tiana throws out her arms as if to say, *look at me.* "I mean, let's be real here. Do I look like a righteous, law-abiding citizen to you?"

I chuckle. "I guess not."

"Exactly. Bethy definitely has more issues with me than I have with her—but that's life, right? Can't be everyone's favourite."

Preaching to the choir, sister.

We climb a set of wooden stairs and step onto a sprawling outdoor deck.

The first thing that catches my eye is the built-in timber bar to the side of the wide sliding doors leading into the lodge. A beer pong table sits underneath the eave, the sticky residue of past games still visible on the deep green surface.

Scattered across the deck are various seating areas—comfortable outdoor couches, plastic sunbeds adorned with worn patio cushions, and wicker chairs arranged in small clusters.

An eye-catching, custom-built seating area quickly draws my attention. A built-in fire pit sits at its centre, surrounded by four wooden day beds with plush cushions covered in thick blankets and fluffy, oversized pillows.

"Pretty cool, right?" Tiana comments as she urges me forward. "Come on. I'll show you something even better."

She leads me across the deck and points to a metal cylinder mounted on the wall.

I blink. "Is that a projector screen?"

"Yep. Got installed last summer. Absolute dream. We host movie nights every Thursday now. The owners are pretty keen on keeping their staff happy. I mean, we spend all day watching rich people enjoy the best life has to offer. It's only natural we'd get a little jealous after a while."

She throws herself onto one of the gigantic pillows scattered about the place. "Some of these added perks definitely help boost staff retention. A bunch of us are ticking off multiple seasons by this point."

I sit down across from her and pick up a soccer ball, rolling it idly between my fingers. "How many seasons have you worked here?"

"This will be my third summer." Tiana holds up her hands for me to toss her the ball. I oblige, and she catches it easily. "I did about a month over Christmas last year, too. Loved it. The decorations around here were next level."

"I bet," I say wistfully, remembering what May told me before another thought strikes me. "What exactly is it that you do here, by the way?"

Tiana spins the soccer ball on her fingertip. "I work at the gym, and sometimes with the entertainment crew," she tells me. "I'm a dancer and performer by trade, so I originally applied for a part-time position as a background dancer and singer. But during my interview, they mentioned the hotel wanted to offer dance classes and asked if I'd be interested in taking on an instructor role. I now teach dance, Zumba and aerobics—and I occasionally cover other classes too."

I guess that explains the toned muscles framing her voluptuous curves.

"Sounds like a pretty cool gig."

"I love it," Tiana concurs. "I get paid to do what I love. What more can you ask for, right?"

"True that," I nod, though the words stir something deeper. I've never had the luxury of considering a proper career, let alone finding something I'd genuinely love to do.

I'm about to ask her another question when the terrace doors slide open, and two girls step outside.

For a moment, I'm convinced they're twins.

They're wearing identical tank tops over tight-fitting mini-shorts—one in light blue, the other in bright pink. Their platinum blonde hair falls in identical, bouncy spirals over their narrow shoulders, each strand curled to perfection.

As they peer over at us, bold lashes and striking blue eye shadow amplify their already similar features.

When they walk in our direction, I feel Tiana stiffen beside me.

"Here we go," she mutters under her breath.

I don't have time to question her before they're standing in front of us, identically pointed eyebrows raised in practised condescension.

"New meat?" the girl in the bright pink top asks, barely sparing Tiana a glance before her glare settles on me.

New meat? What is this, prison camp?

Tiana snorts loudly before responding in a falsely enthusiastic tone, "Oh yes. New meat indeed. This is Miss Chicken McBeefy. Why don't you girls give her a warm, hearty welcome?"

A startled laugh bursts from my lips before I can stop it.

"Oh, *ha-ha*. So funny as always, Hartley," the girl in pink sneers, eyes narrowing into angry slits.

"I thought so," Tiana says brightly, entirely unfazed by the scathing energy radiating from the Barbie Brigade.

"So, who are you, then?" the girl in the blue top asks, folding her arms across her perky chest. Now that she's closer, I notice her face is slightly more angular than her friend's, her tall frame revealing a more delicate bone structure.

I meet her glare with a steady look of my own.

"I'm Elaina," I say, offering a polite nod. "Nice to meet you both."

The girl in pink plasters on a wide, saccharine smile. "And where are you from, *Elaina*?" She draws out my name with an exaggerated lilt, her tone laced with mockery.

"Many, many kilometres from here," I say flatly. The tightness in my smile is starting to ache.

"And what's your business here?" she continues, tapping her foot against the wooden floorboards in a steady rhythm.

"Work."

"Well, *duh,*" the girl scoffs, rolling her eyes. "What kind of work?"

"Oh, this and that," I respond airily.

More laughter bubbles up as their expressions tighten comically.

"Is this a welcome greeting or an interrogation?" Tiana finally interjects dryly. "You girls haven't even introduced yourselves, and yet it's already starting to feel like poor Elaina's a contestant on Jeopardy over here."

She gestures toward the two blondes. "Elaina, let me introduce you to our resident mean girl squad—Clara and Kelsey."

"Pleasure, girls," I say, mimicking Tiana's broad smile.

"You should know you've managed to sniff out the biggest skank in this entire place," Clara sniffs, tilting her head toward Tiana with a self-satisfied smirk. Her pink-painted lips match her top perfectly.

At that, Tiana throws her head back and howls with laughter. "Pot, meet kettle," she cackles, eyes twinkling with mirth.

"Hey, watch yourself," Kelsey sneers, brimming with indignation on her friend's behalf.

"Oh, settle down, little lamb. You'll give yourself an aneurysm with all that pent-up spitefulness," Tiana quips, tossing the soccer ball aside as she pushes off her pillow, completely ignoring their indignant splutters.

"Ladies, this has been fun and all, but Elaina and I have places to be, people to see. And you two"—she flicks a dismissive hand at them—"are definitely not on that list."

She stretches out an arm to help me up. "Ready to go?"

"Never been more ready," I reply, grateful for the escape as I follow after Tiana, who salutes the two fuming blondes as she strides away.

"I'll show you the lodge later," she says as we round the front of the building. "There's too much cattiness polluting the air right now for my liking. And I can't guarantee Miss Shit-For-Brains and her trusty sidekick back there wouldn't follow us inside and cause more of a spectacle."

I don't complain, perfectly happy not to spend another second in their presence. "Should I even ask what crawled up their butts just now?"

Tiana snorts. "You want the grocery list?" She shakes her head, red curls bouncing. "Honestly, they've been like that with pretty much everyone since they arrived a few weeks ago."

"So this is their first season here too?"

"Yep." Tiana rolls her eyes. "Lucky us, right?"

"What do they do?"

"Housekeeping. And thank the Lord for that. Means I don't have to see them much during the day." She picks up the pace as the path widens. "I should probably clarify my earlier statement—they don't act like that with everyone. Just with any girl they see as competition for the guys' attention."

"Ah. Gotcha."

Tiana tilts her head, eyeing me playfully. "You've got some sass in you though, girl. I like that."

"If that's true, I think you bring it out of me. Can't say I've met many girls with more spunk than you."

Tiana chortles. "I'll proudly claim that crown."

Our laughter flows as we cross the lawn, drawing closer to the looming castle walls.

"Should we do a quick tour of the grounds before heading inside to get your employee stuff sorted?" Tiana asks, pointing to a winding path to our left.

"Definitely," I say, excitement bubbling. "I've been dying to see the view from up here since I first laid eyes on this place."

"Oh, it's a stunner," Tiana nods as we head across the driveway, waving to the porter standing guard at the hotel entrance. He smiles back, saluting us.

"That's Greg. Super nice guy. He's worked for the de Águila family forever."

Seizing the opening to learn more about the elusive hotel owners, I ask, "Have you had a chance to get to know the family while working here?"

"I've met them all," Tiana shrugs. "Can't say I know them. De Águila senior only visits now and then, and Mrs de Águila barely spends any time here, so we don't see much of them outside of big events and such."

"What about the son? Isn't he the one running things now?"

Tiana groans. "Don't even get me started on him. *Damn*, is he one hunky piece of male godliness."

She looks genuinely pained for a moment. "What I wouldn't do to get my hands on him—even just for one short hour of pure bliss."

I sigh. "I take it you're a fan, then?"

"Oh, don't get me wrong. He's a total douche twat," Tiana says, surprising a laugh out of me. "Every time he visits—which, considering he owns the joint, isn't all that often—he walks around like he's got a jumbo-sized cucumber stuck up his ass. Acts like the whole world's beneath him, barely spares a glance at anyone—unless you're one of his supermodel flavours of the night."

She tosses a hand in the air. "You know the type—toothpick sized, plastic bunnies with perky, supersized tits and legs a mile long, guaranteed to spread their thighs across his desk in under two seconds flat."

Raising a finger, she interrupts her own tirade. "Though I suppose you can't really judge the poor things for seizing their chance to climb the man, *the legend*, the self-proclaimed God himself, when the opportunity arises. From what I've heard, one night with Domenico de Águila will pretty much ruin you for any other man."

She winks. "Even if that wasn't the case, one look at that gorgeous jawline and taut ass is enough to make any girl's panties melt—and some guys' too, I'm sure."

"Oh, I don't know about that," I quip, casting a glance toward the porter. "I can't see old Greg over there drooling over the boss's bouncy butt cheeks."

Tiana doubles over as she howls with laughter.

"True," she chortles, wiping a stray tear from the corner of her eye. "Admittedly, I might not be speaking for all the guys around here—though I'd bet you just about every single one of them would give their own right butt cheek to look like him, even for a day. As for us girls..." She sighs, leaving the thought unspoken.

When I remain silent, she raises a perfectly arched eyebrow. "You disagree?"

I shrug.

"Girl, you're either blind, or you've never laid eyes on the man before. Which is it?"

I scoff. "Look, he's good-looking and all. I doubt anyone who's actually seen him would say otherwise. But it's just..."

I hesitate, thinking back to the unnerving chill I felt when those azure irises speared through me. "His pretty face isn't enough to draw me in, that's all. If anything, it kind of makes me want to take off running in the opposite direction."

Tiana studies me quietly for a moment.

"You know what?" she muses after a few beats. "If any other girl had said that to me after laying eyes on *all that is* Domenico de Águila, I'd call bullshit. But I actually believe you when you say it."

I smile as we round the corner, following the path as it curves along the gentle slope of a hill.

Tiana might come across as bold and carefree, but something tells me there's a lot more to her beneath her brash demeanour.

"I suppose I can see where you're coming from. Sort of," she concedes as we pass a pair of finely dressed, grey-haired women perched on one of the many benches scattered around the garden.

"Even though we all drool over him, no one actually knows much about him. You pick up bits and pieces from magazines—they love writing about him whenever they can dig up a semi-juicy slice of gossip. But it's not like those vultures count as trustworthy sources. The long-term staff sometimes share minor details, but truth be told, he's a bit of an enigma to us all."

"And let me guess—that only adds to the allure?" I quirk a knowing brow.

"Oh, you bet," Tiana winks. "Nothing like a sexy mystery man to get the juices flowing."

As we crest the small hill, the lush grass separates the castle from the looming cliff edge as it comes into view. We fall into silence as we approach the iron fence.

A silent gasp seizes in my throat as I look across the endless velvet ocean below. Waves crash against the jagged cliffs, their steady rhythm harmonising with the rustling sound of leaves bristling in the evening breeze and the distant cries of seagulls soaring high above the water.

Far below, tiny figures—no larger than ants from where we stand—meander across the sandy dunes and along the beachside pavilion. The town is alive with movement, lights winking to life inside restaurants as they prepare for the afternoon rush.

In the distance, the lighthouse stands tall and unwavering, its presence a silent promise to guide wandering fishermen safely to shore when the sky commences its slow descent into dusk.

"Not a bad view, hey?" Tiana says softly, her voice carrying an uncharacteristic tenderness.

"You can say that again," I whisper, matching her quiet tone. It's by far one of the most picturesque scenes I've ever witnessed.

I follow a large wave as it rolls toward the shore, white foam crowning its crest like delicate lace.

"Do you ever wish you could just float away on a wave?" The words slip through my lips before I even realise I'm speaking. "Leave all your worries behind. Just let go as you drift peacefully toward the horizon without a care in the world, letting the calming beauty of the ocean swallow you whole, until all that's left is freedom and peace."

A heavy silence follows.

Crap. Did I say all that aloud?

I tear my eyes from the sea, forcing a weak laugh that doesn't sound at all convincing. "Sorry. No idea where all that came from. Must be the lack of sleep catching up with me. That, and all the excitement of getting this job. I really can't wait to get started tomorrow. And to see more of this place. It's just... amazing, isn't it? This view? I think I could get lost in it for hours."

I exhale sharply, trying to rein in my rambling. I don't like the knowing look in Tiana's eyes.

"So, where to next?" I blurt.

It's a clumsy pivot, and it's obvious Tiana sees right through it. To my relief, she lets it slide.

"I was thinking I'd show you where you need to head tomorrow morning for your first shift. And maybe the pool and gym area too, so you can come visit me whenever you're bored," Tiana says, a lingering curiosity on her face that I pointedly ignore.

"Sounds great." I scramble for something to distract her when a shrill ringtone pierces the air.

Tiana pats her pockets, fishing out a mobile phone. "Sorry, I gotta take this one real quick."

She steps a few paces away, raising the phone to her ear, and I turn back to the view, leaning my forearms against the iron fence.

The wind whips around me, sending tendrils of hair dancing.

I let my thoughts drift across the ocean, ready to lose myself in the hypnotic pull of the waves once more, when a sharp movement near the corner of my vision pulls me back.

I whip my head around—and collide with a pair of intense, stormy eyes.

For a moment, I lose the ability to think or speak as the intensity of the stranger's gaze captivates me. The world tilts, my thoughts scattering like autumn leaves caught in the wind.

The sheer force of it roots me in place. Something tangible shifts in the air, crackling like a live wire. His eyes, luminous in the blinding light of the sun, are coloured an obscure shade I can't quite pin down, unnaturally vivid against the deep bronze of his skin.

Seconds stretch between us. Hours. Days.

He studies me closely, drinking me in with a look I can't decipher. Beneath his quiet inscrutability, something else looms—a shadow shifting behind his enigmatic cloak.

The longer I look into those magnetic eyes, the more everything around me seems to fall away, my thoughts shattering to pieces that spread out in broken fragments across the patch of grass between us.

I feel exposed. As if his perceptiveness can somehow pierce right through the layers of protection I so carefully keep in place, peeling me apart with a single glance.

I should look away.

I *need* to look away.

But I don't.

I trace the sharp cut of his jaw, dusted in a shadow of stubble. It travels over his golden skin, past the slightly crooked bridge of his nose—once broken, perhaps, and never set properly.

His hair is a deep inky black, tousled and unruly, shorter at the sides in a way that only sharpens the fierceness of his features. A few stray curls tumble across his forehead, careless and alluring.

His lips part almost immeasurably, and I catch the barest flick of movement as the pink tip of his tongue glides along his lower lip, a sharp intake of breath following in its wake. His chest rises and falls in a slow, measured rhythm that somehow syncs with the jagged, uneven cadence of my own.

I stare at his shoulders, at the way his simple white T-shirt clings to solid muscle, stretching over broad shoulders, before dipping to hug the curve of his biceps.

My eyes snap back to his once more.

A shiver runs through me. Goosebumps spread across my arms, down my back, prickling at the base of my spine.

My breath catches.

Abruptly, it's as if a shield slams down between us. His entire presence hardens, any hint of warmth eclipsed by something cold and impenetrable.

His storm-lit irises turn arctic, the wavering light that lingered there only seconds ago extinguished, as if it was nothing more than a mirage—a bewitching figment of my imagination.

With a deep intake of breath, the man lets his eyelids flutter closed for what feels like an eternity, though in reality, it can't have lasted more than a few seconds.

Without a word, he bends down and grips a large burlap sack lying in the grass beside him that I hadn't even noticed.

With a final cutting glance in my direction, he throws it over his shoulder, turns his back, and strides away, never once looking back.

Chapter Fourteen

It's not until the stranger's broad frame disappears in the distance that I realise I've been holding my breath.

A slow exhale escapes me, my chest rising and falling as I gulp down several lungfuls of crisp, salty air.

I feel off-kilter. Dizzy, as though I've just woken from a deep slumber, still trapped in the fog of a dream I can't quite shake.

My fingers tighten around the cold metal of the fence, grounding myself against the sudden unsteadiness threatening to tip me sideways. The sea breeze whips at my hair, and I close my eyes for a moment, letting the relentless pull of the sea steady me.

A voice snaps me back to reality.

"Helloo? Earth to Elaina?"

Blinking, I find Tiana watching me, a curious frown creasing her otherwise smooth forehead.

"Sorry," I mumble, embarrassed. "Totally spaced out there for a second."

"That's putting it mildly," Tiana teases, though her tone is more amused than offended. "I've been talking for the better part of a minute. At first, I thought you were just the silent, listening type, but it didn't take long to realise you were off in La-La Land."

Heat creeps up my cheek, and Tiana grins. "No dramas, chick. It's not a crime to get lost in your own head once in a while."

I give her an apologetic smile, quietly relieved she didn't pick up on the real reason for my distraction. If she knew I'd spent the better part of her phone call ogling a stranger, I've no doubt she'd have a field day with it.

The strangest part is that I can't even recall his face in detail. For how long I'd been staring, you'd think I'd remember every angle, every feature. But all I can grasp are fragments—sharp cheekbones, the curve of his lips, the stubble shadowing his jaw. Like a puzzle only half completed, not yet revealing the full picture.

But his eyes?

Those, I could never forget.

That dark intensity that seemed to pin me in place, threatening to pull me under from an unseen current.

Despite my better judgement, curiosity tugs at me.

"Who was that guy earlier?" I ask, keeping my tone deliberately casual.

Tiana frowns, glancing around. "Who?"

"The guy standing over there a moment ago." I gesture toward the now-empty space. "Tall, dark-ish, olive skin. Black hair, broad shoulders? He had a burlap sack."

Recognition flits across Tiana's face. "Ah. You mean Orlando."

Orlando.

The name somehow fits the guarded man I just locked eyes with. "Is he a groundskeeper or something?"

Tiana shrugs. "Yes and no. He's a bit of an everything-and-nothing kind of guy around here."

My brows knit. "What does that mean?"

She pauses, as if searching for the right words. "Honestly? I still don't know exactly what it is he does. He's been here for years, and he's pretty close to the owners. When I first started, I assumed he was Domenico's personal assistant or something, because I always spotted them together."

She tilts her head thoughtfully. "Mind you, he doesn't look like anyone's PA. If anything, he looks more like a bodyguard. Or a model. But I couldn't think of any other reason why they spent so much time together, or why Orlando never seemed to spend any time around the other staff."

"So he doesn't live in the staff village?"

"Nope."

A strange twinge I can't quite place sweeps through me, but I ignore it.

"He has his own cabin on the other side of the grounds. Off-limits to other staff. The guy sure does like his privacy."

Tiana's words catch me by surprise, and she catches it immediately. "Yep. Like I said, I figured he was pretty high up the ranks. But after a few weeks, I started spotting him all over—lugging bags of soil, working in the gardens, fixing stuff around the gym. Then one of the admin girls lost her damn mind when he suddenly rocked up to an internal stakeholder meeting. In a full Armani suit, no less." She raises an eyebrow. "Man, she wouldn't shut up about him for weeks."

I blink. "And what exactly was he doing there?"

"Apparently? Nothing. Didn't say a single word the entire time. Just sat there, all broody and mysterious. But I ask you—what the hell would a janitor be doing at a stakeholder meeting in a two-thousand-dollar suit?"

"Beats me," I murmur, mulling over her words.

"He's even more of a mystery than the Big Boss himself, truth be told. At least we get *some* gossip about Domenico—catch him out with his lady tramps, hear whispers of his latest exploits. But Orlando?" She shakes her head. "No one really knows anything about him."

Somehow, this doesn't surprise me. One look into his dark, elusive gaze told me enough to suspect that Orlando isn't the type of man to reveal his true self to the world.

Perhaps even less so than I do.

"He's considered a bit of a lone wolf," Tiana continues, stretching her arms over her head with a yawn. "Closed off, broody. Most people tend to leave him alone. At least once they realise he's not like the other guys around here—to the deep-rooted disappointment of pretty much every girl within a hundred-yard radius. You can bet your entire salary that just about every single female staff member here would happily sell a kidney for a shot with Orlando."

I quickly decide to ignore that last part. "The other guys?"

Tiana rolls her eyes. "Yeah. I mean, look at them. Half these idiots are basically here for one reason, and one reason only—to chase pretty girls and screw their way through the summer before heading back to their 'real lives'." She makes air quotes with her fingers.

"It's a common theme, especially with the seasonal staff. No long-term consequences, no real responsibilities. And when people stop worrying about consequences? They get up to all kinds of shit."

She shrugs, then smirks wickedly. "Not that I'm complaining. Some of these boys? Fine as hell. And I'm not one to turn down some good, old-fashioned holiday fun when it's offered up on a perfectly muscular, testosterone-fuelled platter. But I won't pretend that most of them have anything other than sex and stupidity on their brains."

I sigh. A village full of horny boys and territorial girls, all trapped together in one confined space for three whole months.

Delightful.

Tiana grins at the look on my face. "Oh, come on, now. It'll be more fun than you think. The amount of shit you'll witness this summer will blow your mind, chick. And trust me—if you let yourself get swept up in the whirlwind that is this hotel, you'll walk out of here in three months' time a totally different woman. A summer up here, and you'll never be the same again."

She winks. "That, my friend, is the magic of Castillo del Acantilado."

I let out a deep breath, closing my eyes.

You wanted different, Elaina? Well, here's your chance.

When I open them again, I meet Tiana's eager grin as a slow smile spreads across my own face.

"You know what? Why the hell not. Bring it on."

Chapter Fifteen

We spend the next hour wandering the hotel grounds. Just when I think I've seen the height of luxury, every new section of the estate proves me wrong.

Tiana keeps me entertained with stories about her life—her father, the only close remaining living relative she has left, her childhood in southern England as a mixed-race girl born to a British mother and a Portuguese father, and her years working in the creative arts industry.

She nudges me to talk about myself, and I offer carefully curated pieces of my past—fragments of my childhood in Scandinavia, and later, Eastern Europe—keeping any details that might raise suspicion at bay. Every time a white lie leaves my lips, I press on, ignoring the twitch of guilt that knots my stomach.

As Tiana locks up the doors to the state-of-the-art gym, she glances down at her watch, the bright pink strap a stark contrast against her flame-red hair.

"Damn. It's already five-thirty. We better head back to the lodge before we miss dinner."

The sun has begun its slow descent behind us, casting long shadows across the emerald lawn.

As we approach the lodge, warm light spills from the open front door, and the rich scent of garlic and cumin wafts through the air.

Tiana inhales deeply. "*Ooh*, that's right. It's paella night. Come to mama."

With renewed enthusiasm, she picks up the pace, practically bounding up the steps to the front porch.

We walk down a narrow hallway lined with framed photographs of the castle until we reach a wide archway leading into a high-ceilinged dining hall.

A wall of sound crashes over us, laughter, chatter, and music blending into a chaotic din.

I pause for a moment to take it all in.

At least ten rectangular tables stretch across the room, each one flanked by sturdy wooden benches wide enough to fit twelve people on either side. Most are already filled, and the energy in the space is lively and warm.

The hall itself is rustic and airy, with large windows lining the walls offering views of the dense forest surrounding the lodge.

Tiana steers us to a buffet-style serving station, where trays of steaming paella are laid out.

"Let's get in there before the rest of the outdoor crew arrives and steals whatever's left," she advises, piling her plate high.

I follow her lead, grabbing a pair of tongs to load up on salad and warm bread rolls.

Plates brimming, Tiana scans the room before zeroing in on a table near the terrace doors. As we weave through the crowded space, I do my best to ignore the curious stares directed my way. The whispers and lingering glances pressing in from several of the tables we pass make my neck itch.

I focus my sight on the ink swirling beneath the collar of Tiana's shirt, stretching from her upper back to the base of her neck. The design looks intricate, though only a fraction of it is visible.

I make a mental note to ask her about it later.

"Scoot, bitches. This girl is starving," Tiana quips as she drops her tray onto the table, squeezing in next to a girl with glossy black hair and warm, honey-brown skin.

"What's up, T?" A dark-skinned girl with a gorgeous, voluminous Afro greets her. She gives me a quick once-over, tilting her head. "Who's the new girl?"

A slender girl with shoulder-length, curly blonde hair framing her heart-shaped face shuffles her tray down the table, offering me a friendly smile as I sit down beside her.

"This is Elaina," Tiana says through a mouthful of paella. "She just got here this afternoon."

She gestures at each girl around the table in turn. "Elaina, meet Jess, Tess, Rhianna, and Paige."

The girl of Indian descent next to Tiana—Jesmindah, according to her name tag—offers me a warm smile. "Welcome to Cliff Castle, Elaina. It's nice to meet you." Her voice is soft and lilting, a musical accent claiming each word.

"Thanks. It's nice to meet you guys too," I say, returning her smile as I pick up my fork and scoop up a forkful of paella.

"So, where will they have you slaving away, then?" the girl with the Afro—Rhianna, I think her name was—asks, taking a sip of water as she watches me.

"Oh, come on, Rhi. Don't scare her off on her first day," the girl named Tess interjects, shaking her head. "You'll make her think the managers here are slave drivers."

"Depending on where she's stationed, that might not be far from the truth," Rhianna responds, quirking a brow.

Tiana waves a dismissive hand. "The way Elaina's set to bounce between departments, she's bound to run into at least one nightmare manager sooner or later."

Rhianna frowns. "Bounce between departments?"

The girls all turn to me expectantly.

I clear my throat, shifting under the weight of their attention. "I guess you could say I've been hired as an 'everything' kind of person?"

Blank stares.

"Basically, I step in wherever an extra pair of hands is needed—whether it's in the kitchen, the outdoor crew, or somewhere else," I clarify. "But most days, I'll be working with the event planning team."

Tess tilts her head, surprise colouring her pretty face. "I don't remember seeing an ad for that role. Is it new?"

I shrug. "I think so. I came here a couple of days ago to ask about vacancies. One thing led to another, and they sort of created it on the spot."

Paige—the blonde beside me—flicks her curls over her shoulder, her words wrapped in a honeyed southern drawl as she says, "Well, darn, girl. Colour me jealous. I'd just *love* to work in a different department now and again. Shake things up a little. How exciting."

Jesmindah snorts. "Easy for you to say, Paige. You and Tiana both get to do what you love every single day. Some of us have to do *actual* work. You don't have to appease prissy guests all day, busting your ass to cater to their every whim."

"Hear, hear," Tess chimes in, clinking her glass against Jesmindah's.

"You can't really talk either, missy," Jesmindah quips, throwing Tess a knowing look.

Tess tilts her head, all wide-eyed innocence. "What do you mean? I cater to the whims and wishes of the wealthy the same way you do, don't I?"

Jesmindah snorts. "In theory, sure. But let's be real. Customers practically adore you, Tess. Not a day goes by that I don't pick up the phone to find some handsome billionaire requesting you specifically—only to watch him hand you a ginormous tip after you've successfully '*fulfilled his innermost desires*'."

She makes air quotes with her fingers, and the table bursts into laughter.

"Oh, hush, Jess," Tess chides, though amusement bleeds through her scolding. "You're making it sound all sordid. I would never compromise my job to fulfil a guest's '*innermost desires*'. You know that."

She unclips the large claw clip holding her hair in a loose twist, and it tumbles into a tousled bob falling just shy of her shoulders.

Jesmindah sighs dramatically. "True. But still, they all love you on sight. Meanwhile, most guests take one look at me and my wedding ring and assume I'm best suited for all the boring requests—which, by the way, don't pay nearly as well as the more... *innovative* requests."

More laughter follows, and I find myself smiling, despite not fully understanding the inside joke.

Noticing my confusion, Tess turns to me. "Jess and I are concierges, so our job essentially revolves around catering to the guests' every want, wish, and whim."

She nods toward the other girls. "Rhianna and Paige work at the salon and spa. Rhianna's a beautician, and Paige's a masseuse. And I'm guessing you already know what Tiana does."

I glance around at them. "Your jobs all sound really interesting."

Rhianna snickers. "Says the girl who'll be sticking her fingers in all sorts of honey pots over the next few weeks." A mischievous smirk plays on her lips. "And here I thought Miss Harlot and Miss Tart over there were the only ones doing that this year."

We all follow her line of sight, straight to Clara and Kelsey.

At that exact moment, Clara lifts a forkful of chocolate cake in front of a very attractive guy with short, sandy-blond hair and bulging biceps, her smile coy and alluring.

Tiana and Tess dissolve into laughter, while Paige gives Rhianna a pointed look. "That's not very nice, Rhi. Poor Elaina's going to think we're just a bunch of gossiping hens with sex on our brains. Or that we're making fun of her new job," she adds, glancing at me apologetically.

I wave it off with a smile. "My job will probably be far more boring than it sounds."

Paige brightens. "Oh, I hope you get to work with us at the spa sometime. It's absolutely gorgeous and *so* luxurious. You'll feel all pampered and pretty just stepping inside the door. Come by one day and I'll give you a tour."

"I'd love that," I say, already charmed by her bubbly personality.

Rhianna leans forward, resting her elbows on the table. "Will you stick around for drinks tonight, Elaina? Most of us tend to hang out at the lodge in the evenings; play some pool, unwind. It'd be a good way for you to get to know more of the staff."

I hesitate. The thought of meeting yet another wave of new people tonight makes leaves me feeling even more drained than I already was.

"Maybe another night?" I hedge, biting my lip. "I haven't unpacked yet, and I should probably get some sleep before my first day."

“Probably a good idea,” Rhianna nods, unfazed, and I stifle a relieved sigh.

"What about you, T?" Tess asks, eyeing Tiana. "Sticking around for a quick bevvy before hitting the sack?”

"Oh, she'll be hitting someone's sack tonight, alright." Rhianna waggles her brows. "Or rather, licking it."

The entire table erupts in laughter, loud enough that a few people at nearby tables turn to glance over at us.

Tiana shimmies her shoulders. "You know it, girl.”

As the conversation shifts back to playful banter, I scoop up another bite of paella, savouring the rich, spicy flavours rolling across my tongue.

When my plate is clean, Tiana catches my yawn and leans over the table, tossing her napkin down. "Wanna head back to the cabin? I desperately need a shower after all that sticky afternoon heat."

I nod, stretching my tired legs as I push back from the table.

"See you guys later." Tiana nods to the girls as we pick up our trays.

“It was nice meeting you, Elaina,” Paige calls after us. I glance back with a smile, giving the others a small wave before trailing after Tiana through the maze of tables.

By now, nearly every seat in the hall is taken, the energy humming louder than ever. As we pass Clara and Kelsey’s table, an eerie sensation trickles down my spine. Like the sensation of being watched.

I resist the urge to turn.

Until I can’t.

Slowly, I glance over my shoulder—and find myself locked in place by a pair of bright cobalt-blue irises.

It’s the sandy-haired guy from earlier. The one Clara had been so eagerly spoon-feeding.

A knowing smirk tugs at the corner of his mouth as he sizes me up.

Before I can tear myself away from his gaze, a sharp throat-clearing cuts through the moment, and my focus flicks to Clara.

She’s glaring at me. Fury simmers beneath her polished exterior, her scowl darting between me and Mr Blue Eyes, as if his lingering stare is somehow my fault.

The unspoken warning is clear: I do not belong in his orbit.

I snap my head forward and quicken my pace, falling into step beside Tiana.

The heat of Clara’s glower sears my back, but I ignore it, refusing to let myself get caught in whatever game she’s playing.

Not tonight, anyway.

And if I can help it—not ever.

I only catch a glimpse of our cabin as Tiana opens the door before something comes hurtling through the air toward us.

I instinctively duck, sensing the object zoom past as it skims the top of my head before clattering onto the front porch.

Heart racing, I glance over my shoulder and spot a small, rectangular box with black-and-red wrapping, its contents spilling all over the wooden deck.

Condoms.

I barely have time to register the sight before a furious shriek cuts through the air.

A tall, slender woman stands just inside the cabin, her light-brown hair woven into two long braids. Oversized tortoise-rimmed glasses rest on the bridge of her nose, yet there's nothing studious about the blazing contempt etched onto her face.

Her taupe-coloured irises are practically aflame.

"What the hell is wrong with you?" she hisses, her blistering glare locked on Tiana like a heat-seeking missile.

"Chill, Tinkerbell." Tiana strolls into the cabin, as if she wasn't just assaulted by a pack of latex balloons. "What's crawled up your butthole this time?"

The girl—Bethany, I assume—folds her arms across her narrow chest, her jaw twitching as she grinds her molars.

"How many times have I told you to keep your filthy habits away from this cabin?"

Tiana waves an indifferent hand through the air. "Oh, hush, child. This is my cabin too."

She saunters over to her bed and flops onto the pile of clothes. "I'm stuffed. That paella was delicious."

Bethany's hands curl into fists at her sides. For a second, I think she's about to throw something else.

Not wanting to get caught in the crossfire, I step cautiously through the doorway.

Now would be a good time to temporarily make myself invisible.

Fortune, as always, is not on my side as Bethany's scathing glare pivots to me.

"And who the hell are you?"

"Jesus, Bethy," Tiana groans. "Do you have to hate absolutely everyone on sight? Keep going the way you are, and you'll turn into a replica of Harriet one day—*sans* style."

Bethany barely spares her a glance. "Considering she's voluntarily hanging out with you, I'm assuming she's already a lost cause," she snipes.

I gape at her blunt hostility.

Tiana, however, looks downright delighted. A slow, wicked grin curves her lips. "Ah, yes. I do have that irresistible effect on people. Shame your personality's already maxed out on an overdose of sourness, envy, and spite, or you might've benefited from it too."

Without another word, Bethany snatches a book off her bedside table and stomps out the door, slamming it behind her with enough force to rattle the windows.

I remain perfectly still, gaping after her, until Tiana's mischievous laughter snaps me out of it.

"Told you she's a hoot, didn't I?" she snorts, eyes twinkling.

I shake my head. "You can say that again." Walking over to my bag, I pull open the zipper. "I don't think I've ever met so many people in one place who seem to immediately despise me on sight."

Tiana chuckles. "Don't worry, girl. Most people here are pretty chill. It's best to get the whackos out of the way early."

She rolls onto her side as she grins at me. "You've got two main kinds of people in a place like this: the horny, adventure-seeking wildcards, and the stiff, career-chasing text-bookers. Toss them all together, and you're bound to get a few clashes."

I huff out a tired laugh.

"The best thing you can do?" she continues, propping herself up on one elbow. "Just be yourself, go with the flow, and ignore the rest. You can't please everyone, but you sure as hell can—and *should*—make the most of your own life. You don't owe anyone anything except to live your life to the fullest. That, we all owe to ourselves."

Her words settle over me with surprising weight.

For over a decade, I haven't even considered what it means to live for myself. It's been all about survival. Obligation. Fading into the background.

Never just *being*.

But I'm ready for that phase of my life to close. It's my life, and I'm damn well going to make the most of it.

Because if I don't, then why am I even here?

Tiana watches me closely. She must notice something shift in my stance, because her grin widens, and she gives me an approving nod.

“That’s that fiery spark I’ve been seeing glimpses of. Let that fire loose a little more often, and trust me—you’ll do just fine up here."

Hopping off her bed, she throws me a teasing look. "Now, come on, sparkles. Let’s hit the showers."

Chapter Sixteen

I wake the next morning to the unexpected sound of running water.

Blinking groggily, I squint up at an unfamiliar ceiling.

I've woken up in so many different places these past few weeks that it's become a disorienting routine—a moment of confusion before reality settles in and I remember which motel I'm in.

My mouth stretches in a wide yawn as I rub the sleep from my eyes. A few seconds pass before it hits me.

The cabin.

The staff village.

Castillo del Acantilado.

I let out a slow exhale, a tingle of anticipation washing over me. For the first time in ages, I even feel rested.

I've existed in a perpetual state of anxiety for so long, always on edge, running on fumes as I brace for the next disaster to hit. I'd almost forgotten what it feels like to get a full night's sleep.

Reluctant to leave the surprisingly comfortable bunk bed, I peer over the side railing.

Bethany's bed's already immaculately made, the sheets tucked so neatly it looks untouched. I squint toward Tiana's bed, finding her wrinkled sheets empty as well.

What time is it?

A jolt of panic flutters through me. I can't afford to be late on my first day.

Rustling through my sheets, I frantically search for the digital alarm clock I brought with me from Viktor's house.

"It's half past six," a muffled voice says.

Bethany's standing at the foot of her bed, a toothbrush sticking out of her mouth.

"Oh." My heart rate slows. "Thanks."

Bethany disappears back into the bathroom, and I do another quick scan of the room. Maybe I missed Tiana down there too?

Bethany reappears in the doorway, wiping her mouth on a towel. "She didn't sleep here last night."

"Ah." A beat of silence passes between us. "Do you know where she is?"

Bethany rolls her eyes. "I'm assuming over at Dean's—unless that hussy decided to find herself a new plaything last night. Wouldn't surprise me one bit."

I concentrate on climbing down the narrow ladder as I avoid her scowl. I don't want is to start off on the wrong foot with my new roommate any more than we already have, but I'm not about to engage in gossip about Tiana—especially when she's not here to defend herself.

"Right," I say instead, tone even.

Rummaging through my bag for a fresh set of clothes, I glance at Bethany again. "You wouldn't happen to know which cabin Dean's staying in?"

Bethany slathers sunscreen onto her pale skin, her silence loaded. She eventually sighs an exaggerated sigh, every movement oozing bored indifference.

"He's over in cabin 9."

The large bronze number 9 gleams on the cabin door in front of me.

I hesitate. *What now?*

I consider turning around and braving breakfast by myself when the door opens, and a shaggy blond head appears.

It takes a few seconds to recognise the guy who was watching me in the dining hall yesterday as I walked past his table.

He halts the moment he spots me, head tilting. I suddenly feel like a complete fruit loop, standing awkwardly outside his cabin.

His cobalt stare drags over me, something unreadable sparking beneath it. Interest? Amusement?

"You're the new girl."

The gravelly rasp of his morning voice catches me off guard. "I suppose I am."

"Elaina, right?"

I blink. "Yes?" It comes out sounding like a question. *How does he know my name?*

Uncomfortable with the strange tension floating between us, I shift my weight. "I'm sorry, I don't know your name?"

He studies me with a calculating look. "I'm Blaise."

I force a polite smile. "Nice to meet you, Blaise."

His mouth spreads in a wicked grin. It's the kind of grin that sets off warning bells—cocky, self-assured, and far too smug.

"So, princess." His voice drops to a silky purr, and I instantly regret engaging with him. "As much as I enjoy seeing your pretty smile first thing in the morning, I'm assuming there's a reason you're here?"

Heat creeps up my neck at his easy flirtation, and his grin widens.

I square my shoulders. "I'm looking for Tiana. My roommate said she might be with Dean?"

Blaise places a hand over his heart, plump lips forming into a pout. "And here I thought you were here for me."

I give up on trying to hide my blush, which only seems to fuel his obnoxious smirk.

"Surely it's not just a lucky coincidence that I happen to share a cabin with Dean." He leans against the door frame, tone laced with challenge. "You see, princess, I have a feeling I caught your eye yesterday, just like you caught mine."

The audacity of this guy.

Annoyance outweighs embarrassment as I meet his overconfident smirk with cool indifference. "Yesterday? Can't say I remember. Lots of new faces, you know?"

Irritation pulls as me when his posture doesn't deflate in the slightest. If anything, his blue irises darken, glinting with renewed intensity.

Yeah, I'm not playing this game.

Before he can throw another flirtatious remark my way, I tilt my chin up and say evenly, "I won't keep you. But if you could let Tiana know I'll be waiting for her in the dining hall, I'd appreciate it."

Without waiting for a response, I turn on my heel and walk away, ignoring the urge to look over my shoulder, knowing I'll find his glittering gaze still fixated on me.

"H-dawg, how's it hangin'?" Tiana's exuberant voice echoes across the marble floor as we approach the front desk.

Harriet's head snaps up like a whip, glare narrowing with immediate disdain.

"Oh, wonderful. You two." Her words drip with sarcasm. "What do you want? I'm busy."

"Oh, we're fabulous, darling. Thank you ever so much for asking," Tiana chirps, adopting a posh British accent that causes a snort to slip from my lips. I clamp them shut, not wanting to add fuel to the fire crackling beneath Harriet's polished exterior.

"Get to the point or get out of my lobby."

Tiana leans casually against the counter, plucking a random pamphlet from a stand and spinning it idly between her fingers. "We were hoping you could tell us where we might find Corban this lovely Monday morning?"

I have no idea who Corban is, but if it gets us out of Harriet's crosshairs faster, I'm all for him.

Harriet snatches the pamphlet mid-spin and places it back in the stand with excessive force. "He has an office, does he not? I'd suggest you go look for him there."

Tiana rolls her eyes. "You know as well as I do that we're more likely to find Corban hiding in a bush somewhere, snapping photos of a gecko scaling the castle walls or something. And I'd rather not spend my morning scouring the grounds looking for him."

Harriet ignores us, typing away at her computer as if we no longer exist.

Tiana's patience snaps. She slaps a hand down on the counter, making me jump.

"For crying out loud, Harriet. Don't be such a sourpuss for once in your life. We all know your contemptuous glare rarely misses a thing around here, so how about you skip the dramatics and just tell us where he is? Then we can happily be on our way, leaving you to your bright, sunny self."

I brace myself for the eruption.

To my amazement, Harriet merely exhales sharply through her nose. Apparently, the prospect of having us out of her sight outweighs her natural inclination to froth at the mouth.

Without sparing us another glance, she says in a curt, clipped tone, "I saw him heading into the east gardens about twenty minutes ago. You'll probably find him there."

"*Gracias, señora.*" The words trill over Tiana's shoulder as she strides toward a large wooden door at the other end of the lobby. I hurry after her, careful not to make eye contact with the blonde reception dragon in case she unleashes another puff of flames.

"Who's Corban?" I ask as we navigate a high-ceilinged hallway.

"Marketing guy. Handles the hotel's website, social media, stuff like that. He also issues staff passes, which is why we need to track him down."

Tiana fishes out the staff pass clipped to her black denim jeans and scans it against a card reader on the wall. A heavy door marked *Staff Only* clicks open, and we step through.

We emerge into a spacious room with floor-to-ceiling windows. Sunlight pours through the large glass panes, rendering the room stiflingly warm compared to the rest of the hotel.

Peering through an open doorway to the garden, I spot a pair of red Converse sneakers poking out from behind a bush.

Tiana strides over and nudges the airborne shoe with her foot. A muffled grunt sounds from deep within the foliage.

"Hang on." The words are followed by a rapid series of muted clicks.

A moment later, a tuft of messy brown hair emerges from the sea of leaves. The man rolls onto his back, a camera clutched in his hand. I startle as a whoop of triumph bursts from his lips.

My heart skips as he tilts his chin up, eyes crinkling at the edges as he beams up at us.

Holy hell.

This man is, without a doubt, the most aesthetically gorgeous man I've ever laid eyes on.

His thick hair is styled in short, messy waves, casually effortless and perfectly tousled. A faded side part gives him a polished edge, and it's impossible not to notice his eyes—warm amber, framed by unfairly long lashes most girls would trade their grandmother's pearls for.

Even so, his sharp jawline and sculpted cheekbones do a fine job of competing for centre stage. I'm almost surprised there's not a flock of girls standing around him in a circle, drooling.

I'm still trying to process the unfair levels of attractiveness when Tiana snaps me back to reality.

"I suppose there's no need to ask why I find you, once again, sprawled on your ass as you do your best to become one with the vegetation?" Her teasing tone earns her a bright, heart-stopping smile as he accepts her outstretched hand.

"Hiya, T."

With effortless grace, he rises to his feet, brushing away the stray leaves and twigs scattered across his hair and clothes. His right hand still clutches the camera, which he lifts triumphantly into the air.

"You won't believe the shot I just got." His face practically glows with excitement. "Absolute stunner. This one's definitely going on the wall."

"Don't doubt that for a second, Corb." Tiana leans her elbow lightly on his shoulder with familiar ease. "Though, you'd be hard-pressed to top those shots you took of the castle during that insane snowstorm last Christmas."

As Corban chortles, I take in his tall, lean stature. His lightly muscular chest and narrow waist are framed by a simple white t-shirt beneath a light-wash denim jacket, the sleeves rolled up to reveal smooth, strong forearms. His slim black jeans end just above his ankles, effortlessly stylish in a way most guys desperately attempt but never quite achieve.

A vintage watch with a polished black leather strap catches the sunlight as he lifts a hand to scratch his chin.

I drag my eyes back up his athletic frame and find his soft, golden irises on me, curiosity swirling in their warm depths. "Ah, I believe we have a new face here." He offers me a friendly smile that matches his kind expression.

"Sure do. Corban, meet my girl, Elaina." Tiana gestures between us. "Elaina, this is our fabulous resident marketing guru, Corban. He's the wizard behind the staff photos—the man who'll make you wish you could steal your employee ID and use it as your modelling head shot."

Corban shakes his head, laughing good-naturedly as he turns his twinkling eyes to me. "Don't listen to her," he mock-whispers, corners crinkling. "Tiana always gives me too much credit."

"Oh, shush, child," Tiana huffs, swatting his arm affectionately. "You could make a naked mole-rat look like a fluffy Teacup Pomeranian with the way you wield that camera. I swear, Corb, you've got photographer magic in your blood."

I barely stop myself from ogling his damn near flawless face as it splits into another wide grin, exuding the kind of effortless charm that belongs on magazine covers.

Corban's golden eyes shift back to me. "You're a model, then?"

I nearly choke on air.

"N-no. Not at all." My voice comes out higher than intended as I duck my head, letting my freshly cut fringe fall across my face to hide my flaming cheeks.

"She damn well could be," Tiana declares, giving me a deliberate once-over. "You're a stunner, Elaina."

I don't blame Corban when his eyes instinctively trail over my body. To his credit, they barely linger on my curves before he quickly diverts his attention, which only makes me more flustered.

Desperate to steer the conversation in a different direction, I blurt, "Should we get this staff pass sorted, then?"

Corban casts one last look at me before he nods toward the castle. "Follow me, ladies."

Chapter Seventeen

THIRTY MINUTES LATER, I'M standing in the elevator on my way to the eighth floor, dressed in a crisp new uniform. A staff badge with my name printed in neat black font rests against my chest.

As the elevator ascends past the fifth floor, I glance down at the schedule in my hand.

Monday, 10:00am to 6:00pm—Housekeeping, Level 8
Tuesday, 5:00am to 2:00pm—Kitchen, Ground Floor
Wednesday, 9:00am to 5:00pm—Administration, Level 2
Thursday, 7:30am to 4:00pm—Event Planning, Level 2
Friday, 9:00am to 5:00pm—Outdoor Crew, Main Entrance

My stomach flips as a cheery ding sounds from the speakers, signalling my arrival. I fold the schedule as the doors glide open—only to freeze mid-step as I'm trapped by a pair of piercing azure eyes.

Domenico de Águila stands before me, impeccably dressed in a dark grey suit. A blue tie rests neatly against the pristine white collar of his shirt, and his dark hair is slicked back in a smooth, sleek style, not a strand out of place.

His gaze drops to my uniform, a small smile tugging at his lips.

It takes me a moment to register the two men standing behind him, waiting patiently for Domenico to enter the elevator.

I recognise the hulking blond security guard from my last meeting with the elusive Domenico de Águila, his massive frame and stern presence unchanged. The other man is unfamiliar. Younger—late twenties or early thirties at a guess—his clean-shaven jaw and round edges lending him an almost boyish look. His brown hair is gelled back neatly, and his deep brown eyes are studying me with a quiet curiosity.

Domenico's attention lingers on me, glinting with recognition. "Miss Delano," he murmurs, his voice a smooth, velvety caress. "What a lovely surprise to see you again so soon."

"Señor de Águila," I croak, my voice raspy with surprise. "It's—it's nice to see you again too, sir."

An angry beep blares from the elevator—an impatient reminder that I'm blocking the doors.

"I—I'm so sorry, sir. I'm holding you up." I step aside to allow his companions to pass. The brown-haired man gives me a polite nod as he enters the elevator.

To my surprise, Domenico doesn't follow.

"Wait for me downstairs," he instructs, his gaze never wavering from me. "I'll be there shortly. I just need a quick word with Miss Delano here."

"But sir..." The young man hesitates. "Your flight is set to leave in less than an hour. We're already cutting it close. We really need to get mov—"

"I said, I'll be there shortly." Domenico's face hardens with a chilling calm as he fixes the younger man with a stern glare.

He wisely clamps his mouth shut.

"Phone Captain Williams. Inform him we'll be departing in ten minutes and to have the plane ready when we arrive. That'll be all, Lincoln."

Lincoln gives a stiff nod and presses the button for the ground floor.

I frantically search my mind for a way to avoid being trapped alone with Domenico.

Even as my mind scrambles for an escape, I remind myself he owns the hotel. And he's the reason I even have a job here in the first place. I don't want to risk offending him.

Taking a deep breath, I step away from the elevator, wary of the closing distance between us. Domenico towers over me in his perfectly pressed suit, his frame easily surpassing six feet. As the elevator doors slide shut behind me, I glance up to find his piercing eyes locked on me.

"I take it you've settled into your cabin?" His tone is conversational. Friendly, even.

"Yes, sir." I aim for a matching calm tone.

"Excellent, excellent. And someone helped you get organised for your first day, I see?" He nods toward my staff badge.

"They did." I tug at my uniform, suddenly self-conscious.

Remembering my manners, I quickly add, "I wanted to thank you for giving me this opportunity." I lower my chin, unsettled by the intensity simmering in his pale blue stare. "I'm—I'm very grateful, sir."

He gives a small nod but otherwise says nothing, content to let the silence stretch between us.

Confusion churns inside me.

Why would the owner of this grand hotel—a man with a thousand pressing matters on his plate, and who's apparently already late for his flight—waste time lingering in an empty hallway, engaging in small talk with me?

"I wouldn't want to keep you if you're already running late, sir," I offer when he still doesn't speak.

Domenico studies me calmly, vague curiosity simmering beneath his imposing presence. His scrutiny sets my nerves on edge.

I'm silently praying for this uncomfortable encounter to end when he finally speaks.

"I'm flying to Romania to inspect some of my family's ships docked outside of Constanta," he says unexpectedly.

The mention of the Eastern European country sends a jolt through me. If Domenico notices, he doesn't show it.

"We've been having some... issues with our cargo there lately," he continues smoothly. "And I've found that the most effective way to resolve such matters is to put my finger on the very pulse of the problem by handling it personally."

I should be focusing on what he's saying, but I'm momentarily captivated by the appealing cadence of his voice. The rich timbre makes each accented syllable feel deliberately seductive, almost hypnotic.

I realise I've been staring when a smirk shapes the corners of his full mouth.

"That sounds like a very reasonable approach, sir." My voice comes out hoarse.

A small tick of his jaw betrays his displeasure at my response, and my brows crease.

"Yes, well..." His tone shifts, turning cool and detached. The change is subtle but unmistakable, leaving me momentarily wrong-footed.

What did I say?

As if catching himself, he offers me another smile, his voice once again laced with its usual velvety charm. "It can be tiring, travelling so often. I know many would envy the opportunity, but there are times I must admit I'd simply prefer to stay here, at the hotel."

His sigh is soft, almost wistful, yet something about it feels performative—like a line carefully delivered for effect.

If he's searching for common ground, he's missed the mark entirely. Our strange exchange is growing more perplexing by the minute. I'm beginning to understand what everyone's been telling me about this man.

I clear my throat, feeling an odd compulsion not to disappoint him again, even as I have no idea what I did to displease him in the first place. "I can't say I've had the same opportunities to travel as you, sir, but I can understand why you would want to stay here more often."

I take a moment to glance out the window at the end of the hall, where the castle grounds stretch out in the distance. Even from here, the view is breathtaking.

"I've only been here a short time, of course," I continue, "but I'm already overwhelmed by the beauty of this place."

Domenico must pick up on the sincerity in my voice, because his lips curve into what looks like a genuine smile, a trace of pride breaking through.

"I'm pleased you like it, Miss Delano," he says, his voice dipping lower. "I think you'll come to enjoy it even more as time goes by. There are many, many pleasures to be found at this hotel—especially if you happen to find yourself in the right place at the right time."

The cryptic words drip off his tongue like silk. His eyes seem to turn a molten ocean blue, imprisoning me in an intense lure.

Is he... trying to imply something?

A telltale flush creeps up my neck, and I instinctively step away from him. "I'm sure you're right, sir. I—I mean... I'm sure I'll enjoy it. This. Being here. At the hotel. Working here, I mean."

I snap my mouth shut, heat prickling my flushed skin. Before my embarrassment can swallow me whole, the notification of an incoming text cuts through the air.

Domenico frowns as he retrieves his phone from his pocket, finally pulling his gaze from me as he glances down at the screen. I seize the opportunity to put more distance between us, inhaling deeply to steady my frayed nerves.

I watch Domenico's frown deepen as he reads the message.

Sensing my chance to escape, I blurt out, "Please, don't let me hold you up, sir. I already feel terrible for taking up so much of your time. Let me get the elevator for you."

I rush over to the silver doors and swipe my new access card as I press the down button three times in rapid succession. When I turn back around, Domenico's watching me again, something unintelligible flickering behind his smooth mask.

Irritation? Amusement?

He doesn't say another word as we listen for the familiar chime of the elevator bell. As the doors glide open, he steps inside, brushing lightly against my arm as he passes—*was that deliberate?*—before refocusing on his phone.

I've almost convinced myself that our stressful interaction is over when he tilts his face up, and I'm hit with a wave of déjà vu.

The same curious hunger I could've sworn I witnessed in the lobby flares behind his striking blue stare.

"I'm sure we'll meet again soon enough," he croons, his voice low and smooth. His lips tilt into a knowing smirk. "I'll look forward to our next... *encounter*. Until then, you have a good day now, Miss Delano."

The doors glide shut before I can form a single coherent thought, leaving me gaping at my own reflection in the polished silver surface.

Chapter Eighteen

THE NEXT FEW DAYS pass in a blur of activity, my hours filled with a mix of happiness, excitement, and utter exhaustion.

Each day offers a new area of the castle to explore, my mind spinning as I try to absorb every detail. More than once, I find myself lost in the hotel's endless maze of hallways, relying heavily on the floor map Bridget—the strict, no-nonsense HR Manager—gave me on my first day, to navigate the sprawling corridors.

By each afternoon, I'm a tired wreck, crawling up the stairs to the dining hall to devour my dinner, usually accompanied by Tiana and a few of the other girls I've gradually gotten to know over the past few days. Most evenings, I'm passed out in bed before the clock hits eight.

As much as I'm enjoying the job itself, getting to know the people I'm working with has unexpectedly become my favourite part of working here. I've never come across such an eclectic mix of people—all sorts of weird and wonderful personalities from all corners of the globe, gathered together in one place.

It's completely chaotic and wonderfully refreshing.

Thanks to Tiana, I'm slowly finding my place among her lively group of friends—one I'd never have imagined fitting in with before arriving here. I'd grown so used to feigning my way through every encounter that I'd almost forgotten what it feels like to actually enjoy spending time with others.

Even so, I still find myself instinctively pulling back whenever the girls throw inquisitive questions my way. I want so badly to feel comfortable enough to open up more, but for now, I tell myself this is good enough.

As I cross the castle grounds on Friday morning, happiness fills me at the thought of game night with the girls later that evening. My schedule shows outdoor work today, and after days stuck inside, the chance to finally soak up some Spanish sunshine has me buzzing with anticipation.

I'm the first person there when I reach the main entrance at five minutes to nine. From what I've learned about the outdoor crew, they're hardly the types to show up early.

With time to spare, I step inside the cool marble hall to look around for the others, waving to Greg as I pass through the entrance. He returns my greeting with his customary nod, his wrinkled hands clasping the brim of his glossy black porter cap.

Glancing toward the reception desk, I deflate a little at the sight of Harriet instead of Ryan. With no sign of the outdoor guys anywhere, I'm about to head over to the concierge desk to say hello to Jesmindah and Tess when I stop dead in my tracks.

He's here.

Right there, leaning casually against the reception desk, his head down, absorbed in something on his phone screen. He hasn't noticed me yet, even as I stand rooted in place, openly staring at him.

Orlando.

It's the first time I've seen a trace of him since our encounter in the castle grounds, though I've been quietly watching for him all week. It's as if he'd vanished entirely—until now.

Just the sight of him makes my adrenaline spike. I consider retreating back outside when Harriet calls my name.

"Elaina. There you are."

At the sound of her voice, Orlando's head lifts. His stare lands on me like a blow.

My breath quickens, lips parting involuntarily as our eyes lock, holding steady.

He looks entirely unfazed, yet his presence pierces straight through me, just as it did the first time. My mouth goes dry, my chest rising and falling with short, sharp breaths.

What the hell is this guy doing to me?

"Elaina?"

I jump as Harriet calls my name again. "Sorry," I mumble, snapping back to the present.

"Good. Now that I've finally got your attention..." Her tone matches her annoyed scowl. "I'd like you to meet Orlando."

She gestures to the beautiful man strolling casually over to join us. "Orlando, this is Elaina. Elaina, you'll be assisting Orlando today."

The world halts. "I—I thought I was working with the outdoor crew?" My voice comes out squeaky.

Harriet looks peeved. "You *will* be assisting the outdoor department today, yes. With Orlando."

"Oh," I mumble, my pulse fluttering wildly.

"You'll be helping him plant tomatoes, or capsicums, or...something," Harriet adds impatiently.

"I—right." My voice trails off. From Harriet's growing frown, I suspect my awkwardness is painfully obvious.

Orlando remains silent as he watches us, an indifferent expression on his face. Harriet's stare flicks between us suspiciously. "I'll leave you two to it, then," she says eventually after serving me yet another stern look.

She gives us her back as she turns to assist a middle-aged woman approaching the reception desk in an eye-catching, bright pink dress that's at least two sizes too small. It perfectly matches the diamond-studded collars adorning the two little Shih Tzus trailing behind her.

I dodge Orlando's penetrating gaze as I study them. When I finally gather the courage to look at him, he's assessing me impassively.

I force an awkward smile. "Hi. I'm Elaina. I think we, uh... met briefly the other day?"

If you could even call that a meeting.

He remains immovable as the silence stretches uncomfortably between us.

"So... We'll be working together today?"

I shift. Still nothing.

As embarrassment presses down on me, Orlando finally bends to pick up a large cooler bag at his feet. Without a word, he walks straight past me as he heads for the exit.

Wonderful. Not only does this guy turn me into a blathering mess just by existing, but apparently, he's also a rude, dismissive mute.

After a moment's hesitation, I follow him outside, trailing several steps behind. I consider quickening my pace to catch up with him, but a flashback to his cold, detached wall of silence convinces me otherwise.

A heavy quiet settles over us as we step into the early morning sunlight. Orlando keeps a steady pace, offering no sign that he's even noticed I'm following him.

Until suddenly—

"You coming, or what?"

I jump at the sound of his voice—rich and deep, with a faint rasp that lends a rough edge to his words. My heartbeat quickens again, even as frustration prickles beneath my skin.

I pick up my pace, falling into step beside him as we walk along a winding path through the garden. He makes no further effort at conversation, and I resign myself to the awkward silence that follows us all the way across the grounds.

Before long, the outline of several greenhouses comes into view, framing a sprawling, vibrant garden. Rows upon rows of leafy vegetables stretch out before us, bordered by neat gravel pathways that wind between garden beds.

I take it all in, impressed by the scale of this place.

Orlando stops in front of a wooden shed and swipes his staff pass over a card reader before pulling the heavy door open. He disappears inside, calling over his shoulder, "Can you flick the light on?"

"Of course," I say quickly, following him into the dim interior.

It takes a few seconds to adjust after the bright glare outside, and I fumble along the wall until I find the switch. The room floods instantly with cool white light from a row of low-hanging bulbs dangling from steel beams in the ceiling, illuminating the cramped space in a flickering glow.

I glance around, admiring the meticulously organised shelves lining the walls, stacked high with bags of soil and wooden containers filled with seeds. Along the side wall, gardening tools hang from sturdy metal hooks, each shovel, trowel and rake placed in immaculate rows.

Orlando pulls out two pairs of gardening gloves from a shelving unit, tossing one pair in my direction. I catch his eyes rolling as I fumble to grasp them, one glove slipping through my outstretched fingers to land softly on the dirt-speckled floor.

Without waiting for me to retrieve it, Orlando loads a few tools into a bucket and strides past me without a glance. "Close the door behind you."

I shut the door firmly as I step out after him. Orlando has already reached one of the empty garden beds, laying out the tools along the edge. The faint scent of fertiliser fills the air.

"Let's go get the tomato plants," Orlando mutters as I approach and immediately heads in the direction of one of the greenhouses. It's as though he can't tolerate standing next to me for more than a few seconds at a time.

Suppressing a sigh, I follow after him.

The greenhouse feels stiflingly hot as I step through the frosted glass door. Beads of sweat gather along my neck almost instantly.

The interior is spacious, with long tables arranged in neat rows, each surface covered with more exotic flowers and seedlings than I could ever hope to identify, even with my above-average knowledge of horticulture.

Orlando stands beside a table laden with trays. I keep a deliberate distance as I walk over to join him, but I can't stop the grin that spreads across my face as I take in the tiny seedlings pushing through the white-speckled soil, bursting with life.

Orlando finally spares me a side glance. "These are the seedlings we'll be planting today," he says, gesturing toward the tiny peat pots. "Grab a trolley, fill it with as many trays as you can, and take them over to the garden bed. Be careful not to grab any eggplant seedlings by mistake. We're not planting those for another week or so."

I glance at the adjacent tables, spotting at least twenty more trays of vibrant green seedlings.

"You got it," I reply cheerfully, pulling on my gardening gloves as I make my way to the trolleys. Genuine excitement fills me as I stack a trolley high with sprouting seedlings, carefully wheeling it down the dirt path to the freshly ploughed bed.

Orlando steps onto the soft soil, expertly raking it into even rows with practised strokes.

"Can I help with that?" I ask cautiously, hesitant to interrupt but craving an excuse to hear the deep cadence of his voice again.

He pauses briefly, meeting my eyes properly for the first time since we left the hotel lobby. "It's fine," he replies evenly, resuming his task. "I prepared the soil yesterday. Just needed a final shuffle before we start planting."

Shrugging, I watch the fluid motion of his arms as he grips the rake firmly, its metal prongs gliding smoothly through the soil. It's impossible not to notice his muscles tensing with each languid stroke, his biceps flexing subtly beneath his loose-fitting t-shirt.

Soon, a sheen of sweat skims his golden skin, highlighting the veins along his forearms. He's undeniably fit—broad shoulders tapering down to a lean waist, toned chest beneath his black shirt, and muscular thighs visible through the fabric of his grey track pants.

Despite his impressive build, his height makes him more athletic than brawny. He must stand around six-foot-two, towering over my much shorter five-foot-six frame.

I avert my gaze as he steps onto the path next to me.

"All right," he says, using one of his gloves to wipe the sweat from his forehead. "Have you planted tomatoes before?" He regards me coolly.

I fight the urge to glance down as I catch a trickle of sweat gliding down his broad neck. "Sorry—what?"

Orlando exhales loudly. "Tomato plants. Have you ever planted them before?"

"Oh. Yes, actually," I rush. Something tells me he wouldn't be too pleased if he had to teach me.

"Good." He nods. "Then we should be able to get this entire lot planted by the end of our shift. Want to watch me plant a couple first?"

The fact that he's voluntarily offering instructions—without an edge of irritation—surprises me. I wouldn't call his tone friendly, but the timbre of indifference usually lacing his voice has lessened, if only slightly.

"I'd be happy to watch you do one or two, just as a refresher." I attempt a small smile.

He doesn't return it, but he also doesn't scowl.

Progress.

"Follow me."

I watch as he picks up a trowel and kneels in front of the garden bed, dragging it through a patch of soil before digging a moderately deep hole. Picking up a tomato seedling, he gently squeezes the sides of the peat pot to loosen the dense soil, then lowers it into the hole with smooth, practised movements. He scoops a layer of fresh earth over the edges, patting it down lightly before moving on to the next one.

By the time he's started on the third seedling, I grab my trolley and roll it to the opposite side of the container, mirroring his actions with my own seedling.

We work in silence, moving down each row with steady, unspoken coordination. The hours slip by, only briefly interrupted when Orlando grabs two bottles of water from the cooler bag and silently hands me one. I accept it with a grateful nod, gulping down the icy liquid as the sun rises higher, heat pressing down in thick waves.

The repetitive nature of the task is meditative. Despite the growing burn in my shoulders and arms from the unexpected use of dormant muscles, I don't mind the silence. It's surprisingly easy to fall into rhythm alongside him, the quiet companionship making the work feel less tedious.

When more than half the seedlings are nestled beneath the sun-baked soil, Orlando finally checks his watch. "It's almost one o'clock. Wanna break for lunch?"

I straighten, stretching out my aching back. My stomach growls in answer, and I glance at my wrist out of habit before remembering that I left my beloved Cartier watch behind in Russia.

"Sounds good," I say, surprised at how famished I suddenly feel.

As I dust loose soil from my thighs, curiosity tugs at me. I've never seen Orlando in the staff lodge before.

"I brought lunch with me," he says, as if reading my mind. He nods toward the cooler bag.

I try not to let my disappointment show. If he brought his own lunch, it means he won't be coming back to the lodge with me. Not that I really expected him to.

Pulling off my gloves, I'm caught off guard when he bites his lip, hesitation tightening his expression. With a resigned shrug, he adds, "I brought some food for you as well. So you wouldn't have to walk all the way back to the staff village."

I gape. "You did?"

He shrugs again as he scratches the back of his neck, clearly uncomfortable. "You can head back to the lodge if you want. But there's food here for you, if you'd rather stay."

My cheeks pull into a grin before I can hide it. "Thanks, Orlando. That's really kind of you." I roll my stiff shoulders. "I think I'll take you up on that. My back's already killing me, and something tells me I'll need all the strength I can get this afternoon."

I glance over at the seemingly never-ending pile of unplanted tomato seedlings, suppressing a groan.

For the briefest second, Orlando's mouth tilts—somewhere between a smile and a frown—but it disappears almost immediately.

Without another word, he grabs the cooler bag and heads toward a narrow path leading further away from the castle.

I push myself to my feet, nearly stumbling as my legs protest after hours spent crouched in the dirt. Shaking off the numbness, I follow after Orlando, content to walk behind him in silence. After working across from the man all morning, I feel more relaxed in his presence, despite his broody demeanour.

The path winds through a quiet stretch of greenery, the air cooling as we pass under the shade of the trees. After several quiet minutes, the distant sound of waves crashing against rock reaches my ears, and the trees give way to a small clearing.

A wooden bench sits a few metres from the cliffside, facing the sea. A short fence marks the edge of the ridge, its low placement maintaining an unobstructed view of the breathtaking horizon.

A tired sigh escapes me as I sink onto the bench, my muscles groaning as I let my body relax for the first time all day. Closing my eyes, I tilt my face toward the salty breeze drifting in on the waves.

"This is heaven," I murmur, stretching out my sore limbs. "Feel free to leave me out here for the next three months. I might die of hunger, but it'd be a happy death."

A quiet snort makes me crack open an eyelid. Orlando's gazing out at the ocean, the corners of his lips twitching with something resembling amusement.

The reaction is so foreign on him that it startles me.

"Well, look at that," I quip before I can think better of it. "You can smile after all."

His eyes slowly shift to meet mine, the faint trace of humour still lingering there. "Rarely," he admits dryly, though there's a flicker of something warm beneath his usual detachment.

He reaches into the cooler bag and pulls out two bottles of lemon lime and bitters, condensation beading along the bottle necks.

"Figured we deserved something more invigorating than bottled water after working our asses off all morning." He twists off the cap and takes a deep swig.

I eagerly accept mine, unscrewing the top before taking a sip. The tangy fizz slides down my throat, instantly refreshing.

A quiet groan of appreciation escapes me. "Holy crap," I mumble, wiping a stray drop from the corner of my mouth. "That's the best thing I've ever tasted."

I don't miss Orlando's glance flicking over my lips as I take another large gulp.

We sit in silence for a few moments, the golden sunlight warming our skin as the ocean stretches endlessly before us.

Right here, in this moment—with the breeze in my hair, my muscles aching in the best way, in the quiet company of a man I barely know but undeniably and inexplicably feel drawn to—everything feels peaceful.

I sip my drink as we watch the waves gently roll along the water's surface. Despite the space separating us, I'm intensely aware of exactly where my body ends and his begins, as if my skin can sense the heat radiating from him without ever making contact.

My ears tune in to the rhythmic flow of the water below, memories drifting in like the tide. A pang of sadness pierces my chest unexpectedly, and before I can think better of it, I find myself voicing a memory I haven't allowed myself to revisit in years.

"When I was little, my dad used to take me to the beach almost every week. It was kind of our thing," I say softly.

From the corner of my vision, I sense Orlando's head turning toward me, but I keep my focus on the horizon, afraid I might lose my nerve if I look at him.

"He would take me down to the water's edge and race me as we tore off our shoes and socks, then hold my hand as we sprinted into the water, letting the cold waves lap around our calves. He'd always find this one spot where the water was cloudy and murky from the waves stirring up the sand," I continue, voice barely above a whisper.

"Then he'd carefully lead me to another spot, where the water would be crystal clear, and we could gaze upon the abundant life teeming beneath the surface. He would ask me to close my eyes, and as I listened to the sound of the waves cruising along the water's edge, he'd tell me to be like water."

Take a deep breath, sweetheart, and feel the gentle caress of the water as it flows beneath you. Feel its energy. Millions of individual droplets forming together to create one unstoppable force. The water gives and takes, clouds and cleanses—and through it all, it never stops moving. It's a force to be reckoned with. A force to both admire and revere; that humbles and mystifies in equal measures. Be like water, my daughter, and your impact on this world will be limitless.

I sigh wistfully, a sad smile forming on my lips. "Whenever I think of my dad, I always think of the ocean, and those precious moments by the beach. For years after he passed away, the words he spoke to me felt like the only thing I still held inside my heart that would give me enough strength to persevere. To keep on fighting and never stop living. To be like water."

I stop talking as emotion catches in my throat. Closing my eyes, I draw in slow, steadying breaths, acutely aware of Orlando observing me.

The quiet air surrounding us is charged, yet oddly comforting.

Though Orlando says nothing, I sense a subtle shift in his energy, as if something in him has softened slightly.

I don't know what it is about this moment that made me share this small piece of myself—a piece I've never shared with anyone else. But to my surprise, I don't regret telling Orlando. It's a simple memory, but one that kept me alive when nothing else seemed to matter. It felt good to voice it out loud.

After a long pause, I open my eyes, turning slowly to face him.

Orlando's features remain carefully guarded, but they're softened by the unexpected compassion colouring the edges of his green-tinted irises, which I now notice are speckled with traces of grey and gold in the midday sun. As our eyes lock, the colours seem to merge in a fluid dance, transforming from an impenetrable darkness to a liquid, mesmerising, golden hue.

"I'm sorry about your dad, Elaina," he says quietly.

The sincerity behind his words stirs something in me as the soothing lilt of his accent turns my name into something beautiful and exotic, making each syllable sound like a caress.

"Thank you," I reply, my voice barely above a whisper.

Orlando holds my gaze for a moment longer before he looks back to the horizon. Silence falls between us once more, but this time, it feels lighter.

After a while, Orlando reaches for the cooler bag, resurfacing with two gigantic rolls wrapped in aluminium foil.

"Roast beef or falafel?" His casual tone breaks the quiet spell.

I smile. "Falafel sounds great."

"A veggie girl, huh?" Orlando muses, pulling out two salad containers and handing me one.

I unwrap my roll and take a tentative bite, unable to hold back the groan of pleasure as the flavours burst in my mouth.

"Holy crap," I mumble, wiping a stray drop of yoghurt from my mouth. "What is this sorcery?"

Orlando trails the tip of my tongue as it glides across my lips, his irises turning a shade darker as his mouth parts ever so slightly. As if catching himself, he clears his throat and turns back to his lunch.

Finishing my sandwich, I pick up my drink and lean back on the bench, grateful Orlando seems content to linger here for a while longer.

I relax completely, allowing myself to enjoy the quiet company as the blazing sunshine streams down on us from a clear, cloudless sky. I stretch my hands in the air and let my eyelids flutter closed, listening to the soothing sounds of bird song and the gentle rush of waves.

"I come here a lot." Orlando's sudden words are unexpected, and I glance over at him, quietly observing his unreadable expression. "Whenever I want to get away. Most of the staff don't know it exists, since there aren't many facilities out this way."

He pauses, a pensive air settling over him. "And you can't beat the view. It makes me feel like I'm all alone at the edge of the world."

A quiet thrill passes through me at the thought of Orlando bringing me somewhere so private—to a place he usually keeps to himself.

Encouraged, I cautiously keep the conversation flowing. "How long have you worked here?"

He shrugs. "Long enough."

Not exactly forthcoming, but at least he hasn't shut me down yet.

"And do you enjoy it?" I press. "Working here, I mean?"

Another shrug. "It's a good job. Pays well, and the surroundings are beautiful. Should be enough for anyone, right? I have no reason to complain."

I consider his words, sensing there's far more to them than he's willing to impart.

I try another approach. "I suppose you must know the de Águila family pretty well, having worked here for so long?"

His jaw twitches, the barest indication of annoyance. "Well enough."

Getting answers from this guy is like drawing water from a mirage.

"Where did you live before you started working for them?"

I immediately know I've asked the wrong question when his expression hardens, a shadow ceasing hold of the air around us.

"What is this?" he snaps. "Did I inadvertently sign up to appear on Oprah or something? Want my whole family history while you're at it?"

I'm completely blindsided by the sudden shift in mood. "I—I'm sorry," I stammer, searching for words to undo my mistake. "I didn't mean to—"

My sentence dies under the chilling force of his scathing glare.

One wrong question, and we're right back where we started. Even further back, if that's even possible.

I wish I could rewind time, bring back the softer Orlando from moments ago. The cold detachment emanating from him now chills me to the bone.

He tears his gaze away as his anger bleeds into the space between us, and we finish our drinks in stony silence.

Orlando stands without looking at me, grabbing the empty bottles and tossing them into the cooler bag. I'm surprised when he waits for me to rise before marching off in the direction of the greenhouses.

We walk side by side, the tense silence heavier than ever. My mind scrambles, replaying our conversation over and over as I desperately try to pinpoint exactly what made him snap.

I should've known better than to push him. All I wanted was to understand him a little more. Instead, I've managed to drive him even further away.

I don't even know why it bothers me so much. Even after spending half the day with Orlando, I'm still at a loss to explain what it is about him that captivates me so inexplicably.

His smooth skin and cool gaze. His guarded nature and raw edges. His dark, soulful eyes. All of it draws me in, completely and inexplicably, every detail pulling at me, even as I try to ignore it.

By the time we approach the greenhouse, my stomach is knotting with unease. Every movement feels awkward and unnatural. I long to break the prickly silence, but the fear that he'll snap at me again keeps my lips tightly sealed.

And beneath it all, a flicker of irritation slowly begins to simmer.

Giving up on finding a way back to where we were before, I pick up my pace as I shuffle over to the garden bed and pull on my gloves. I don't glance up as I feel Orlando's presence across from me.

He remains unmoving for several long seconds, but I stubbornly refuse to give him the satisfaction of acknowledging him.

I keep my hands busy, firmly focused on my task as I ignore the burning sensation of his stare. If he expects me to placate him or offer an apology for asking a harmless question, he's deeply mistaken.

When it's becoming painfully clear that I have no intention of meeting his brooding scowl, I hear him release a quiet sigh before he finally moves back to his side of the container.

We work in silence until the sun has travelled all the way across the sky, the final rays dipping behind the edges of the castle walls standing sentinel in the distance, creating long, drawn-out shadows across the vegetable patch.

I don't ask what time it is. I don't ask how long we've got left. I just keep working, walking back to the greenhouse to fill up my trolley two more times, until every single seedling has found a home in the rich soil.

It must be hours later when I finally look up to find Orlando watching me. I quickly break his stare as I focus on gathering my tools.

Another sigh escapes him as he rises slowly, collecting his own tools. I'm grateful for the distraction as we return everything to its designated spot on the wall inside the shed.

"Take the gloves with you," Orlando says quietly as he catches me glancing around for a place to put them.

Startled by his voice after hours of silence, I turn too abruptly, and the back of my foot hits the edge of a timber pallet stacked with bags of soil.

I brace for the fall, but Orlando catches me by the waist before I can tumble.

My breath hitches as his touch scorches my skin, the warmth of his strong fingers burning through the thin fabric of my shirt as I regain my equilibrium. I lift my chin to find his face inches from mine, worry edging his features.

"Are you okay?" he asks, all traces of hostility absent.

"I-I'm fine," I stammer, heart hammering. "Thanks."

Taking a quick step back, I feel the loss of his touch like a sting as the added distance forces him to let go.

For a moment, we simply stand there, pulsing tension stretching around us.

I catch a hint of regret before his guarded expression shutters it away. "You're welcome," he murmurs softly.

My pulse is still racing as we finish cleaning our equipment, but neither of us speak again until we step outside the shed.

"I'll walk you back to the castle," he offers, not quite meeting my eyes.

I nod subtly. "Okay."

We walk together through the fading daylight, the only sounds coming from the gentle rustle of trees and our steady footsteps on the gravel path. The sun's dipping low in the sky, casting everything in soft hues of orange and gold.

When we finally reach the rounded driveway, Orlando places a hand on my arm, emotions fortified by a mask I can't read.

"Thanks for your help today." His voice is low and gravelly. "You were—a great help."

"No problem," I murmur, unsure how to interpret his shifting moods.

"Will you be fine walking back to the lodge by yourself?" His voice is still carefully measured.

"It's a short walk. I'll be fine."

He nods, looking almost... disappointed?

"Okay, then." His jaw ticks as he angles his head away from me.

The evening light plays across his face, once again making it impossible to pinpoint the exact colour of his eyes. They seem to change every time I look at him.

He hesitates briefly, like he's about to say more, but then gives his head a small, nearly imperceptible shake. "Goodnight, Elaina."

"Goodnight, Orlando."

He offers me one final nod before turning his back to me. Without another word, he walks away, heading back down the darkened path we just came from.

My stare remains fixed on his broad shoulders until the encroaching shadows swallow him completely.

Chapter Nineteen

I tug self-consciously at my floor-length, navy-coloured dress. The too-high slit separates the silky material all the way up to my lower hip, exposing far more skin than I'm comfortable with.

I've spent the entire evening fidgeting with it in a futile attempt to avoid the lewd gazes of the men lounging in stuffy leather chairs at the other end of the room, jovially sipping aged whisky from crystal tumblers as they laugh at each other's crude jokes.

Fools, *I think to myself as I watch them with thinly veiled disgust, frustration simmering under my skin at the memory of Viktor's not-so-subtle insistence that I wear this ridiculous dress for his pretentious excuse of an evening. It's a good thing their attention isn't currently trained on me, or even these impotent halfwits might pick up on the disdain that's undoubtedly written all over my face.*

A prickle creeps down my neck—the unmistakable sensation of someone's unwanted eyes on me.

I glance to my left and meet the assessing stare of Mikhail, one of Viktor's trusted goons. The knowing glint in his soulless irises tells me my contempt hasn't escaped his vigilant notice.

Sliding on my well-practised mask of indifference, I allow an arrogant smirk to pull at my lips, cocking an eyebrow as I boldly meet his probing glare.

A flash of annoyance cuts through his otherwise stony features.

Satisfaction tugs at me. I know Mikhail's just itching to scurry off to Viktor like the obedient little lapdog he is, whining that his master's favourite pet is misbehaving again. And yet, his frustration is one of the few things in this wretched environment that brings me any semblance of amusement.

Sadly for him, this 'pet' has no interest in dancing to the tune of some boneheaded bodyguard turned sycophantic thug.

Across the room, the mindless chatter of the women reaches an unbearable pitch.

"So then, I went over to her and said, straight to her face, 'Are you really going to pretend you didn't just openly flirt with my husband right in front of me? After everything you've done to our family?' And if you can believe it, she had the nerve *to purse her thin lips together and say, 'Pamela, I would never lower myself to your level, let alone take your sloppy seconds—even if your husband were the last man on earth.' And let me tell you, I barely restrained myself from slapping that bitch across her smug little face right then and there, in front of the entire gala. How dare she! So, I went straight to my husband and—"*

I roll my eyes, exhaling sharply as their grating voices drill into my already throbbing headache.

Lifting my wine glass to my red-stained lips, I take a deliberate sip—not because I enjoy the taste, but because it gives me an excuse to avoid being dragged into their pitiful conversation.

I promised myself I wouldn't drink tonight. I've learned to always keep my wits about me at these gatherings. But I don't know if I can endure another minute in the company of these dim-witted airheads without at least a mild buzz dulling my senses.

The assembly consists of the usual suspects: self-important, haughty wives who continue to accompany their slimy husbands to these insufferable events, despite the men's numerous indiscretions.

Even with Viktor's relentless attempts to force me into his perfectly curated social circle, I still feel like an outlier. An ill-fitting puzzle piece jammed into the wrong set.

Not even bleach-blonde hair dye, eye-wateringly expensive makeup, and extravagant, form-fitting dresses can make me feel, or act, as if I truly belong in their world, much to Viktor's chagrin.

But it isn't just my failure to engage with these women that ignites Viktor's anger.

He sees the way his circle of 'associates' look at me. The way their lecherous stares drag over my curves, hands twitching in their laps as they suppress the urge to reach out and grasp what they so rapaciously desire. The dark hunger in their expressions, the excited gleam. The way their fingers inconspicuously clasp at their bulging crotches when they think no one's looking.

They're so used to taking what they want without consequences. My only consolation is their knowledge that Viktor would chop off more than just their hands should they ever dare.

If only that meant his wrath was reserved solely for them. That they were the ones punished for their inability to keep their covetous eyes and hands to themselves.

I shudder, unbidden memories clawing to the surface.

I think back to the last gathering Viktor hosted, less than two months earlier. The bruises on my skin lingered for weeks, forcing me to wear less revealing clothing than Viktor usually demands.

Thankfully, the dress he picked out for me tonight covers every faint trace of those old wounds, even as it highlights every smooth curve of my slender frame.

The blatant contradiction gnaws at me.

Not for the first time, I wonder why Viktor insists I wear such revealing outfits, only to punish me at the slightest touch of someone else's gaze on me.

I suspect the answer is as cruel as it is calculated.

Many of those looks are directed at me simply because Viktor has made me into something none of these men can ever have.

Untouched and untainted. Innocent and pure.

A wholesome, edenic gift only Viktor gets to claim. A prize wrapped in silken temptation, dangled before them like an alluring snare—not for their taking, but to remind them of their place. Cleverly presented to stoke their envy.

And through envy, command their respect.

Because in their world, power isn't just measured in wealth or violence.

It's measured in control.

And Viktor has made sure that every man in this room knows that he alone has earnt the prize for wielding it.

A roar of laughter erupts from the group of men gathered in front of the grand stone fireplace in Viktor's pristine mahogany study. I watch the self-satisfied smirk stretch across Viktor's face as he basks in their amusement at whatever witty comment he just made, soaking up their admiration like a predator lounging in the glow of its own dominance.

If only he were always this content. If only the fleeting joy he finds in the respect and flattery of these men was enough to keep his temper at bay.

Here, Viktor is in his element—like a jock at a frat party, the undisputed king of his domain. All eyes are on him, attention rapt, spellbound by his words, his looks, his every gesture. Each of them waiting, hoping, to be the one he singles out next, the one graced with his approval.

To be acknowledged by him is a mark of status.

And Viktor knows it.

He's measured with his praise, strategic with his punishments, wielding both admiration and fear with precision. He thrives in the delicate balance between charm and menace, and I can't deny that he's good at it.

I've watched him rise through the ranks of the organisation with ruthless efficiency—even as he works tirelessly to keep me as oblivious as the other women in this room, most of whom serve as decorative distractions valued for their beauty rather than their brains.

Yes, Viktor keeps me within reach more than the other men do their wives and mistresses. Sometimes, he even demands that I remain in the room when business is discussed, though that's mostly because he still believes I don't understand any Russian. And because he enjoys the power of parading me as a superior species—cleverer, prettier, and more desirable than the vacant-eyed, surgically perfected women his associates have settled for.

But he still doesn't want me to know the full extent of who he is.

Of what *he is.*

Of what he's capable of.

He only wants me to know enough to fear him.

Viktor's not a man who acts in haste. He relishes a spectacle, thrives in obscurity and scheming, and savours delayed gratification. I've come to learn it's one of his most dangerous traits.

As if sensing my thoughts, Viktor lifts his chin ever so slightly—the only command needed to summon his men into action. Instantly, his house manager, Simon, appears at his side, as if he had been lurking in the shadows all along.

"Simon," Viktor commands, his voice silky with authority. "Would you kindly escort the ladies to the sitting room?"

"Right away, sir," Simon replies smoothly, nodding to the other housekeeping staff. Without hesitation, they move to shepherd the women through the wide doors leading into the grand entryway.

I turn to follow, ignoring the cold, impassive stares of the two goons flanking the door, when Viktor's voice calls out behind me.

"Not you, lapochka*."*

My feet halt mid-step.

I close my eyes, despising the all-too-familiar endearment rolling off his slippery Russian tongue, like honey laced with poison. Inhaling deeply, I school my features as I turn back to face him, meeting the curious, hungry leers of the men still lingering in the room.

The heavy doors close behind me with a foreboding thud, sealing me inside the stifling room.

"Is there anything I can do for you, my love?" I ask, my voice carefully even, though every syllable grates against my pride. I internally recoil at the nauseating nickname Viktor insists I use whenever we're in the presence of his associates.

A cruel smile spreads across Viktor's rough yet undeniably handsome face.

"Oh, indeed there is, lapochka."

There's something different in his tone tonight. A shadowed callousness, barely suppressed by his outward charm. The subtle shift sends goosebumps prickling across my skin.

"Please, dear one." He beckons me forward with a flick of his long finger.

My pulse skitters in warning. Still, I obey.

I take a few unsteady steps toward him, careful not to wobble on the high-heeled satin stilettos he insisted I wear to match my dress.

Viktor catches my clammy hand in his and turns me into a slow pirouette with effortless control, allowing the men to take in every inch of my body, artfully exposed in the skin-tight dress.

Allowing them to look. Allowing them to covet.

"Is she not exquisite, my dear friends?" Viktor declares with theatrical grandeur, his voice laced with pride.

A chorus of murmured approval hums through the room, though I know it's not me they truly admire.

It's what I represent. Not a woman. Not a person.

A prize.

Viktor's arrogance was not born from love or adoration. His pride stems from the power that possessing me grants him in this room. I'm the untouchable jewel—a pretty, virginal damsel on his arm, a coveted rarity none of these men can ever have.

They only desire me because they cannot own me. Because in their world, untouched means unclaimed.

And to them, that's the greatest temptation of all.

Viktor moves behind me with deliberate, unhurried steps, his fingers trailing lightly along my lower back.

"When my dear Isabella here came into my life five years ago, I knew instantly that she was special," he croons, his voice thick with satisfaction.

A chorus of 'Absolutely' and 'Hear, hear' ripples through the gathering of men, their rapt focus tracking Viktor's every measured movement.

Viktor circles me slowly, his touch feather-light and suffocating. His fingertips glide up my spine, a whisper of pressure that sends a wave of unease crawling over me.

"I knew even then that she was a rare beauty," Viktor continues. "Even more so for her untouched innocence, unspoiled by the greedy hands of others. Such a treasure is a rare thing for a man to find in this age of exhibitionism and flagrant sexuality. I dare you, my friends, to find such a rare jewel yourselves."

A shiver rolls through me as his hand skims the back of my neck, his fingers moving in soft, deliberate strokes. The sensation is deceptively gentle. Practised.

And it only makes my stomach twist tighter.

My spine stiffens as his palm coasts over my shoulder, tugging idly at the delicate strap of my dress.

"Such a rare treasure..." His voice lowers to a near whisper, but the weight of each syllable presses down on me like a heavy stone.

"Viktor, please." I'm barely able to summon my own voice. I don't even know what I'm pleading for. I just know that whatever he has planned tonight, I don't want any part of it.

Viktor ignores my quiet plea as his fingers continue to drift along my shoulder blade.

"In appreciation of such a remarkable gift, I have been practising the art of delayed gratification for some time now."

A murmur of amusement spreads through the room. The men are hanging onto his every word.

My breath catches as Viktor's gaze dips to where the curve of my breasts peeks out from the provocative sweetheart neckline.

His grip abruptly tightens as he tugs at the strap of my dress. The fabric slips, falling to rest limply against my arm.

"For six years, I have restrained myself, controlled my desires, patiently waiting for the day I get to claim my reward." His voice is silky, but the underlying hunger is impossible to miss.

A fresh wave of unease crashes over me.

"Oh, there have been temptations, my friends. Bozne moy, *have there been..." His tone darkens with feigned lament. "More than I can count, and almost more than I could bear at times. But, you see, I was lucky to learn a valuable lesson early in life."*

The men shift in anticipation, bodies tensing, eager to hear the grand philosophy Viktor has elected to bestow upon them tonight as he slowly builds his crescendo.

"The core of true power lies in unwavering self-control, gentlemen," he declares, pausing to let his words sink in. "A power I have mastered. And so, I continued to wait."

The other strap of my dress slips past my shoulder.

I lift my hands instinctively, gripping the fabric where the smooth velvet clings to my chest, my fingers trembling as I clutch the delicate material.

I feel their eyes on me as the men drink in the spectacle unfolding before them, lusting to see what will happen next, feeding off the slow, calculated unravelling of their leader's prized possession.

"Let go, girl."

The sudden reappearance of Viktor's harsh, unforgiving tone jolts me. Without warning, his hand yanks at the smooth folds of my dress.

The rip of expensive silk shreds through the silence.

I gasp as the fabric tears along the edge of my right breast, exposing even more of my pale skin to the avaricious male gazes devouring my body with intensifying desire. For the first time tonight, I'm thankful the dress is tight enough for the fabric to cling helplessly to my trembling frame.

A hush falls over the room.

The men watch silently. Waiting.

I stand rigid, my arms stiff at my sides, my skin crawling beneath the weight of their attention.

Viktor circles me like a lion savouring the breath before he pounces. His footsteps echo against the polished floors, each measured step drawing out the torment, stretching it thin, like a taut string ready to snap.

"The problem is, you see," he muses, "that I am not a man content to settle for a bad deal. I do not fail. I do not lose. I do not invest my time and effort without ensuring I receive a worthy return. Only then, my friends, do self-control and delayed gratification mark the true signs of a powerful man. And so, my darling lapochka..."

He stops before me. Despite every instinct screaming at me to keep my face down, I make the mistake of looking up.

The second our eyes lock, the bottomless darkness of his cruel depravity glints wickedly, and my blood turns to ice.

In the chasm of his cold stare, wild hunger dances in those glacial blue depths.

Viktor takes a graceful step closer to me until we're standing chest to chest, our bodies nearly touching as his breath ghosts across my cheek. His hands brush my waist, fingers grazing over the smooth fabric as he languidly trails his hands upward.

My breath seizes as his thumbs skim the swell of my breasts.

The slow, deliberate pull of the zipper snakes down my rib cage.

He's going to undress me. Here. In front of all of them.

A rush of panic explodes in my chest, terror seizing my limbs, and I react without thought.

The slap lands before I even register my own movement.

The sharp crack as my palm connects with Viktor's cheek reverberates through the room, leaving a deathly silence in its wake.

Everything goes eerily quiet. No one makes a sound. No one moves.

I know I should run, but it's as if I have lost all control of my body. I stand frozen, my terrified orbs fixed on Viktor's rigid frame. On the small, ominous tick of his jaw.

Oh my god...

What have I done?

Agonisingly slowly, Viktor tilts his chin up to look at me. Ice floods my veins at the fierce intensity glittering there. A bone-chilling combination of hatred, excitement and indisputable, unadulterated madness.

I should run. I know I should run. Now.

But my feet are fused to the floor, my breath lodged in my throat as I stare at him—at the danger blooming within him like a poisonous flower.

In a flash, his hand lurches out, seizing the skirt of my dress. The fabric rips away in a violent surge.

A strangled cry escapes me as I stumble forward, slamming into his chest. His grip tightens, fingers biting into my arms. Wild, unhinged hunger flares behind his irises, his lips twisting into something monstrous.

A feral grin.

He shreds more of the dress, the torn blue satin scattering across the floor, leaving it ragged and frayed, the remnants of a broken illusion.

"Viktor, please," I sob as tears stream down my cheeks.

I doubt he even registers my pleas through his primal craze. When his stare collides with mine, all I see is diabolic, boundless depravity.

As he lifts his clenched fist, I hold firm beneath the shadow he casts and wonder what he sees in my watery gaze. If he sees the hatred there.

Abruptly, his features soften inexplicably. I flinch as he gently strokes the back of his knuckles against my wet cheek.

I close my eyes, letting the pool of tears trail down my face onto his cold skin.

With the speed of a trained fighter, Viktor's palm comes crashing down with a ferocious intensity, hitting me on side of the forehead with a vicious, bone-rattling whack. The force of the blow is enough to temporarily blind me as the edge of his silver ring slices my skin open.

Pain explodes behind my eyelids, white-hot agony radiating through my skull.

The room lurches.

The floor disappears.

And then—

Nothing.

A cold, weightless void swallows me whole as my body crumples to the cold timber floor.

I jolt upright with a sharp gasp, my body slick with sweat as the sheets cling to my damp skin.

Blinking rapidly, I fight to erase the vision of Viktor's face floating in the air before me—the way his eyes burned with undiluted fury and terrifying, ravenous madness. But the image refuses to fade, as if seared into the backs of my eyelids.

It's the first time I've dreamt of that night since arriving at the castle, though the dream itself is all too familiar. It seems no matter how many miles I put behind me, those haunting images will follow me like a phantom, slipping into my thoughts whenever I let my guard down.

A loud snore rumbles through the room.

I crawl to the foot of my bed and peer over the edge. In the dim light, I can just make out Tiana's curvy frame sprawled across her mattress, her fiery hair fanning in wild waves around her. Her pale yellow tank top is scrunched up around her navel, and her quilt lies in a tangled heap on the floor. She must've kicked it off in her sleep again.

I glance over at Bethany's bed. A tuft of light-brown hair pokes out from beneath her blanket, her body eerily still in slumber.

Relief trickles through me. *I didn't wake them.*

I settle back onto my pillow, counting slowly to fifty. As my heartbeat gradually evens out, I feel foolish for thinking, for even a second, that the nightmares would disappear so easily.

This dream—*this memory*—is a stark reminder that I'm still not free.

Viktor's men are still out there, looking for me.

I know it. I *feel* it.

At times, I catch myself peering into dark corners, searching for shadowed figures lurking beyond the light. I tell myself it's irrational. Paranoia, even. But that doesn't stop my pulse from quickening every time I catch a looming silhouette in the corner of my eye.

On autopilot, my fingers trail over the small scar stretching across my forehead—the last mark Viktor left on me. Even now, weeks later, a phantom ache lingers beneath my temple, as if my body refuses to forget the intense pain that shattered through my skull until I was convinced my brain was being cleaved in two.

I peer through the narrow gap in the side railing again.

My bag lies on the top bunk of Bethany's bed, tucked beneath a pile of spare blankets. For the first time in weeks, my mind drifts to the scrolls of paper hidden inside it, buried beneath an old jumper in case anyone ever tries to look inside.

The temptation to retrieve them claws at me, but I push the thought away almost as soon as it comes.

If either of the girls were to wake up and find me hunched over those scrolls in the middle of the night, it would undoubtedly raise all kinds of questions. Questions I'm not prepared to answer.

Better to leave it be for now. The last thing I need is either of them getting curious enough to take a peek when I'm not around.

I squeeze my eyes shut, willing my thoughts to quiet as I pray for sleep to claim me once more.

But when the morning light seeps through the sheer curtains hours later, I'm still wide awake.

Chapter Twenty

I WAKE TO THE sound of *Sunday Morning* by Maroon 5 blaring from Tiana's portable speaker in its usual spot on the vanity.

Squinting through the gaps in the bed railing, I spot Tiana swaying her hips back and forth to the music as she coats her long lashes with mascara.

"Didn't think I'd ever have to remind you of all people, but it's Saturday today," I mumble groggily, flopping back onto my mattress and pulling my pillow over my head.

It fails to muffle Tiana's bark of laughter.

"Morning, sleepyhead. Get up. It's a beautiful day, and it's our first full day off together in over two weeks. We're not wasting it by sleeping in all morning."

I grumble something unintelligible, making no move to get up. I haven't been sleeping well—not since I woke up from my reoccurring nightmare a few nights ago—and my body feels like it's been wrung dry.

"*Come ooon,*" Tiana sing-songs, yanking at my duvet until it slips off the bed to pool onto the floor.

"Okay, *okay!* I'm getting up. No need to get nasty," I grumble, stifling a massive yawn as I stretch my arms above my head. I immediately feel the aches and pains coursing through every spent muscle in my body.

Yesterday was another full day of planting zucchini seedlings with Orlando. Another tense shift spent in absolute silence—the third so far—followed by yet another restless night.

I'm convinced my poor muscles will need at least a week to recover.

Sitting up, I rake a hand through the tangled mess of my hair after tossing and turning all night, wincing at the knots.

Yawning widely, I muster up the energy to drag myself out of bed and make my way down the ladder—only to collide with Tiana as she skips over to me, looking effortlessly gorgeous and put-together.

She's wearing a snug black skirt that stops about mid-thigh, paired with a bright yellow, short-sleeved top and a pair of espadrille wedges. A yellow-and-orange hairband pulls her wild mane of curls away from her face, a few artful strands left loose to frame her striking, violet-blue irises.

"If this is how most people here dress for Saturday morning breakfast, I fear my own planned attire would leave me severely under-dressed," I quip.

"Oh, I'm not dressing up for breakfast," Tiana chirps, grabbing a bright red handbag from a hook on the wall. She throws it over her shoulder, the colour popping against her red curls and yellow top.

Somehow, she totally pulls it off.

"The girls want to hit the beach tomorrow, and *someone* failed to bring a bathing suit with her," she tuts, giving me a pointed look. "So, we're heading into town today to get you one. We'll stop by some shops, grab lunch—make a day of it."

She bends in front of the mirror to apply a fresh layer of lipstick, giving me a brief moment to compose my thoughts.

While Bethany remains steadfast in her mission to ignore me, Tiana has effortlessly slotted me into her tight-knit circle of friends. Not once have the other girls made me feel like an outsider, even with my somewhat shy and reserved demeanour.

They treat me like I've always been one of them.

And I couldn't be more grateful, though it still catches me off guard some days.

Tiana straightens, smacking her glossy lips together with satisfaction. "Ready for a girly day of shopping and gossip?"

A genuine smile spreads across my face. "Count me in."

The sun's already high in the sky as we make our way across the hotel grounds. I fall into step beside Yao Min, a petite girl I met on my first day working in housekeeping. She's a total sweetheart, her tiny frame and sleek, poker-straight hair complementing her sweet, soft-spoken nature. She smiles at me as we walk together in comfortable silence while Tiana, Tess, Paige, and Jess walk ahead of us, chatting animatedly. The only one missing is Rhianna, who was rostered on for an early shift.

As we approach the edge of the cliff where I first laid eyes on Orlando, I gape at the beautiful stone archway curving over a wrought-iron gate, its sand-coloured blocks draped in a tangle of vibrant green vines.

Tess pulls the gate open to reveal a narrow staircase carved into the stone. The moment we step through, we're engulfed by rugged cliff walls, the path snaking downward in a series of steep, winding steps.

The town below is momentarily hidden from view, but small windows offer fleeting glimpses of the water glinting in the distance as we carefully descend the steep climb. We cling to the metal railings attached to the wall on either side, our voices echoing against the cavernous rock.

"Okay, that was seriously awesome," I gush when we finally reach the bottom, breathless from the long trek.

Tess swipes her staff card across a discreet electronic reader embedded into the stone, and with a metallic creak, the second gate swings open, granting us access to a paved path at the far end of the beach.

"Right? The staircase was originally built so that supplies and materials purchased from the ships docking in the harbour could easily be transported to the castle. Once the townsfolk developed easier means of transportation, they sealed it off to keep intruders from sneaking onto the estate. The de Águila family eventually reopened it when they started using the place as a vacation home. Now, it's an exclusive entrance point to the town for guests—and staff, when we're lucky enough to get away with using it."

I glance back at the archway, admiring how seamlessly it blends with the rugged cliffs.

Tiana skips up beside me, tossing her arm around my shoulder. "You say you like it now, but let's see how much you love those stairs when you have to climb back up after a long day at the beach."

Tess chuckles. "The hotel has a shuttle to and from town for guests who don't want to use the stairs. Staff can take it too, if there's room. We'll probably use it tomorrow. No way am I lugging all my stuff down all those steps. And I'm definitely not dragging it all back up again."

Our chatter carries on the gentle breeze as Paige leads us down the stone pathway to the beachside boulevard.

We stop at a quaint gelato shop nestled at the corner of a rustic, terracotta-roofed building. The scent of fresh waffle cones and sugared fruit fills the air as we step inside.

I groan with delight as the first spoonful of cherry-and-vanilla flavoured gelato melts on my tongue, the creamy sweetness bursting across my taste buds.

Bolstered by the sugar rush and the warmth of the bright, sunny day, we continue down the cobbled sidewalk, our laughter weaving through the hum of passing tourists and locals.

Paige suddenly lets out a squeal of excitement. "This is it," she announces, pushing open the door to a small boutique with mannequins draped in breezy, floral dresses displayed in the floor-to-ceiling windows.

We pile in after her, the scent of fresh linen and flowery perfume surrounding us.

"This place has the best bikinis and summer dresses you'll find anywhere in town," Paige beams, grabbing my hand. "And they always have amazing sales on."

I glance around the welcoming space, taking in the racks of colourful clothes. The sight of it all should make me excited.

But Viktor's slippery voice slithers through my mind, as crisp and cool as if he were standing right beside me.

Perfection, lapochka. Always strive for perfection.

His demand echoes in my head, the rigid rules of my old life still imprinted in my bones.

Viktor never let me wear clothes that I wanted to wear. Everything had to be tailored to perfection. Expensive and flawless. Dull, neutral tones. Stiff, pristine fabrics. Not a crease in sight.

I was never allowed to dress comfortably.

Never allowed to feel like *myself*.

“Elaina, over here.” Paige waves me over to a display wall lined with swimwear hanging from metal hooks.

“I’ll grab someone to reach those gorgeous pieces up on the top rack.” She walks over to the counter to flag down a staff member, and I take advantage of her distraction as I discreetly glance at a price tag.

To my relief, it’s not as bad as I feared.

Still, I hesitate.

Until I have a few more pay checks under my belt, I’ll have to be careful. The small pile of money I’ve got tucked away in my duffel bag is all I’ve got left.

I know it’s irrational—this creeping paranoia that everything could be ripped away from me at any moment. But the feeling just won’t shake.

I need to be ready to leave at a moment’s notice.

Just in case.

Even so, I do need a bikini if I’m going to join the girls at the beach tomorrow. And surely, one small purchase won’t hurt too much in the long run.

Right?

Chapter Twenty-One

TWO HOURS LATER, WE'RE seated at a small cafe near the harbour, scanning the seasonal lunch menu.

Shopping bags crowd our table—mostly Tess's and Tiana's—overflowing with clothes, shoes, makeup, and sunhats.

I managed to snag two bikini sets on sale, as well as a gorgeous yellow summer dress that I found tucked away at the back of the shop at fourty percent off. I threw in a cheap pair of sandals and even managed to find a pair of running shoes at sixty percent off. I can finally throw away the oversized, scuffed-up pair Iris gave me.

"I don't know about you guys, but I'm definitely getting the shrimp salad," Tess declares, pushing her sunglasses up onto her head as she peers down at the menu.

"*Ooh*, I was thinking of ordering that too," Paige trills. "The food here's always fresh, and I never say no to a shrimp salad."

Jess clicks her tongue. "Shrimp's not really my thing. I'm going with the lamb and tzatziki sandwich."

We take turns walking up to the counter to place our orders. By the time I return to the table, the girls are already deep in conversation.

"...acting like an absolute ass," Jess grumbles, her voice thick with irritation. "I swear, that boy's never going to grow up."

"Who are we talking about?" I ask as I settle into my seat.

"Blaise," Tess says, rolling her eyes. "He's been acting like a total tool toward Jess again."

I glance at Jess. "I didn't know you had an issue with Blaise."

Jess crosses her arms. "It's more that he has an issue with the fact that I'm married."

My brows furrow. "Why in the world would that be a problem?"

Jess exhales sharply. "Because Blaise is convinced he's the greatest thing to ever crawl out of a woman's vagina since Jesus was born," she deadpans, making the other girls snort with laughter. "Second only to the belief that he's God's greatest gift to women, and nothing and no one will ever be able to resist him. Apparently, this privilege somehow grants him a licence to say and do whatever he wants."

She grinds her molars together. "When he found out I was married, he took it as some kind of personal challenge to test my loyalty. He's constantly pretending to seduce me. You know, touching me inappropriately, wolf-whistling when I walk by. But yesterday, he really outdid himself.

He came up to the concierge desk acting like a twat as usual. When I told him to fuck off, he said, and I quote," she pauses for dramatic effect, "that if I'm not up here to 'fuck around with irresistible guys like him', I must have a pussy as dry as the Sahara desert. And if that's the case, I might as well head back to my husband, throw on a sari, and spend my days in the kitchen making naan bread as I'd be good for nothing else."

I blink at her, jaw slack. "You're not serious," I gasp, outrage sparking through me.

"Oh, dead serious," Jess huffs.

"Blaise's a total dick." Tess shakes her head. "He's been a cheating wanker ever since he started working here last summer. I can't believe they hired him back this year."

"I can't believe he hasn't been fired for harassment," I mumble, appalled that the hotel would allow someone like him to stick around. "Surely there have been complaints about him, if he's willing to take it that far?"

Paige twists a golden curl around her finger. "His uncle's one of the de Águila family's biggest business partners or something."

"Ah. So that's why he's always walking around this place like he's invincible," Tess grumbles, tapping her long nails against the tabletop. "I was wondering what gave him his God complex."

The waitress arrives with our drinks, and I take a long sip of my iced latte, savouring the cold relief against my parched throat.

"Well, from what I've seen lately, Elaina's the one who needs to look out," Tiana quips, a bitter smirk tugging at her lips.

I pause, straw still in my mouth.

Tess voices my question before I can ask. "What does Elaina have to do with Blaise?"

Tiana throws her hands in the air. "Oh, come on. Don't tell me I'm the only one who's noticed the way Blaise practically drools every time she walks into the staff lodge."

We all stare at her blankly.

Tiana huffs. "Seriously, y'all need to be more aware of your surroundings. Blaise is practically obsessed with Elaina. He won't shut up about her whenever I stay the night at Dean's, always bugging me about what she's up to, where she's from, whether she has a boyfriend, what makes her 'tick'."

"T, you haven't said a thing about this to me," I whine, even as a jolt of unease coils in my stomach. I've caught Blaise eyeing me more than once this week, though I've done my best to ignore his penetrating stare every time I walk past his table.

Tiana waves off my concern. "Oh, relax. I already told him you have zero interest in his tiny dick and hairless balls."

The table erupts into laughter.

"He already has enough pussy floating around him as it is, what with Clara and Kelsey trying to wriggle their way into his little posse," Tess scoffs, faking a gag. "How anyone can strive to become a revolving plaything for those guys to bounce around between themselves, I will never understand. I mean, I'm not one to judge," she adds, holding her palms up. "I like sex just as much as the next girl. But to lower myself to that level? Never."

"Amen to that, sister," Tiana cheers, and the two clink glasses.

Paige grins mischievously. "Speaking of boys and sex..." Her focus shifts to me. "Have you set your sights on anyone yet, Elaina?"

All eyes snap to me.

My cheeks burn. "N-no," I blurt, taking a huge gulp of my iced coffee for something to do with my hands. "Definitely not."

"Oh, but you *must* have seen someone you liked the look of?" Paige presses in her sweet Southern twang. "There are so many cute boys working here. You're bound to find someone you fancy sooner or later."

A very specific face flashes through my mind—dark hair, green-speckled irises, strong arms flexing beneath the glow of the sun.

I shove the mental picture away.

"Nope," I reiterate, a tad too quickly.

"What about Corban?" Tiana says slyly, one eyebrow raised provocatively, and I give her a stern look.

"What about Corban?" Paige shifts beside me. If I'm not mistaken, there's a hint of tension stiffening her posture.

"He seemed pretty smitten with you that day he helped us sort out your staff pass," Tiana presses, grinning wickedly. "He could barely take his eyes off you, girl."

I shake my head. "You're overplaying it."

"Oh please," Tiana scoffs. "I've never seen him so adorably bashful around anyone before. He's normally pretty easy going. And"—she looks dramatically around the table—"he thought Elaina was a model."

"Because you led him to believe I had a freaking modelling portfolio," I remind her, exasperated. My words can barely be heard over the squeals of excitement from the other girls. I notice Paige doesn't join in.

Tess fans herself, her perfectly manicured fingernails flicking through the air. "Who's complaining? I don't know about you ladies, but I certainly wouldn't mind Corban Hart getting all sweet and gooey for me." She feigns a theatrical, girly sigh.

Tiana raises her glass to me. "I think it's safe to say that yet another babe has officially arrived at Hotel Acantilado. And by the looks of it, she's going to take the boys by storm."

She winks. "Welcome to the crazy hotel life, babe. We're all thrilled to have you join our little summer adventure."

"Hear, hear," they all shout in unison, lifting their glasses to meet hers.

I lift my own glass with rosy cheeks, a round of shrill clings ringing through the air as we clink them in the middle of the table.

Chapter Twenty-Two

"Tell me, ladies—is this heaven or what?"

I tilt my head to look at Tiana as she stretches out on her sunbed, her toned legs curling as she arches her back like a cat.

I glance down to my sundrenched body, where a faint tan line has already started to form along the edges of my bikini bottoms.

Compared to the other girls, who are all stretched out on their own sunbeds, I'm practically a ghost. I guess I never really stood a chance against Rhianna's rich, chocolate-coloured skin or Jess's golden, chestnut hue. But even Paige, despite her otherwise fair features, has a natural glow that makes me look even paler by comparison.

Guess my Spanish roots have some catching up to do.

I consider pulling out one of Tiana's magazines from the cute tote bag she lent me this morning, but the warmth of the sun, the rhythmic crash of waves, and the distant hum of laughter lull me into contentment. I sink lower onto my sunbed, too relaxed to move.

A sudden sharp noise startles me, jolting my body upright. My sunglasses slip down my nose to land awkwardly halfway across my nose. I pull them off, lifting onto my elbows as I squint against the glare of the sun.

A volleyball lies in the sand a few meters away. From the nearby court, a tall figure jogs toward us, arm raised in an apologetic wave.

"Sorry, ladies!" The deep, unmistakable drawl of an Australian accent carries over the breeze. The guy reaches down to grab the rogue ball, flashing us a boyish grin. "Didn't mean to scare ya."

"Damn it, Hayden," Tess huffs, throwing her water bottle at him. "You nearly gave me a heart attack."

Hayden laughs, catching the bottle mid-air with ease. "You can't blame a guy for *accidentally* throwing a game for a chance to get an eyeful of you fine ladies lounging in your tiny bikinis." His lopsided smirk is all charm and mischief.

Paige giggles as Tess fires back a retort that makes Hayden's booming laughter float across the warm sand. I flick my sunglasses back over my eyes so he won't notice the way they wander over his athletic frame.

He's definitely good-looking, with light brown, tousled hair, sun-kissed skin, and bucketloads of boy-next-door charm.

"Oi, mate. Hurry up!"

Hayden glances over his shoulder, waving at a group of players throwing their hands in the air. I try to make out who's playing but quickly look away when I register Clara and Kelsey standing in the middle of the court with their hands on their hips, faces ablaze as they glare over at us.

I have to admit, I'm impressed they're managing to play volleyball with the matching scraps of fabric covering their gigantic breasts. If I tried to jump with one of those frilly things, I'd be giving the whole beach a nipple show.

"Yeah, yeah. Give me a minute," Hayden hollers, tossing the volleyball into the air as he delivers a perfect serve, sending the ball flying back toward the court. "Get someone to cover for me for a sec, will ya?"

Turning back, he grins down at Tess. "Hiya, Reynolds. How 'bout you join us for a game?"

Tess lets out a huff. "No chance, *mate*. Have you seen this body?" She gestures to her long, slender frame. "These limbs are built for sunbathing, not volleyballing."

Hayden takes his time drinking in Tess's tanned curves. "From where I'm standing, that rocking body looks like it's more than capable of a number of different physical activities."

His wicked smirk widens as Paige and Jess let out scandalised squeals.

"Aw, c'mon, Reynolds," he pleads, peering at Tess with puppy-dog eyes. "At least take a swim with me?"

"Uh-uh. No way." Tess shakes her head vehemently.

Before Hayden can ooze more charm, another voice cuts in. "What's up, ladies?"

Dean appears behind Hayden. His whisky eyes squint in the bright sun, his wet hair causing drops of water to slide down his absurdly sculpted chest. His board shorts hang low on his hips, sunlit water glistening along the deep grooves of his torso.

I swear I hear Tiana swallow.

His eyes rake over her curvy body, visibly appreciating her golden skin shimmering under a layer of suntan oil. She shoots him a teasing wave with the tips of her fingers, and he lets out a stifled groan before not-so-subtly adjusting his bulge through his board shorts.

I muffle my giggle, though another part of my body—a part I haven't paid much notice lately—tightens at the thought of having a man look at me the way Dean's looking at Tiana right now.

"Hey, sexy," he says gruffly, walking over to stand beside her sunbed. "Should've known you'd be down here today."

"*Eek*, Dean. Move over, you're dripping all over the place," Tiana shrieks as tiny droplets fall from his hair to land on her taut stomach. As she squirms to avoid them, her boobs wriggle provocatively, and I catch Dean soaking in each movement with rapt attention.

A devilish grin spreads across his face. "Oh, you want *more* water on you, did you say?"

Before Tiana can protest, Dean launches himself on top of her, pressing his wet body to hers.

"Dean, get off!" Her laughter rings through the air as her shrill squeals pierce my eardrums.

Ignoring her protests, Dean scoops her up into his arms like she weighs nothing. With Tiana flailing wildly in his arms, he takes off running toward the water.

"Dean, I swear to God—"

Hayden must take Tiana's high-pitched shrieks as his cue to follow suit, because he wastes no time rushing over to Tess, swiftly lifting her from her sunbed until her lithe body flops against his chest. "Might as well go two-for-two."

"Hayden, you put me down right this second, you hear?" Tess wails, hitting him on the chest as her sunhat flies off her head. Hayden just laughs as he rushes down the beach after Dean.

I chuckle as we watch the boys stampede into the waves, with Tiana and Tess hanging on for dear life, their squeals cutting off as they're submerged in the clear, turquoise water.

"You guys want to take a dip, too?" Paige asks through her giggles as she sits up and adjusts the straps of her yellow bikini top.

"I'll come willingly before I'm dragged there against my will by some other horny fool," Rhianna snorts.

"I'll come, too," Jess yawns, slowly rising from her sunbed. "I need a splash of water to wake me up. You coming, Elaina?"

"Nah, I'm good." I reach for the bottle of sunscreen at the foot of Tiana's chair, slathering a fresh layer onto my chest, where the sun has left a faint red tinge.

"Minnie, you wanna come?" Paige turns to Yao Min, who's been engrossed in her book at the far end of the row of sunbeds.

"Oh, no, I just can't right now." Yao Min sighs dreamily, her nose practically pressed to the crisp pages of her paperback. "The heroine's about to catch her husband with her best friend, right after she had this incredible moment with her high school sweetheart, who's just outside their house, pining for her, and.... Oh, I simply can't put this book down until I find out what happens next!"

Smiling to myself, I recall Yao Min animatedly gushing about her obsession with raunchy romance novels over breakfast last week.

As she once again loses herself in her book, I sigh contentedly, watching Paige, Rhianna and Jess leisurely walk across the sand to where Dean, Hayden, Tiana and Tess are splashing around in the water.

"Yo, Elaina!"

I glance up, surprised to see Corban striding in my direction, a camera hanging loosely from a strap slung over his shoulder.

My gaze flicks over his shirtless torso, and it's impossible not to appreciate the way his body narrows perfectly from his well-defined chest to his slim waist, his hipbones creating a tantalising V above the line of his dark-blue board shorts.

"Hey, Corban," I call back, waving as he walks up to my sunbed. "How's it going?"

"Really good. Hard to complain when you get to spend the day on the beach in beautiful weather like this." He gestures to the cloudless sky, the sunlight glinting off his golden skin.

"Can't argue with that." I adjust my sunbed into an upright position to see him better.

"You mind if I sit?" He nods toward the foot-end of my lounger.

"Go ahead." I curl my legs to give him more space as he sits, placing his camera down on the towel beside him. "Been out taking photos?"

His eyes light up. "All morning. Got some great shots of the guys playing volleyball. I probably have hundreds of photos from previous games, but still..." He shrugs. "I'm always looking for new content for my portfolio. And honestly? Any day I get to be out and about snapping pictures is a good day in my books."

His whole face lights up as he talks, his voice alive with a passion so genuine it's hard not to be drawn in.

"That's really cool," I say, meaning it. "I'd love to see your work sometime. Tiana always gushes about your talent. She showed me some of your shots of the castle you posted on the hotel's social media pages. They're truly amazing, Corban."

His lips stretch into a wide smile, crinkling the corners of his eyes. "Thanks, Elaina. I've put a lot of effort into building our media platform over the past couple of years. It's been really great seeing the positive feedback."

He pauses, then glances down briefly, looking uncharacteristically shy. "I'd be happy to show you some of my other work sometime, if you're serious about wanting to see it? I always appreciate a fresh pair of eyes and a new perspective. Helps me figure out what to improve."

I smile at him. "Of course I'm serious. But I doubt I'm the best person to give you any constructive criticism. I'll happily admire your work, though."

His grin broadens. "Cool. Maybe I can bring my portfolios to the staff lounge one night? If you ever hang out there. I haven't seen you around much up until now..." He cuts himself off, looking a little sheepish.

I tilt my head, oddly flattered. "Yeah, I've kind of collapsed into bed every night this week." I shrug. "The girls are hounding me to stop being such a bore, though, so I suppose I should make more of an effort. Otherwise, I wouldn't put it past them to physically drag me from my bed in the middle of the night."

"With Tiana as your roommate, that wouldn't surprise me one bit." Corban shakes his head, chuckling. "She's a firecracker, that one."

"The loudest and most exuberant in the pack."

We chat for a while, his easy-going energy making conversation feel effortless. He tries to ask about me, but I deflect each question as subtly as I can, steering the focus back to him. He doesn't push, though the curiosity in his eyes is unmistakable.

As I look down at the water's edge, listening to his melodic voice describe the misty winters of his hometown, a quiet ache settles in my chest.

Will there ever be a day where I don't have to be afraid of opening up to someone? Will there ever be a time where telling someone the truth about myself won't be the equivalent of signing my own death warrant?

I don't have an answer.

But for today, at least, I'll pretend.

Chapter Twenty-Three

I JOLT AWAKE AS a loud bang tears through the cabin, making the windowpanes rattle.

Disoriented, I peel my cheek from where it's glued to the page of the book I borrowed from Yao Min, scrambling to piece together what's going on through the fog of sleep.

I have no idea what time it is, but the heavy cobwebs clogging my brain tell me I've been out for at least a couple of hours.

By the time I made it back to the cabin after dinner, drained from a long day in the scorching sun, the girls were already half-drunk, downing shots like champs. They practically begged me to stick around, but all I wanted was a cool shower before crawling into bed with a good book.

I shake my head to clear the grogginess, just as another loud slam echoes from somewhere inside the cabin.

Even in my sleep-fogged state, I know it's definitely not Bethany making such a ruckus. When Tiana and I got back this afternoon, she'd whipped around to glare at us, announced she was heading off for a few days to visit her family holidaying in Léon, and stormed out with her weekend bag slung over her shoulder.

I can't say I expect to miss her much while she's gone.

I squint through the bedside railing, trying to make sense of the commotion. I must've forgotten to switch off Tiana's bedside lamp earlier. Its tempered glow casts a soft light over the otherwise dark room.

It takes a moment for the image before me to cut through the thick fog clouding my brain.

"Oh, Dean, yes. Keep doing that, just like that. That feels... oh, that feels *so good.*"

The staggering view of Tiana's boobs bouncing wildly just a few metres away abruptly assaults my exhausted senses. They're barely contained by her red tank top as Dean grinds against her, his jean-clad erection pressing into her with wild abandon. His bear-like paws are digging into the sides of her bare waist as he holds her small frame against the wall, her legs wrapped around his middle as she clings to his neck, mouths fused together in a messy, passionate kiss.

Fuck. Not again.

I'm paralysed, completely at a loss for what to do.

I'm not exactly keen on interrupting them a second time—they'll think I'm some kind of peeping Tom. But I can't just sit here and watch them, either. Because that *would* make me a peeping Tom.

Flustered, I clear my throat hesitantly, but the sound is instantly drowned out by another series of loud moans.

"Fuck, baby. You're so fucking sexy. Your pussy feels so goddamn wet grinding against my cock."

I clamp my mouth shut, desperately searching for a way to escape this clusterfuck of a situation before it escalates any further.

Silent despair claws at me as Tiana releases another depraved moan, curls bouncing around her face as Dean pulls his hands from her waist to rip her tank top from her chest, revealing a lace-covered bra. He unhooks it with practiced ease, letting the red fabric drop in a heap at his feet.

My eyes go round as Dean bends his head and darts his tongue out, softly gliding the wet tip across Tiana's taut nipples. She arches her back, thrusting her breasts into his face.

"Oh, yes, Dean. Oh my god, that feels amazing." She moans, yanking at his hair to pull him even tighter into the soft swell of her cleavage.

A rush of heat blooms deep in my belly, trailing a slow burn to my core. My mind goes fuzzy, and my voice seems to have gotten caught somewhere in my throat.

Everything slows down, and yet, somehow, it all seems to move at a rapid pace that I can't keep up with.

I know I shouldn't be here right now, but I can't seem to tear my eyes away.

Tiana's nipple slips from Dean's lips as he guides her petite frame down onto the floor. Letting go of her for a moment, he claws at his own belt before grabbing the edge of his t-shirt, ripping it over his head in one swift move. His pants and boxer shorts drop next, discarded in a blur.

I gasp as my gaze zeroes in on his long, hard shaft, the wet tip jutting out to point directly at Tiana, who looks at it with sultry hunger. Dean doesn't waste a second before picking her back up, his strong body moving them easily over to the bed while he kisses the side of her neck.

His biceps bulge as he throws her down on the mattress, the motion making Tiana's boobs jiggle as she spreads her legs for him.

I feel myself grow hot as Dean's eyes cloud with heady, unadulterated lust, his pupils capturing every wobble with enraptured desire.

"Fuck, baby. I could come just looking at your gorgeous tits bounce," he rumbles as he stalks forward, his voice low and gravelly.

"I'd much rather you use that fine cock of yours in a more mutually favourable way," Tiana purrs, her voice dripping with sex as she glides her fingers along her chest, gently tugging on her own nipples, before sliding them down to her stomach, stopping when she reaches the edge of her panties. She pulls the material down her thighs with slow, deliberate movements, allowing Dean to take in every second of the show.

The moment the lacy material slips from her toe to sail to the floor, Dean loses it.

He rushes forward, halting only to pull a condom from the pocket of his jeans. He tears the packet open with his teeth, rolling it onto his thick shaft in record time. Lifting Tiana's hips into the air, he slams into her, drawing a cry of pure pleasure from them both.

My own pulse quickens as I watch Dean's firm ass clench and unclench with each powerful thrust, his deep groans growing louder and more frequent. Tiana's eyelids flutter as her pleasure builds, frantic moans ringing wild and unrestrained through the cabin.

I doubt either of them would notice if I climbed down and walked straight past them out the door right now. The fact that they've both likely drunk their own body weight in alcohol tonight probably doesn't help their inhibitions.

It doesn't take long for Tiana's groans to rise in pitch. Dean immediately picks up the pace, hips slamming against hers as he pounds into her.

Loud, wet slurps echo through the room.

"Oh God, Dean. I'm gonna come. *I'm gonna come!*"

Breathless, I watch as Tiana's eyes roll back into her head. Her back arches as she tips over the edge, coming loudly around Dean's cock, her jumbled words barely discernible as Dean reaches his own climax with a final, powerful thrust.

"Oh, fuck. Baby, that's it. Oh, yeah, that's it. Fuck, yeah. Fuck. *FUCK!*"

His whole body jolts, back-muscles rippling as he empties himself into the condom. An eternity seems to pass before he finally collapses on top of Tiana, panting heavily into the abrupt silence.

I hadn't even realised I was holding my breath until my chest hitches, lungs screaming for release.

I duck my head behind the railing, silently praying neither of my two unwitting companions notice me, now that the haze of lust and sex has lifted.

A tight pressure had lodged itself in the pit of my stomach, and without even touching my panties, I know they're completely soaked.

I hear movement below and chance a quick glance over the railing.

Dean's peeling the condom from his slick, half-erect dick, tossing the glistening rubber lazily onto the floor at the foot of the bed.

I cringe.

Gross.

Crawling under the sheets, Tiana rolls over to turn off the bedside light, throwing the room into darkness.

I don't dare move, terrified even the smallest rustle of sheets will alert them to the fact that I just witnessed their loud, sweaty thrust fest.

I try to ignore the throbbing that's settled low in my pelvis, barely stopping my fingers from slipping underneath my pants to touch the only place I know might relieve some of this building pressure.

Before long, I hear their breathing growing heavy, and moments later, I'm almost certain they've both fallen asleep.

I brace on my elbows, tugging the sheets beneath me as I crawl back up to my pillow and gently lie down on my back.

A soft snore from somewhere in the cabin tells me Dean's definitely fast asleep, and if I've learned anything about Tiana over these past few weeks, it's that she sleeps like the dead, especially when she's been drinking.

I sigh in relief, wriggling side to side to get more comfortable.

The relief is short-lived. Twenty minutes later, it's clear I'm not going to get any sleep tonight—at least not feeling the way I do now.

I keep picturing Dean's taut muscles as he thrust into Tiana, their joint groans of pleasure echoing in my ears.

With a sigh of defeat, I let my hand glide along the smooth curve of my stomach, past the edge of my panties. A soft gasp escapes my lips as my palm slips beneath the soft silk.

My eyelids flutter shut as I swipe a finger through my wet folds. Another rush of heat floods my core as I surrender to my own inner desire, my pulse racing as my mind conjures the image of dark, brooding, green-speckled eyes boring deep into mine.

Chapter Twenty-Four

I'M METHODICALLY SCOOPING SPOONFULS of fruit and yoghurt into my mouth when Tiana appears at the staff lodge the following morning. With a loud sigh, she drops heavily onto the bench across from me.

"Morning, sunshine," I chirp, barely hiding my smirk as I take in her untamed hair and puffy eyes. "Don't you look like butterflies and rainbows this morning?"

"Shoot me," Tiana grumbles, reaching over to snatch my still-steaming mug of coffee and downing half the cup in three large gulps.

"By all means, help yourself," I mumble, my tone hovering somewhere between annoyed and amused.

"I feel like a block of cheese that got left in the fridge to rot until mould grew on it, and then that cheese was eaten by a mouse, and then that mouse died from the contamination it caught from the mouldy cheese, and then that dead mouse was eaten by a cat—and then that cat crawled into my mouth and died there," she says tonelessly, her expression dead serious, and I burst out laughing.

"Guess it's safe to say over-dramatisation doesn't run in your gene pool," I joke, chuckling as Tiana flops her head onto the table, a stifled groan escaping from somewhere beneath her tousled mane.

"Girl, I had *way* too much to drink last night," Tiana mutters unnecessarily, peeling her forehead off the table to squint at me with bloodshot eyes. "I know I'm no longer eighteen or whatever, but holy cheese balls, did this round hit me harder than a rough, uncut, C-grade porno."

I fixate on dipping my spoon into my yoghurt, struggling not to blush like a ripe tomato at that colourful metaphor, considering what I witnessed last night.

Luckily, Tiana seems too engrossed in her own self-pity to notice anything around her. I quirk my lips as another loud, pitiful moan penetrates through the blanket of red curls.

"Let me get you another cup of coffee," I say when I finally take pity on her.

I head over to the coffee stand to make fresh cups for us both. As I'm stirring a heaped spoonful of sugar into Tiana's cup—I figure she could use a little extra sweetness today—my skin tingles at the awareness of someone standing behind me.

I shift to the side to allow whoever it is access to the coffee machine.

"Sorry. I'm taking up the whole counter this morning," I say, a sheepish smile already forming as I glance up—only to find Blaise's assessing eyes leering back at me.

My smile dissipates.

"Oh, don't move on my account. I certainly don't mind you standing there in those tight little shorts, baby cakes," Blaise drawls, his blazing irises trailing over my body in a slow, deliberate assessment.

Baby cakes? Seriously?

Is this guy for real?

"I was done anyway, so..." I grab both cups from the counter and move to step away. I couldn't care less that I didn't even get to add milk to my coffee. I'd drink liquid tar right now if it helped get me away from Blaise faster.

"Why in such a rush this morning, princess?" Blaise croons in a would-be wounded voice as he swiftly moves to block my path. "After all, I walked all the way over here just to say good morning to you."

A teasing smirk plays at the corners of his mouth. I feel my annoyance seeping to the surface, but the last thing I want is to cause a scene in the middle of the staff lodge with about two dozen people to witness it.

"In that case—good morning," I say evenly, giving him a tight-lipped smile. When he doesn't move out of the way, I sigh, letting the annoyance show on my face. "I should probably get back to my table now."

I shoulder past him, bumping into him as he leaves no space for me to get through. I don't even care that a slosh of coffee splashes onto the hem of my light blue top, leaving a large stain.

I faintly catch his low, rumbling laughter as I hurry across the room, his leer following me every step of the way back to my table.

I shudder. *Can't he find someone else to obsess over with that creepy stare?*

Shaking off the uneasy feeling, I sit down and slide Tiana's cup in front of her, sipping on my own brew as I relish the bitter taste.

It matches the direction my mood has just taken.

Tiana picks that moment to completely side-track my thoughts.

"Hey, Els. You weren't in the cabin when Dean and I got back last night, were you?"

It's a miracle I stop myself from spluttering coffee all over the table.

"Last night?" I echo, my voice pitched slightly higher than normal. "Nah. I couldn't sleep, so I went for a walk. You were both fast asleep by the time I got back. Why do you ask?"

Tiana's shoulders droop in relief. "Thank the Lord for that," she sighs, wiping imaginary sweat off her forehead. "We were going to stay in Dean's cabin, but Jackson was already there, merrily banging some chick's brains out. So we decided to head back to my cabin instead. Let's just say that in the heat of the moment, we kind of forgot to check whether anyone was already there before we... well, you know."

She winces comically. "Sorry, but not sorry?"

"What are you guys talking about?"

Yao Min sits down next to me, carrying a bowl of oatmeal and the biggest mug of tea I've ever seen.

"Just reliving the glory of Dean making me see God last night," Tiana chirps, savouring another gulp of coffee.

"Oh, joy." Yao Min's voice drips with sarcasm. "Just the conversation you want with your morning oats."

"With your love for steamy romance novels, I'd think you'd adore a good ol', down 'n dirty play-by-play first thing in the morning, Mins," Tiana teases, nodding her head at the book clutched in Yao Min's hand, which is aptly titled *The Scarlet Lover*.

As Yao Min opens her mouth to reply, I glance up at the large wall clock.

"Shit. I better get going," I say, downing the rest of my coffee. "I have to head back to the cabin and change before work now, thanks to Mr Moneybags over there."

"Are you working with us again today?" Yao Min asks eagerly.

"Sorry, Mins." I offer her a regretful smile. "I'll be working with the event crew for the foreseeable future."

A spark of excitement ignites within me as I say the words. The fact that I've been rostered with the events team for the next two weeks tells me they have a big event coming up—and I can't wait to throw myself into another project.

"So, as you can all appreciate, this event is absolutely crucial for the hotel, and it's vital that everything goes off without a hitch."

Cindy's heels tap against the floor with each step as she struts back and forth across the room, her arms folded behind her back, her posture rigid.

"The de Águila family has invited a number of important people to this event, including the family's most prominent business partners, as well as both current and potential future investors. And they will all be here to enjoy the finest things this hotel has to offer. It simply must shine during the entire event."

Her sharp look cuts over all of us. "Alright, then. Lisa, Tim, Phillip—you will work with me on the event program. Madison, Tara and Sophie will look after catering. Alison and Tina—you girls will take main responsibility for the guest list. Matt, can you work with the reception crew to coordinate rooms for all the guests? We'll need to make absolutely sure there are no glitches when guests arrive. You know the drill—VIP guests get private cabins and suites, prominent guests get ocean views, and so on."

She walks around the room, separating everyone into groups until she stops in front of me. "Elaina, you will be working on decorations with Emma and Keisha."

She pauses, looking firmly at all three of us. "Girls, I cannot stress enough how important it is that the entire hotel is perfectly presented. That means we need to spruce up not only the main hall, but every other area as well. The lobby will need fresh flowers every day. The gardens must be meticulously maintained. Each flower bed must be free of weeds. No matter where a guest goes, they must be blown away. Understood?"

We nod vigorously.

Enthusiasm blooms in my chest as the meeting wraps up and everyone splits into smaller groups.

Just a few short weeks ago, I had absolutely nothing I cared about.

Now, I'm finally doing something with my life. Here, my input actually matters, and I'm positively giddy at the prospect.

I might not be saving lives, but this daydream is more than enough for me.

At least for now.

I'm humming along to Jim Stärk's *Morning Song* as I'm walking across the lobby on Thursday morning when someone calls my name in a low rumble. The unexpected sound halts me in my tracks.

Orlando's leaning against the polished marble walls, arms crossed, his face carefully arranged in its usual smooth folds.

"Yes?" I respond wearily.

He lifts one eyebrow but otherwise doesn't respond.

For some reason, this irritates me to no end.

"Is there anything I can help you with?" My tone is cool and sharp. "Because if not, I'm already late for a meeting, so I'll just be on my wa—"

"You're not working with the events team today," he says evenly, cutting me off.

I frown. "Yes, I am."

"No," is all he says before pushing off the wall and heading for the front entrance.

"Right. Were you planning on telling me what I'm supposed to be doing, then?" I call after him, my clipped words aimed at his back.

He glances over his shoulder, pausing for barely a second to throw me yet another impassive stare. "You're working with me." He doesn't spare me another look before he turns away again and walks out the door.

I stand frozen for a solid ten seconds, contemplating whether to simply ignore the infuriating man and head on to my meeting.

With a big sigh, I roll my eyes and follow after him.

Hurrying my pace, I catch up to him by the time he's halfway across the driveway.

"You know, this habit of yours of walking away from me without a word, leaving me to run after you like a stray, is becoming a bit of a recurring feature," I say in a falsely cheerful voice as I fall into step beside him. "Let's not make it one, shall we?"

All I get is a twitch of his lip.

"So, Señor Sunshine, what's on the agenda for today?"

My unusually bold bravado is fuelled by lingering frustration with this man. The fact that my pulse still quickens at the thought of spending another full day with him irritates me to no end, but I resolve to put all my energy into zoning out the unwelcome emotion.

I don't want to be attracted to him right now.

Instead, I keep my attention fixed on the path ahead, steadfastly ignoring my fluttering heart.

"Señor Sunshine, huh?" Orlando echoes, a hint of amusement colouring his gravelly voice.

"Well, I did consider calling you Mr Shitting Rainbows, but in the end, I decided that would be giving you too much credit."

To my astonishment, Orlando bursts out laughing.

The light sound is such a surprise, a stark contrast to his typical broody demeanour, that I find myself staring at him, mesmerised by how his smile completely transforms his usually stern features. A small dimple even appears in his cheek, and for the first time since I met him, the shadows that always swirl in his eyes seem to melt away, replaced by a glint of shimmering light.

"I suppose I deserved that one," he chuckles, shooting me a side glance, humour still glittering in his slate-green irises.

Be still, my heart.

Luckily, he keeps talking, giving me a chance to blink away the image of his dimple.

"To answer your question, we'll be planting squash and eggplants today."

"*Ooh*, I've never planted eggplants before." I'm genuinely excited at the prospect of learning something new.

Orlando smiles, clearly pleased by my excitement. "Tomorrow, you'll help me harvest the broad beans. I checked them yesterday, and we'll want to get on it while they're at their peak."

"I'm—I'm working with you again tomorrow?"

"Yep," is all he says.

We walk the rest of the way in silence, enjoying the warm sun on our skin. There still hasn't been a day of rain since I arrived in Cliff Bay, and the temperature's been climbing steadily each week. At this rate, it's going to be sweltering by mid-summer.

When we arrive at the greenhouses, Orlando nods toward the shed. "I asked the admin guys to update your staff pass in the system so you'll have access to the sheds and greenhouses."

I blink at him. "Really?"

I'll be needing regular access to the sheds and greenhouses?

He nods. "I was out here this morning, getting everything ready for us." He points to a patch up newly dug earth, where two full trolleys of seedling trays stand waiting. "If you ever need anything else, though, you should have access to the tools shed now. Oh, and I brought you this."

He walks over to where his cooler bag's sitting in its usual spot in the shade. "I figured you'd need something casual to wear."

He gestures to my buttoned-up, short-sleeved white blouse as he bunches up a gigantic, navy blue t-shirt in his hands and tosses it at me. "I'd hate to see that pretty top of yours ruined after a full day out here with me."

A waft of cologne hits me as I grab the t-shirt mid-air. I immediately recognise the warm, earthy notes of Orlando's alluring scent clinging to the fabric. The thought of wearing his shirt does something strange to my heart.

"You're lucky I decided to wear sneakers and black tights today," I chastise him as I head for the tool shed, pulling out my staff card. "Now give me a minute to change into this thing, and then you can start bossing me around again, Señor Sunshine."

Chapter Twenty-Five

"Oh my god. How horrible."

"Can you even imagine? That's my worst nightmare, for something like that to happen to me."

"It's terrifying. Makes me grateful I didn't end up going on that Contiki tour a couple of years ago. Who knows what could've happened on a trip like that?"

I frown as I step out of the elevator bank to find the rest of the events crew huddled in front of the TV, absorbed in some news program airing on the screen.

"What's going on?" I ask the group as I walk over to the coffee machine to pour myself another cup—my third of the day. This job is going to turn me into a caffeine addict, but the extra boost is definitely needed today.

I've spent the morning running errands for Cindy all over the hotel, and even had to make a quick run to town for supplies after we discovered an entire box of decorative lighting had been left next to a leaking fridge in the storage room.

"Oh, you're not going to believe it," Lisa squeals, her plump face flushed with horrified delight. "They've been talking about it all morning. It's on every channel. Do you remember that sixteen-year-old girl who disappeared while holidaying in Spain with her boyfriend? About four years ago now. It was all over the news back then. They never found her, and she was eventually presumed dead. Turns out she was kidnapped and sold into the sex trade! Can you imagine?"

It's as if a huge rock drops into the pit of my stomach, and the sip of coffee I just swallowed turns to ash in my mouth.

"What's... what's her name?" My voice is barely louder than a whisper.

"That's her there." Lisa points to the TV, where an image of a pretty girl with dark hair and big brown eyes appears. The description beneath the picture reads, *'Annabelle Sullivan (16), before her disappearance'.*

Bile climbs up my throat as my body floods with recognition.

Breathe, Elaina, breathe.

I tear my eyes from the TV to find Lisa watching me, her curious stare eagerly awaiting my reaction. "That's just... wow," I croak, my throat suddenly bone dry.

"I know," Lisa exclaims, her eyes round as saucers. "It's all so terrifying. But guess what? She managed to escape!"

It's a miracle I don't spill my coffee all over the floor.

"What?! I mean—*how?*"

"We don't know yet," Sophie, a sweet but shy girl says in her thick, French accent. "The police have only given the media breadcrumbs. Apparently, she's in pretty bad shape, but they're trying to get as much information from her as possible. They're hopeful she might be able to tell them more about how, and where, the trades happen. Maybe even provide names of some of the people involved."

Lisa bounces in her seat, as if we're discussing the next celebrity couple to hit the gossip magazines rather than the interrogation of a girl who's been trapped in the flesh trade for the past four years.

"What if they manage to get enough information to take down one of those awful sex trafficking rings?" she gasps. "That would be the takedown of the century."

I swallow hard, trying to clear the knot lodged in my chest. "Yeah, that would be... amazing."

I gingerly place my coffee cup on my desk. Clearing my throat, I call out to no one in particular, "I think I'll grab an early lunch today."

No one responds, too wrapped up in the news report to notice.

I barely register my surroundings as I make my way down to the lobby and out the front doors.

I vaguely catch the sound of laughter in the distance, but I don't stop to see who it is as I walk toward the staff village at a clipped pace, cutting across the freshly mown grass to save time.

As I open the door to cabin 15, I'm relieved to find the room empty. I rush over to Bethany's bunk, climb the small ladder, and yank my bag toward me with rough movements. Unzipping it, I fumble around until I find what I'm looking for.

Pulling out the large roll of papers, I spread it across the bedsheet with some effort. As my hands glide over the top page, the material feels rich and smooth beneath my palm, as if coated in a thin layer of film.

The navy background is contrasted by thousands of thin, white lines extending in all directions. I make out a series of tunnel-like outlines forming a circuitous framework around hundreds of different-sized squares. A large, oval-sized area dominates the centre of the page.

As my eyes adjust to the odd colours and shapes, it's clear I'm looking at a blueprint, most likely of some sort of town or city.

I shift the paper aside to glance at the sheet beneath it, revealing yet another blueprint—this one a more detailed layout of what appears to be the same city. I recognise the oval-shaped area, this time located on the left-hand side.

Unlike the first, this blueprint has a white background, and the various buildings drawn across it have been rendered with an almost bi-dimensional appearance.

I flick through the remaining sheets of paper, finding comparable blueprints displayed on every page—some from similar aerial perspectives, others from more isometric points of view.

A few offer a much closer view of a specific block or square, though I can't tell where they would fit on the larger map. For all I know, they might not even depict the same city.

That suspicion only grows as I reach the bottom half of the pile, uncovering a new set of blueprints that bear little resemblance to the first. These drawings are covered in a myriad of strangely curved lines and perplexing, multi-dimensional layers I can't even begin to understand, let alone the random numbers and letters dotted along each separate line.

If only I knew what these blueprints were for.

The sound of footsteps thudding against the outdoor deck startles me so much I nearly fall off the ladder. Scrambling to gather all the documents, I hurriedly stuff them into my bag a second before the door flies open.

"Oh, hey, Beth," I say, cheeks flushed as I meet Bethany's cold glare. "We weren't expecting you back until tomorrow."

A suspicious frown tugs at her brow as she glances from me to the bed and back again.

"What do you care?" she snaps, folding her arms across her chest. "And what are you doing up there, anyway?"

"I-I was just looking for something. In my bag." On impulse, I grab a random shirt that I suspect belongs to Tiana, judging by the bright orange colour. "This one."

"Well, now that you've found it, do you mind getting off my bed?" Bethany snipes as she strides over to the bathroom. "I'm exhausted from my trip, and I really need to take a nap. And you climbing all over my bed is going to ruin that plan. Don't you have some other place to be? Some stupid guy to charm?"

My jaw has barely dropped low enough to gape before she disappears into the bathroom, slamming the door behind her with a deafening bang.

Chapter Twenty-Six

WITH THE BIG EVENT fast approaching, the events team kicks into full prep mode, scurrying to get everything ready in time.

I expect Cindy to keep me within arm's reach at all times, so it catches me off guard when I arrive at the castle Monday morning to learn I'll be splitting my time between decorating sessions and landscaping work for the next two weeks.

Landscaping work with Orlando.

As much as I enjoy the days I get to work with Keisha and Emma, who have accepted me into their work duo wholeheartedly, I still feel a tug of excitement each time I walk into the lobby to find Orlando waiting for me, cooler bag in hand.

We've fallen into a routine of sorts on the days we spend together.

Each morning, we walk to the vegetable garden, where Orlando heads off to get seedlings while I collect the tools we need from the shed. We work quietly, side by side, until lunchtime, when we'll head over to the lookout to take in the view and devour whatever food Orlando's had the kitchen staff prepare for us that day. Then we'll return to the vegetable patch and work in silence once more until the sun begins its lazy descent across the evening sky.

Orlando still doesn't say much, and we mostly work in silence. Even our lunch breaks are largely quiet. But it's a comfortable silence. There's a different dynamic between us now than when we first met.

Orlando doesn't seem as distant, and his face is more relaxed when we're together. Less guarded.

It's no surprise that all the time I've been spending with Orlando hasn't gone unnoticed.

"What's he like anyway?" Rhianna asks me one Friday afternoon as I slip into the dining hall late, muscles aching from a backbreaking harvest of cabbages and white onions.

"Who?" I say innocently.

"*Duh*. Orlando, of course. You're, like, the only person in this entire hotel who can actually say you know him."

I snort. "I wouldn't call it *knowing him*. He's mostly quiet and broody and barely even talks when I'm around."

If only she knew how much I want *to know him better.*

"But you must've learned something about him in all that time you've spent together?" Paige queries, and I glance up to find six faces turned my way, their curiosity practically humming in the air.

"Not really," I shrug. "We barely talk at all."

The girls groan in unison.

"Damn," Tess moans, her shoulders slumping in disappointment. "I was really hoping for some goss on that hunk of a man for once. All this cloak-and-dagger mystery surrounding him makes him way too appealing. Someone ought to let something slip that'll take him down a few notches."

"Straight up," Tiana agrees. "If there's anything that man doesn't need, it's more sex appeal."

Tiana shoots me a curious side-eye when I don't immediately join in on the fervent nods of agreement from the other girls. Averting her look, I busy myself with my Spanish omelette.

"Even though he's clearly not much of a talker, I still wish you'd get a shot at jumping that fine ass. In all the years I've worked here, I've yet to see him give a single girl so much as a second look." Rhianna looks glum. "Tough luck, chick. Guess we're all stuck in the same boat when it comes to Orlando—the one he has no intention of ever boarding, apparently."

I force a laugh, even as my heart sinks in my chest. I glance around, taking in the room full of unquestionably attractive women.

If Orlando's never shown an interest in any of these girls...

I aim for a light-hearted tone as I say, "Good thing he's not really my type. He's good looking and all, but I don't really see him that way."

Good thing I've learnt how to lie through my teeth, too.

"Gosh. I can't imagine Orlando *not* being anyone's type," Paige gushes in a slightly breathy voice, a small giggle escaping through her gloss-tainted lips. "He's gorgeous."

"That he is." Rhianna points her fork at Paige as if to emphasise her agreement, a bit of omelette dangling precariously from the tip. "Even I can admit that, even if I'm partial to the ladies myself."

"Luckily for us, he ain't the only good lookin' bastard around here." We all look at Tiana, who claps her hands together decisively, an electrified gleam in her indigo eyes. "Don't forget this crib is practically teeming with sexy men just itching for us to jump their bones. What say we all stick around for movie night tonight, slosh down a few bevvies, and do some window shopping?"

Tess raises her glass of water in a mock toast. "Girl, you know I'm always up for some quality window shopping."

"*Ooh*, and they're showing *The Lucky One* tonight," Paige squeals. "As a die-hard Zac Efron stan, I'm definitely in."

"You know I'm always up for movie night," Jess mumbles through a mouthful of salad.

"Sure," Yao Min chimes in. "But only because it's a romantic drama. I got so bored with that superhero movie last week."

Tess feigns indignance. "I swear, Minnie, you're the only person in this room who can watch the Avengers movies and *not* like them. If not for the action, then surely you can't ignore the superhero hotness factor?"

As Tess and Yao Min bicker amicably, Tiana glances over at me, that dubious gleam still shining in her irises.

"Whaddaya say, Els?" She wriggles her eyebrows suggestively. "No more sneaking away from us. One more night, and I'm going to take it personally. So, what's it gonna be? You staying out tonight or what?"

I don't get a chance to respond before Rhianna jumps in and drawls in her usual dry tone, "Honey, if it wasn't already clear, that wasn't really a question. You're sticking around tonight, whether you like it or not."

I roll my eyes. "Alright, alright. You've all convinced me. Or forced me, more like it. But nevertheless, I'll stay."

The girls all cheer, and a wide grin breaks across my face.

Chapter Twenty-Seven

I'M MELTING INTO MY beanbag, sore muscles groaning with relief, when two loafer-clad feet appear in my peripheral vision.

I glance up to meet twinkling amber eyes smiling down at me.

"What's up, Elaina?" Corban greets me, stretching out his arm to hand me a fresh bottle of cider. I accept it gratefully.

"Hi, Corban." I return his smile as I take a sip of cider, relishing the refreshing feeling as the sweet, apple-flavoured liquid slides down my throat. "Oh, that's good," I sigh contentedly. "Thanks for bringing me a fresh bottle. I've been too lazy to get up and fetch one."

Corban flops onto the beanbag next to mine, previously occupied by Tiana until she deemed the movie too boring and joined Dean on one of the terrace couches for an impromptu make-out session.

"No problem," Corban says, looking pleased as he sets his beer down and shuffles deeper into the beanbag, arms resting behind his head. A few minutes pass in comfortable silence as we strain to catch the movie's dialogue over the surrounding chatter.

"I haven't seen you around lately," I say after a while as Corban takes a sip of his beer.

I catch the small smile ghosting across his lips. "Yeah? It's been really busy this past month. I've taken to ordering food from the kitchen most days so I can eat at my desk." He rubs his face tiredly, and I notice the outline of dark rings circling under his eyes.

"Sounds rough," I say, sympathy lacing my voice. "I hope they're not working you so hard you don't get any time to rest."

He shrugs. "The boss is really pushing for publicity ahead of the big event, so I've been doing my best to keep up with social media—nudging journalists, getting articles out there about the hotel, that kind of thing."

I nod in understanding. "No kidding. My team's definitely feeling the pressure. I swear, Cindy's going to collapse from overexertion any day now."

Corban chuckles, and my gaze lingers on his mouth for a second longer than is strictly appropriate, appreciating the way his full lips part to show off perfectly straight, white teeth.

"Thankfully, it'll all be over in a couple weeks' time," Corban sighs, taking a long gulp of his beer. The faint outline of his Adam's apple bobs up and down as he swallows.

Setting his empty bottle down, he turns to face me. "How're you finding it here so far, anyway?"

A genuine smile spreads across my face. "I love it," I say truthfully.

Corban's eyes twinkle. "I'm glad." He studies me for a few beats. "Can I ask what brought you here?"

He doesn't seem to notice me stiffening, too busy trailing his eyes down the golden strands of my hair, currently wrapped in a fishtail braid curving along my shoulder blade to rest somewhere near my navel. When he looks back up at me, a faint, rosy shade tints his cheeks.

"Well, I—" I falter, deliberating how to answer his question. "It was actually a coincidence that I ended up here. I found myself at a loose end in my life, and I decided to... change things up. So I packed a bag, jumped in my car, and let the road take me where it wanted. And it took me here."

Corban looks impressed. "I'll say, I admire a woman who has the guts to pack up her life and head out on the road all by her lonesome self." His bottom lip juts out the tiniest bit as he dips his chin in quiet approval. "That's pretty cool, Elaina."

I manage a small smile. "Thanks."

I turn back to the screen and pretend to watch the movie.

"So where did you live before—"

"What about you? How did you end up here?" I interrupt before Corban can finish the rest of his sentence.

Corban looks puzzled for a moment. "A childhood friend of mine worked here one summer a couple of years ago. He raved about it for weeks when he got back. Seriously, he couldn't stop talking about it."

He chuckles. "Probably because of how often he got laid while he was here, if we're being honest. But even so, when he began the application process to come back the following year, he urged me to apply with him. I was only looking at casual positions initially, figured something in the outdoor crew would be my best bet. But as it turned out, they had a position open in the media team."

A reminiscent smile tugs at his mouth. "I already had some experience that partially qualified me for the position, and with James putting in a good word for me, I managed to land the job. And that was that. I've been here ever since."

I smile. "Funny how life turns out sometimes."

Corban nods, looking contemplative. "Sometimes, I feel as though life's little more than a string of random coincidences, all jumbled together in one, crazy, beautiful mess that makes up the course of your life. You think you have a plan, and then—*poof*. Life throws you a curve ball, and you're suddenly veering off course at breakneck speed, finding yourself navigating down an entirely new path you never suspected, or even knew about until that very moment."

His words echo through me, causing the fine hairs on my arms to rise as goosebumps scatter across my sun-kissed skin.

In a raspy voice that can barely be heard over the surrounding noise, I quietly reply, "It sure does seem that way sometimes."

Corban smiles softly at me, though a slight frown shades his brow.

"So," I say, hoping to keep him talking. "What you're doing now, for the hotel—is that the type of work you want to do in the future as well?"

Corban shrugs, looking almost abashed. "Well..." he says, dragging out the word. "I definitely want to continue this line of work, just on a larger scale. But I'm also hoping I'll be able to do more artistic work on the side."

"Artistic? In what way?"

He smiles sheepishly. "I take a lot of my own photos, outside of the work I do for the hotel. You know... portraits, still photos, stuff like that. Portrait photography's my favourite. My true passion, if you will. I'd love to make it as an artistic photographer specialising in portraiture. I seem to have a knack for identifying unique characteristics in the people I photograph."

He beams at me. "I love trying different methods of lighting, angles and focal points to highlight distinguishing features. It's amazing what you can capture with a camera if you know how to use it properly."

He inhales a deep breath, his gaze trailing along my cheekbones. I sit oddly still as I watch him watch me. When his eyes graze my lips, I swear a hint of heat flares there, but by the time I blink, it's gone, making me wonder if I imagined the whole thing.

Tilting his head to the side, Corban's expression turns assessing.

"What?" I ask, squirming under his intense amber stare. "What's with the head tilt?"

Corban laughs. "Sorry. I've been told I have a tendency to assess everyone around me when I'm in photographer mode." He looks sheepish again.

"Ah, is that what that was?" I tease.

I'm expecting his soft laugh again when his face turns serious. "I was actually thinking how you would make the perfect portrait model."

I choke on my cider. "I'm definitely not model material. At least not in the ordinary sense of the word," I wheeze out, thrumming my fist on my chest to release the liquid lodged in my throat. "If I'm model material, your professional eye must be searching for something very different."

"Actually, I think you're breathtaking."

The matter-of-fact tone of Corban's words catches me off guard, and I catch a flicker of vulnerability in his eyes. "When I first met you, I actually believed Tiana when she said you were a model. I wouldn't have been surprised for a second if you were."

I'm left blushing profusely as I grasp for something witty to diffuse this sudden tension between us, but before I can recover, a chorus of giggles and loud whistles erupts around us.

We break eye contact just in time to find Zac Efron and Taylor Schilling locked in an epic make-out session on screen. My blush deepens as the two actors tug at each other's clothes, their heated kiss dissolving into a steamy sex scene beneath a stream of water cascading down their slick bodies.

I resolutely keep my attention fixed on anything but Corban's handsome face as mortification settles over me like a living thing.

"Aww, what do we have here?"

A deep voice cuts through my embarrassment, the familiar taunting lilt sending shivers down my spine. A moment later, Blaise's broad frame blocks my view of the screen as he looms over us.

"Hart and Delano. How cute," he quips, his trademark smirk curling his lips.

"What do you want, Blaise?" Corban asks in a resigned voice. The hint of annoyance in his flat tone surprises me. I don't think I've ever heard Corban speak to anyone with anything other than friendliness before.

"Easy, Hart. There's no need for impoliteness."

"And here I thought that's the only language you comprehend," Corban replies dryly, not a trace a humour in his voice.

Blaise clicks his tongue, shaking his head from side to side in mock disappointment. "Now, now, Corbie. No need to get snarky just because I interrupted your piss poor attempt at flirting with the pretty girl," he says snidely, his impish grin widening.

I glance at Corban's reddening ears and the tightening lines around his mouth and feel my own annoyance rising to the surface.

Blaise only smiles wider, clearly revelling in our discomfort. "I guess I can't blame you, golden boy. I mean, the girl's smokin'." His cobalt stare skitters across my body, the same appreciative glint I've seen lurking there before flaring bright.

Moving his eyes slowly from my chest to my face, they gleam with malicious venom. "But if you ask me, she doesn't look all that impressed by your weak game. Sorry about that, spud. Perhaps you better leave the seducing to us real men from now on? Girls tend to grow out of their 'nice guy' phase by the time they hit high school, I'm afraid."

I gape in horrified anger, lips parting to say something—*anything*—to get this overbearing, cocky twat to shut up, when a cackling laugh rings out across the terrace.

Tiana strides confidently toward us, her fiery mane bouncing off her bare shoulders as she throws her head back in an exaggerated cackle. Fixing her sights on Blaise, she wipes an imaginary tear from the corner of her eye.

"Oh dear. Did I actually just hear you compare yourself to a *real man*? One who thinks he has any clue how to seduce a woman at that?"

She bursts into another bout of deep belly laughs. A few people nearby titter as they glance between her and Blaise.

"Why do you always rock up where no one wants you, Hartley?" Blaise snaps, shooting daggers at Tiana as she flops onto a beanbag, looking utterly unbothered as she crosses her legs.

"Could it be, dear one, that it is *you* who has an unfortunate tendency of forcing your pompous ass on people who want nothing more than to escape the presence of your pimply backside? They say outward projection is unhealthy, you know?"

The redness seeping across Blaise's cheeks deepens as Corban and I howl with laughter.

"How dare you speak to me like that? You filthy slut," Blaise hisses, a livid gleam rippling in his glacial stare. "You'd be *lucky* to get a glimpse of my ass. We all know you've been frothing after it forever, Hartley."

The cocky smirk is back on his face, but an unsettling crudeness darkens his features.

His comments trigger a genuine bark of laughter from Tiana.

"Oh my... You really are deluded, aren't you, sweetie?" She shakes her head at him. "What must it be like to walk around with a head so inflated with self-importance that there's no room for anything else? And to my great misfortune, I was already unlucky enough to catch a glimpse of your pale butt cheeks squeezing tight as you pumped your STD-riddled cock in and out of Susie in the showers last week."

A small squeak carries across the terrace, and I turn my head to see a girl with mousy brown hair stiffen in her lounge chair, looking utterly mortified.

Blaise barely spares her a glance as he glares at Tiana, who cocks an eyebrow at him, tutting mockingly. "You shameful little boy."

Blaise's ominous scowl narrows on her. "What I do, or who I fuck, is none of your goddamn business, slut," he snarls.

Tiana peers up at him with equal amounts of humour and nonchalance painting her pretty features. "Actually, bonehead, it kind of is my business, since you happen to be dating someone I consider a friend."

My eyebrows shoot up to my hairline.

Blaise has a girlfriend?

Blaise rolls his eyes and spits on the ground. "Fucking women. Always so goddamn sappy and emotional, making a big deal out of the smallest shit. Get this into your tiny little brain, Hartley. My relationship with Savannah and how I choose to conduct it is none of your fucking concern. Got it?"

Tiana snorts disdainfully, eyes turning cold. "'How *you* choose to 'conduct your relationship'?" she parrots, glaring at Blaise like he's a mole growing on her toe. "Do you even hear yourself? Let's put to the side for a moment that you seem to believe you're the only one who should be 'conducting' anything in your relationship." She makes air quotes with her fingers, her body language growing increasingly angry.

"Are you really trying to convince me—convince *yourself*—that repeatedly fucking around on a sweet girl who loves you to death, and who has no fucking clue what your cheating ass is up to up here, is your idea of 'conducting your relationship'? Like you're both in on it, and Savannah's perfectly content with you sticking your filthy dick in just about anything with tits?"

Blaise's entire body stiffens, but Tiana doesn't let him speak, spitting words at him through gritted teeth, her voice seething.

"Seriously, Blaise. Don't even try to pretend Savannah would be okay with this. She loves you, for some fucking stupid reason, and she'd be devastated if she had any clue about your escapades. How would you feel if you found out Sav was fucking around with some other dude right now?"

Blaise tries to look unaffected, but he's too slow to hide the spark of fury flaring in his icy blues.

Tiana crosses her arms, smirking. "That's what I thought. So it's a one way street, is it? You're the only one who can fuck around as you please, but she has to remain wrapped around your dick, and your dick only? Charming, Blaise. Real charming."

Blaise's eyes turn arctic as he glares at Tiana with unconcealed contempt. "You're one to talk, Hartley. You're not exactly shy in the intimacy department, are you? I've lost count of the number of guys you've spread your legs for up here. A couple more, and you'll be giving all the other girls a run for the title of 'Slut of the Season'."

Blaise's lackeys aren't the only ones laughing now. I glance at Tiana to gauge her reaction, but she looks just as unaffected by Blaise's crude words as she does about everything else that would make most other mortals crumble from humiliation.

"That's the best you can come up with, Bloom?" she huffs, rolling her eyes. "That's honestly pathetic. I'm a free woman. I don't have a guy pining for me at home, lovingly thinking I'm a saint while I do my worst to be a sinner. I can fuck whomever I please, whenever I please, and it's not hurting a goddamn soul."

Getting up from her beanbag, she takes three angry steps forward until she's standing right in front of Blaise, her face centimetres from his.

"That said, whether you believe I'm a slut or not—which, frankly, I couldn't care less about, as your opinion means about as much to me as the half-eaten potato I threw in the garbage after dinner last night—I'm actually a one-man-at-a-time kind of girl.

Every guy I fuck knows exactly what it is we're doing and what we want from each other. Despite what you may think, I'm not in the habit of throwing myself at the next available guy five minutes after wiping another guy's cum from my vagina—unlike you."

A ripple of giggles and hushed whispers spreads through the crowd, most of whom have already abandoned the movie to watch the real-life spectacle unfolding before them.

For one taut, heart-stopping moment, Blaise looks like he might actually hit Tiana. Then his gaze sweeps across the terrace, clocking the enraptured eyes glued to him, and he lets out an almost imperceptible breath.

His posture relaxes, and that cold, smug smirk slithers back into place.

"Aw, that's cute. I didn't know you were the jealous type, T. Acting out because you finally realised that when the time comes, it'll be your friend's pussy I'm filling instead of yours. Newsflash, pumpkin—I wouldn't fuck you with a ten-foot pole, even if they fired every other girl at this hotel."

With those parting words, Blaise's vile smirk vanishes as he gestures to his two lackeys to follow him. The three of them head toward the far end of the terrace, where Clara and Kelsey sit primly, surrounded by the same group of guys I've seen with Blaise in the food hall.

Both girls are fixated on us, following Blaise's every move. Clara's pouty lips are pursed, her pointy nose scrunched in a resentful scowl as she glares at me.

If looks could kill, I'd be little more than a fried shrimp by now.

I frown. Tiana's the one who just roasted him. Why is her scowl directed at me?

Blaise turns mid-step and shoots me a cheeky wink.

Oh.

Bile climbs up my throat as realisation hits me.

"What a douche," Corban mutters, glaring at Blaise's retreating back.

"When has he ever not been?" Tiana sighs, huffing as she flops back down onto the beanbag.

I watch as she sinks into the slouchy fabric and closes her eyes.

"Thanks for speaking up, T," I murmur, just loud enough that the people around us can't hear. Curious glances still flick our way, tongues no doubt wagging with all sorts of rumours.

Tiana opens one eye, smiling tiredly as she flashes me one of her signature winks, albeit with a little less gusto than usual. "Don't mention it, girl. Trust me—I'd seize any opportunity to call out that pigheaded peacock on his moronic dumbness."

"He's lucky we're not all getting in line behind you to punch him in the balls at this point," Corban mutters sourly, his voice carrying a gloomy edge I'm not used to hearing from him.

"Hey," I say gently, nudging his shoulder until his troubled eyes meet mine. "Let's forget about Blaise for tonight. He's not worth our time. I'll go get us another drink, and then we'll enjoy whatever's left of this movie—even though I no longer have a clue what's going on."

That makes him smile. "Sounds good, Els."

The fondness in his voice as he calls me by my nickname settles inside me.

Despite the chaos of tonight, my heart feels lighter knowing I have friends like Tiana and Corban by my side now.

Chapter Twenty-Eight

*P*LEASE, BRAIN, PLEASE. LET *me sleep.*

I toss and turn in bed, my tired body refusing to let me rest.

After Blaise's little show, no one was feeling in a particularly festive mood. Deciding to head to bed early, it took less than a minute before I could hear Tiana's breaths slowing. I've been listening to her faint snores for the past three hours, struggling to calm my racing mind.

It keeps spinning with a million thoughts, continuously pulling me back to the surface whenever I tiptoe around the edges of unconsciousness. Any hope I had of sleeping slipped away the moment I remembered leaving my access card back at the lodge. As strict as the hotel is about keeping our passes secure, I know I'll get in serious trouble if I lose mine.

After another fifteen minutes pass without an ounce of tiredness seeping in, I let out a sigh of resignation, accepting that my conscience won't let me rest until I've retrieved the card.

I pull off the sheets and crawl to the edge of the bed, carefully climbing down the ladder so I don't risk waking Bethany. Tiana's peaceful slumber doesn't worry me—I could throw a party in here without her stirring.

Draping one of Tiana's sheer white cardigans over my modest tank top and shorts, I ease the door handle down with exaggerated slowness, wincing when the wooden frame squeaks as the door glides open.

I finally take a deep breath as I tiptoe outside and close the door behind me, relishing the fresh night air filling my lungs.

The staff village is peacefully quiet as I walk along the dirt path. The partying must have died down some time ago. The steady stream of people stumbling past our window earlier made it hard to relax, but I haven't heard a sound in well over an hour.

Reaching the edge of the lodge, I climb the wide staircase to the terrace, yawning as I pull the cardigan tighter around me to fight off the cool breeze.

The dim night lights set along the terrace railing cast a soft glow over the muted outlines of chairs and tables, guiding me through the dark space. I spot the beanbags Tiana, Corban and I lounged in earlier, still grouped together in a small circle.

I'm headed in that direction when a loud cry rings through the air, curdling the blood in my veins.

I whirl around, blinking rapidly for several long seconds before I fully comprehend what I'm seeing.

Bodies—naked, sweat-slicked bodies—glide together with slow, languid movements, gleaming skin illuminated by the fading glow of the fire pit, where only a pile of smouldering embers remain.

My stare locks on a woman crouching on all fours, her hands and knees resting on the smooth surface of the wooden deck. Her naked body is partially obscured by two men, one standing with his erect dick inches from her face, the other behind her, his crotch pressed firmly against her bare ass.

At first, I'm too stunned to recognise who I'm looking at, until the girl lets out a loud moan when one of the guys thrusts into her. As she throws her head back, I catch a glimpse of pale blonde hair and narrow, bony hips.

Holy shit. It's Kelsey.

Kelsey lowers her chin, her mouth sealing around the first man's cock as he glides it over her puckered lips, begging for attention. At his deep groan, I let my eyes trail up his bare chest and immediately recognise Finn—a tall, red-headed Irishman who works with Blaise on the outdoor recreation team.

He's biting down on his lower lip, eyes closed as Kelsey sucks him off.

The guy thrusting into her from behind has his pants pulled down to his knees. I can't see his face clearly from this angle, but I'm almost certain it's Jack, one of the other guys always hanging around Blaise.

His right hand clasps the side of Kelsey's narrow waist as he guides her lithe frame against his pelvis in hard thrusts, his left hand circling her hip as he fingers her clit with rough movements.

Kelsey's clearly enjoying the attention, her loud moans muffled by Finn's cock filling her mouth.

Forcing my eyes away from the thrashing threesome, they drift over the dying embers of the fire to land on Blaise's muscular frame lounging across the plush cushions.

His hand's grasping Clara's platinum locks as he guides her head up and down in his lap, eyes hooded with lust. His blue irises gaze down at her plump lips as they glide along his thick shaft, her bare boobs bouncing against his thighs. His abs tense with each bob of her head.

As if sensing the weight of my stare, his head snaps up, locking on me. The hand grasping Clara's hair freezes momentarily as his body visibly stiffens.

I'm half cloaked in shadows, the only illumination emanating from the subtle night lights. But by the way his stare cuts through the darkness, I know he can tell someone's standing here.

I watch with bated breath as he narrows his eyes, squinting through the gloom.

My heart sinks when his mouth gapes, his face jolting with recognition. A crude smile slowly spreads across his lips.

At that very moment, Clara's mouth glides off his dick with a loud smack. She licks her swollen lips as she gazes drunkenly up at him.

"What's wrong, baby?" she croons, her hand gliding up his bare thighs to clasp the base of his cock. "You want me to suck it harder? Faster? Tell me how to please you, baby."

Blaise shakes his head curtly, keeping his probing gaze on me for another long second before he glances down at Clara, a smirk still teasing the corners of his mouth.

"Just get the fuck on with it," he snaps, his tone harsh and demanding. Shock twists my gut as Clara lowers her head again, sucking his length back into her mouth without complaint.

Blaise grabs hold of her hair as he thrusts his hips in time with her increasing rhythm. I have no idea how she's managing not to gag from the rigorous movements as Blaise slides his cock deeper and deeper down her throat.

Rooted in place, I feel a strange dissonance rise in my chest. Shame and fascination coils within me.

There's nothing violent or forced about what's unfolding in front of me. And yet, the memory of another night—another girl—claws at the edges of my mind like a splinter I thought I'd buried.

This is different, I chant internally. *They're choosing this. All of them. They* want *this.*

The pleasured moans piercing the air send a trickle of heat pooling low in my belly, followed by a suffocating wave of guilt and confusion crashing in behind it.

Kelsey's loud shriek yanks me back to reality.

What the hell am I doing standing here, watching their illicit spectacle like some kind of voyeur?

I mentally block out the guttural grunts reverberating around me as I yell at myself to *look away*!

But my eyes drift on instinct, catching on Blaise as he yanks Clara's mouth off his dick, leaving her dazed and confused.

Before she can protest, he tugs her upright by her arms until she's standing in front of him, not a single item of clothing covering her naked body.

His hands shift to her hips, spinning her around before dragging her bare ass back onto his lap in one swift motion.

Both sets of eyes flutter closed as Clara sinks down onto him, an exaggerated moan spilling from her red-painted lips as she throws her head back, like she's starring in her very own porno.

I shouldn't be watching this. I really *shouldn't be watching this.*

But the image has seared itself onto my brain before I can tear my eyes away.

Blaise clasps his hands over her large breasts, pulling her ass hard against his pelvis in rapid, rhythmic thrusts. The sharp slap of skin meeting skin mixes with Clara's pleasure-drunk cries echoing through the night air—so loud I'm shocked the rest of the staff village hasn't come running to search out the source.

My brain screams at me to run, to escape this madness, but my feet remain rooted to the floor.

I'm horrified. And yet... I can't look away.

Blaise's face twists in a grimace of raw pleasure, and I catch sight of his cock glistening with Clara's arousal as it slides in and out of her.

A rush of heat stirs in my core, unwelcome and undeniable, just like it did the night I inadvertently watched Tiana and Dean.

It's wrong. It feels *so wrong*.

But my body doesn't seem to care.

As if spurred on by Clara's loud shrieks, Kelsey's own pants grow more intense, joined by a chorus of hoarse grunts from her two companions. Her lips slip off Finn's cock as she pants, "Oh my god, oh my god, oh my god!"

She detonates, writhing against Jack as she collapses onto her forearms. Finn quickly clasps his cock, fist pumping incessantly until he explodes, squirting cum all over Kelsey's exposed breasts.

Watching her friend come undone seems to be all Clara needs.

Practically bouncing off Blaise's lap, she lets out a loud, drawn-out cry, tossing back her blonde mane as her boobs lift high into the air, pleasured shrieks ripping into the night sky.

Her body trembles as wave after wave courses through her.

As Clara clenches around his cock, Blaise finally tears his clouded gaze from me, his eyes drooping to the spot where their bodies connect. A muffled, "Fuck," is all the warning he gives before a low, throaty groan escapes his lips.

I watch his hips jerk violently as he empties himself inside her, their guttural cries merging as they ride out their releases.

His body finally relaxes, intense pleasure slowly fading from his expression.

Suddenly, the night is eerily quiet. The absence of lust-filled moans, so loud just seconds ago, is jarring, the silence crashing over me like a slap.

A wave of confusion and disgust barrels through me, cutting straight through the lingering haze.

I need to get the hell out of here.

Blaise's cerulean gaze burns my skin as I whirl around and bolt for the stairs, all thoughts of my access card forgotten.

Chapter Twenty-Nine

"Miss Lindell? Mr Lencovich wants you to join him in his study."

I glance up from my book to find Simon standing in my doorway, his gaze angled slightly above my right shoulder.

He always avoids looking me directly in the eye. I wonder if that's Viktor's doing, or if Simon's simply terrified of what Viktor would do if he ever caught one of his male staff looking at me for longer than absolutely necessary.

Not that there's any cause for worry with Simon. For as long as I've known him, he's always gone above and beyond in his service for Viktor. It's likely why he's still here, rather than lying dead in a ditch somewhere.

That, and his unwavering loyalty. I'd love to be a fly on the wall if Simon was ever brought in for questioning by the police. No matter how hard they'd push, they wouldn't get a word out of him. Guaranteed.

I should know. When I first arrived here, I did everything in my power to trick Simon into spilling information.

He didn't crack once.

I shudder at the memory of the day Viktor came to find me in my room to confront me about my little 'detective project', as he called it. I never asked Simon about Viktor ever again.

"Miss Lindell?"

I sigh, resigned. "Give me a moment and I will be right out, Simon."

Simon gives me a curt nod before closing the door, leaving me to my own miserable thoughts. Knowing I don't have long, I put my book on the nightstand and climb off the bed. Walking over to the floor-to-ceiling mirror, I glance at my appearance.

It's become a habit to do this whenever Viktor is home—especially when he calls for me. If he ever sees me looking anything other than immaculate, I'm sure to hear about it. And if he's in a particularly bad mood, he'll find some other creative way to punish me.

Deciding he'll likely disapprove of my cute but plain blouse, I quickly change into a lace-covered silk shirt and slip my feet into a pair of high-heeled boots. After smoothing down a few stray hairs that have managed to escape my high ponytail, I cross the room and open the door to find Simon waiting patiently for me.

Without a word, he turns and walks over to the large staircase. I follow him silently, cursing him every step of the way, even though he's only doing his job.

But he knows as well as I do that Viktor's summons rarely bode well.

As we climb the steps to the entrance hall, I spot Viktor's goons standing guard at the front door, looking bored. I still don't understand why Viktor maintains twenty-four-hour security at every entrance to the large, three-story house—he already keeps me under constant surveillance. But I'm not stupid enough to ask.

Ignoring the invasive stares from the two guard dogs, I keep my focus locked on Simon's back as we walk across the cream-coloured tiles, the click of my heels providing an eerie backdrop to our awkward little march.

Rounding the corner, the sound abruptly cuts off, padded by the plush carpet covering the old floorboards lining the dark hallway to Viktor's study.

As we reach the wide mahogany door, Simon lifts his hand and knocks gently before turning the doorknob. He steps aside with practised ease, giving me room to enter.

Viktor's sitting behind his desk, a thick folder gripped in his large hands. I recognise it instantly as one of the reports landing on his desk every day at five, like clockwork.

His brow is furrowed in concentration as he scans the pages, but as I quietly step into the room, he sets the folder down and folds his hands. With a curt nod to Simon, the door closes behind me with a heavy snap.

"Ah, my dear Isabella." His deep voice rumbles through the quiet space, powerful and commanding. He has always had the ability to demand the attention of an entire room with a single word.

Although his tone is calm, his words gentle, I feel the suppressed tension radiating from him.

"You called for me?" I say softly, keeping my tone light and demure, void of even the slightest trickle of unease.

Viktor rounds his desk, moving to the gilded bar cart in the corner. He pours himself a tumbler of whisky from an amber-hued bottle. "Yes. I wanted to talk to you. I have something I wish to... discuss with you."

I don't miss the calculated pause he injects into his sentence.

"Of course," I reply curtly, knowing less is more. Words, in Viktor's hands, are weapons—ones he will use against me later the moment I slip up, giving him an opening to do so.

Viktor walks across the room to stand next to the old fireplace, his back to me. He doesn't gesture for me to join him like he usually does, so I remain standing where I am, awkward and wary, but grateful for the distance between us.

'So, little mouse. I have noticed that you have been very quiet lately. Is there anything on your mind that you would like to tell me?" Viktor's tone is smooth and poised.

The hairs on my neck rise.

Little mouse. *It's the nickname Viktor gave me when he discovered I'd been prying for information about the organisation, and Viktor's role in all of it.*

I wanted to know more about the man whose house I was living in. A man I had gradually started to distrust.

Each time he uses the nickname, it's a sickening reminder of what he did to me that day—the first time I got a true glimpse of who Viktor Vladimir Lencovich really is behind the mask.

I still recall the words he spoke to me, right before the first blow struck.

"You, my dear Isabella, are like a tiny, little mouse. Crafty and guileful. Covert and stealthy. Quietly, you scatter around the house, hiding in the shadows, only spotted when you want to be—*or* when you are finally lured out of your hiding spot by a tantalising piece of cheese.

The thing about mice, lapochka, is that there is always a larger predator lurking around the corner, patiently waiting to catch that innocent, little mouse. And remember this, my dear Isabella—the mouse always gets caught in the end.

Because, you see—a mouse can never resist that delicious, tempting slice of cheese, even if they know, deep down, that the cheese is only there to draw them out. And before the mouse can grasp what hit it, its sly little body gets caught in the mice trap. And when it does... the poor little mouse's insignificant life is over in the blink of an eye."

Shaking off the memory, I rack my brain as I frantically try to piece together what Viktor could've possibly found out that he wants me to confess to.

I've been so careful...

"Tell you?" I inflict an air of puzzlement into my voice as I fold my hands, willing my trembling fingers to still as my pulse hammers violently. "I always tell you everything, my love. Oh, actually," I pretend to interrupt myself. "Gloria from the flower shop was hoping to take next Friday off to attend her grandson's school play. I told her I would cover for her. I was meaning to tell you."

Thankfully, my comment is enough to district him—even if it's just temporarily.

"You told her you would cover for her?" Viktor's voice has taken on a cold, ominous note, causing a shiver to run down my spine. "And you did not think it would be prudent to ask me for permission before you decided to commit to this agreement?"

I bite my lip, bowing my head contritely. "I'm sorry, Viktor. I know I should've asked you first. But Gloria was so upset about her grandson's play, and I didn't want to let her down. She's been working a lot of hours lately, and you know how important she is for your shop. So I thought you would be happy that I agreed to help—"

"Enough!" Viktor's sharp bark cuts me off, and I immediately fall silent.

The fire crackles merrily, a jarring contrast to the oppressive stillness that presses down on us. I keep my gaze fixed on the floor, hyper-aware of Viktor's pervasive eyes on me.

When a deep sigh escapes him, I finally glance up, trying to gauge his temper.

"I suppose you will have to go now, as you have already made a commitment," he says evenly, though the trace of displeasure lingers.

He takes a long sip of whisky, angling his body toward the fireplace. The flames cast flickering shadows across his face as he watches them devour the ash-coloured logs.

"I do not like breaking commitments, Isabella," he declares eventually. "It is a sign of weakness. It tells people that you are not a person of your word. That you will not follow through on what you say. And in this life, lapochka, honour and respect are everything. If you do not have respect, you have nothing."

I stay quiet, wary of his strange mood. He's acting differently tonight. Calmer.

It sets me on edge.

When he finally turns to regard me, his stance is resolute. "I am glad you brought this up tonight, little mouse."

My stomach twists. "Y-you are?"

"Mmm," he hums. "It is actually a good example of what I wanted to discuss with you this evening." He swirls the whisky in his glass, studying me with unsettling precision. I stay unnaturally still, hiding any indication of my growing trepidation. "Perhaps you already know what it is I wish to talk to you about, little mouse?"

I shake my head, keeping my expression carefully blank.

"No?" He sighs, as if disappointed in me, yet I know him well enough to recognise the brewing excitement sparking behind his arctic irises. It's the same excitement I've glimpsed there many times before. The same fevered exhilaration that emanates from him each time he prepares to shatter my world a little more.

"Have I not given you everything you could wish for, Isabella? Have you not had a good life since I found you, filthy and starving, in that desolate parking lot three years ago? I let you work. I feed you. I clothe you. I provide a roof over your head. I've bought you more dresses, shoes and jewellery than most women could pray to afford in a lifetime. Yet you shy away from my touch. You flinch from the weight of my gaze. I see it in your eyes every time you look at me. I feel your reluctance each time you are near me."

His eyes glide over my body, lingering on my every curve.

"You have grown into a beautiful woman, Isabella. Still so young, yet already undeniably a rare beauty. I am a patient man, little mouse, and I will continue to be patient for a little while longer. I will not rush. I will persevere until it is the right time—when there is no longer a trace of juvenescence in your exquisite face, not a vestige of preadolescence in your luscious curves. When the desire for your unspoilt youth no longer carries any power, overtaken by the temptation of your blooming womanhood. A temptation so strong that I can no longer trust my associates will be able to curve their ravenous appetites. When having you will serve me a stronger purpose than resisting your youthful warmth currently does—then, and only then, will I finally have you for my own, my sweet lapochka."

As Viktor finishes his monologue, his penetrating eyes meet mine, locking me in place.

"Ah, my little mouse. I see the reluctance in your eyes, that rebellious foreboding shining back at me. You want to defy me. Perhaps even escape, if the chance presents itself. You eat from my table, yet you do not repay me for my kindness. You never intend to. It is as clear as day. One need only look at your captivating face to know it.

But, my dear little mouse, it is time you learn that I do not take well to disobedience. It is time you learn, little mouse, what I do to those who do not come willingly."

As if on cue, a loud knock rattles the door.

"Vkhodi", *Viktor barks, and it glides open.*

A girl stumbles into the room, her thin legs wobbling precariously as they struggle to balance on a pair of silver-coloured stilettos. Mikhail and Ivan follow closely behind her, the door shutting behind their broad backs, locking us in.

The girl looks utterly terrified as her huge, brown irises skitter frantically across the room, as if desperate to locate an escape route. Her long hair looks almost black in the dimly lit space as it flows limply over her frail shoulders, a few loose strands getting caught in her black eyelashes, which have been generously coated with a thick layer of mascara.

In fact, her entire face has been heavily made up, the bright pink of her eye shadow matching her short-skirted dress. Peering more closely at her, I realise she can't be more than eighteen or nineteen, though someone has clearly gone to great lengths to make her look older.

But her youthful, innocent eyes betray her, her adolescence made apparent by the unmistakable terror cloaking her pale face.

She looks as if she hasn't had a proper meal in months. Her slender arms wrap protectively around her scrawny waist, as if she's trying to shield herself from the very air surrounding her. I barely stop myself from flinching when I spot the stark outline of collarbones protruding from the taut skin across her chest.

She visibly cowers beneath Viktor's scrutiny, her shoulders high as she tries to sink into herself.

She looks sad and pitiful—a gaunt shell of what was once likely a very beautiful young woman.

The knot in the pit of my stomach twists painfully.

"Ah, finally," Viktor announces, his voice authoritative as he eyes his two goons.

"'Pologies, boss," Ivan grunts, his voice gruff as he scratches at his shabby, week-old stubble. "Snuff told us his crew ran into some issues at the border, so the last lot came in 'bit later than expected."

He pushes the girl further into the room, and I have to bite my tongue to stop from calling out as she nearly falls flat on her face, her skinny ankles wobbling dangerously as they balance on her ridiculously high heels.

Viktor trails a slow, calculated glance over her gaunt frame, his manner contemplative. The girl still refuses to meet his cold stare, panicked eyes flashing to her feet as she drops her chin.

A small teardrop escapes from beneath lowered lashes, sliding down her pale cheek to fall forlornly to the dark floor boards.

"This is from the last group?"

"Yes, boss." Ivan's large, dumb head nods fervently. "You said you wanted a fresh one, so figured we'd better grab one of 'em before they get processed through the system. You know how it goes with the best ones, with 'em havin' to go out quick to satisfy demand."

Viktor nods, his focus back on the girl. "And the substance?"

"'Bout twenty minutes ago, boss."

"Excellent." A satisfied look flashes across Viktor's rugged face as I frantically try to piece together their conversation.

Before I can wrap my head around their cryptic words, Viktor gives a curt nod. Without another sound, Mikhail and Ivan shuffle out of the room, closing the door firmly behind them.

I don't dare make even the smallest sound as silence engulfs us once more, terrified of what will happen when the tension swallowing the room eventually breaks.

The poor girl is visibly shaking now, her arms clutched weakly around herself.

Viktor's the only one who seems perfectly at ease as he walks over to the bar trolley to refill his glass. Spinning it around in his large hand, he finally speaks.

"Isabella, I would like you to meet... I'm sorry, dear one. I do not know your name?"

Viktor pretends to look contrite, even as a self-satisfied smirk glints on his lips. "Oh, well. No matter, no matter. What do such silly details really mean in the end? I think I will call you... Ivanka." He nods to himself. "Yes, I think that will fit you nicely, dear one. I have always liked the name Ivanka. It has a certain... flare to it."

I feel my blood simmering at the subtle condescension in his voice, but the girl doesn't react. That is, until her body suddenly sways precariously.

I rush across the room and grasp her by the arm to stop her from toppling over. Her skin feels unnaturally hot and clammy against my palms, and I instinctively let go. I was expecting her skin to feel cold from the way she was shivering only moments before.

I watch her nervously as her body sways from side to side, her limp hand trailing absentmindedly up her sunken abdomen to scratch at a faint rash working its way from her chest to her neck.

I startle as Viktor appears beside me. He stretches out his arm to clasp the girl's jaw in a firm grip, yanking her chin upward. The hard line of his mouth tightens as he studies the dull emptiness in her vacant eyes.

Her vacant, strangely clouded eyes that were perfectly clear and alert, albeit terrified, only minutes before.

"Is she alright?" My voice sounds weak and distant through the loud thrumming in my ears.

"She is fine," Viktor replies, not a hint of concern in his voice. "In fact, she is just about ready."

Ready? Ready for what?

I watch with wide, horrified eyes as Viktor grabs the girl's arm and pulls her roughly across the room, disposing her beside one of the leather couches by the fireplace. She looks even more fragile next to Viktor's bulky frame, his huge paw dwarfing her bony arm.

Callously casting her down on the armrest, he walks behind her and forcefully pulls at her zipper until the dress falls unceremoniously down her body in a pink cascade.

She's completely naked underneath, not a trace of clothing covering her slender physique. Now that her body is no longer covered by a layer of clothes, I'm shocked to discover just how frail she actually is.

While her body has not yet lost all resemblance of curves, her stomach is hollow, not a hint of fat trimming her narrow waist. Her ribs protrude through her pale, almost translucent skin, and her breasts are small and bruised, as if they were recently groped with excessive force.

As I take in the purple-and-yellow marks covering her thighs and abdomen, my stomach turns.

Nausea overtakes me as I spot other parts of her body where large, blotchy bruises peek through, some purple or yellow in colour, other reddish-pink—each a vivid contrast to her otherwise opaque skin.

I spent enough time living on the streets to know what causes these types of bruises.

Fists and needles.

I stare at her blank face, expecting embarrassment, or even shame, at having her body on full display, needle marks clearly visible. But her expression is completely void of any emotion. She simply stands there, shoulders slightly hunched, hands hanging limply at her side, eyelids drooping as she stares unseeingly into the distance.

I slowly replay Viktor's and Ivan's words in my head.

'And the substance?'

''Bout twenty minutes ago, boss.'

And then it dawns on me.

They drugged her.

My entire body seizes in an instant, an eerie chill spreading through my entire body.

"Viktor..." I whisper, heartbeats quickening. Before I can say another word, Viktor pushes the girl's back with force until she sprawls ungracefully over the armrest.

Holding her body down with one hand, he uses his other hand to undo his belt. As he lets his pants fall to his knees, I catch a swift glimpse of his thick, hard cock before he thrusts into her, a loud, satisfied grunt rumbling from deep within his throat.

A tiny twitch of her brow is the only indication that the girl even notices Viktor entering her, her eyes continuing to stare vacantly into the empty air.

"Viktor, what the fuck?!" I scream, my voice laced with panic.

I no longer care if he gets angry at me. I'm not going to stand here and watch this happen.

"Viktor, get off her! Stop it! What the hell are you doing?!"

Viktor only thrusts harder into her, a self-gratified smirk pulling at his lips.

The bastard's getting off on my panic.

Without thinking, I dart across the room and pull helplessly at his shirt in a useless attempt to drag him off her. Viktor halts his relentless thrusting long enough to throw out his elbow.

The sharp edge cracks across my temple, sending me sprawling to the floor.

I vaguely register Viktor shouting for Mikhail and Ivan as I scramble to sit back up, my vision blurry as I try to regain my balance. I faintly hear a loud slam from somewhere behind me before strong arms unceremoniously drag me to my feet.

It takes a flurry of rapid blinks before the room finally comes back into focus.

To my horror, Viktor is still thrusting his hips violently against the girl's naked backside, creating a nauseating slapping sound with each heaving plunge. Her body has gone entirely limp. I'm not even sure she's conscious anymore.

"Viktor, stop," I shriek again, not caring if the entire neighbourhood hears. "Please! Please, stop. You're hurting her!"

My screams are muffled by a hand clamping over my mouth. I gag at the smell of stale tobacco seeping from Mikhail's meaty paw. I know it's him from the imprint of his large silver ring pressing against my upper lip.

A deep, throaty chuckle draws my panicked face back to Viktor.

A light sheen of sweat is spreading across his forehead, his raspy voice laced with unadulterated pleasure.

"I want you to remember this moment, little mouse. Soak in it. Let it imprint on your mind. Did you really think I would let you slip away from my grasp, after everything I have done for you? Did you really think you could shy away from me—avoid my gaze, withdraw from my touch—without me noticing?"

Chuckling at my useless attempts to break free from Mikhail's tight hold, Viktor adjusts his stance as he clasps the girl's hips in an even firmer grip, using his giant hands to pull her body forcefully against his pelvis. His throaty grunts are coming more rapidly now.

"I always get what I want, lapochka. Always," he rasps in a husky voice.

As his keen pants grow more incessant, he fixes his merciless stare on me, lust-filled eyes locking onto my terrified, furious glare. "You will do well to remember that, little mouse. Because if you do not give me what I want willingly, I will take it by force."

Feeling a desperate sob climb up my throat, I close my eyes tightly, fighting to block out Viktor's guttural moans mixing with the nauseating sound of flesh hitting flesh.

This is a nightmare, *I tell myself over and over again.* This is just a nightmare. I will wake up soon, and all of this will have been a bad, horrible dream.

"LOOK AT ME!"

Viktor's roar thunders through the room, and I flinch, squeezing my eyes even tighter, willing it all to go away.

"I SAID, LOOK AT ME!"

Mikhail clasps his other hand across my jaw, pressing down hard until I can no longer tolerate the pain.

I open my eyes reluctantly.

Viktor's expression is ablaze with a lethal mix of fury and pleasure, his excitement fuelled by the profound horror bleeding from my eyes.

His face contorts as a ripple of intense pleasure surges through him.

With a series of deafening, guttural moans, he empties himself inside the pale, lifeless body slumped over the cold, leather-clad armrest as broken tears stream down my face.

"Elaina! Els, wake up!"

My eyes fly open.

Tiana's blurry face floats above me, her eyes wide with concern.

She's clasping my shoulders in a firm grip. When she notices I'm awake, she lets go and slides back across the bed, giving me room to sit up.

Utterly disoriented, I cover my face as I gasp in air, sharp breaths drowning my throat as I fight to slow my galloping heart. As my palms touch the sides of my cheeks, a cold, wet trail trickles down my cheeks.

It takes me several breathless seconds to realise I'm crying.

Pulling the scrunched duvet from beneath my sweat-slick body, I clasp the edge of the sheet and use it to wipe away the stray tears.

"Elaina... Fuck, are you alright?"

I peek out from behind the duvet.

Tiana's watching me cautiously, her eyes swimming with relief and worry.

"Thank God you woke up, or I don't know what I would've done," she whispers, her voice trembling slightly. "I was trying to wake you up for at least a minute before you finally opened your eyes."

I swallow hard, hands trembling, gaze hazy and disoriented.

"I'm fine," I force out. The tight pull of Tiana's lips tells me she doesn't believe me.

I yank the bed sheet back over my face, hating her scrutinising look.

"Are you sure?" she ask quietly. "That... that sounded like a pretty bad dream, Els. You were talking in your sleep. You were kind of yelling, actually."

I wince, breaths shaky as my heart pitter-patters in my chest. "I'm so sorry, T. I didn't mean to wake you."

She scoffs. "I don't care about being woken up, Els. I care about whether or not you're okay. You were thrashing around, yelling out nonsense. At one point, I thought you were going to throw yourself out of the bed. What kind of dream was that, anyway?"

I grab my water bottle from the small wall shelf and take a huge swig to buy time. I down half the bottle before finally looking back up at Tiana. "To be honest, I can barely remember."

A doubtful frown mars her pretty face.

I clasp my fingers tightly around the base of the water bottle. "Honestly. It's always been like that for me. I never recall my dreams."

Tiana clicks her tongue. "Oh, come on, Elaina. That's total bullshit. How can you have a dream like that and *not* remember it?"

I fumble with the sheets still clutched tightly in my fist. "It was all so messy and confusing. I suppose I remember small glimpses of it. But I don't really want to remember, you know? It definitely wasn't a good dream, whatever it was. I'd rather just forget."

Tiana's frown softens, and she reaches out to grasp my hand. "Of course. I get that. I'm sorry, Els. I didn't mean to push you. You just scared me, is all."

I squeeze her hand back. "It's okay. I know I did, and I'm sorry. I'll try not to have any more nightmares in the future." I force a tiny smile, and the knot in my stomach loosens a fraction as her lips pull into a gentle grin.

You're okay, Elaina. You're safe.

I chant the words over and over as Tiana climbs back down the ladder and lies down on her bed, throwing the room into darkness once more as she switches off the bedside light.

Viktor won't find you here. You'll never, ever have to go through another night like that, ever again.

As I roll onto my side and force my eyes shut, I offer a silent plea to the universe that I'm right.

Chapter Thirty

I barely contain my smile when I spot Orlando's broad frame leaning against the stone fountain in front of the castle on Friday morning, a week out from the big event.

"Morning, boss man," I call out once we're close enough to talk, lifting a hand to block the glare of the rising sun as I squint at him. He offers little more than an imperceptible nod, but I still catch the faint warmth stirring beneath his otherwise composed exterior.

I halt a few meters away, careful to leave a comfortable distance between us. Even so, my breath catches, as it always does, when his gaze makes its usual sweep over my body, taking in my simple outfit.

I keep my eyes on the proud eagle standing sentry above us as I ask, "So, what are we getting our hands dirty planting today?"

His posture shifts immeasurably at the word *dirty*, and the familiar flutter of butterflies stirs in my stomach.

"We're not planting anything." He nods for me to follow him as he heads in the opposite direction of the vegetable garden. "You up for helping me with a different project today, *sirena*?"

A frown creases my brow as I quicken my steps. "*Sirena*?" The unfamiliar word feels strange on my tongue.

Orlando turns to face me, and my heart lurches at the sudden intensity sparking behind his guarded demeanour. Small flecks of gold mingle with prominent swirls of green and grey in his irises. Once again, it's as if they can see right through me.

When he speaks, his voice is low and deep, gravel threading each word.

'Yes. *Sirena*. It means 'siren' in Spanish. In ancient Greek mythology, sirens were known to be seductively beautiful creatures. With their beguiling looks and captivating allure, they had the ability to enthral men with their very presence until they went mad with lust. The ultimate temptation—and the ultimate danger."

His voice cuts through the space between us, rich and unexpected, the weight of his words striking me as much as their poetic cadence.

My heart pounds faster, its erratic rhythm slamming against my rib cage. His stare burns into mine, holding me captive.

Orlando's lips twitch in an almost imperceptible smile, the faint sparkle in his eyes hinting at amusement.

"Why do you look so surprised, *sirena*? Do you not think you're beautiful?" His direct question catches me off guard even more than his earlier words. "Do you not think you're alluring? Entrancing'? Capable of spiralling a man's mind until he no longer knows good from bad. Safe from dangerous. Truth from a tempting illusion. Capable of shattering hearts and bewitching minds?"

I stand rooted in place, dumbfounded, as he saunters across the lawn at a languid pace.

"Maybe you should," he tosses over his shoulder when I don't respond.

I can't seem to form words. They're stuck, thick and unmoving on my tongue.

"Now, come along, sirena. Time to work."

For the rest of the day, we move from one flowerbed to the next, trailing a path through the hotel grounds. Sweat trickles down Orlando's forehead as he works with a hefty hedge trimmer, his strong hands expertly manoeuvring the tool as he trims the dense hedges flanking the winding walkway.

I spend most of the day on my knees, pulling weeds and wilted flowers from the garden beds, occasionally planting fresh seedlings in place of the ones I remove.

Orlando's more talkative than usual, sharing stories from past hotel events and making me laugh with his whispered commentary on the questionable fashion choices of the more eccentric guests wandering past.

Beneath his lingering reservation, a tentative friendship is beginning to take root between us. The growing thread of familiarity makes my heart skip—though it's nothing compared to the swoop in my belly each time he offers one of those wary, yet undeniably beautiful smiles.

When lunchtime finally rolls around, we settle beneath the shade of a large oak tree, its densely leafed branches providing welcome relief from the blazing midday sun.

I let out a squeal of delight as Orlando pulls two large containers from his cooler bag, packed to the brim with juicy chicken and topped with generous dollops of sour cream, salsa, and guacamole.

"Mexican bowls," I whoop, snatching one of the containers out of his grasp. "Oh, it's been a minute since I had one of these."

I lift the bowl to my nose to sniff at the contents, eyelashes fluttering as I relish the mouth-watering aroma of spices and zesty lime.

"Who would've though such a simple gesture would be met with such spirited enthusiasm?" Orlando quips through a crooked smile. "If I knew I'd get this kind of response, I'd bring you lunch every day, just to see that look on your face."

I clamp my mouth shut before something slips out that I'll regret, ducking my head as I dig into my food to hide the heat creeping up my cheeks.

Several minutes pass in peaceful silence.

"So, what's really going on with you, sirena?" Orlando's deep voice cuts through the quiet.

The unexpected question catches me off guard, and I nearly choke on a piece of lettuce.

My voice is croaky as I wheeze out, "What do you mean?"

Orlando quirks a brow, as if to say *Oh, come on, now.*

"I'm fine?" My response wavers, more a question than an answer.

He gives me one of his signature poignant stares. "Don't play coy, Elaina." Those sharp, perceptive eyes gleam greener than ever, cutting straight through my performance. "I've been watching you all day. I can tell something's off."

I huff. "What're you on about?" If anything, we've talked more today than all our other shifts combined.

"Don't think I've missed all those vacant stares into thin air, your mind a million miles away, caught up in something far away from here," he says without missing a beat.

The rebuttal catches in my throat.

Oh... I didn't think he'd noticed.

"Come on, Lainey. Just tell me what's going on. I know something's playing on your mind, so you might as well spill. I'm going to keep bugging you either way until you spit it out."

The ease with which he utters the unexpected nickname nearly distracts me from his question. But even Orlando's gentle words and steady presence aren't enough to drown out the vivid flashes from last night's dream, clouding my already mercurial mood.

"I—it's nothing really," I mumble, lowering my chin to avoid his astute gaze. "Just a weird dream. It threw me off a little, that's all."

I can feel him watching me, tracking my every reaction. "What kind of dream?"

When I don't respond, he reaches out and gently hooks a finger under my chin, carefully turning my head to face him.

"What kind of dream, sirena? What has your mind drifting so far away, lost in unsettling thoughts?"

I momentarily lose myself in his eyes, pulse steadying at the tenderness shimmering there. He gives me a small, encouraging nod, his hand lingering lightly on my skin, and something inside me suddenly aches to open up. To tell him what I've been through. What I've lost. What I'm running from.

How alone I feel.

How *scared* I feel.

I know I can't tell him everything. But in that moment, I feel an inexplicable need to tell him *something*.

For some unexplainable reason, I want him to know something about me that no one else knows. Something that will connect us in some small, perhaps insignificant way, but a connection all the same.

I close my eyes, drawing strength from his gentle hand on mine, his patient eyes on my face, his quiet presence, ready to listen—to absorb even the smallest fragment of the hurt I carry on my tired shoulders.

A hurt I now realise I never managed to hide from him, despite my steadfast attempts to do so.

"Before I came to Cliff Castle, I lived in a place where I... let's just say it left a lot to be desired."

I pause, choosing my words with care. "The person I lived with was... very controlling. He wouldn't let me leave the house without supervision. He would track my every move, dictated where I went, what I wore, who I spoke to, what I was allowed to say. If I ever stepped out of line, he'd find some manipulative, calculated way to punish me."

An image of Viktor floods my mind—his maniacal eyes as he pushed himself into the lifeless girl, the flickering light of the dying fire ghosting across his face as it contorted into a mask of cruel, gratified pleasure.

I squeeze my eyelids shut, fighting the sting of tears as my hands tremble. "Last night, I dreamed about one of those times. It brought it all back, and now..." I draw a shuddering breath. "I can't seem to shake it."

"Is that why you ran away?"

I snap my head back to him as a wave of panic crashes through my chest. Orlando's watching me cautiously, his expression unflinching.

"Ran away? Wh-what makes you think I ran away?" I say in the most brazen voice I can muster.

Orlando's lips tighten. He doesn't buy it.

"It was just a hunch," he says. "But I can tell from your face I've hit the mark."

I pull away, zeroing in on a stray ant trudging across the manicured lawn, clinging to the distraction as I try—and fail—to steady my galloping heart.

"I don't really want to talk about it," I mumble at last, my voice barely audible.

To my relief, Orlando doesn't press me.

He folds his arms loosely around his knees, staring into the distance as he speaks.

"I've always found it fascinating how people who've never faced hardship in their lives seem so quick to judge those who weren't as lucky. It's no easy feat, stepping out of the dark and seeking the sun. Yet people who've never known the dark think it's as simple as moving your legs forward and effortlessly walking into the light.

They don't understand how paralysing the darkness can be. How it can ensnare you in its gloom, its cold hands numbing your entire body until your muscles fail you, your mind betrays you, and you're truly convinced there's no way out."

When his eyes meet mine, I feel them on my skin like a physical touch.

"Not everyone finds the courage to escape what feels inescapable. You may not know it, Elaina, but by breaking free from whoever caged you, you've already shown more courage than most people will ever show. You don't need to tell me all the dark, distorted details of your past for me to see that. You story is yours, and yours alone. It's up to you who you share it with. I just hope you never forget how resilient you are."

I'm left speechless as Orlando falls quiet, his thoughts once more drifting back to the horizon.

As much as I want to let his words wash over me, to soak in them until they sink into the deepest part of me, I know I won't be able to stop the tears from falling if I do.

So instead, I lock his words tight inside my chest for now and focus on calming my breaths.

Several minutes pass in silence before I finally work up the courage to glance at Orlando again.

He's watching me, carefully gauging my reaction. His expression is as unreadable as ever, yet I find myself lost in his stormy eyes, mesmerised by the shift from subtle shades of mossy green to slate grey. He doesn't look away, capturing me in his orbit.

A soft breath escapes his lips as our eyes tangle.

Neither of us moves, our chests rising and falling is unison as we remain locked in place, oblivious to the world around us.

For one suspended moment in time, it feels like we're the only two people in the world.

And for the first time since my nightmare wrenched me from sleep this morning, my thoughts are far, far away from Viktor and his cruel depravity.

Orlando tilts his head slightly, and I feel the weight of his gaze settle on my mouth. I draw in a sharp breath as his body shifts imperceptibly closer. As if pulled by instinct, my body leans in to meet his, unable to tear my eyes from his as they bore into me.

His gaze drops to my lips again...

A piercing ring shatters the silence, jolting us from our trance.

Orlando gives his head a small shake as he pulls a phone from his pocket. I don't miss the way his lips flatten into a thin line as he checks the screen.

When his eyes lift back up to mine, it's like a shutter has dropped, sealing off all warmth.

The tug inside my chest betrays my disappointment.

Without a word, he lifts the phone to his ear, his presence still anchored to mine.

"¿Puedo llamarte más tarde? Estoy... ocupado ahora mismo."

Even with my broken Spanish, I manage to piece his words together.

Can I call you back? I'm busy right now.

A blush creeps across my cheeks at the reminder of what, exactly, he was *almost* busy doing—though the annoyed look now clouding his face makes the dreamlike moment feel like an illusion.

His eyes slip away from mine as he listens, his attention suddenly absorbed by the call.

"¿Domingo? Eso es más temprano de lo que pensaba. No te esperaba hasta el miércoles. ¿Todo salió bien en Constanta?"

My ears perk up.

Sunday. Earlier than I thought. Not expecting... until Wednesday. Everything... well in Constanta?

The words stand out amid the fluid stream of Spanish. My mind instantly jumps to what Domenico de Águila said before he left for Romania.

Constanta. That's where he said he was going. It has to be him on the other end.

But Orlando turns his back to me, his voice dropping lower, and I can't make out the responses on the other end—only the occasional, rich murmur of the other speaker, the words completely lost on me.

"Eso es... buenas noticias, supongo. ¿Has arreglado el transporte de vuelta al hotel o necesitas que alguien te recoja?"

Good news. Transport. Hotel. Pick up.

The pieces land in fragments, barely enough to construct a full sentence. I strain to catch more, but all I get is the rhythmic cadence of what I now faintly recognise as Domenico's voice, rich and smooth as it rumbles through the speaker.

"Bien. Nos vemos el domingo, entonces. Mándame un mensaje cuando llegues. Podemos... discutirlo con más detalle."

Good. Sunday. Message. Discuss... details.

I don't need to understand the rest to feel the weight in Orlando's voice as he holds the phone to his ear for a few more seconds before ending the call.

"Was that Dom... señor de Águila?" I ask.

Orlando's head snaps up, his glare sharp and sudden.

"Why would you think it's him?" His tone is laced with suspicion.

The hostility coating his words stops me short. "I-I don't know," I stammer, shrinking back when his eyes narrow. "H-he told me he was going to Romania—to Constanta—before he left, so when I heard you mention it, I thought..."

I trail off, the rest of my sentence catching in my throat as a flash of anger breaks through Orlando's exterior.

"He told you?" he parrots, voice low and dangerously cool.

"Uhm... yes?" I hesitate, watching him carefully.

"Ah. I see." Orlando nods once. "Guess I missed the part where you two became best friends."

A flare of irritation sparks in my chest. "We're not 'best friends'," I bite out, imitating his sarcastic tone. "We met—by coincidence, I might add—on my first day here, and he mentioned he was going to Romania. That's all."

From the ripple passing over Orlando's face, I know I'm not the only one annoyed.

"Funny," he says, tone dry. "I was under the impression very few people knew he was headed there, so forgive me if I'm a little surprised he added you to that rather intimate list of confidants."

"It's not like I asked for him to impart the information." My voice has taken on a frustrated edge, slowly rising with the weight of his accusatory tone. "Why do you care, anyway? What's so bad about me knowing where Domenico was headed?"

Orlando's eyebrows climb even higher on his forehead. "*Domenico*? Oh, so you're on a first name basis now, are you? How sweet."

I throw my hands in the air. "Christ, do you hear yourself? Why are you being like this?"

"*'Like this*?" He echoes my words with something resembling a tight smile tugging at his lips, but there's not a trace on humour there. "Is there a particular way I'm supposed to behave now? Did I miss a memo?"

Shoving aside the sting of his callousness, I let the anger rise to the surface.

"You know what? Screw you," I bite out. "I'm over tiptoeing around you, waiting for you to switch from one personality to the next, never knowing which version of you I'll get. One second you act like we're friends, and the next, you look at me like you can't wait for me to get out of your face. It's *exhausting.*"

I drop my fork into the bowl, suddenly no longer hungry. "No wonder no one else here actually knows you, or even really likes you," I seethe. "You push everyone away, and I was a fool to believe, for even a second, that you actually wanted to get to know me. Clearly it was a mistake for me to try to get to know you. I should've known you'd end up treating me the same way you treat everyone else. Silly me for thinking any different. Lesson learned."

I push to my feet and grab my bag from beside me. It catches on the edge of the bench, and the force of my tug tears a seam in the beige fabric

"Where are you going?" Orlando snaps as I march away, his voice sharp with frustration.

"Away from you," I yell into the open air, refusing to turn around. I already know what I'll see in his cutting glare.

Without another word, I take off toward the staff village, leaving Orlando behind.

Chapter Thirty-One

"Els?"

I look up from the book I'm unsuccessfully trying to read and spot Tiana heading my way, her sandals clicking against the timber floorboards.

I've been holed up in one of the lounge chairs outside the lodge ever since I stormed off from Orlando, pretending to be engrossed in my book whenever someone walked past so I wouldn't have to talk to anyone.

In truth, I've spent the entire time replaying our argument over and over, trying to make sense of it.

I still can't wrap my head around what happened. It all shifted so quickly. One minute we were laughing and having fun, sparking that intense, unexpected moment between us—and the next, it was like a switch had flipped.

What could've possibly triggered him so much? From the fragments I managed to interpret during his call with Domenico—though his one-sided responses weren't exactly illuminating—the call sounded innocent enough.

But something must've happened to spark such a drastic shift in his mood.

Tiana flops onto the ottoman at the foot of my lounge chair, and I scoot my feet aside to give her room. "What a rare treat seeing you here so early," she teases. "I wasn't expecting you for at least another couple of hours. What gives?"

I shrug. "I—Cindy let me take an early day," I lie, turning back to the book in my lap. "Delivery delay."

"Wow." Tiana looks genuinely surprised. "That's an unexpected turn of events. Don't get me wrong. Cindy's a total gem, but I don't think I've ever heard of her letting people off early. That woman always has a never-ending laundry list of things to get through."

I laugh uncomfortably. "Yeah, well ... We were all surprised. No complaints, though."

I don't give her a chance to push. "How was your day?"

"Don't even ask," Tiana groans as she lies down across the ottoman. "I had to do six classes in a row today, since Tanya's unwell. I'm knackered."

"Guess it's an early night for you tonight, then?" I say, peering over the edge of the book.

Tiana rolls over on her side to pin me with a pointed glare.

"Are you kidding? It's Friday, girl. We've both been busting our asses all week. It's finally our chance to cut loose. Early night, my French tush. Tonight, you and I are getting hammered."

"How's the event planning coming along? I bet they're keeping you busy over there. We've barely seen you in our department for weeks now."

I smile at Sandy, a cheerful American girl from housekeeping, as I take a sip of my gin and tonic. I wince as the searing liquid assaults my taste buds and remind myself not to let Tiana mix my drinks for the rest of the night. I won't last another hour at this rate.

"It's going pretty well," I tell Sandy, shouting to be heard over the blaring music. "Cindy's been keeping us all on our toes. There's still lots left to do, but I think it's coming together nicely."

Sandy chuckles. "I bet. I can't even tell you how many times they've told our team how important it is for *'every room to be positively spotless'* when the guests arrive next week."

She rolls her eyes. "If they took this event any more seriously, they'd have to tear the place down and rebuild a new castle to make sure everything lives up to their lofty standards."

I giggle, then shrug. "I suppose it's understandable. From what Tina and Alison told me about the guest list, I can appreciate the pressure they're under to make sure everything goes off without a hitch. This place would be impossible to manage without substantial investor funding, even for a family as wealthy as de Águilas."

"Oh! I was meaning to ask Alison about the guest list," Sandy squeals, eyes lighting up. "You have to tell me who's coming. Is it true Justin Bieber's going to be here?"

We're interrupted as Tess and Jess wander over, fresh bottles of cider in hand.

"What's up, ladies?" Tess greets as Jess offers me a smile. "Figured we'd join you. It's getting a tad too... *exhibitionistic* over there for our taste."

We glance toward the far end of the terrace, where Kelsey and Clara are dancing in the middle of a large group of guys, all watching with wide, salacious grins as the two blondes shimmy provocatively around a makeshift pole. Several of them whoop loudly as Clara whips off her bright pink crop top to reveal a matching bra, her ample breasts straining against the lacy fabric as she sways her hips to the pulsing beat.

I wince, already turning away when a prickle of unease shoots across my skin. Scanning the circle of guys, it doesn't take long to find Blaise's crude eyes watching me.

"What's the deal with you and Blaise, anyway?"

My focus snaps back to the girls as I meet Tess's inquisitive look.

"Absolutely *nothing,*" I grumble.

"Doesn't seem like he's got that memo. His eyeballs have been permanently glued to you all night." She glances over, catching him staring again.

"Don't I know it," I mutter darkly, irritation lacing my voice.

I have a strong suspicion our unintentional encounter on the terrace the other night has something to do with Blaise's increased interest in me tonight.

"He's barely looked away from you for more than ten seconds at a time," Tess snorts, rolling her eyes. "I've seen him pull moves before, but his fixation on you definitely takes it up a notch."

She leans in and lowers her voice. "Tiana's theory is that he's obsessed with you because you're just about the only person around here *not* screwing your brains out like a cat in heat."

I choke on a sip of gin.

Coughing, I wipe away the liquid spluttering down my chin with a napkin Jess hands me as I glare at Tess with wide, watery eyes.

Tess guffaws. "It's true, though. It's what you get when you put a bunch of young-blooded, horny guys in close proximity to a cackle of hormonal ladies. But you, my friend, seem to be the only one not bitten by the lust bug."

An unbidden image of Orlando floats into my mind.

"Are we talking about Elaina's unnatural ability to abstain from the thick cloud of pheromones engulfing this place?"

Rhianna's loud voice rings over the music as she saunters over to us, her usual Afro tamed into two massive space buns atop her head.

My shoulders lift in a would-be casual shrug. "I'm just not after that kind of thing right now."

Understanding flashes across Tess's face. "Ah. Bad relationship?"

I lower my gaze to the tumbler in my hands. "Something like that."

Her smile turns sympathetic. "I had one of those once, too. Took me a long time to get past it. But I did eventually, and so will you." She gives me a gentle smile. "Trust me. One day soon, you'll feel a hundred times lighter for leaving the bastard behind, whoever he is."

A familiar voice cuts in behind us.

"Did I just catch you discussing Elaina's recent meanderings in the Sahara Desert?"

Tiana smirks as she appears on Tess's left side, carrying a tray of shots filled to the brim with an inky-coloured liquid.

I arch a brow. "Sahara Desert? Really?"

She cackles as she balances the tray on the timber railing. "Anyone who can ignore the melting pot of male exquisiteness around here and resist ogling every single one of these fuckboys—and fucking at least a good handful before summer's out—has clearly decided to live out their days drying out their poor vag in the desert."

Tiana's eyes dance as the girls hoot with laughter.

"Oh, leave her alone, T," Tess giggles.

"Don't you talk, missy." Tiana darts a narrow-eyed look at Tess. "Don't think we haven't noticed the way you've been eye-fucking Hayden lately."

To my surprise, Tess looks more pleased than embarrassed. "I can assure you, there's more than eye-fucking going on there," she retorts, adding a cheeky wink.

Tiana lets out a delighted squeal. "I knew it," she cries, lifting her palm for a high five. "Nice going, chick. He's *smokin'*. Go get it, girl."

Tiana snatches the shot glasses from the tray and hands one to each of us. "This calls for celebratory shots. Cheers to Tess getting her rocks off with Hayden. To me for getting thoroughly screwed on a regular basis by the magnificent Dean and his super-sized dick. And to Elaina, for having more self-control than a monk."

Snorting, I lift the tiny glass to my lips and pour the contents into my mouth. The taste of liquorice assaults my taste buds, and I wince as the salty liquid glides down my throat.

"Now we're talking," Tiana hoots, pumping her fist in the air. Dean appears behind her and snakes one hand around her waist, carrying a second tray of shots in the other.

"Evenin' ladies," he croons, giving Tiana a seductive kiss on the neck. "I was coming over here to get you girls fired up with some shots, but I can see you're already well ahead of me."

A twinge of unease stirs in my chest as Tess and Tiana cheer. I'm not convinced another shot, so soon after the first, is the wisest move.

Before I can decline, Tiana grabs two glasses and hands one to me, clinking hers to mine.

"Cheers to an awesome night, Els," she hollers, a beaming smile brightening her face. "I'm so happy you're here tonight. It's about time you join in on the fun around here."

Her genuine happiness is contagious, and I can't bring myself to stomp on her excitement.

So I flash a wide grin, throw my head back, and down the entire shot in one swift swallow.

Chapter Thirty-Two

"Now, tell me. I've always wanted to know... How big is it? I mean, we've all seen that gigantic bulge in his pants that he never really tries all that hard to hide. But I've never been able to confirm the true size of it, you know?"

I snort at Tiana's intrusive questioning, causing my latest sip of beer to fizzle uncomfortably in my nose.

"Girl, that bulge is *all* for me, so hands off," Tess teases, bumping Tiana's shoulder playfully. "And from what I've heard, you've got more than your hands full with your own sizeable bulge over there." She nods toward Dean, who's in the middle of a game of beer pong with the outdoor crew.

A loud cheer rings around the table as Dean manages to sink the small, orange ball into the other team's cup.

As one of his teammates slaps him on the back, I catch him sneaking a peek at Tiana, following the sway of her hips as they move seductively to the music blasting from the speakers. I've caught him throwing her heated glances all evening, seemingly unable to keep his eyes off her.

Dean's undeniably good looking, in that muscular, brutish kind of way. While I'm not attracted to him, I can't deny the small stab of envy I feel at the way he's constantly drawn to Tiana, desire and lust written all over him.

I've never had anyone look at me like that before.

As if the world wants to explicitly disprove my inner dialogue, I catch Blaise studying me from across the room for what must be the twentieth time tonight. There's undeniable lust dancing in his icy blues, but unlike the flirty grin Tiana flashes Dean's way, the intensity in Blaise's calculating stare sends a chilling ripple coursing through me.

Another tray of shots sails toward us, this time courtesy of Rhianna. I finally raise my hand in protest.

"Time out, girls," I shout over the loud music. "I need some fresh air before downing any more of these lethal things." My words come out slightly slurred.

Waving away their protests, I stumble down the side of the house until I reach the front porch. Rounding the corner, the thrumming of music and laughter fades to a distant hum.

I inhale deeply, fighting to clear the fog from my mind. The cool night air feels refreshing against my flushed face.

I let my eyelids drift shut, enjoying the trickle of wind as it slides across my cheeks.

A loud moan snaps me out of my peaceful lull.

I blink against the dim light, eyes slow to adjust, and spot a couple pinned to the front entrance of the lodge. They're tangled in a tight embrace, mouths fused together, practically dry humping the door off its hinges.

The pair seems entirely too engrossed in each other to notice me standing less than ten metres away. I tip toe past them and head down the porch steps, wincing as I lose my footing and nearly fall down the short drop.

Regaining my balance, I take a few tentative steps along the paved road leading to the castle before making a snap decision to veer off the path.

Padding across the slightly damp grass, I skirt the edge of the tall trees, admiring the meticulous elegance of the castle grounds in contrast to the untamed beauty of the surrounding forest.

I slowly make my way along the thick line of trees, careful not to trip over any protruding roots. The distant glow of the private cabins lining the hill near the cliff's ridge catches my eye, just as a faint noise from somewhere behind me breaks the quiet.

Squinting through the darkness, I can just make out the outline of three people walking in my direction, their features obscured by the dim light.

"Where are you traipsing off to, baby cakes?"

I stiffen as a paralysing shiver slivers down my spine.

Blaise's face looms through the murky darkness, Finn and Jack flanking him.

I instinctively take a step back.

Pulling my cardigan tighter around me, I ease to the right, aiming to walk in a half-circle around them.

An arm shoots out, blocking my path.

"Aw, don't tell me you're leaving us already, princess?" Blaise croons in my ear. "Not after I came all the way out here to find you." He tsks, tongue clicking with mock disappointment.

I pull away from him, forcing down the unease twisting my gut. "I need to get back to the lodge now, so I'll see you boys lat—"

My words are cut off as Blaise grabs me by the waist, hauling me to him until my back hits his hard chest.

"Blaise, let me go," I yelp, struggling against his firm hold. But his grip is too tight, his arms too strong.

"Here's the thing, princess," Blaise purrs in a low voice, his mouth so close I can feel his hot breath teasing my earlobe. "You've been strutting around this place for weeks now, showing off your tight little body, driving me crazy. Now, I don't mind a good cock tease now and again. It makes the reward all the more sweet. But a man's patience has its limits, and sooner or later, you gotta deliver the goods, baby cakes."

I push against his unyielding grip, fear rapidly blooming in my chest. "Blaise, this isn't funny," I snap, agitation masking the dread coiling inside me. "Let me go!"

Blaise only laughs. "Oh, come on now, princess," he whispers softly. "I've seen the way you look at me. I know you want me, just as badly as I want you. You just don't want to admit it to yourself. But I'm here to ease your mind. There's no need to fight it any longer. I can see right through you, baby cakes. I know you're dripping for me, so why even try to hide it?"

A jolt of revulsion rips through me.

Oh my god. He's delusional.

And he's not joking around anymore.

Panic claws at my chest.

"Blaise, please," I gasp, my laboured breath coming out in quick, shallow bursts.

"But if I let you go, you'll only run away from me again," Blaise hums, his whisky-tinted breath tickling my cheek. "And didn't I just tell you I'm growing weary of this little game of hide and seek we've been playing?"

Blaise pins my arms to my front, using his free hand to slide my cardigan down my arms.

"Hey, man. Maybe this isn't such a good idea?" Jack says from somewhere behind Blaise, hesitation marring his voice.

I zero in on his face in the dark, latching onto the flicker of doubt written there.

"Shut the fuck up, Adams, or I'll make sure your wimpy ass gets thrown out of this place before the sun rises," Blaise snaps, and Jack falls quiet, his head bowed.

I search for his eyes again, desperation clawing at my throat, but he evades my silent screams.

I turn my imploring gaze to Finn, but his features remain carefully stripped of any emotion.

"Don't stress it, princess," Blaise whispers, his lips tracing the outline of my neck. Tears press against the back of my eyelids as he toys with the edges of my cardigan, pulling it off with deceptive tenderness. The soft fabric floats to the ground while his hand smooths down my body, ghosting over my thigh.

Blaise trails the edge of my skirt as I wriggle helplessly in his unrelenting grip, his fingers slow and deliberate as they graze my bare skin.

In that moment, I feel utterly, hopelessly alone.

I steel myself for a final attempt to break away, knowing there's no escaping what's about to happen next if I fail—and stumble forward when Blaise's arms suddenly fall away from my waist.

Disoriented by the abrupt release, I drop to my knees on the cool, wet grass.

Adrenaline crashes through me as I blink to clear the black spots dancing in my vision. Someone yelps behind me, and a loud smack ricochets through the air.

I spin, stomach coiling, bracing for hands to seize me.

Two blurry figures stand opposite each other, their broad silhouettes etched against the darkening sky.

"*What the fuck*, man?!"

Blaise's voice rings through my haze, and his shape finally comes into focus as he raises a hand to his face, wiping away a trickle of blood from the corner of his mouth. Glaring at the other man, his words seethe with anger as he bites out, "You're gonna pay for that, asshole!"

Finn and Jack close in behind him, fists clenched. My eyes dart to the unknown man, my stomach sinking.

Whoever my rescuer is, he's about to fight three men at once.

No sooner has the thought crossed my mind than the stranger moves with unexpected swiftness. The force of his blow catches Blaise off guard.

I gape in horror as Blaise flies through the air, arms flailing as he tumbles to the ground.

Shouts of protest erupt as Jack rushes over to Blaise's crumpled form, shaking his shoulders as he tugs at his arm. Finn remains standing, his fists raised to fight, though his dilating pupils betray his trepidation.

"Enough."

A sharp gasp slips from my lungs as the biting word slices through the air.

Orlando?

A mix of relief and fear seizes my heart as I finally recognise the tall frame and broad shoulders I've admired more times than I care to admit these past few weeks, though his figure is mostly concealed beneath a hooded jacket.

Orlando takes three commanding steps forward until he's looming over Blaise. The icy fury radiating from his towering presence is enough to make Finn and Jack retreat, clearly thinking twice about taking on Orlando without their pathetic leader, who's currently too busy writhing on the ground.

"In nearly nineteen years at this hotel, I've seen plenty of people just like you come and go." Orlando's voice carries a chilling air of suppressed rage.

The stifled irritation directed at me in the past is nothing compared to the unbridled fury emanating from him now as he glares down at Blaise with unadulterated disgust.

"Entitled little shits who think the world owes them something, simply because they were born into wealth—a monetary foothold gained through absolutely no effort or skill of their own.

Because of your stacked wallets and cushy trust funds, guys like you think you can control and manipulate anyone unlucky enough to cross your path. That you can make people bend to your will with no more than a lazy snap of your spoilt little fingers."

"Fuck you," Blaise snarls as he spits on the ground. A dollop of slime skims the edge of Orlando's shoes, and a wide, wicked grin spreads across Blaise's face. My stomach clenches at the blood staining his pearly white teeth.

"Mr Perfect, always skulking around like you're better than everyone. Just because you're daddy Águila's favourite little pet."

My brows knit together. *Daddy Águila's favourite pet?*

"Careful, Bloom." Orlando's voice is deadly calm, his attention fixated on Blaise with razor-sharp intensity, fists clenching at his sides. "Even your pea-sized brain should know better than to flap your lips about things you have no clue about."

But Blaise only grins wider, his eyes gleaming. "Oh, *please,*" he scoffs, amusement curdling his voice. "Everyone knows the only reason you're even here is because your precious daddy used to suck up to de Águila senior. It's not like anyone would bother keeping filth like you around otherwise."

Orlando takes a slow step closer to Blaise, his face a stony mask of fury. Blaise stumbles backward, but the moron's too stupid to keep his mouth shut.

"I always wondered who you were, back when my uncle first brought me here. Dirty, dark skin. Fuck all words to spare for anyone but Domenico. Shit-for-brains, and an even shittier attitude. And not a hint of interest in the things any normal teenager should've been drooling over—like all the babes parading around here, tits out, tight little bodies begging to be fucked."

Blaise's wicked grin is still firmly plastered across his face, even as he shakes his head with mock incredulity.

"When I eventually found out who you were, I figured you were just putting on a front for de Águila senior. Acting like the nice, reliable poster boy, ready to carry out your dear daddy's shitty jobs right alongside the old man.

But even at Domenico's private parties, you always just sat there. Stiff and sour-faced, chasing away every piece of ass bouncing on your lap with that miserable pout, even when they were practically throwing themselves at you. God only knows why they bothered in the first place. Must've thought you had money too, with how tightly you were wrapped around Domenico's cock, even back then. They should've sensed your wimpy ass wasn't even worth the wasted bit of space your ugly mug takes up."

I flinch as every twisted word burrows into me. I should want to relish every detail about Orlando—I get so few of them from him. But the venom in Blaise's voice scrapes against my heart as he spits them out like dirty secrets.

"Are you gay, is that it?" Blaise sneers. "Were you frothing at the mouth for Dom's dick while he was busy sticking it into every tight hole he could find?"

His malevolent grin stretches wider. "Maybe you and your dad were both pining for cock. Is that why you signed up to do the de Águilas's dirty work? Or was it the money? That small taste of 'the good life'? All the things your low class, punk-ass self knew you'd never belong to.

I guess even you knew better than to pretend to fit in, huh, cloister boy? I probably shouldn't complain. Your weird-ass celibate act left plenty of pussy for the rest of us to devour."

Blaise grabs his crotch and crudely thrusts his hips as he laughs boorishly.

A twitch of Orlando's fingers is the only visible reaction he gives, but his body emanates a chilling, motionless fury.

It's a testament to Blaise's stupidity that he doesn't catch on.

"But if it wasn't for the pussy, or Dom's dick, then it had to be so you could stick around with your old man, huh?" Blaise's tone drips with condescension. "I remember how you used to trail after him like a lost puppy, when you weren't busy playing Domenico's faithful lapdog. Used to look up to the old fool and everything, didn't you?"

He laughs, loud and derisive. When his stare locks on Orlando, the pure malevolence in his face is unmistakable.

"Still don't know how that good-for-nothing fuck managed to fool de Águila senior into hiring him. Makes no goddamn sense. Must be something you inherited—slithering your way into cushiony positions far above your station. Filth like you doesn't deserve that kind of luxury. At least the old man got what was coming to him in the end. I'm still waiting to see if you'll follow suit."

Finn and Jack don't even have time to flinch before Blaise hits the ground, fists flying as Orlando looms over him.

I watch in horror as Orlando pounds his knuckles into Blaise's face, again and again until blood sprays from his nose, painting the grass in jagged streaks of maroon.

Grabbing him by the collar, Orlando yanks him upright and slams his back against the thick trunk of a tree.

"Now, listen here, you little shit." His face hovers inches from Blaise's, ferocity dripping from every syllable.

Blaise's widening eyes finally betray his fear.

Oh, you've fucked up now, boy.

"You know *nothing* about me, or my father. Your filthy mouth isn't even worthy of speaking his name. I've worked my ass off to earn everything I have, and so did he. What would a pathetic ass-wipe like you know about hard work? Everything you have was spoon-fed to you on a silver platter. You wouldn't recognise hard work if it grew a pair of tits and begged to suck your malformed little cock."

Blaise's lips barely parted before Orlando slams him against the trunk again, forcing a whoosh of air from his lungs with a pained "*Oomph*".

"This isn't a dialogue, fuckwit. This is a monologue, so listen carefully." Orlando drills his glare into Blaise's round, terrified orbs, trapping him in an unbreakable stare.

"We both know the only reason you're even here after all the shit you've pulled is because of your uncle's ties to Mattia. If it weren't for their business relationship, your misogynistic ass would've been booted five minutes after your arrival. Now, when I woke up this morning, severing the de Águila-Bloom alliance wasn't exactly on my do-to list."

Orlando shrugs, his bottom lip jutting out as if to say, *Oh well, shit happens.*

"Thing is, I also wasn't planning on catching you out here, frothing at the mouth as you force yourself on a woman who's clearly fighting tooth and nail to escape you. So I'd say that drastically changes things."

Despite the terror written across his face, Blaise can't seem to help himself. He lets out a derisive snort, wheezy and warped from the pressure against his throat.

"Yeah, right. As if you have the power to do any such thing."

I brace for Orlando's fury to erupt, but instead, it morphs into a cold smile that sends chills rippling through me.

"Oh, I think you'd be surprised by what I can make happen around here if I put my mind to it," he says in a low, eerily calm voice.

Without warning, he lets Blaise go, leaving him spluttering on wobbly legs as he struggles to regain air in his lungs.

"But by all means," Orlando continues, eyebrow raised in challenge. His tone's almost airy now. "Doubt me. I dare you. That way, we'll both know by tomorrow night whether I'm telling the truth or not."

Blaise glares at Orlando, breaths coming out in laboured pants. Blood and saliva mixes as he spits on the ground.

"No?" Orlando presses. "I thought so."

Blaise drops his gaze, humiliated rage burning in his eyes as pride and fear wage war.

Orlando sighs tiredly. "Unfortunately, the breakdown of the relationship between your uncle and the de Águilas would hurt them too. Not as much as it would damage your family's precious societal standing, of course. But if I can help it, I'd rather not let your stupidity bleed onto them. So, here's what's going to happen."

He takes a sharp step forward, and Blaise stumbles back, tripping over his own feet in his haste to retreat. I would've laughed if the air wasn't so strung with tension.

"You will stay far, *far* away from Elaina from this moment on," Orlando declares, his voice no more than a whisper, yet the chilling sobriety in his tone dispels any doubt about the gravity of his words.

"You will not speak to her. You will not look at her. And you will never, ever lay a hand on her ever again. As far as you're concerned, she doesn't exist."

Orlando takes one final menacing step toward the cowering trio.

"Now... I do not give two shits who you fuck, Bloom. If someone willingly lets you dip your cowardly cock inside them, that's their business. I can't cure poor taste. But if I ever get so much as a whiff that you're forcing yourself on another woman, you'll have a hell of a lot more to answer for than the biggest financial loss of your family's history falling squarely on your shoulders. Because once I'm done with you, you won't be physically capable of enjoying so much as a blowjob ever again. *Do. I. Make. Myself. Clear?*"

Reluctantly, Blaise dips his chin by the barest inch.

Orlando eases back, giving Blaise and his thugs just enough room to slink past.

I track their scuttling retreat until the darkness swallows them whole.

Only then do I finally take a full breath.

"Orlando?"

Orlando stays rooted in the same spot, watching the cluster of trees where Blaise cowered only moments before. He doesn't turn around, his fists remaining clenched at his sides.

"Orlando, are you okay?" I slowly rise to my feet and take a cautious step closer to him.

"What the hell were you thinking, Elaina?" The furious snarl cleaves through the lingering tension.

"I-I was just—"

"What kind of fool walks out here alone, at night, unprotected?"

I instinctively step back as he spins to face me, fury blazing in his expression. "Do you have any idea what could've happened—what *would've* happened—to you tonight if I hadn't been here?"

Despite the tremors still running through me, my hackles rise at the harshness of his words.

"I'm not a fool," I bite out through clenched teeth, my gratitude evaporating as heat rushes to my cheeks.

"Then what do you call what you just did?" Orlando growls.

"I was just getting some fresh air." My own voice is rising now. "When did that become such a sin?"

"There's fresh air everywhere, Elaina," Orlando snaps, gesturing sharply. "There are a hundred places near the lodge you could go to 'get some fresh air'. Anywhere where there's people around. Yet you decide to a stroll out here, with nothing but the looming forest for company?"

I groan as humiliation feeds my annoyance. "I-I... You are so damn exasperating!"

I want to scream at him, hit him, launch myself at him.

Instead, I spin on my heel and march in the direction of the lodge.

"Where the hell do you think you're going?" His thunderous voice slices through the dense night air as he stalks after me.

I ignore him. The echo of his footsteps trailing me barely breaks through the thrumming in my ears.

"Elaina! For fuck's sake, stop acting like such a brat."

That's. It!

I swirl around, every venomous insult I can think of gathering on the tip of my tongue—and almost crash into Orlando's firm chest as he charges toward me, his towering frame much closer than I'd anticipated.

His arms shoot out, gripping my waist as I stumble back. Despite the fury clouding my senses, a shiver of heat races down my spine at his touch.

The sensation only fuels my anger.

"Stop yelling at me," I shout, voice ringing through the darkness as I pull on his arms to break free. "Stop yelling at me, stop calling me names, stop insulting me, stop treating me like a child, stop following after me. Just *stop* all your bullshit and leave me the hell alone!"

"No."

His laconic response pulls me up short. I'd been bracing for a spew of angry words to come pouring from his mouth, but instead of the blazing fury that had just filled his eyes, his onyx irises now hold a cautious, almost jaded look.

"I—*what?*" My hands tremble as adrenaline rushes through me.

"No," he repeats, his hands still firm on my hips.

I battle the thick haze fogging my brain as I try to make sense of this moment.

I swear the corners of his mouth twitch as he studies me, sensing the confusion mingling with my mounting frustration. But just as quickly, the veil returns, any openness vanishing behind that familiar wall of stoicism.

"No, Elaina. I'm not going anywhere. Not before you tell me what's going on with you."

I scowl. "Other than the glaringly obvious detail that I was almost just assaulted? Because that one's sitting pretty high on my list of things *going on* right now."

His grip tightens as annoyance slips back into his expression. "I'm not talking about what that fucker almost just did, Elaina. As fucked up as that is, Blaise isn't the catalyst for the dark shadow that's been following you around since the first time I saw you."

I swallow hard as pressure builds in my chest.

"I have no idea what you're talking about," I mutter, tone sharp, even as my body betrays me, shivering under the weight of his words and the heat of his touch.

"Come on, Elaina. Don't take me for a fool. You ran from something, and I want to know why. What did you run from, sirena? What makes you so sad? So guarded? So afraid?"

"I'm not scared, or sad," I yell, insincerity bleeding through my fierce words. "And even if I were, it's none of your damn business!"

"I'm making it my business."

I gape at him, disbelief colouring my words. "Are you for real right now? You think you can just snap your fingers and I'll spill my entire life story to you like some obedient little fool? Just like that?"

A shadow passes over him. "Stop avoiding the question, Elaina."

A maniacal laugh escapes me. "Right, right. Well, before I obey your command, *my Lord*—how about you tell me one single personal thing about your life history, huh?"

The icy cloak slips back over him in a flash, and I eagerly press on.

"Let's start with how you came to work for the de Águilas, shall we? Or how about the 'dirty work' Blaise was referring to? I'm guessing he wasn't talking about literal dirty work, like digging soil and planting fucking tomato seedlings all day. So what was he talking about, Orlando? Might as well tell me, since we're all about sharing now."

"*Enough.*" The biting chill in Orlando's voice cuts through the tepid night air, but this time, I refuse to back down.

"No, Orlando. *Not* enough." I meet his steely gaze head on. "This isn't a one way street. Whenever I ask you anything remotely personal, you shut down on me. Push me away. In fact, it's like you suddenly can't stand the sight of me, all because I'm trying to get to know you. Just because I actually try to give a shit."

Tears suddenly pool at the corners of my eyes. I wipe them away angrily, fighting to keep a steady voice.

"Being your friend is a total mind fuck. It's a never-ending, fucking roller coaster. I don't even think friend is the right word for this fucked up thing we have going on. Perhaps 'spasmodic acquaintance' would be a better description."

"Elaina—"

"Elaina, *what?*" I cut him off, voice lethally sharp. "What will it be this time? You going to use some clever trick to distract me again? Force me to divulge my secrets while you remain a solemn mute? Pretend to be my friend until you suddenly decide it's too much effort and you do another one-eighty? No way. I'm done."

"Elaina, if you would just let me—"

"Stop. Just stop, Orlando. Stop with your false words and your false smiles. This back and forth between us is obviously never going to change. I don't even know why I bothered trying. Just leave me alone. Please. Another couple of months and you'll never have to see me aga—"

My words are severed as Orlando yanks me to his chest—and before I can even think to protest, his mouth crashes down on mine.

Time grinds to a halt as his lips claim me, his woodsy scent flooding my senses. His chest presses against my body, strong arms cinching me tighter until there's no space left between us.

My mind spirals, struggling to make sense of the sudden, searing kiss. The tip of his tongue grazes my lower lip, and I part for him without thought. I gasp as his tongue slides over mine, tasting of strawberries and mint.

Helpless against the pull he has on me, an involuntary moan slips from my lips as his hands glide down my lower back. The sound spurs him on, and he deepens the kiss, sending sharp jolts of desire tearing through every nerve ending.

His hands continue their exploration, sweeping over the curve of my ass to clasp my thighs as he lifts me effortlessly into his arms. My legs lock around his waist, arms draping around his neck, and his grip shifts back to my waist as he carries me forward until my back meets the rough bark of a nearby tree.

The world falls away as our tongues tangle, my body catching fire beneath the heat of his hands on my bare skin. His thumbs graze along my ribs, sending waves of heat surging through me, and my heart skips several beats as his growing hardness presses against the silky softness of my panties.

I gasp as another rush of desire sparks beneath my skin. My hips rock against his hard length of their own volition, desperately pleading for more friction.

With a final, maddening swipe of his tongue, Orlando pulls his mouth away, leaving me reeling.

Breathing heavily, he lifts his hands to cup my face as his heated eyes bore into mine.

"You drive me crazy," he whispers fiercely. His minty breath comes out in short bursts as his chest rises and falls, each movement causing his taut muscles to brush against the outline of my breasts. "Fuck, Elaina. Every time you open that smart mouth of yours, you drive my entire body fucking wild."

I can't pull my eyes from the scorching intensity dancing in his molten irises, a spellbinding mixture of emerald green and shimmering silver. My core melts at the brazen desire spiralling in their depths.

I whimper as his mouth descends on mine again, his lips more forceful than before. My hands drag over his broad shoulders until I'm clutching his silky hair, fingers raking through the tousled waves. The light stubble along his jaw rasps against the delicate skin of my chin, a delicious contrast to the smooth glide of his tongue across my swollen lips.

The entire world could burst into flames and I wouldn't notice.

In this moment, all I can see, feel, and breathe is Orlando.

The pull in my core deepens, fevered bursts of fire dancing across my skin—until he suddenly pulls away again.

A low whimper escapes me at the loss.

I watch him through a haze of lust as his head swirls to the side, peering intently into the engulfing darkness. Following his line of sight, I squint until faint lights appear in the distance, their shimmering glow drawing steadily closer.

The rush in my ears fades enough for me to catch the dim sound of a motor running, and it takes my clouded brain a moment to catch up.

The lights must be emanating from one of the hotel's complimentary transport carriages. It's headed down the road leading to the private cabins at the edge of the nearby cliff.

Turning to face me, Orlando rests his forehead against mine, sighing in resignation. His chest still moves rapidly with his quickened breaths.

"Never a moment of privacy in this place," he mutters, though his words carry a faint tinge of amusement. Locking eyes with me, he raises a hand to cup my face, giving my cheek a soft stroke with his calloused thumb.

"Perhaps it's for the best," he muses, the corners of his mouth lifting ever so slightly. "I would think two physical assaults are enough for one night, wouldn't you?"

A small giggle bubbles up, and warmth floods my belly as his mouth pulls into a grin.

"I love that sound," he says softly, tracing my bottom lip with his thumb. His eyes follow the motion, and desire stirs inside me once more as they darken.

Tearing his gaze from my mouth, he glances over his shoulder at the approaching carriage, its headlights now illuminating the dense line of trees edging the forest. Sighing, he looks back to me, and his molten eyes burn straight through me.

"Meet me at the lookout tomorrow afternoon, at six. I want to show you something."

Not trusting my voice, I can only nod.

With one last, searing kiss to my lips that makes my head spin all over again, Orlando whispers, "Now, head back to the lodge, sirena. Straight back to your cabin, okay? No detours. Get some sleep, and I'll see you tomorrow, beautiful."

Sliding down the length of his body, I'm acutely aware of the hardness of him grazing against my skin as I unwrap my legs, grateful for his steady grip on my waist. Spinning me so my back is to him, he delivers a soft slap to my ass.

I stumble along the grass-laid path on shaky legs, casting repeated glances over my shoulder as my thoughts whirl and collide in a tangle of emotion.

At the edge of the village, I pause to draw a deep breath before turning around one last time.

The night has nearly devoured the castle grounds, but Orlando's silhouette still lingers against the silvery wash of moonlight.

I hold his stare as I step backward, unwilling to look away.

He watches every movement carefully, vigilant eyes tracking my steps until the darkness finally swallows us whole.

Chapter Thirty-Three

"Els?"

"Huh?"

I glance up to find Tiana looking at me, one eyebrow arched in amusement.

"Anyone home there, darlin'?" Her lips twitch.

I peer up at her sheepishly. "Sorry, T. Got lost in my own little world there."

A world where Orlando's hands are roaming all over my body, his tongue teasing my lips as his warm mouth devours mine in a heart stopping kiss...

"No shit," Tiana laughs, grabbing a baguette from the buffet tray. "I've called your name about six times already. Even sourly old Glenda in accounting would make for a more engaging conversational partner than you this morning. Another minute of your mindless wandering into La La Land and I was considering slapping you across the face with this spatula to verify you weren't actually sleepwalking."

I mock gape. "Well, as you can see, I'm perfectly awake now, thank you very much. So no egg-covered spatula bitch slapping, please. It's seven-thirty in the morning, for Pete's sake."

Tiana snorts as she dumps a pile of scrambled eggs onto my plate before scooping another large spoonful for herself. "What has you so mesmerised this morning that a pack of wild rhinos could've stomped through this place without you even batting an eyelid?"

Before I can conjure up a plausible reply to her colourful question, she slams her tray down on the counter and whirls to face me, eyes bulging. "Oh my God. Did something happen last night?"

Shit.

"I—I..." My brain scrambles for anything my perceptive minx of a friend won't immediately catch out as a bald-faced lie.

"I knew it," she squeals, iolite irises glittering. "I wondered what happened when you suddenly disappeared. You were gone for so long, and then you never came back to the party... You were meeting someone, weren't you? *Who? Where?* Spill the beans, chica!"

Heat rises in my cheeks as I scramble to blurt out that she's got it all wrong—and praying she doesn't see the truth glowing on my face—when her eyes suddenly go wide.

"Did someone come back to our cabin with you?" She gasps. "Oh my God. You sneaky, little fox! Was he still there when I got there, doing the nasty with you, and I didn't even notice?"

I can't help my burst of laughter. "Calm down, Charlie. You're way off base here."

Maybe not 'way off', but...

Her shoulders droop. "Damn," she grumbles, a small pout forming on her glossy lips. "I was sure I'd finally get some sizzling details from you. With all that suppressed sexual energy you've got brewing over there, I'd bet good money it'll be a wild ride when all that passion finally gets the green light to escape."

"Oh, shut up."

We make our way to our usual table, where Jess, Rhianna and Paige are already seated.

"Morning, ladies," Tiana sings as she sits down next to Rhianna.

"Hello there," Rhianna greets us through a mouthful of cereal. "How're we all feeling this morning?"

"Thoroughly screwed," Tiana chirps, flashing Rhianna a brazen wink. "In all the right ways, if you know what I mean."

Jess rolls her eyes with a fond huff. "We always know what you mean, T."

"I'm just sayin'. There ain't no better bedtime ritual than having the D or the T all over your favourite intimate parts," Tiana says, unabashed.

"The D or the T?" Paige scrunches her button nose, looking adorably confused.

"She means the dick or the tongue, Paige," Rhianna explains, laughing when Paige's mouth opens in a silent *oh*. "And I'd like to add a second T for 'tits' to that list, for the record."

"I'm inclined to agree with Tiana," Tess chimes in as she sits down next to Paige. "There really is no better bedtime ritual to guarantee a good night's rest."

"Of course you agree," Paige sighs. "You're sleeping with Hayden. Who wouldn't be happy to wake up next to him every morning? He's *so* dreamy."

"Oh, Paigey," Tess chuckles, giving Paige a side hug. "When are we going to get you a mister, huh? It's a travesty that someone with as much hope and faith in love as you has no one special to direct all that loveliness toward."

"Oh, I'm sure it'll happen one day," Paige mumbles shyly, and I briefly recall the longing glances I caught her throwing Corban's way when he passed through the dining hall at lunch last week.

"You make sure to hold off for someone special, Paige. You deserve someone as wonderful as you are, and you shouldn't settle for anything less," I blurt out, surprising myself.

Judging by the doe-eyed look on her face, I've surprised her too.

"I second that," Jess nods, clinking her tea cup against my coffee cup.

"Speaking of someone special—in all the wrong ways," Rhianna cuts in, her chocolate eyes zoning in on me. "I thought I had Blaise pegged by now, but clearly I was wrong, because that boy is infatuated with you, girl. I couldn't believe the amount of times I caught him eyeing you last night."

She shakes her head, looking bewildered. "If I didn't know any better, I'd think the resident bad boy has a serious crush on you, Elaina."

At the mention of Blaise, a wave of nausea twists through me, and my appetite vanishes.

"Ugh, that guy's such a tool," Tiana growls. "I'd tell him to keep his filthy hands off you if I didn't already know he doesn't stand a chance." She pretends to throw up on her plate.

I fight down the bile in my throat as the phantom touch of Blaise's heated palms on my body flashes through me.

I expected the aftershocks of yesterday's chilling encounter to keep me awake all night. But each time a vivid reminder of Blaise's hot breath on my neck fought to penetrate my mind, the memory was instantly replaced by the lingering caress of Orlando's fingers trailing the outline of my waist. Each chilling recollection of Blaise's arm entrapping me in his suffocating embrace was replaced by Orlando's searing gaze. Each whispered delusion escaping Blaise's crude mouth replaced by the lingering echo of Orlando's soft lips as he devoured my mouth and swallowed my fevered gasps.

"Damn, girl. You really are out of it today." I meet Tiana's worried gaze across the table. "Are you sure you're okay, hun?"

For a breathless second, I consider telling her about yesterday. About Blaise, Orlando, their fight, *our kiss*... all of it. The sudden urge to drag her out of this room and let all the confused, jumbled emotions trapped inside me spill out into the open seizes hold.

But as quickly as the urge appears, the unspoken words stall on my tongue.

If I tell Tiana what Blaise tried to do last night, I know she won't let it go, no matter how much I beg her to. And when she storms over there to drown him in curses in front of this entire room full of people, all hell will break loose.

At that point, who knows what Blaise will do in retaliation.

As far as I'm aware, Blaise hasn't so much as glanced my way since he sauntered into the hall about half an hour ago, flanked by his two buddies. The thought of what Orlando might do to him is likely the only thing stopping him from trying anything again.

But if Blaise's secrets are spilled out into the open, there's nothing stopping him from continuing what he didn't get to finish last night.

"Yeah, T. I'm good." I give Tiana my most reassuring smile. "Just tired."

"That makes two of us," Rhianna mutters with a wide yawn, pulling Tiana's troubled gaze off me. "I'm dead on my feet. What I wouldn't give to have today off."

As the girls fall back into easy conversation, my eyes involuntarily trail across the sea of bodies until they land on Blaise, his light blond hair standing out from the others at his usual table. His demeanour is uncharacteristically quiet and sullen, and it's impossible to ignore the dark bruises marring his usually handsome face.

As if he can feel the weight of my stare, his cerulean blues flash to mine.

In the split second it takes for me to rip my gaze away, his glare darkens with an intense fusion of desire and loathing.

As I lower my head to the half-eaten food on my plate, I fight to regain control of my racing heartbeat, not entirely sure which of those two emotions I'm more scared of.

The sun is still high in the sky as I make my way across the castle grounds at a quarter to six that afternoon. The hours have crawled past at a snail's pace all day as I anxiously anticipated seeing Orlando again.

When the massive wall clock finally showed three o'clock, I excused myself, telling the girls I needed a shower and a nap to sleep off the lingering remnants of last night's alcohol.

Luckily, Tiana was too busy making out with Dean to follow. When she inevitably interrogates me on where I disappeared off to tonight, I'll serve up some passable excuse.

I walk past the vegetable garden, memories of the many hours I've spent there with Orlando flooding my mind. As excited as I am to see him, nerves twist in my stomach. I have no idea which version of him I'll be facing tonight.

Everything feels so different now.

I try to steady my breathing as the canopy of leaves blocks out the sun, casting dappled shadows across the path. Pushing through the thick cluster of trees, I know I'm close to the lookout.

I round the final bend, and my heart stutters as Orlando's broad frame comes into view.

At least he showed up.

In that moment, I realise a small part of me hadn't expected him to. After all, it's not like he's shown much care for how his shifting moods have affected me before.

The beautiful smile that spreads across his face when he spots me makes my heart stumble. It's subtle, but there's a quiet warmth in the way his eyes drink me in, his gaze drifting slowly down my body. I flush under the appreciation shining in their jade-and-silver depths.

"Hello, sirena," he says softly, and the quiet warmth in his deep voice sends goosebumps prickling across my skin. "You look... beautiful."

He leans forward and places a gentle kiss on my cheek, his soft lips lingering on my skin. As his mesmerising scent engulfs me, I fight the overwhelming urge to press my lips to his.

He lifts his hand to stroke a loose strand of hair behind my ear, and my eyelids dip at the sensation of his fingers trailing the length of my neck.

"Have you had a good day so far?"

"Y-yeah. It—it was good," I whisper, lust mixing with my already heightened emotions. "How was your day?"

"Long."

Not as long as mine felt.

"Thanks for meeting me here," he says after a moment, and I glance up at him shyly. "I want to show you something, but before I do, I wanted to ask you....

He pins me with a serious look. "Are you okay, sirena? Truly okay? After last night and... everything that happened?"

His worry is so sincere that the knee-jerk response of 'I'm fine' catches in my throat. I'm not even sure if he's asking about Blaise, or about the kiss—or both.

Teeth gritted, he takes my silence as his answer. His shoulders roll, as if to shake off his agitation. "The thought of what nearly happened to you yesterday... It makes me want to find that fucker and punch his face in until he can't see straight for the rest of his sad, miserable life."

Catching my hesitation, he gently tilts my chin. "I'm sorry. But I need to know—are you okay, sirena?"

Breathless from his proximity, I can only nod.

"I'm glad to see that beautiful light hasn't deserted your eyes." He scans my face as his thumb strokes along my jawline. "If you're ever *not* okay, promise me you'll tell me. Can you do that?"

When I hesitate, his eyes cloud with swirls of grey.

"Orlando..." I falter. How can I even begin to express the muddled thoughts spiralling through my mind?

"I can't thank you enough for appearing when you did yesterday. For *what* you did. But I—I feel so confused about all of this. About you, and what happened with Blaise, and everything afterward. I just—".

Orlando places a finger over my lips, halting my words. "I know, sirena. I know I haven't treated you the way you deserve. I know I've been an asshole, and I don't blame you for being wary of me. Honestly, I'm a little surprised you even showed up today, though I really hoped you would."

He bites his lip, and something akin to guilt pulls at his downcast mouth.

"I know I probably don't deserve it, and it might already be too late, but... will you come with me today? Will you give me a chance to show you a small part of my life, and why this castle means so much to me? A small part of... who I am, I guess."

He looks almost bashful as his head dips toward his feet. Hesitation paints his face when he looks back at me.

My heart softens at the first sign of vulnerability he's ever shown me.

My heart screams at me to be careful. My brain yells that I'm the moth, drifting too close to the flame.

And yet, I willingly dance along the sparks of the smouldering embers, a breath away from catching fire.

I nod.

His devastating smile makes my heart soar, and any lingering traces of hesitation flutter away on the wind.

Chapter Thirty-Four

"Wow."

It's the only word that comes to mind as I glance around the vast room, the shimmer of silver, bronze and gold reflecting from every surface.

"I said the same thing the first time I saw this place," Orlando nods, his hand resting on my lower back as he guides me along the aisle lined with ancient artefacts.

"I can't believe they've been able to preserve all of this," I say, wonder filling my voice as I walk up to a display case exhibiting a magnificent ornate sword. The steel blade is marred by cuts and crevices, betraying its bloody history.

The sword is one of hundreds of similar items dispersed around the vast space, some hanging from hooks embedded in the rugged stone walls, others resting in glass enclosures stretching the length of the room.

My attention catches on an enormous shield hanging beside a daunting suit of armour, each metal plate carefully assembled to give the illusion of a medieval knight standing sentry. Squinting, I can almost trick myself into believing cold, deadly eyes stare back at me from behind the small slits carved into the metal visor.

Drawn to the shield, I admire the elaborate coat of arms embellishing the heater-shaped escutcheon—a magnificent eagle donning a crown, its feathered wings spanning the length of the shield, shaping the middle line into a swirling 'A'.

"That's the de Águila family coat of arms," Orlando says as he walks up behind me. I swallow a sharp breath when his strong hands glide lightly along my waist, his chest pressing against my upper back. His warm skin brushes the underside of my arm as he points to the majestic eagle.

"*'Águila'* means eagle in Spanish. Many of the artefacts you can find in this room are pieces of armour that were actually used in battle by the de Águila's ancestors and their soldiers, some going back centuries. Señor de Águila's grandfather—Domenico's great grandfather—dedicated substantial time and resources to collecting artefacts from notable events throughout Spanish history. He curated the majority of the vast collection the family owns today."

"It's incredible." I stare in wonder at an array of daggers and tapered poniards displayed atop a white satin cushion. The inbuilt spotlights illuminates the intricate carvings on each handle. "I've never seen a collection like this before. It feels like we've walked into a museum."

"You wouldn't believe how many museums have attempted to entice the family to part with these treasures over the years. They used to display the collection in one of the downstairs halls. It was a major draw when the hotel first opened."

"Why did they move it up here?"

"One too many attempts at theft." Orlando shrugs. "It's not exactly a secret how valuable this collection is. I guess some guests just couldn't help themselves. These days, the family only provides access to visitors they wish to impress—royalty, state officials, potential business partners and the like—and only ever in the presence of security guards."

Pivoting to face him, my frown betrays my confusion. "And yet, you let me up here?"

Orlando shrugs again. "Are you going to steal anything?"

I snort. "Doubtful."

That begets another smile. "I just had a feeling you'd enjoy seeing it. You seem to have a keen interest in the castle, and a genuine appreciation for its history."

The smile I give him is wide and unadulterated. "Thank you, Orlando. For showing me this, and for trusting me not to—what was it? *Steal anything?*"

I grin when a laugh escapes him. "You were right. About me enjoying this, I mean. I might just save the stealing for another day, though."

He chuckles. "Well, the tour's not over yet, sirena. We've barely even scratched the surface." His mischievous wink sends shivers of pleasure tingling down my spine.

Clasping my hand, he guides me through the massive doors and into the hallway. We wind through long corridors and climb several curving staircases, each cavernous passage leading deeper into unfamiliar corners of the castle.

As much as the antique light fixtures and timeworn portraits intrigue me, I'm mostly drawn to the feeling of Orlando's warm, calloused hand wrapped around mine. So when he suddenly lets go to pull his staff card from his back pocket, I can't help the small sting of disappointment.

"Just around the corner here..." he mutters, a moment before we come to a halt in front of a pair of wide-framed double doors. I hear the faint click of the lock unlatching as Orlando scans his card and pulls on the massive metal handle, stepping aside to let me through.

As I walk through the door, I'm surprised to find a narrow, circling stone staircase. A glance through a small window confirms my suspicion that we're entering one of the castle's spiralling turrets.

"Come on," Orlando urges, and if I'm not mistaken, there's a note of excitement in his usually measured voice. "We're almost there."

"Almost where?" I ask, starting the steep ascent. My thighs protest with every step, my pulse rising to a soft pant. I make a mental note to increase my weekly runs.

"What kind of guy would I be if I spoiled the surprise mere minutes before we get there?" Orlando teases.

Glancing over my shoulder, I catch the playful gleam in his expression. "Something tells me patience isn't your strong suit, sirena, so maybe it's in both our interests for me to teach you some."

"Oh, shush you," I scoff, my stifled voice betraying my giggle. "I'm as patient as they come. I just like to be prepared, is all."

That earns a snort from him. "Ah, just prepared? Right, right, I'm sure that's it."

Still snickering, he gently grabs my waist to halt my laboured climb as we reach a narrow landing.

"Give me a minute. I just need to grab something."

Holding up a finger, he scans his card over a reader on the wall, unlocking an inconspicuous door set into the stone wall. As he slips inside the small space, I peer over his broad shoulders and frown at the confined storage closet.

A moment later, he backs out holding a tall ladder.

"What in the world do we need a ladder for?"

He flashes me a cheeky, and all too mesmerising, smile. "Wait and see."

Beckoning me forward, we continue up the final flight of stairs.

I expect him to take us through the only visible door, but instead, he grabs a long metal rod from a hook on the wall and uses it to pop open a ceiling hatch I hadn't even noticed.

Positioning the ladder so the metal frame stretches into the chamber above, Orlando grips the edges and gestures for me to climb. "Up you go, sirena. I'll be right behind you."

Tentatively, I step onto the narrow rungs, reassured by the steady strength of his grip anchoring the frame. As my head breaks through the opening, I frown, scanning the space.

It's empty—completely bare except for a wide opening on one end, where the soft light of the late evening sun spills through.

I climb the rest of the way up and wait for Orlando, my gaze drifting to the way the corded muscles in his forearms flex as he ascends. Stretching to his full six-foot-two height, he takes my hand and gives it a gentle squeeze. "Ready?"

"Hit me," I reply, slightly breathless.

With another wink, he leads me toward the open archway and into the warm air outside.

I've barely taken five steps across the stone-paved patio when I stop abruptly, breath catching in my throat.

The entirety of Bahía De Acantilado stretches out before us. The rugged cliffside below the turret drops dramatically toward the coastline, cradling the edge of the beautiful coastal town. Beyond it, the white-speckled beach curves into the distance, embraced by the shimmering turquoise water.

I tentatively walk forward and rest my hand on the stone fence curving along the open space, mesmerised by the nearly three-hundred-and-sixty-degree vantage point. Glancing across the castle grounds, my eyes land on the private cabins basking in the golden rays of the waning evening sun, perched proudly atop the cliffside ridge. Far in the distance, I can just make out the roof of the staff lodge nestled amidst a sea of trees.

"Oh my..." The words escape as barely more than a whisper.

I thought I was already enamoured with this place from the resplendent views around the castle, but the panorama from up here is something else entirely. It's made all the more breathtaking by the sky above us—an azure canvas slowly bleeding into shades of yellow, orange, and pink as the sun begins its descent into sunset.

Orlando doesn't say a word. He just stands beside me, our arms a breath apart, taking in the view in quiet companionship.

I tear my eyes from the horizon when he steps away, striding across the terrace to pull open a hatch set into the stone floor. From the hidden compartment, he retrieves a thick blanket, letting the trapdoor fall shut with a muted thud before spreading the blanket across the terrace.

He gestures for me to join him.

Any lingering nerves melt away as I walk over and settle beside him, turning once more to admire the kaleidoscope of colours painted across the sky.

I don't know how long we sit there, wrapped in silence, surrounded by beauty.

When I sense Orlando watching me, I tilt my chin to meet his appraising look. The weight of it slams into me—the teal hue of his irises in the dimming light steals the words from my tongue.

"Beautiful," Orlando murmurs, his tone almost solemn.

I nod, glancing back up at the shimmering sunset. "It really is."

"Not the sunset. The way you watch the sunset."

My gaze snaps back to his, searching for the emotions veiled behind his guarded exterior.

Meeting my intensity head-on, he continues. "Not just the sunset, but the whole world around you. It's like you find peace in the simple act of absorbing nature. From all the times I've observed you, that's when you seem most at ease.

You always look like you're carrying a heavy weight on your shoulders, slowing you down and dimming your spark. But when you're out here, in the open air, it's like you toss that weight aside and finally let yourself breathe. It's beautiful. I think I could watch you watch this sunset for hours without growing tired of it."

I watch him intently, his words wrapping around me like a warm breeze. I'm caught off guard when his image suddenly blurs, and I quickly swipe at the unexpected tears pooling in my eyes.

"If that's true," I whisper, "then I have you to thank for guiding me to another place where I can find peace—even if just for a moment."

He hums. "It's actually been nice, sharing some of my favourite spots with someone else. With you." His candid tone betrays his surprise, as if he didn't know the truth of his own words until he spoke them aloud.

"So this is yet another hidden gem you haven't shared with anyone else?" I ask quietly.

Orlando nods. "Just you, sirena."

"Why?"

The question blurts out before I can stop it, and my hand flies to my mouth. A flicker of amusement dances across his face, but instead of brushing it off, he seems to give it real thought.

"At first, I think I was hoping it might soften that haunted look in your eyes. It's what I do when something's weighing on me—I seek out nature and solitude. That first time I brought you to the lookout, it seemed to work. I might've gotten a little addicted to the way your eyes lit up, your whole face coming alive with wonder and contentment. After that, I just... wanted to see it again. To coax that look back whenever I could."

He hesitates. "But besides that, the fact is—I like spending time with you, Elaina."

He exhales wearily, and when our eyes meet, confusion and vulnerability churn in the depths of his gaze.

"There's something about you. Something that draws me in. Fuck, I've been drawn to you since the very first moment I saw you. I could list a dozen reasons why anyone would be. You're kind. Thoughtful. Hardworking. You care deeply. You always put others first. And, Lainey... you're fucking gorgeous."

My heart lurches.

"Sirena, you captivated me from the moment your bewitching eyes met mine. And I haven't been able to get you out of my head ever since."

His eyes flicker across my face, gauging my response. A breeze spins through the air, sending tendrils of my hair dancing between us. He gently tucks one strand behind my ear, his finger barely grazing my cheek.

"What have you done to me, sirena?"

His face hovers inches from mine, the heat of his body stoking something deep inside me.

Kiss me, I plead silently, lashes lowering to the soft curve of his lips. My breath hitches as we lean closer, gravity tugging us together—

A loud honk blares from far below, and we jolt apart like magnets of opposite poles.

"Bloody cruise ships," Orlando mutters, pulse visibly ticking in his jaw. "Do they have to announce their arrival to the whole bloody world?"

Despite my own frustration mirroring his, a snort escapes me. The absurdity of the untimely interruption is too much.

I slap a hand over my mouth to trap the giggles building in my chest.

He glances over, his scowl softening at the sight. And then we're both laughing, deep and unfiltered as the tension dissolves, chased away by the wind and the sound of our shared laughter.

Even as I wipe tears of laughter from my cheeks, the heat still simmering in my core bristles at the untimely interruption.

"Can I ask you something?" I say once our chuckles fade.

Orlando lies back with his arms folded behind his head. I trace the tight coil of muscle along his triceps as he closes his eyes. "Ask away, sirena."

He sighs as I hesitate.

"Elaina, I won't snap, whatever it is. I know I've been a jerk, and I can't promise I'll always manage my temper. But I won't push you away just for asking. I promise."

Another breath escapes him, heavier this time. "Just... bear with me if I'm not ready to answer something yet, okay? I want to open up. I want us to get to know each other, but—it just might take some time."

I swallow down my doubts, heart steadied by his honesty.

"When Blaise said your dad 'got what was coming to him'..." I pause. "Did he mean—did your father... pass away?"

Silence stretches between us as he chews on his lower lip. When he finally speaks, his tone is flat.

"Yes. Almost fifteen years ago." His throat bobs. "He was a good man. Kind. A hard worker. Loyal." His voice cracks slightly on the last word.

I stay quiet, letting him work through whatever emotions he's fighting back.

When his breathing evens out, I find the courage to ask another question.

"And... what about your mum?"

His gaze skims over me, deliberating., before he shuts his eyes again. "My mum was Colombian. Met my dad on holiday in Puerto Rico and never looked back. She didn't have any family left, so it didn't take much to convince her to move. They had me not long after."

"You were born in Puerto Rico?"

"Yep," he says, popping the 'p'. "Lived there until I was seven. My mum—"

He falters, and I wait. "My dad worked as a diplomatic liaison for the Puerto Rican government. He grew up poor, but earned a full scholarship to study international relations and political science in America. When he finished, he brought his education back with him. That's when he met my mother.

After climbing through the system, he landed the liaison job. He quickly gained access to classified intel—Puerto Rico's ties with the US, trade deals, security operations, and so on. In other words, exactly the kind of intel the Puerto Rican cartel needed to smooth drug exports and trafficking routes into the States."

Orlando places his arm across his brow to shield his eyes from the waning light of the sun. "Before long, they started threatening my dad to give them information. Sent letters to our home, had people follow him—stuff like that. I still remember this one time..."

He swallows hard, and the sorrow on his face makes my heart ache even before I know what he's going to say.

"My mum would always take me to this bakery every Saturday morning to buy me a *quesito*. It's a type of puff pastry filled with cream cheese—my absolute favourite treat as a kid.

This one Saturday, we were standing in line waiting our turn. I'm bouncing around on my toes, impatient for the old man in front of us to hurry up. I can still remember the intoxicating smell wafting through the place. It would make even a pastry hater's mouth water, I tell you."

My lips tip up, but the smile fades almost as quickly. I know this isn't going to be a happy story.

"We'd just walked up to the counter when the doors flew open, and three men in balaclavas stormed in, heading straight for us. Stupidly, my first thought was that I couldn't understand why they were wearing so much clothing when it was so hot outside. When they pulled out rifles, I figured they were there to rob the bakery. I remember thinking, *Of course. This bakery has the best quesitos in town. They must have plenty of money in the till.*"

He chuckles, though there's no trace of humour in his voice.

"Next thing I know, one of the men shoves me across the room so hard my head slams into a table, and I collapse onto the floor. By the time I manage to pull myself up, the room swaying before my eyes, they've already beaten my mum to a pulp."

He pauses, and though I can't see his expression behind his arm, I can only imagine the weight of the memories flashing through his mind.

"Even through the dizziness, I launched to my feet and started kicking and screaming with everything I had, fighting to reach her. The fuckers just laughed at me. One of them yanked me up by the ankle like a pig and let me dangle there, yelling and crying for them to leave my mother alone. Then they dropped me beside her and threatened to come for my dad next if he didn't listen to their warnings."

I push down the sadness threatening to swallow me whole, my heart aching for the boy he once was. I give him a moment to gather himself before I whisper, "And... did he? Heed their warnings?"

The weight of Orlando's sigh is answer enough. "No. No, he didn't."

He swallows hard. "Like I said, my dad was a loyal man. He refused to betray his country, refused to compromise his integrity. Instead, he hired a full-time security team to protect my mum and me. " He pauses, voice tightening. "In the end, it didn't matter. They managed to install a bomb in her car while she was at work. She died instantly."

His voice breaks on the final word, and the sight of this stoic, guarded man shattered by grief splinters something inside me.

"Orlando..." I whisper. "No words I say could ever make your loss, or what you went through, any easier. So I'm not going to pretend to know the right thing to say." I swallow. "I'm just so deeply, terribly sorry for what you had to endure. For the brutal way you lost your mother. I—"

I hesitate, then follow my gut.

"I lost my parents young, too. Abruptly. So I understand, at least a little, the kind of wound that leaves behind. The toll it takes on your heart. How hard it is to get back up. I wouldn't wish that sorrow on anyone. And it breaks my heart to know you lived it. To lose someone so dear, in such a violent way—it's just not fair."

I exhale, a defeated note to my words. "But then, the world isn't always fair."

Letting my words trail off, we sit quietly side by side, listening to the lapping waves rippling across the water far below. I find I'm not at all discomforted by the silence after the dark and harrowing memories we just shared. The gentle quiet between us is solaced by a sense of unity and understanding, born from the knowledge that we both carry the burden of painful memories. Perhaps not the same pain, but a kindred sensation nevertheless—enough to discern the lingering scars we both carry.

Scars that will never fully heal.

Despite his soft tone, I still startle when Orlando finally breaks the silence. "Do you want to talk about them? Your parents?"

Sensing my hesitation, he continues. "I'm not expecting you to tell me anything just because I told you about my parents. You were right yesterday, Els. When you told me off for expecting you to share personal details—pressing you to tell me things I wanted to know, without ever reciprocating."

He runs a hand through his hair, leaving it adorably dishevelled. He's never looked more handsome as the warm light from the fiery sunset dances across his golden skin, illuminating the vibrant colours of his arresting eyes.

"I meant it when I told you I want another chance to show you a part of my life here. Show you more of myself. Because I truly want to get to know you, sirena. What I was trying to say is, that if you want or need someone to talk to—about your parents, your past, anything at all—I'm here.

I don't want to pressure you to share anything you're not ready to talk about. I know I need to earn that right, and for that to happen—for you to trust me—I need to show you I'm worthy of your trust. Which can only happen if I open up too. I just hope you can bear with me when I inevitably fuck up from time to time. I'm very new to this sharing thing, and I'll be a rough work in progress. But I promise you, I'll try."

The knot of anxiety slowly loosens in my chest, replaced by a hesitant glow of lightness at the realisation that this withdrawn, broody, beautiful man feels drawn to me, the same way I am to him.

In one evening, Orlando has made me feel more seen, more understood, than anyone else ever has.

The realisation is enough to knock the wind from my lungs.

Swallowing down the emotion tickling my throat, my voice carries a slight tremble as I whisper, "I appreciate that. So much. More than you could ever know."

He places his hand over mine in silent acknowledgement, and my body answers with a searing warmth.

"So, rather than pressing you for information about what led you here, would you be interested in knowing how I landed here in Bahía de Acantilado?"

I nod eagerly, thrilled to find out more about this enigmatic man.

"When my mum got killed, Dad was beside himself. He felt responsible for her death, and the guilt and grief were slowly drowning him. Then one day, the doorbell rang, and Señor de Águila was standing on our doorstep."

He shakes his head, as if the memory still bewilders him. "It was surreal. This well-dressed, well-groomed, obviously wealthy stranger shows up outside our humble home, out of the blue, telling my dad he wants us to move to Spain so my dad can come work for him."

I gawk. "Hold on a second. How did he...? I mean... how could he... why would he... *how*?"

Orlando chuckles. "That reaction right there? Picture that times ten, and you'll have a pretty clear picture of what my dad and I looked like."

He shrugs. "Turns out Señor de Águila was in Puerto Rico on a business trip and just so happened to hear about my mother's murder through one of his business connections, who worked with my dad at the time. Apparently, it came back to Señor de Águila how loyal and trustworthy my dad was. After all, his wife was killed because he didn't want to betray his own government. And if there's one thing Señor de Águila values, it's loyalty."

The air around us seems to thicken as Orlando speaks those words, though I can't quite decipher the weight they hold.

"My dad was sceptical at first, but after some coaxing, Señor de Águila was able to convince him. To be honest, I'm not sure my dad would've said yes if he wasn't so miserable in Puerto Rico after we lost my mum. Our house, our street, our town—everything reminded us of her. My dad completely lost his passion for his work. How can you be expected to dedicate your life and loyalty to a place that literally caused your family to be torn apart? I think he was worried that if we stayed, he'd decline further and further into his depression. So he took a leap of faith, with the hope that wherever we were headed, it would lead to something better than what we were leaving behind."

I let the silence settle between us for a moment. "And did it?"

Orlando sits quietly for several seconds. "You tell me, sirena."

I let my eyes sweep across the majestic landscape, once again mesmerised by the beauty of this gorgeous little town. "Well… I'm sure Puerto Rico is nothing to scoff at, but at least you can't complain about the views here. Especially from this vantage point."

"Fair point well made. This is probably my second favourite place on this entire property," Orlando sighs wistfully, leaning back on his elbows as he glances up at the dimming colours above us. The sun has nearly vanished beyond the horizon, darkness rapidly consuming the last remnants of light clinging to the castle walls.

"Only your second favourite?" I ask, half teasing, half intrigued. "What's your number one?"

"Patience, sirena. All in good time." The playful tone is back in Orlando's voice.

My excitement sparks. "Does that mean you'll show it to me?"

Orlando doesn't immediately answer my question. Instead, he watches me intently, as if trying to read something I haven't yet said aloud.

"I just might. But"—he glances down at his watch—"not tonight. It's already late, and trust me, we don't want to rush this next one. And anyway, there's still one more stop on the list of places I wanted to show you tonight, if you're up for it?"

Anticipation hums in my chest at the realisation that our night together is not yet over.

"Lead the way."

Chapter Thirty-Five

"I'M SERIOUSLY NOT GOING to be able to walk straight tomorrow," I lament as we descend yet another set of stairs. My calves are on fire, and my thighs threaten to give out on me any minute.

"Not much further now. I promise," Orlando calls, his words swallowed by the thick walls rising up around us as we tentatively make our way down into the cool, dry air lingering in the lower levels of the castle.

I'm grateful for the light strips recessed into the risers of the stone staircase, illuminating each step as I nearly falter on a slightly uneven ledge. Orlando reaches the ground before me and offers his hand, gently guiding me down the last few steps. Only when my feet are firmly planted on the floor do I finally look up.

A sweet, faintly musky scent invades my nostrils as my eyes sweep across the dim space, softly illuminated by warm lights shining from cast iron sconces on the stone walls. A cluster of antique leather settees to our right encircle intricately carved wooden tables, each donning a matching coaster rack with the de Águila family coat of arms emblazoned on the surface. But that isn't what captures my attention.

With wide eyes, I take in the floor-to-ceiling glass wall stretching along the entire left side of the room, separating us from a cavernous stone vault filled from floor to ceiling with wine racks.

"Bet you've never seen a wine collection quite like this one, huh?" Orlando says as I shake my head in awe, admiring the formidable chamber. "It's supposedly one of the biggest private collections in the world."

"I can certainly believe that," I say softly, taking in the seemingly endless shelves housing what must be several thousand bottles of wine, each row stretching far into the spacious room—so far I can't even make out the back of the chamber from our current vantage point.

"Want to take a look inside?"

I pivot to face Orlando, eyes wide. "We're allowed to do that?"

He flashes a smug grin. "I am. When are you going to realise that I have the infinite power to unlock all kinds of secrets and wonders around this place?"

I feign a husky voice. "Oh, I suppose around the same time it strikes me how incredibly humble you are."

Huffing out a laugh, Orlando places a warm palm on my lower back as he guides me to stand in front of the glass door to the vault. It measures at least three metres tall by two metres wide, framed by a solid wooden frame matching the timber shelves within. Keying in an eight-digit code on the digital keypad, the door slowly opens with a soft whoosh.

We're immediately hit by a strong, earthy scent—an entrancing mix of oak, stone and leather, tinged with a lighter, almost fruity undertone. I inhale deeply, savouring the nuanced hint of tannins wafting in the air.

Soft shelf lighting bathes the wide array of bottles in a gentle glow, highlighting intricate labels and accentuating varied hues of red, white and pink.

Orlando leads me down aisle after aisle, pointing out notable bottles in the collection and telling me their fascinating backstories.

I have to clutch my stomach from laughing when Orlando animatedly tells the story about the time Domenico's grandparents travelled to France, intent on paying a small fortune to acquire a rather rare collection of wines from an eclectic French collector, only to be forced to participate in a play the owner had written himself—and insisted on performing in front of the entire household at his mansion—before he would agree to part with his collection.

As we reach the rear wall, Orlando pulls out a black-tinted, red-capped bottle from a shelf lined with identical bottles, tilting the off-white label toward me so I can read.

"Medalla Real, Gran Reserva, Cabernet Sauvignon. Santa Rita, Maipo Valley, 1982." I pronounce each word carefully, tracing my finger over the ageing label.

"It was the wine my parents drank at their wedding," Orlando says in his usual calm voice, yet the sad smile tracing his lips reveals his bittersweet emotions. "Señor de Águila secured several bottles as a present to my dad for his loyal service a few years after we moved from Puerto Rico. My father vowed to drink one bottle every five years on their anniversary in honour of my mum's memory. He only got through two before he passed away."

He doesn't look at me as he speaks, tracing his thumb absentmindedly over the faded label on the elegant bottle. Gently placing my hand on top of his, I wait until he lifts his chin to look at me.

"I want you to know how honoured and grateful I am for everything you've shared with me tonight. It cannot have been easy for you, and the fact that you're trying... it means the world to me. I'm relishing every little glimpse of your life you've given me—where you come from, who you were, and who you are today. The good, the bad, the ugly—all of it. That said, I don't want you to feel any pressure to share more with me tonight than you already have. Not unless you want to."

Detecting his unspoken gratitude, I give his hand a gentle squeeze. "Just know that I'm here for you, if you ever do feel the need to talk. About your dad, or your mum, or anything at all. I promise that your stories, and your pain, will always be safe with me."

I don't know what I expect. A trace of a smile, perhaps, or a silent nod of appreciation. What I don't anticipate is the smouldering fire in his eyes, searing through me and stealing my breath.

Placing the bottle back on its shelf, his intensity never strays from me as he takes two purposeful steps closer until our bodies are no more than a few inches apart.

"What are you doing to me, sirena?" Orlando whispers, his voice low and gravelly, sending shivers down my spine. "You're so goddamn beautiful. Inside and out. You drive me fucking crazy, Lainey."

As his eyes dip down to my mouth, tracing my tongue as it slips out to wet my suddenly dry lips, I know he's finally going to kiss me again.

My heart beats so loudly in my chest that Orlando must be able to hear every thud against my rib cage. He slowly eases his head closer to mine, and without even realising it, my head tilts forward to meet his.

Our lips are millimetres apart...

A faint noise from somewhere nearby causes us both to freeze, though I don't miss the low growl Orlando emits from somewhere deep in his throat.

Staying completely still, our faces inches apart, we strain to listen for any discerning sounds in the otherwise quiet space.

Just when I think the noise must have come from somewhere above us—though the immeasurably thick stone floors should've swallowed every whisper—the unmistakable thud of approaching footsteps reaches my ears. From the frantic look on Orlando's face, I know I'm not imagining it.

"Shit. Over here," Orlando mutters in a fervent whisper, pulling me along the back wall until we reach a small sliver of space between two large wine shelves near the end of the row. "Come on. In here. Quickly."

"What?"

"*Shh!*" Orlando hisses as he urges me forward, glancing over his shoulder. "We have to hurry or they'll know we're here."

"But I thought you were allowed to come here," I protest in a loud whisper, even as I slip into the narrow gap.

"I am. But trust me when I say that we *do not* want them to find us here." Orlando eases into the sliver of space after me, leaving my thoughts churning with his cryptic response.

I barely have time to register the closeness of our bodies when a shrill, womanly laugh cuts through the silence from somewhere on the other side of the glass wall. I glance, wide-eyed, at Orlando as he places a finger across his lips.

"It's quite the collection, I can assure you." The unmistakable cadence of Domenico de Águila's musical voice reaches us over the faint sound of the passcode being entered into the keypad. My heart starts thrumming for an entirely different reason.

"So you say, though I still doubt it's as large as Lucien's."

I don't recognise the saccharine female voice accompanying him, but the whiny, high-pitched edge to her ostentatious words, delivered in a posh British accent, immediately grates on my nerves.

Domenico scoffs above the soft swoosh of the vault door opening. "I can assure you, dear Cynthia, that it is. You know Lucien's flair for embellishment. Have you not learned by now that Lucien always polishes his own halo to give it that extra shine? In fact, devil's horns may be a more apt description."

Two sets of footsteps echo through the cavernous vault as Domenico and his companion make their way down one of the aisles.

"I saw his collection at his chateau in France when he took me there on his helicopter last summer, and it was quite impressive. He picked me up directly from my flat in Knightsbridge, you know? You might want to take some notes, Dom."

I scrunch my nose at her haughtiness, but Domenico just chuckles. "Is my private jet not sophisticated enough for you, Cyn? You prefer helicopters now?"

"I didn't say that. Though I must admit, having to travel all the way to the private airstrip is somewhat of an inconvenience."

I glance at Orlando to see him rolling his eyes, the distaste on his face mirroring my own.

"I would suggest convenience is something Lucien knows all too well. For instance, whilst he might have a rather large collection of wines and whisky, he could never be bothered to 'inconvenience' himself enough to seek out the rarer and, inevitably, more valuable collectables. Whereas I tend to favour quality over quantity. Take this Vega Sicilia 'Unico', 1962."

The reverberation of their footsteps abruptly halts.

"It's a true gem from the Ribera del Duero region, produced by the famous Bodegas Vega Sicilia and renowned for its meticulous make and unparalleled ageing potential. This 1962 vintage is particularly rare, crafted during a time when production techniques were evolving across Spain, resulting in a wine that embodies the essence of its terroir and the mastery of its makers."

The clink of the bottle being placed back on its shelf chimes through the vault. "Or, if we walk over here..."

Their footsteps recommence before halting once again, this time much closer to our hiding spot.

"That range of wines you see up there, with the matching labels, are all Clos Mogadors—a 1989 vintage from Priorat in Catalonia. A testament to René Barbier's pioneering spirit in revitalising the Priorat region. Made from old-vine Grenache and Carignan, with a touch of Cabernet Sauvignon and Syrah. We hold almost every bottle still in existence from the 1989 vintage, which represents a pivotal moment in the rebirth of Priorat as one of Spain's most esteemed wine regions."

"Not bad," Cynthia concedes, though her tone remains unimpressed. "Though knowing you and your taste for all things exquisite, I expected you to hide some reasonably valuable bottles down here."

"Like I said, *mi querida*, I'm partial to quality. That said..." Domenico trails off, and I strain to hear his next words over the rhythmic sound of footsteps getting closer—one set firm and measured, the other a snappy click-clack of heels across the dark, wood-panelled floor.

When Domenico speaks again, his voice is buttery soft and oozing with seduction. "My fondness for quality does not mean I sacrifice quantity. This wine collection is but one example. My penchant for women is another."

My eyes widen at his blunt admission, and I expect the woman to take offence, but she surprises me by responding, "Ah, yes. Yet another thing you and Lucien have in common. Your unquenchable thirst for women. The same women more often than not, or so I've heard. I suppose present company already proves that rumour true."

Domenico tuts, his lilting voice velvety smooth, and much closer than before.

"My dear Cynthia. As much as Lucien enjoys the pretence of competing with me—and notwithstanding the many women we have, admittedly, shared—I can assure you there's no competition. You see, when Lucien fucks his women, he's usually more interested in his own pleasure and self-importance than he is the woman's. When I fuck my women, they will be too preoccupied finding a way to walk straight the next day to think about anything else."

Speechless, I catch the knowing smirk playing on Orlando's lips, even as he rolls his eyes again. I get the feeling this isn't the first time he's heard Domenico speak like this.

"Despite what Lucien attempts to share far and wide, I can assure you that no woman's pussy would ever be as satisfied with his limp dick poking into them as they would be with the thrust of my cock between their lush thighs. Now, tell me, dear Cyn... isn't that exactly why you are here? To find out if the tales are true? To satisfy an appetite our dear, old friend Lucien didn't quite manage to quench, despite his many acclaimed prior conquests?"

"Well," Cynthia purrs in a voice that can only be described as sultry. "Since you're offering..."

Placing a finger across his pursed lips once more, Orlando carefully leans his head to the side as he peeks around the edge of the shelf. Following his lead, I glance over my shoulder and ease along the narrow gap until I'm just able to spot the dimly lit aisle.

An audible gasp escapes me as I lock onto a tall, slim woman, her red-painted nails clasping Domenico's sizeable crotch through his tailored charcoal suit pants. I whip my head back to Orlando, who cuts me a sharp, warning look.

I mouth a silent sorry.

Orlando casts me another warning look before shifting his attention back to the amorous duo entwined mere metres from where we're hiding. I let a few seconds pass before I follow suit.

From this angle, I have a perfect view of Domenico's growing erection as the blonde-haired woman rubs him through his pants. I watch his hands glide along her thighs and over her perky ass before caressing the small of her back. His nimble fingers reach the zipper of her lacy, bright pink dress, and with one quick pull, he yanks it all the way down.

A small shimmy from Cynthia is all it takes for the dress to slip past her waist, pooling at her feet to leave her naked and exposed in the middle of the aisle.

I can't deny that she has a beautiful body. Her skin is smooth and creamy, with gentle curves framing her hips and thighs—in stark contrast to her silicone-infused boobs, which jut from her slim frame like perky watermelons.

Domenico's darkening expression fills with lust as he grasps one breast in his palm, kneading her pebbled nipple with delicate fingers.

The soft moan escaping Cynthia's lips sends a flutter rippling through my lower abdomen, and my own nipples tighten as Domenico lowers his head to capture the pink bud in his mouth, seductively flicking his tongue over the peaked nub.

Cynthia's loose curls spill down her upper back as she tilts her chin up, her moans growing more urgent as she rubs herself against Domenico's groin. I watch, enraptured, as his erection swells until the bulge strains against the restricting fabric.

Pulling away from her, Domenico swiftly unbuttons his pristine white shirt and yanks it off, followed by his pants and boxer briefs. I clasp my hand over my mouth to stifle another audible gasp at the sight of his thick, erect cock, mesmerised as a drop of pre-cum forms on the silky-smooth tip.

In my periphery, I sense Orlando's chin tilting toward me, but I purposefully keep my eyes averted, trying to hide the furious blush creeping up my neck behind the loose strands of hair framing my cheeks.

My breath catches as Domenico spins Cynthia around, giving us a full frontal view of her gigantic breasts, before he bends her forward and plunges into her in one swift thrust. I wince at his roughness, but the scream of pleasure that reverberates through the room tells me Cynthia doesn't mind in the slightest.

Within seconds, Domenico's low grunts accompany the mewling whimpers slipping from Cynthia's lips. Despite the treacherous situation we're in, the low pull in my core is impossible to deny as the sultry cadence of colliding bodies reverberates all around us.

It's strange, how my body can still respond so fiercely, heating with desire when the memory of what I witnessed in Victor's office should've stolen this from me.

As if of its own accord, my focus drifts back to Orlando. My chest clenches as his dark green eyes meet mine, softened to a slate-coloured hue in the dim light of our confined hiding place.

Suddenly, I'm acutely aware of the nearness of his body. His hand tracing my arm as he pulls it back to his side. His chest softly brushing mine when he draws in a deep breath.

I inhale a lungful of air to steady my quickening pulse, and his eyes darken to a silvery lustre as the curve of my breasts skates across the hard ripple of his muscles.

A shiver courses through me, unravelling my thoughts and drowning my senses in a hazy blur. His gaze lingers on my mouth for a heartbeat before his eyelids flutter closed, and he sucks in a shaky breath, tilting his head almost imperceptibly from side to side.

I suddenly wish, with a fervent intensity, that I knew the thoughts racing through his mind.

Orlando tentatively eases his large frame away from the opening to our narrow hideaway. The movement of his right leg between our crammed bodies causes the edge of his upper thigh, thick with muscle, to rub against my pelvis. The unexpected contact sends a jolt of electricity through my entire body.

Before I can stop it, a husky moan slips through my parted lips.

Orlando goes rigid at the exact moment I do.

My heart takes off at a fast gallop. I don't know if the deafening thrum pounding in my ears stems from the realisation that the gyrating couple behind us might've heard me, or the undeniable fact that Orlando definitely did.

My face burns with heat, intensified by Orlando's leg still lightly tracing my upper thigh. I tentatively listen for any signs that Domenico or his female companion heard us, but the loud guttural grunts reverberating through the chamber silence my worry.

I keep my chin lowered, attempting to ignore the heat simmering low in my core amid the flurry of frantic thoughts darting through my mind.

Unable to ignore the mounting tension between us, I hesitantly tilt my head up, stealing a glance at Orlando through lowered lashes. The heat blazing through me from the molten intensity radiating from him steals my breath away.

Time stands still, the air thickening as our eyes lock. My lips part, chest rising and falling in sync with the frantic pulse of my pounding heart as Orlando's nearness scorches me, flooding my core with heat and setting every nerve alight.

The tension crackling between us is enough to knock me off balance when he finally moves—but rather than pulling away as I expect, he shifts closer.

With measured, deliberate movements, he eases his leg up and down. The slow friction of his upper thigh brushing against my crotch in a languid, torturous rhythm causes a wave of heat to ignite me from within, leaving me breathless under his touch.

"*Oh-h...*" A whispered stutter escapes me as a fevered surge blooms in my belly, coiling tighter with each passing stroke of his leg. My pelvis moves of its own accord, hips instinctively rolling in slow, tantalising circles against the firm ridge of Orlando's muscular thigh.

The friction builds, igniting my insides with liquid fire that sends shockwaves of sizzling heat surging to the surface—an inferno of desire and lust consuming me from within.

I tip my head back against the wooden frame of the shelf, eyes fluttering shut as I surrender to the sensations flooding through me. As if sensing the tension coiling tighter inside me, Orlando quickens his pace, his body grinding against mine with increasing pressure.

Then, unexpectedly, he hits a nerve deep, deep inside me.

A sensation stronger than anything I've ever felt before seizes hold of me as liquid fire surges straight to my core. A hitched moan spills from my parted lips, shuddering into the charged air between us.

"Fucking hell, sirena. You're killing me," Orlando mutters hoarsely as his hips inadvertently thrust forward. I jolt as something large and firm brushes against my thigh.

Instinctively, I glance down at the narrow space between our flushed bodies, landing on the pronounced bulge straining against the confines of his clothing.

Before I can fully process what I'm doing, I subtly shift my hip to the side, letting the inside of my upper thigh brush against the firm ridge of his denim-clad pelvis. The guttural groan that rumbles up his throat is like a spark to dry kindling, igniting something deep and insatiable inside me.

In a swift motion that sends my lust-fogged mind reeling, Orlando abruptly pulls his leg back. A protesting whimper rises to my lips, but I barely have time to bite it down before his pelvis is pressing against mine.

The pulse of his rigid cock against my centre, even through the thick denim barrier, is the most devastatingly erotic sensation I've ever felt.

Somewhere at the fringes of my awareness, I faintly register Domenico and Cynthia's escalating groans as they near their release. But every nerve in my body is ensnared by the uncontrollable wave of pleasure tearing through me as Orlando rocks his erection against my core.

"Oh, fuck. Lainey... *fuck*." The words tumble from Orlando's lips in rapid succession, his voice no more than a raspy groan as his hands clasp my waist, strong arms grinding my body against his with increasingly fervent movements.

"Oh my God. Orlando, I—I... *oh!*" I'm barely conscious of the breathless words spilling from my mouth as the pull in my abdomen intensifies, burning into a blazing inferno. With each thrust of Orlando's hips against my sex, a familiar tension coils deep in my belly, gathering momentum as it spills into every nerve, every cell, until fire ignites in my veins, searing through my limbs.

"Yes, yes, yes! Oh, yes, right there, baby. That's it, right there. Fuck me harder, baby. Fuck me hard and fast. Oh yes, just like that!"

In any other situation, Cynthia's screeching voice would be akin to nails on a chalkboard. But in my current state of sensory overload, the knowledge that she and Domenico are fucking like rabbits mere metres from where Orlando and I are tangled up in our own fevered rhythm only fuels the furnace burning through me. Their uninhibited noises only stoke my arousal.

"Goddammit, Elaina. You're so fucking beautiful," Orlando groans as his rigid cock grinds over my clit, and I shift to meet the full weight of his desire, searching out eyes drunk with lust.

His face is mere inches from mine, our lips no more than millimetres apart as our heated breaths mingle in a dense cloud of unbridled want.

My panties are completely soaked, my breath hitching with each teasingly tormenting thrust against my most sensitive spot.

"Orlando, I'm... I can't—I'm... I think I might—I... Orlando, I can't... I don't—*oh my God.*"

Breathless whispers tumble from my lips in a jumbled, incoherent rush as tension builds, the pressure mounting to an almost unbearable peak.

I've lost all sense of what's happening to my body, my mind too clouded with lust to make sense of anything around me. All I know is that I'm being pulled higher and higher, teetering on the edge of an unstoppable precipice I could tumble over at any moment, with no way to stop it.

"Oh, yeah, baby. That's it. Fuck yeah. Keep bouncing on my dick, Cyn. Just like that. Oh, I'm gonna come so hard, baby. I'm gonna come. I'm fucking coming... I'm—*f-f-fuuuck*!"

"Yes, yes, *yeeees*!"

The sound of Domenico's and Cynthia's joint release is my undoing.

With a final, desperate moan of pleasure, I'm propelled over the edge, free falling into an ocean of ecstasy as Orlando's mouth descends on mine.

I vaguely register the noises tumbling up my throat as wave after wave of euphoria crashes through me, swallowed by Orlando's fevered kisses as his mouth devours mine. His luscious lips are the only barrier muffling the frenzied sounds pouring from deep within me.

The ripples of pleasure seem endless, each thrust of Orlando's hard length against my pulsing sex igniting fresh jolts of electricity through my veins.

Though it can't have been more than a minute, it feels like hours before the cresting pleasure finally begins to subside.

Spent and trembling, I melt into Orlando's arms, my damp forehead pressed to his firm chest as I struggle to pull in enough air to steady my racing heart.

As the rush in my ears gradually fades, the surrounding noises come back into focus. The haze of lust recedes just enough for clarity to return, allowing worry to creep in once more.

I strain to pick up any sounds from the two people in the room with us.

A sharp smack, like a palm striking flesh, breaks the momentary silence, followed by a soft squeal.

"Come on, Cyn," Domenico says to the sound of a zipper being pulled. "Let's grab a few of these bottles and bring the party back to my suite. I have a few friends on speed dial who I'm sure would love to join us."

I fail to make out Cynthia's response as the echo of their receding footsteps ricochets through the room, followed by the distinct clank of the vault door opening and closing.

I remain frozen, acutely aware of Orlando's warm body pressed against mine as silence envelops us once more. The weight of what just happened wraps around me like a tangled knot.

Desperate for something to anchor my focus, it skates across his torso to land on his crotch, where the outline of his hard-on still visibly strains against his jeans.

Suddenly, the realisation that I came right here, in this confined space, in front of Orlando, with our boss mere metres away—and Orlando *didn't*—flushes my cheeks with embarrassment.

"Oh my God. I'm so, so sorry." The words blurt out of me before I can stop them. "That was... I can't even... God, I'm so embarrassed. They were right there, and you haven't even—I just... Christ."

"Hey, hey, hey. Slow down there, sirena."

Orlando trails a finger under my chin and gently tilts my face up until I have no choice but to meet his beautiful irises, still sparkling with visible heat.

"That," he says, his tone heavy with sincerity, "was the hottest, most erotic thing I've ever witnessed in my entire life." There's not even a hint of hesitation in his voice. "I'm about ready to burst in my pants right now."

The ball of anxiety in my chest lessens slightly, replaced by the familiar fluttering in my lower belly as the fervent intensity pouring off him sears my insides.

I glance down at his still noticeable bulge as uncertainty creeps back in.

"I—uhm... I could, you know..."

Orlando shakes his head. "Not tonight, sirena."

He softens his words by placing a gentle, sweet kiss on my lips.

"I want you. Believe me, I want you so fucking bad. But I want the memory of your face as you come to be the last picture ingrained on my brain when I fall asleep tonight. There will be plenty of time for everything else later."

Placing a final, swift peck on my swollen lips, he clasps my hand in his as he helps me ease out of our little hiding spot—a spot that will, forever and always, be emblazoned in my memory.

Chapter Thirty-Six

When I wake the next morning, it takes a moment to register why I'm feeling so damn good.

My first thought is that I must've gotten a better night's sleep than any in recent memory. But even that doesn't account for the overwhelming sensation of floating on cloud nine.

All at once, memories of last night crash into me, igniting a tidal wave of electrified butterflies taking flight in my belly.

Holy crap. *What actually happened last night?*

A small giggle bursts from my lips, the sheer insanity of the evening flooding my mind.

Orlando made me come last night. He made me *come.*

We listened to our boss fuck, hiding from sight like naughty teenagers, while he rubbed his rock-hard erection against my clit until I burst into flames, dissolving into the most intense orgasm I've ever had.

Holy. Shit.

A blinding smile pulls at my cheeks, and I barely suppress another giggle. I'll already have a hard enough time explaining the shit-eating grin I can't seem to shake. If Tiana hears me giggling on top of that, she definitely won't leave me alone until she drags the truth out of me.

But when I glance over the edge of my bed, I find the small cabin empty. Tiana's sheets are crumpled as always, and from the usual mess on her bed—clothes and makeup strewn in a jumbled heap—I can't tell whether she even slept here last night.

Stretching with a contented sigh, I pull myself out of bed and head into the bathroom, gathering my hair into a messy bun as I brush my teeth in the small sink. Tossing body wash, a towel, and a change of clothes into one of Tiana's tote bags, I slip on my flip-flops and head out the door.

The morning breeze tickles my hair as I make my way to the showers, humming to myself the whole time.

I find the shower room empty—not surprising, since it's still early on Sunday morning. Choosing a stall in the back, I step inside and pull the curtain just as I hear the entrance door swing open.

Still humming softly, I hang my towel on the hook fastened to the tiled wall before slipping my silk top over my head and placing it inside the tote bag. My fingers find the elastic waistband of my matching sleep shorts, but before I have a chance to pull them down, the shower curtain flies open.

I yelp, instinctively pulling the towel in front of my chest.

Whirling around, I'm ready to confront whoever thought it would be funny to launch a peep attack at seven in the morning on a freaking Sunday—but my words catch in my throat as I meet Blaise's crystal blue gaze, zeroed in on me with unsettling fervour.

"Hello there, princess."

Before I can scream, his hand clamps over my mouth.

I stumble as he shoves me roughly back into the shower stall, pulling the curtain shut behind us. A gasp rips from my lungs as my back slams against the cold tiles, but I have no time to recover before his brooding frame presses against my body, his glacial stare burning into me.

"Here I was, thinking I'd have to bide my time before I got another chance to catch you alone. But barely a day later, here you are, traipsing down the path right in front of me, looking entirely too delicious."

Panic surges through me, my protests muffled beneath his palm as I thrash against his firm hold, but it's useless. My hands are too busy clinging to the towel with a death grip. I refuse to let it drop, knowing it will leave me completely exposed with my bare chest pressed against Blaise's pecs.

Judging by the heat flaring in his irises, my futile struggles only excite him more.

"What was that?" He lifts his palm from my mouth for no more than a second, but it's enough.

"Fuck you, you deranged lunatic!"

I expect my words to anger him, but all they do is entice a wicked smirk.

"I must say, princess, the word *fuck* sounds entirely too appealing slipping from those plump, luscious lips. It's putting all sorts of naughty pictures in my head."

As if to drive the point home, he grinds his erection against my pelvis. I can feel every inch of his semi-hard length through my thin silk shorts, and I gag against his palm as he stiffens with each stroke against my crotch, still tender from yesterday.

Despite the similarities to last night—his large body pressing into mine, his erection grinding against my centre—this moment is *nothing* like yesterday, in all the ways that matter.

Surely, Blaise wouldn't try to force himself on me again? Not here. Not where anyone could walk in at any moment.

I level him with my most venomous glare, praying I'm right. His eyes glint with dark amusement, aquamarine depths swimming with arousal.

"Oh, princess," he murmurs. "If I didn't think you'd bite my tongue off, I'd give anything to kiss you right now."

He's deranged. That much is obvious as I fight against my rising panic.

I have to act before he gets so worked up that he stops caring about consequences.

I shift my leg, aiming to slam my knee into his crotch. Before I can get far, he blocks the attempt with his own leg, pinning my thigh to the cold tile wall.

"Ah, ah, ah. None of that, baby cakes. I followed you in here for a reason, and it's very important that I get to say what I came here to say."

His icy blue stare pins me in place. Against all logic, my curiosity piques. He almost looks disappointed when I stop wriggling beneath him.

"Tell me, princess. Have you told anyone about what happened Friday night?"

He doesn't wait for my response before continuing.

"Now, I need you to understand something. If you lie to me, things will take a very, very bad turn for you. If you think you can get away with deceiving me—that it'd be worse to tell me the truth now than to lie and have me find out later—you're sorely mistaken. Trust me when I say that it's *not* in your best interest to deceive me. So, I'll ask you again, and you will tell me the goddamn truth. Did. You. Tell. Anyone?"

I shake my head vehemently, hoping he reads the sincerity on my face. He studies me for several long moments, his cobalt glare penetrating me, searching for deceit.

He must not find any, because his whole body relaxes slightly.

"Good. Do you promise not to scream if I remove my hand?"

I nod, and to my surprise, he lets go, his hand sliding down to rest against the bare skin of my waist. It takes everything in me not to recoil from his touch.

"Now listen carefully. Not a single fucking soul can know about Friday night. Do you understand?"

"Yes," I whisper, as if speaking too loudly might set him off.

"In case you're ever tempted to forget that answer, let me make it crystal clear for you."

Blaise moves his mouth even closer to mine. "There were only five of us there that night. Jack and Finn won't say a word. They don't have the balls to cross me. That leaves you and Mr Stick-Up-His-Ass."

An ugly sneer warps his deceptively handsome features. "You may think that prick is your knight in shining fucking armour, coming to your rescue like a damn superhero. But let me tell you something, princess—I know things about that man that would make your silky soft skin crawl."

He trails a lone finger from my waist to my stomach, triggering a ripple of goosebumps.

"You may see me as the villain right now, baby cakes, but let me assure your pretty little heart—I'm far from the worst sinner lurking in the dark corners of this castle. You'd do well to remember that."

With an unsettlingly gentle kiss on the tip of my nose, he finally lets me go.

Flashing me a brazen wink, he rakes his eyes over me one last time before disappearing from sight.

I listen as his footsteps echo across the tiled floor.

I don't realise I'm holding my breath until the door slams shut behind him.

Chapter Thirty-Seven

No matter how hard I try, Blaise's words echo through my mind all morning. Even as I eat breakfast alone, I can't shake the sense of him watching me from his usual table. Every so often, I glance over to find him laughing with his friends or openly flirting with Clara, acting as if I don't exist. But despite the performance, I catch him stealing quick glances my way as he pretends to scan the room.

He's keeping his distance.

Good.

Desperate for a distraction, I scan the dining hall for the other girls. None of them have shown up for breakfast today, which is unusual—the one day I actually mind the solitude.

Tiana's still absent when I return to our cabin. I could go looking for her—she's probably with Dean, like she usually is after a night of drinking. But that risks running into Blaise again, and I'd rather avoid that at all costs.

Restless, I make a split-second decision to go for a run. I promised myself I'd increase my weekly mileage. Might as well start now.

Lacing up my shoes, I fasten Tiana's running belt around my waist, clip in my water bottle, and head out the door.

The moment my feet hit the pavement, I feel lighter. The sun'sstill low in the sky, but the humidity's rising steadily. It's going to be a scorcher.

I keep a steady pace as I cut through the gardens. It's early enough that most guests are either still in bed or enjoying the breakfast buffet in the hotel restaurant, leaving the grounds blissfully empty. Even though I'd wished for company, I suddenly appreciate the quiet.

Deciding to take full advantage of my day off, I reroute toward the beach instead of my usual loop around the castle grounds. My thighs are already protesting by the time I reach the bottom of the stone steps, but the ocean breeze on my flushed skin quickly rejuvenates me.

I take off down the path skirting the beach, letting the rhythm of my strides and the steady thud of my breath anchor me. With every drop of sweat sliding down my back, the gnawing unease from this morning begins to melt away.

That is, until I reach the outskirts of the harbour.

"...late yet again. I thought I made it abundantly clear there would be consequences if this happened again."

"I—I'm s-sorry, boss. It's like I told ya, we r-ran into trouble at the fence again. It's g-gettin' harder to get 'em across these days, even with the new system in place."

"Well, Mr Grimes, isn't that exactly what we pay you for? To ensure they *do* get across, no matter what? If not, then tell me, Lenny—what do we even need you for? My family already went to great lengths to establish this new trade route for you. Without our assistance, your business would've collapsed long ago. And I don't think I need to spell out what would happen if that was to occur."

I stop dead in my tracks, my stomach lurching.

My subconscious registers the voice before my brain catches up.

"I—I s-swear it won't happen again, boss. I'll personally make sure of it."

"I'd suggest you do that, Mr Grimes. Because there are much bigger and vastly more important moving pieces to consider in this rather intricate cabal we're all tangled up in. And in the coming weeks, your precision and scrupulousness will be of the utmost importance if we are to ensure all the cards align."

A cold shiver spreads down my spine despite the sweltering heat.

Halfway down the wooden pier, Domenico de Águila stands facing a much shorter man in an ill-fitted suit, sweat trickling down the man's weathered forehead as he stammers excuses. I don't recognise his ruddy face, but his darting eyes and hunched shoulders scream distress. Domenico, by contrast, is perfectly composed, his gaze locked on the man like a predator sizing up his prey.

But it isn't the sight of Domenico that makes my heart slam against my ribs.

At first, Orlando doesn't notice me, his concentration centred on the tense conversation unfolding before him. He stands slightly behind Domenico, his stance sharp and controlled.

If I didn't know better, I'd mistake him for Domenico's bodyguard. He looks effortlessly composed, dressed in fitted black chinos and a dark grey button-down with the top button undone, the metal clasp of his belt catching the morning light.

His face remains expressionless, betraying nothing of his mood.

I edge forward, careful not to draw attention as I keep my eyes on Orlando. The wooden boardwalk creaks beneath my weight, and I wince.

Neither of the men have noticed me yet, and I'd prefer to keep it that way. Tension hums in the air, sharp and brittle, even from this distance.

But luck isn't on my side.

Orlando's attention snaps to me, flaring with surprise before hardening into something unreadable. I lift my hand in an awkward wave, offering a hesitant smile. Even with Blaise's words from this morning echoing in my brain, my body reacts instinctively to Orlando's presence—nerves coiling tight, heat pooling in my core as memories of last night rush to the surface.

He doesn't smile back. Instead, his jaw tightens, muscles tensing as a shadow passes over him.

The flutter in my chest dies instantly.

Domenico follows Orlando's line of sight until his baby blue eyes land on me.

"Ah. Miss Delano. What a delightfully unexpected surprise."

To my dismay, he dismisses the flustered man at his side and strides toward me, leaving his short companion to shuffle after him. My glance cuts to Orlando, who somehow looks even more displeased than before. His lips move, as if he's cursing under his breath, before he straightens his posture and trails after them.

"Buenos días, señor de Águila," I murmur as Domenico reaches me, resisting the absurd urge to curtsy.

"Oh, my dear Ms Delano," Domenico croons, flashing me a devilish wink. "There's no need for such formality. We're not at the hotel among guests, after all. You may call me Domenico."

"Uhm... yes, sir—I mean, Domenico."

His grin widens. "*Maravilloso*. Much more intimate, wouldn't you say?"

Heat crawls up my neck as my tongue seems to tie itself in my mouth. Thankfully, Orlando and the wheezy stranger catch up to us, sparing me from answering. The short man takes me in with open curiosity, while Orlando's glare stays fixed on the boardwalk.

Domenico gestures to the nervous man. "Lenny, allow me to introduce you to the charming Miss Elaina Delano. She's one of my valued employees at the hotel. Miss Delano, this is Mr Lenard Grimes." He motions behind him. "And I'm not sure if you've had the pleasure of meeting Mr Álvaro ye—"

"We've met," Orlando interjects tersely. He gives me a curt nod. "Elaina."

That's it? That's all he's giving me, after last night?

Fine. Two can play at that game.

"Orlando." My voice is clipped, matching his cool detachment. His brows lift a fraction, and I feel a flicker of satisfaction.

Domenico tuts theatrically. "Ah, but of course. Miss Delano has been helping you with the gardens, has she not? *Dios mío*, how could I forget?"

His tone sets off a quiet unease in my chest. Why in the world would someone with as many employees and responsibilities as Domenico remember something so trivial?

Does he keep tabs on Orlando? On me?

Domenico steps closer, placing his hand on my shoulder as he gestures to the massive yacht docked in the harbour.

"You see that boat over there, Miss Delano? Her name is *El Gran Sueño*. My pride and joy."

"She's beautiful, si—Domenico," I mumble hoarsely, trying and failing to ignore the uncomfortable heat rushing through me from his unexpected nearness.

Glancing briefly at Orlando, I'm surprised to find his posture more rigid than I've ever seen it, his shrouded stare shooting daggers at the spot where Domenico's hand connects with my bare skin.

Oblivious to Orlando's scorching glare, Domenico continues. "Isn't she? Have you ever had the pleasure of spending a gorgeous, sunny day cruising crystal blue waters aboard a luxury yacht, Miss Delano?"

"I can't say I've ever had the opportunity."

Domenico clicks his tongue. "Ah, such a shame. It's truly an experience one can never tire of. Say, would you be interested in joining us on deck, sweet Elaina?"

"Domenico..." Orlando's tone is low and gravelly—a quiet warning. "You have important matters to discuss with Mr Grimes. Perhaps today isn't the best day?"

A long moment passes between them, silent but charged.

"I suppose you're right," Domenico concedes, though he doesn't look pleased. "Today is, perhaps, not the best day for visitors to accompany us."

Turning to me, he lifts my hand to his mouth, brushing a feather-light kiss over my knuckles. "Another time, perhaps. Enjoy your day, Miss Delano. Mr Grimes, shall we?"

Without another word, he spins on his heel and strides down the pier, expecting the short man to follow.

When they're both out of earshot, Orlando finally looks at me. "Elaina—"

"Don't." My curtness slices through his words.

I thought we were past this. I thought, after last night...

I guess the joke's on me.

Determined to stay composed, I steel myself, erasing every trace of emotion. "I don't know what's going on here, and honestly, I don't care. So why don't you tag along after your boss, and we can skip the part where you feed me some vague excuse that doesn't actually explain anything. You know, the part where you act like a completely different person less than twelve hours after your lips were on mine?"

I know I'm probably angrier than I should be—Blaise's confrontation this morning has scrambled my emotions—but I refuse to let that soften my stance.

Orlando's jaw tightens, though a glimmer of regret slips through.

"Elaina, I'm sorry, okay? Please don't be mad. I promise I—"

"Orlando. Just—don't. I really don't want to hear it right now."

He steps forward, but the moment I shift back, he hesitates. Frustration etches itself across his face, his hands twitching at his sides, as if fighting the urge to reach out.

After a glance over his shoulder, he exhales sharply. A quiet growl slips from his lips as he looks at me imploringly.

"Please, Lainey. Can we talk later? I know this looks bad, and I hate that I have to go right now, but I promise I can explain lat—"

"Sure, Orlando. Whatever." I inject as much indifference into my voice as I can, though I don't sound nearly as detached as I want to. "I'll just add it to the list of things you never seem to find the right time to explain."

Without waiting for a response, I turn on my heel and take off in the direction of the castle, locking my sights on the cliffs in the distance as I force my legs to move faster, putting as much space between us as I can.

I make it to the stone steps before the first silent tear slips down my cheek.

Chapter Thirty-Eight

"I swear, if I keep on eating like this, I'm going to gain at least five kilos before the summer's over." Tiana rubs her perfectly flat, toned stomach with a satisfied sigh.

"Oh, hush," I scoff, giving her a playful shove. "You could gain double that and still be one of the fittest people I know. And you know damn well curves look good on you."

"Oh, you sweet little sugar plum," she coos. "How did my ego ever survive this place before you?"

I laugh. "Like anyone could tear you down, even if they tried."

Tiana links her arm through mine as we stroll through the staff village toward our cabin. She has, albeit unknowingly, kept my mind off Orlando for most of the day, dragging me into endless rounds of ping-pong and card games with Rhianna and Jess.

"I'm serious, though," she groans. "That lasagne? I swear to God, that's what dreams are made of."

I hum in agreement, acknowledging that my belly is fuller than usual. The quality of the staff meals here still amazes me.

"Elaina?"

I freeze.

His deep, rumbling voice sends an involuntary jolt through me, halting me mid-step. Tiana yelps as my abrupt stop yanks her backward.

"Girl, what the hell? You alright?"

Spinning around, my stare locks onto him immediately.

Orlando leans against a tree at the edge of the clearing, half-hidden in the shade of the sprawling branches. Pushing off the trunk, he takes a slow, measured step toward me.

"Uhm... is that *Orlando*?" Tiana whispers, following my line of sight as she squints into the trees. "What in the world is he doing here?"

I force my face into a mask of indifference, unwilling to let her see anything I don't want to explain. "I don't know," I say, loud enough for him to hear. "Taking an evening stroll, perhaps?"

Orlando exhales, shifting his weight as he stuffs his hands into his jeans pockets. "Elaina, can I talk to you? Alone?"

I bite my lip, my brain at war with itself. One part of me wants to run over to him, throw caution to the wind, and sink into the comfort of his strong arms. The other part screams at me to flip him off and walk away, triumphant in my indifference.

Dramatic? *Maybe.*

Justified? *Absolutely.*

Glancing at Tiana, I nearly burst out laughing at the shocked disbelief stamped across her face.

"Uhm, girl?"

My lips twitch. "Yeah?"

"Tell me something... Why, in the name of all that's scrumptious, is *Orlando Álvaro* asking to talk to you? Alone? At"—she checks her watch—"nine o'clock at night?"

Suppressing a sigh, I know I'll only make it worse if I refuse. This situation's already suspicious enough as it is.

"Your guess is as good as mine," I say lightly, feigning nonchalance. "Probably something work-related, with the big event coming up next weekend."

Ignoring Orlando's watchful glare, I gently pull my arm from Tiana's. "I'll meet you back at the cabin in a minute, okay?"

Tiana backs away slowly, her suspicious look flitting between Orlando and me. "Sure," she enunciates, drawing out the word. "You holler if you need me, though, okay?"

I give her a composed smile. "Sure thing."

Still eyeing us like we're up to something, she eventually sighs and heads toward the cabin. As soon as she's out of earshot, I press my fingers against my temples.

"You could've just waited until the next time we ran into each other, you know?" I mutter. "Who knows what Tiana's going to think now, with this little stunt?"

My words are cut off by the sound of laughter echoing through the evening air. Three figures make their way down the terrace stairs in our direction. Orlando tugs gently on my arm, nodding for me to follow him.

Against my better judgement, I do.

We walk a short distance along the side of the lodge, stopping when we're safely hidden from the main path. The dim glow from the lodge windows casts enough light for me to make out Orlando's features as he turns to face me.

"So... I take it you haven't told Tiana about last night?" His voice is careful and measured. "About what happened between us?"

I sigh. "No. I haven't told her anything."

"Why not?"

The question catches me off guard. "I—I guess I assumed you wouldn't want me to."

Guilt flashes across his face, and before I can stop them, more words flow from my mouth. "But it's not just that." I shrug. "I'm a private person. When it comes to things like this... I don't share easily, so I probably wouldn't have said anything, even if I did think you wouldn't mind."

He studies me as something unspoken passes between us.

"Elaina," he murmurs, voice low and steady. "I know I don't have the right to ask this when there's so much I haven't told you. But I still want to know—why did you think I wouldn't want you to tell your closest friend about us?"

Us. That one little word sends a surge of butterflies through me.

Might as well lay it out.

I sigh. "Besides the fact that I never know where I stand with you, because you switch from hot to cold more often than a malfunctioning thermostat?" My tone is sharp but honest. "I figured you wouldn't want people knowing because of how much you separate yourself from the rest of the staff. They were all practically itching to tell me how you barely spare any of them a glance when I first started working here."

I shrug again. "I guess I just assumed you wouldn't be thrilled about everyone knowing we've been... doing whatever the hell we've been doing."

Orlando grimaces as he rubs a hand over the back of his neck.

"Look." He hesitates. "I'm glad you haven't told her. But not for the reasons you might think."

His hands slip back into his pockets as he meets my confused frown with a veil of resignation.

"That first day we worked together..." he says carefully. "I didn't know, at the time, that Domenico was the one who hired you."

My brows crease. "And why does that matter?"

He exhales slowly, tension tightening his jaw. Whatever this is, he's struggling to come out with it.

"Domenico is... complicated," he finally says. "He's one of the most intelligent people I know, but he's also impulsive, ruthless, and driven by his own desires. More often than not, that last one is what gets him into trouble. He doesn't let things like morality or propriety stop him, and he usually makes decisions based on gut instinct. Or... *other* bodily reactions."

In any other circumstance, I might've found the remark funny. As I look at Orlando, my lips don't even twitch.

"And?" I press when he doesn't continue. "What does any of that have to do with me?"

Orlando mutters under his breath, running a hand through his hair. "Man, how can I even explain this to you in a way that makes sense?"

"At this point, any explanation is better than nothing," I grumble. "I don't need polished. Actually, I'd prefer the raw version."

He closes his eyes, exhaling sharply, then nods.

"The first thing you need to know is that my relationship with the de Águila family is... layered. When señor de Águila hired my father, Dad became integral to his various business ventures. As Domenico and I grew up, Domenico was always expected to take over the de Águila empire. Mattia began grooming him for the role of CEO from an early age, dragging him all over the world to meet business contacts and see their operations firsthand. Technically, Domenico wasn't supposed to tell me anything... but we were best friends."

Orlando shrugs, contrition flickering faintly in his expression. "He kept some things from me, but I still knew enough—and Mattia knew it. So when my father died, Domenico pulled me into the fold to take his place."

I have no idea where this is going, but I find myself drawn in. The de Águila family is largely a mystery around here, and Orlando's voluntarily peeling back the curtain to their elusive world.

"Mattia wasn't happy about it. He tried to oppose the idea at first. Quite vehemently, actually. But Domenico was adamant."

"Why?" I blurt, curiosity overriding caution. "Didn't he like you or something?"

Orlando smiles, but there's no humour in it. "It's not that he didn't like me. He just didn't get me. Never has. It's like, no matter how hard he tried, he could never figure me out. I don't think Mattia has ever been certain whether he can—"

He stops himself, jaw tensing, as if catching something before it escapes.

"Anyway, it doesn't matter," he rushes out, slamming the door on whatever thought nearly slipped out. "Domenico wouldn't hear of anything different. It was one of the only times I've seen him openly defy his father. Nic was taking over more and more by that point, and he insisted on surrounding himself with people he trusted. His father couldn't argue with that. He'd insisted on the same thing when he was in charge. So I became Nic's right hand, the same way my dad had been for Mattia."

A crack of shattering glass cuts through the moment, filtering through an open window above us—a sharp reminder this conversation isn't meant for curious ears. Without a word, we step deeper into the shadows edging the forest.

As much as I want to understand why he's telling me all this, I don't want him to stop. For once, I'm glimpsing a part of Orlando I suspect he rarely lets anyone see.

The trees dim the fading light as Orlando continues.

"Because Nic trusts me, and because of everything he's done for me over the years, I do what I can to repay that trust. I doubt I'd even still be here if it weren't for him. He lets me do the work I enjoy—gardening, working the grounds, spending most of my time outside. He only pulls me in for... other things when he needs a second opinion, or whenever he needs someone at his side he knows won't betray him. And as much as I prefer to keep my distance from the rest of it, I owe him my loyalty when he calls for it."

Orlando exhales, rolling his shoulders, as if shedding a weight only he can feel. "I say all this because over the years, I've come to know Nic better than anyone else. And when you first started working here, I had no idea he even knew who you were. Not until he made a comment about you."

His Adam's apple bobs as he swallows hard, and my stomach tightens. "What kind of comment?"

He hesitates, then shakes his head. "Nothing I want to repeat."

I scowl, indignation flaring. "Why? Because you're still keeping things from me?"

His mouth flattens, though his voice stays gentle. "Not because I want to keep things from you, Lainey. But because repeating what Nic says behind closed doors won't do anyone any good. Suffice it to say, once I realised he was talking about you, my blood boiled. When it became clear you'd somehow captured his attention..."

I frown. "So let me get this straight. You ignoring me, acting like a dick, and whatever the hell that was down at the docks today—it's all because you're, what? Jealous?"

The growl that rumbles up his throat is equally daunting and alluring, and a spark flares inside me.

"Trust me, Elaina. You don't want to draw the attention of Domenico de Águila. I may not know everything about you, but I know enough to guarantee you that this family isn't one you want to be entangled with any more than necessary. As long as you're just another worker, you're safe. You'll just be another face in the crowd to them. But Lainey... I know Nic. I know what he's like when he sets his mind on something. Or someone."

"But—but..." My thoughts are churning. "Why would Domenico even care to notice me?" I shake my head in bewilderment. "Sure, he remembers my name, but he's like that with everyone, right? I mean, you saw what he was like last night, in the wine cellar, with that woman. I can only imagine what he's like behind closed doors, if that's how he acts with people around. And that blonde bombshell he fucked? She's way more his type than I could ever be."

Something flashes across Orlando's face at my bold words, but he lets me ramble, unwavering as his eyes stay fixed on me.

When my words finally falter, he declares in a low, gravelly voice, "Nic's a good man. A great friend. But he's used to getting whatever he wants, and whoever he wants, with the flick of his fingers. And when something presents a challenge, he tends to get a little... fixated."

I swallow hard. "So because I'm not throwing myself at him like everyone else—"

"You've caught his interest," Orlando confirms, voice tight. "I saw the look in his eyes today at the docks. I've seen it before. I fucking know what it means. And Elaina, as much as I love the man, I don't want him anywhere near you."

His hands capture mine, strong and warm, grip firm but not forceful. "You ask if I'm jealous? You're goddamn right I am. I can't stand the thought of another man touching you. Not after what that fucker almost did to you that night."

A sharp breath hitches in my throat as his grip tightens.

"Elaina, I don't know how or why, but I'm becoming more protective of you than I've been of anyone in my entire life. If I thought Domenico, or Blaise, or any fucking man in this place was good enough for you—if I truly believed any of them could make you happy—I swear, I wouldn't stand in the way. No matter how furious the thought makes me."

His voice drops to a whisper, thick with raw truth. "Not if Domenico, or someone else, was who you truly wanted. I would never stand in the way of your happine—"

"He's not who I want." The words tumble out before I can stop them, and the moment they leave my lips, I feel the depth of their truth.

Orlando stills, his hands tightening around mine, the air charged with something unspoken.

Lust? Desire?

Hope?

Whatever it is, the way he's looking at me in this moment sends a pulse of heat straight to my core.

"I fucking hope not."

And then he's kissing me. Finally, he's *really* kissing me.

His soft lips are rough and hot, moulding again mine, and I can't help the groan that escapes as his tongue slips past my lips, tangling with mine in a seductive dance that ignites a wildfire inside me.

His calloused hands skim up my thighs to rest on my hips, dragging my shirt with them until his warm fingers glide over bare skin, sending shivers of arousal rippling through me with each touch.

I don't even realise my hands have wandered to his chest until I'm gripping his fitted t-shirt with both fists, pulling him closer, desperate for contact as our bodies meld together, touching at every point.

Somewhere in the back of my mind, I know there's still so many unanswered questions. Blaise's words from this morning still linger, and everything that has unfolded today only proves how much I still don't know.

But right now, I can't bring myself to care. In this moment, I let myself drown in him, locking away my doubts and fears in a steel box buried deep in my chest.

We kiss for seconds, minutes, hours—or at least, that's what it feels like. By the time our lips finally part, my breath is ragged, my lips swollen and tingling from his rough stubble.

"Fuck, sirena. You drive me fucking crazy, you know that?" Orlando sighs deeply, resting his forehead against mine as we wait for our racing hearts to slow.

We stand like that for several long minutes, his palms still on my waist, my fingers still clutching his shirt.

When he finally straightens and takes a reluctant step back, his hands don't leave my body, grounding me in the warmth of his touch.

"I wanted to see you tonight," he murmurs. "I know I still haven't told you everything. I know you have questions. But I needed to see you, even if you didn't want to speak to me." He hesitates, then exhales. "I'm leaving for a few days."

Disappointment slams into me. "You're going away?"

"Yeah. Just for a few days." Resignation tugs at his tone, as if he hates the thought as much as I do. "Domenico needs me for some business negotiations. I—it's not something I can get out of. We'll be back the day before the party."

Lowering my gaze, I swallow the unexpected wave of dejection curling in my stomach.

Orlando's hands cradle my cheek, tilting my head up until I have no choice but to meet his eyes.

"I'll find you when I get back, and we'll talk, okay? I can't promise to tell you everything. Not all of it is my secret to share, and my loyalty to Domenico means there are things I'm bound to keep in confidence. But we will talk, Elaina. I promise you that. I don't want to lose this—whatever this is between us. I don't even know for sure what *this* means, or if I'm even ready for it. But I do know I'm not willing to lose you."

His silver-green eyes bore into mine, his words chipping away at my defences, crumbling the walls I've so carefully constructed.

My body leans into his, drawn by a force stronger than reason. When he presses a soft, lingering kiss to my forehead, I want to drown in his cedar-tinted, earthy scent.

His breath tickles my skin as he exhales. "I hate to ask anything of you, sirena, but until we've had a chance to talk, until we figure this out, can we keep this—us—between you and me? Just for a little while longer?"

Before I can pull away, though I'm not even sure I want to, he presses his lips to mine again, quick and firm.

"Please, just trust me. It's only until I can sort out some of this mess. Gossip spreads like wildfire in this place, and right now, I need you to trust—I mean, I *hope* you can trust me when I say it's best if no one else knows about us. Just for now."

I bite my lip, hesitating for only a moment before nodding. I may be a fool—a big one at that—but in this moment, I choose to give him the benefit of the doubt.

For now.

Relief eases the tight pull of his brow, and he lets out a slow breath—like he just stepped off a ledge, unsure if he'd land in calm waters or be dragged under by the tides.

"Thank you, gorgeous girl."

With one final, swift kiss to my lips, he spins me around. "Now, back to your cabin, sirena. Dream the sweetest of dreams. An when you open your eyes, it'll be one day closer to the moment I get to see your beautiful face again."

My shaky feet take me past the first row of cabins in a haze.

When I glance back, I'm not surprised to see Orlando's dark silhouette still standing where I left him, once again watching until I've made it safely back to my cabin.

Chapter Thirty-Nine

"Holy cheese-on-a-cracker, Els. You look *smokin'*!"

I give Tiana a nervous smile, running my clammy palms across the fitted bodice of my floor-length dress. "You really think so?"

"Understatement of the decade, chick," Rhianna pipes up from where she's perched on Tiana's bed, flicking lazily through a magazine. Paige claps her hands together excitedly, her eyes bright.

"You look absolutely gorgeous, Elaina," she sighs happily, reaching out to twirl one of the loose curls spilling over my bare shoulders around her dainty finger. "I'm a wonder with a curling iron, if I do say so myself."

"Damn straight, you are. I'm considering bribing you into coming home with me this autumn so you can be my personal hairstylist," Tiana says as she moves behind me to admire the gemstone-studded barrette keeping my hair secured in an intricate half-up, half-down style. Delicate loops and twirls gather at my crown before cascading in spiralling ringlets down my back.

Using my fingers, I gently swipe a perfectly curled strand away from my brow, where a section of my long-layered fringe has been left loose to frame my heart-shaped face. I turn to glance at my reflection in the full-length mirror, barely recognising the woman staring back.

Hesitation glimmers in familiar hazel irises, the swirls of brown, amber and subtle blue accentuated by the gold-shimmered glitter dusting the upper edges of my smoky eyelids. Dark eyeliner and thick lashes lend a boldness to my look I'm not used to.

I pull at the edge of my raspberry-tinted bottom lip with my teeth, trailing my subtly contoured cheeks to the sweetheart neckline of my sable-coloured gown. The intricately pleated bodice wraps around my torso in delicate swirls before gracefully unfurling into a cascade of ruffled layers, pooling into an obsidian waterfall.

I still don't know if wearing this dress tonight is the right move, but as waves of smooth fabric skim beneath my shaky palms, I can't deny it's the most exquisite piece of clothing I've ever worn.

Viktor may have forced me into opulent dresses on many occasions, but even those garments pale in comparison to the craftmanship woven into every inch of this extravagant gown.

When Tiana and I returned to our cabin earlier in the afternoon, there it was—hanging off the railing of my top bunk, enclosed in a luxurious garment bag of soft silk.

Up until that moment, I'd been content to wear the pale blue dress Tess had kindly offered to lend me, paired with a set of wedged heels from Tiana's expansive collection. But the second I spotted the Castillo del Acantilado crest stamped across the note dangling from the hanger, elegant cursive writing sprawled across rich, cream stationary, the sinking feeling in my stomach told me exactly who the dress was from.

Dear Miss Delano,

I hope you will do me the honour of wearing this gown for tonight's event.

Cindy has informed me of the valuable contribution your delicate touch has made in bringing this evening's festivities to life, and it would bring me the greatest pleasure to honour your hard work by seeing you grace this joyous occasion in the most exquisite of dresses—which, from the moment I spotted it, I knew would suit you perfectly.

Your presence, adorned in this attire, will surely elevate the splendour of the evening.

Until then...

Yours sincerely,
Domenico de Águila.

As nausea and disbelief churned in my gut, my only saving grace was that Tiana was too busy gawking at the lush fabric to notice the note before I hastily stuffed it beneath my duvet.

I concocted a quick explanation—Cindy must have sent it, after arranging for members of the event crew without formal wear to borrow dresses from the hotel's collection. It wasn't a complete lie, though I highly doubt anything in storage matches the quality and elegance of this statement piece.

Tiana flat-out refused to let me even glance at Tess's dress after taking one look at Domenico's gown. I guess I can't blame her for thinking me mad for still wanting to wear the light-blue, modest dress. As pretty as it is, it pales in comparison to the ebony gown now draped across my frame, highlighting my subtle curves in all the right places.

There's also the gnawing suspicion that Domenico would not take kindly to having his generous, though disconcerting, gesture refused.

Once Tiana convinced me that I had no choice but to wear the dress—threatening bodily harm if I didn't listen—she immediately called in reinforcements, declaring that a dress like this deserved more than a basic French braid and a hurried swipe of foundation.

Three hours of meticulous plucking, curling, and primping later, I barely recognise myself. This bold, dramatic look is a far cry from my usual modest appearance, and my twitchy fingers yearn to pull on the absent plait that ordinarily drapes across my shoulder.

But as I take in the voluminous spirals cascading down my back, each loop catching the golden strands in my caramel blonde hair, I can't deny the tentative spark of excitement I feel.

Viktor always preferred my formerly platinum locks streaming down my back in an unbroken deluge of pin-straight tresses.

Now, as I take in my appearance, I feel different. Free. *Beautiful.*

A prickle of tears suddenly threatens to blur my vision, and I blink rapidly as I pretend to smooth the skirt of my dress to avoid Tiana's sharp-eyed glance.

"Go on then, girl. Give us a twirl!"

Biting my lip, I clasp the outer layer of the skirt and spin. The fabric flares seductively around me like a rippling tide, while the beads sewn into it glitter like tiny stars in the late afternoon sun streaming through the open window.

Paige sighs. "Gosh. You're stunning, Els."

"Thanks to you," I say earnestly.

"Oh, it was nothing." Paige waves off my gratitude, though her eyes sparkle with delight.

"My girl's gonna leave a trail of men in her wake tonight, that's for sure," Tiana crows as she high-fives Rhianna. "Girl power, baby!"

As their laughter fills the room, I turn back to the mirror once more, inhaling deeply as I force air into my lungs. The transformation is empowering, but there's only one person whose attention I truly want to capture tonight.

The thought of Orlando sends a complicated tangle of emotions through me—a sensation I've become far too familiar with over the past few weeks.

I haven't seen or heard from him since our whispered conversation and heated kiss on Sunday night. He told me he'd be back yesterday.

But he never appeared.

With every passing hour, the unease tightening my chest grew heavier. I fought to keep my thoughts on work, on the event preparations, but every time my gaze drifted toward the ballroom entrance, hoping to catch sight of him, the disappointment only dug deeper.

I want to trust him.

But doubt lingers with every new tug of disappointment. A nagging whisper has taken root in the back of my mind, growing louder ever since my run-in with Blaise. Insufferable git that he is, he still managed to crawl under my skin, leaving behind threads of doubt and mistrust I don't want to feed.

I can't ignore the whispered voice warning me that my heart will never be safe, especially in the wavering grasp of the gorgeous, mysterious man who's captured every stuttering thud since the moment I first saw him. The voice telling me he will only let me down. That I'm walking a dangerous line—one that can only lead to heartbreak.

I shake my head, steeling my wavering pulse as I push the uncertainty aside. Tonight is about the event. About the work we've all poured into making this evening a success.

If all else fails, I will focus on that.

No matter what happens, I will get through this night with my head held high.

Chapter Forty

Glitz and glamour shimmer all around me as my eyes scan the room, taking in the vibrant fusion of people crowding the vast space. Every guest is dressed to the nines, draped in dazzling outfits, each piece likely worth more than I'll earn all summer.

The sheer level of extravagance is hardly surprising, given the exclusive nature of tonight's attendees. In just an hour, I've seen more celebrities than I ever expected to encounter in my entire life.

For the past three days, the staff lounge has been buzzing with anticipation as actors, musicians, athletes, influencers, and politicians from across the globe descended upon the hotel for this prestigious event.

Even as some of Hollywood's most prominent stars waltz past me, plucking flutes of champagne from passing trays, I barely register them. My thoughts remain elsewhere, scanning the sea of elegantly dressed figures for the only face I want to see tonight.

I thought I'd spot him instantly. He'll undoubtedly be by Domenico's side. And while I haven't spotted Domenico yet, there's no way Mr Casanova himself would miss this event. It's far too important for the castle and its ambition to secure its place among Europe's finest luxury hotels. Cindy's made that abundantly clear, with her relentless warnings of impending doom should anything go awry tonight.

As if summoned by my thoughts, Emma's voice murmurs beside me, "Smile and pray, girls. If this event doesn't go off without a hitch, Cindy will have our heads."

"We've done everything we can to plan this down to the last detail. Whatever happens from here on out is mostly out of our hands," Lisa replies, though she contradicts herself by glancing at her watch every few seconds, counting down to the start of the speeches.

If I had been responsible for tonight's schedule, I suppose I'd be just as tense. At least most of my tasks were completed ahead of time.

"Man, I really hope Tim and Phillip are staying on schedule. The speeches should be starting soon. Has anyone seen Domenico yet?" Lisa asks, craning her neck to peer past a group of cackling women edging toward a cluster of well-known actors near the open doors to the garden.

I've been too preoccupied searching for Orlando to pay much attention to the conversation, but at Lisa's question, I tune back in.

"Nah, haven't seen him," Keisha replies, scanning the room with an appreciative nod. "Though, with all these celebrities here, Domenico's got some serious competition for once. Is that Hero Fiennes Tiffin I see over there?"

"Oh my God, where? I *love* him," Emma squeals, bouncing on her toes before she catches herself. "I just adored him as Hardin—"

I tune out their chatter again, my eyes sweeping the room once more.

Where the hell is he?

Orlando's absence unsettles me, though I'm not entirely sure why. Lisa seems equally on edge, but I doubt it's for the same reason.

"They should be here by now," she mutters, mirroring my movements as she scans the clusters of guests. With another quick glance at her watch, she looks toward the entrance. "I might check with Tina and Alison, see who's been checked off the guest list so far. We can't start the speeches if we're still missing key guests, let alone the main speaker."

She strides toward the door, and for a brief moment, I consider following her. Before I can decide, a presence looms behind me.

My heartbeat quickens as I spin around, nearly stumbling as I come face to face with a camera lens.

"Say cheese, beautiful."

A bright flash momentarily blinds me, followed by the soft click of the shutter.

"Sweet baby Jesus, Corban. You scared the hell out of me," I gasp, though a smile takes over as his wide, mischievous grin peeks out from behind the lens.

"Sorry, Els," he chuckles, lowering the camera to his chest, where it hangs securely from a thick strap. "I couldn't resist. You look like you belong out there with the high society crowd, not slumming it with us lowly employees."

His eyes glint with amusement, but as they linger on my gown, his humour fades. "Seriously though. You look stunning tonight, Elaina."

"Thanks," I murmur, flustered by the sincerity in his admiring gaze.

Sensing my discomfort, Corban smoothly shifts the conversation. "Not a bad turnout so far."

Grateful for his ability to ease my nerves, I let out a breath as my shoulders relax. "As good as we could've hoped for. Though the night is still young."

Corban's mouth curves with suppressed laughter.

"What?" I ask, narrowing my eyes.

He fights back his smirk. "Nothing. I just like the way you phrase things sometimes. It's unusual. Almost old-worldly."

I stiffen.

"Hey, Els. I'm sorry. I didn't mean anything bad by it," Corban adds quickly, noticing my reaction. "I like the way you speak. That's why I noticed. It's just different from how most people here talk, that's all. I'm sorry if I offended you."

His unease makes me regret my knee-jerk reaction, and I force my posture to relax as I offer a reassuring smile. He couldn't know that his innocent comment dredged up the memories I've fought to bury—haunting reminders of Viktor's expectations, his imposing presence, his sharp words and calloused actions disciplining me into behaving exactly as he wanted.

I was always the youngest in the group of wives and girlfriends at the social gatherings he dragged me to, and as his *sokrovishche*—his *treasure*—his demands were strict and unyielding.

"No, I know. It's all good. I don't even know why I reacted like that," I say, shaking off the uneasy feeling. I squeeze his arm lightly, relieved when his stance relaxes again. "Got any good photos yet?"

"Just captured a masterpiece a few seconds ago," Corban teases, winking as he gestures toward his camera. My cheeks heat for the second time since he walked over.

"Jesus, Corban. Are you trying to make me blush tonight?"

His grin turns wicked, though there's nothing but laughter and friendly mischief there.

Or maybe friendly isn't quite the right word.

"Sorry, Els. You're just too easy to tease." He taps my nose with his index finger.

I swat his hand away, sticking my tongue out at him, and his dazzling smile reappears.

Turning back to the room, Corban sighs and grips his camera. "Guess I better get back to work. Plenty of famous faces still waiting to be immortalised. But before I do..."

Corban's arm slides around my waist, pulling me effortlessly against his side as he angles the camera lens toward us. He leans in, his freshly shaven jaw brushing against my cheek, and the smooth warmth of his tanned skin sends an unexpected shiver through me.

This time, I'm ready for the flash. Forcing my lips into a wide grin, I hold the pose as Corban fires off several quick shots.

"You're not posting those anywhere, right?" I ask warily as he pulls back, pressing a series of buttons to scroll through the images.

I can't afford to have pictures of me circulating online.

"No, no. Just for my personal collection," Corban reassures me, but his words barely register as a slow warmth unfurls along my neck, pulling my awareness across the room.

Familiar, piercing, and utterly captivating silvery-green eyes lock onto mine from across the sea of bodies, and I suck in a sharp breath.

Orlando stands amidst a cluster of men, his presence commanding, even from a distance. Dressed in a perfectly tailored, ink-black suit with a matching ebony shirt, the only splash of colour comes from the dark silver of his tie. Its muted shade makes his eyes stand out even more.

But it's not just the colour that makes them striking. His expression is a storm of restrained emotion, an inferno of chaos and fiery intensity.

And then his attention shifts.

His smouldering glare slides from me to Corban, darkening to something lethal. His already taut features sharpen as his jaw tightens, his stance turning rigid. Even through the swarm of people between us, I can feel the suppressed tension rolling off him in waves.

How long has he been standing there?

How much did he see?

For someone who insisted only days ago that no one could know about us, he isn't exactly hiding his animosity at another man's proximity to me.

My pulse stutters as I glance at Corban, relieved to find him engrossed in his camera, oblivious to the silent battle raging just beyond his lens. A tiny smile lingers on his lips as he studies the photos he snapped of us, completely unaware of the fury aimed directly at him.

Orlando's unrelenting glare remains locked on us, and I know it's only a matter of time before Corban will notice.

"I think those ladies over there wouldn't mind you pointing that lens in their direction for a moment," I murmur, tilting my chin toward a group of women to our left.

They've been fluffing their hair and batting their lashes in Corban's direction for several minutes, all but salivating at the idea of being captured by his astute photographer's eye.

They aren't the first people I've seen blatantly seeking out the cameras tonight, eager to secure proof of their proximity to wealth and fame.

Corban rolls his eyes. "Here we go again. I was nearly assaulted earlier by two women offering... let's just say, very *creative* favours if I managed to capture them with Tom Holland and Timothée Chalamet in the background."

He shudders theatrically before winking playfully. "As you said, the night is young. Let's see how insane these requests get before it's over. Catch you later, Els."

I watch his retreating form, barely stifling a laugh as the women pounce on him the moment he's within reach, swarming him with eager smiles and fluttering lashes. His look of mild horror makes me snort as I turn back to Orlando.

The laughter dies in my throat.

Orlando drags a slow, hungry gaze down my body, lingering shamelessly on the delicate silver pendant dipping beneath my neckline before flicking back up to meet my eyes. His lips part slightly, his mouth moving in a silent whisper as he mouths, *You're breathtaking, sirena.*

The unspoken words sear my skin, as surely as if he'd whispered them directly in my ear. A ripple of heat moves down my spine.

I take a tentative step toward him, but stop short when he subtly shakes his head.

The warmth in my chest is instantly doused, doubt creeping in before I can stop it. But before my thoughts can spiral, Orlando gestures to the group of men at his side with the barest tilt of his head.

I immediately spot Domenico. He's in the centre of the circle, surrounded by a handful of men laughing loudly at something he just said. Now that I'm no longer hyper-focused on Orlando, I tune into their voices cutting through the room—booming, boisterous, and completely unaware of anything around them.

When I glance back at Orlando, he's discreetly scanning their reactions, confirming none of them caught our exchange. Looking back at me, he nods ever so subtly in the direction of the hallway entrance as he mouths, "Bathrooms. One hour."

I give the smallest nod of understanding.

His face doesn't change, but something in his posture shifts as he turns back to the group of men, seamlessly rejoining the conversation.

My heart pounds as I force myself to move, my heart skittering inside my chest.

One hour.

Giddy with anticipation, I rejoin Emma and Keisha, praying that the next hour passes quickly.

Chapter Forty-One

An hour later, I'm pacing outside the entrance to the women's bathroom, anticipation coiling in my stomach as I wait for Orlando to appear.

I lost sight of him when he followed Domenico into the gardens for an impromptu photo shoot, and I was too wary of being caught lurking in the background to follow.

Peering down the long hallway, I listen to the distant hum of music and laughter drifting from the ballroom, my ears attuned to approaching footsteps. The bathroom door behind me swings open, and I nod absently at a tall woman in a striking red gown as she exits, watching her disappear through the entryway to the party.

Strong hands suddenly appear out of nowhere, wrapping around my waist as I'm yanked around the corner. A startled yelp escapes my lips as I whirl around, my hands lifting to protect myself—only for my breath to catch as Orlando's mouth crashes down on mine.

His lips are fervent and insistent, searing away my surprise as he pulls me flush against him, eliminating the space between us. A shaky exhale slips from me as I melt into his embrace, my fingers grasping at the lapels of his suit jacket for balance.

His tongue teases the seam of my lips before slipping inside, coaxing mine into a slow, intoxicating dance. The kiss deepens, breaths turning ragged as our bodies press closer. His hands slide down my back, skimming over the curve of my waist before settling on my ass in a firm grip.

With effortless strength, he lifts me into his arms, and my legs instinctively wrap around his waist. A low groan rumbles in his chest as my core presses against the hard length tucked beneath his suit trousers.

"Holy fuck, sirena," he pants, voice rough with desire. "You're killing me in that dress."

He moves forward until my back meets the cool stone wall, using it as leverage to press himself against me. Heat sparks through my veins as his hands roam, exploring every curve of my body.

He barely pulls away, breath hot against my lips as he darts a quick glance around the corner. Satisfied we're alone, his hands return to my waist, sliding up to graze over my breasts, his mouth following the path his fingers chart.

"Oh god, Orlando," I exhale in a breathy moan, my body thrumming with anticipation. I want him to tug the fabric down, to feel his warm mouth on my skin, taking me apart piece by piece. Even through the barrier of my dress, the graze of his thumb across my nipple sends bolts of pleasure coursing through me.

"I want you so bad, Elaina," he groans, need building in his voice. His lips skim the hollow of my throat, breaths teasing my skin. "I want nothing more than to throw you over my shoulder and carry you back to my cabin right now. How the hell am I supposed to get through the rest of the evening with a fucking boner tenting my pants? You drive me insane."

His heated words are like fuel to the fire already burning inside me. My hands slip between us, tugging his shirt free from the waistband of his trousers. Eager fingertips trail over rigid muscles, mapping every ridge and dip of his sculpted torso.

"Take me there. Now. Please," I whisper, my voice laced with raw desperation. I barely recognise this version of myself, but I know with absolute certainty that I've never wanted anything more in my life.

Orlando groans, his forehead pressing against mine.

"I can't. Fucking hell, *I can't*," he mutters, pained self-restraint dripping from each syllable. "Domenico needs me tonight. He'll notice if I disappear. *Fuck!*"

The curse barely slips from his lips before his mouth crashes down on mine again, devouring my breathy gasp as he grinds himself against me.

Stars burst behind my eyelids, and my head tilts back against the stone as a low moan escapes.

"I'm going to come if you keep doing that," I whimper, heat flooding my cheeks.

The sound of approaching footsteps shatters the moment.

Orlando's body tenses as muffled laughter mixes with the sharp clickety-clack of heels echoing down the corridor.

"You've got to be kidding me," he growls. His heavy exhale bleeds frustration into the narrow space between us. "Is it so fucking difficult to get a moment alone in this massive castle?"

We stay frozen, ears tuned as the drunken giggles of two women bounce off the stone walls.

My legs remain wrapped around Orlando's waist, reluctant to let go. My body's still buzzing from the intensity of our stolen moment, but the sharp sound of more approaching footsteps quickly forces reality back into focus.

Orlando pulls back slightly, pained emerald eyes locking onto mine. His grip tightens for a fleeting second before his lips part.

"I want to take you back to my cabin tonight."

My heart stutters.

"I've never taken anyone there before," he admits, his fingers tracing slow, feather-light patterns along my waist. "But I want you there with me. Just us. Where no one can interrupt us."

His thumb brushes against my cheek, his voice a seductive whisper as he leans closer. "I want to watch your eyes spark in the firelight as I whisper in your ear how breathtaking you are. I want to feel your body against mine and taste every inch of you. I want to kiss you until the moonlight fades and the sunrise paints your skin in gold. Will you come with me, sirena?"

My breath catches. His voice—low, rich, and edged with that intoxicating accent—draws a visceral quake through every nerve-ending. I can barely think, let alone speak.

I can only nod.

A slow, tantalising smile flashes across his face before he dips his head to brush the softest kiss against my parted lips—a mere whisper of a touch, yet more intimate than any other kiss we're shared tonight.

"Good."

With a final, meaningful look, he lowers my feet to the ground.

"I'll find you before the night is over," he murmurs, his fingers lingering on my waist for a heartbeat longer. "Until then, *mi sirena*."

With a devilish wink, he disappears around the corner, leaving me with trembling knees and a racing heart.

Chapter Forty-Two

No matter how hard I try to act unaffected, I repeatedly seek out Orlando in the crowd over the next hour.

I talk and laugh with the girls, sway to the music flowing from the speakers, and gossip shamelessly about the celebrities scattered around the ballroom.

And yet, a molten fire has been burning me up from the inside all night. The memory of Orlando's hands on me makes it impossible to stay present, every thought centred on the man who's slowly and irrevocably infiltrating my heart.

As *Big Energy* by Latto pulses through the room, luring more than a few people onto the dance floor, I steal yet another peek in his direction.

His face remains expressionless, but his posture is relaxed as he stands beside Domenico, who is deep in conversation with yet another cluster of high-profile guests. A tall, long-legged blonde has hooked her claws into the illustrious hotel owner for the evening, her fire-red nails digging into his arm, a *come-fuck-me* look radiating from her lust-filled eyes.

"Looks like Boss Man's already lined up his catch for the night," Keisha comments, and I look over to find her capturing the same scene. Luckily, she doesn't seem to have picked up on the real reason why my eyes have been tracking Domenico's side of the room all evening—a reason that has little to do with the CEO himself, and everything to do with the brooding man standing beside him.

"Let's see if he can limit it to just one hussy tonight," Emma quips, joining us with three flutes of champagne in hand. I accept the glass she offers and take a slow sip, revelling in the delicate bubbles sliding down my throat. I'm already on my fourth glass and counting.

I know I should probably slow down, but the smouldering inferno simmering low in my belly, and the nervous anticipation of going back to Orlando's cabin later tonight, is making me all kinds of jittery. So far, the steady stream of champagne seems to be the only thing keeping the tingling nerves at bay.

"Wanna see if we can snag some hors d'oeuvres from the kitchen before all the good stuff's gone?" Emma asks, eyeing a tray of skewered prawns sailing by.

"Oh, hell yes," Keisha moans, rubbing her belly. "I haven't eaten anything since this morning. I'm starving."

Feeling my own stomach rumble in protest, my empty belly echoes her sentiment. I move to follow the girls through the back entrance to the kitchens when a prickling sensation at the back of my neck stops me—the kind that makes the fine hairs on my arms stand on end.

It's a sudden, creeping sensation telling me I'm being watched.

Turning, I scan the room, skimming over the throngs of dancing guests as the eerie feeling only intensifies. A cold tingle slithers down my back, and my fingers tighten instinctively around the stem of my glass.

And then, I see him.

At first, my brain struggles to place the greased-back hair and cold, assessing stare boring into me from across the room. But the longer I hold his gaze, the more vivid the sickening realisation unfurling within me becomes.

I know this man.

The ghost of a memory slowly ignites from deep within the recesses of my mind.

Simon, his customary grey suit immaculate, his usual stoic air in place as he leads me into Viktor's office.

A group of men, Viktor among them, standing in a tight circle around his large mahogany desk, peering down at an array of polyester-coated blueprints. A snatched glimpse of white lines, overlapping geometric shapes stretching across a navy background.

A ripple of revulsion shivering down my spine as my eyes briefly meet those of a short, thick-necked, barrel-chested man with bushy brows and a protruding belly. Crooked teeth poking out beneath a lewd, cynical smirk. Thick, stubby hands resting atop his stomach. A fleeting, heavy-lidded wink shot my way.

A salacious, canine grin that disappears the moment Viktor lifts his head.

As I stare into those cold, twisted eyes across the sea of people, I immediately know it's the same man.

I don't think. I don't wait.

I just run.

Darting for the exit, I weave between the clusters of guests, my breaths coming fast and uneven. Panic claws its way to the surface, screaming at me what I already know.

It's over. They've found me. They'll come for me.

And when they do...

No. Not now. Please, not yet!

But I can't afford to lose myself to the desperation drowning my heart. I have to put as much distance between myself and that man as possible.

I'm three metres from the door when—

"Oh! There you are, Elaina."

I pivot, nearly losing my balance as Cindy appears in front of me, accompanied by a tall, elegant woman with a sleek, A-line bob framing her strikingly sharp face. Her shimmery dress clings to her body like a second skin, the ebony colour matching the glossy sheen of her hair.

"I've been looking for you," Cindy chirps, fingers curling around my arm before I can bolt. "I wanted to introduce you to one of our most valued sponsors for this evening. Colette, meet Elaina Delano. Elaina, this is Collette Valois, the CEO of VelourLocks."

Cindy yanks me forward with a proud smile, oblivious to my face screaming for escape. I barely register her words as she rattles on about my role in tonight's event, my eyes busy scanning the room for signs of him.

But when they dart across the crowded hall, I don't see him anywhere.

And somehow, that's even worse.

Colette extends a slim, manicured hand, her manner one of polite indifference. I grasp it reluctantly, wanting nothing more than to flee this conversation.

"It's a pleasure to meet you, Ms Valois," I force out, wringing my lips into a tight smile.

"Likewise," Colette replies in a languid, bored tone, her French accent thick. She swiftly withdraws her hand, rummaging through her purse for a pack of cigarettes.

Cindy, clearly oblivious to my panicked discomfort and Colette's obvious disinterest, launches into a long-winded monologue about VelourLocks' upcoming partnership with the hotel. I nod absently, scattered throughs elsewhere as my heart hammers in my chest.

I can't keep standing here. *I can't stay here.*

"I desperately need to visit the ladies' room," I blurt, cutting Cindy off mid-sentence. "Will you excuse me?"

Without waiting for a response, I slip through the doors and sprint down the hallway.

The sounds from the party fades as the stone walls echo my pounding footsteps. My heels slam against the marble floor as I weave down corridor after corridor, pulse thundering in my ears.

I turn the last corner that will lead me to the lobby—and freeze.

He's already there, casually leaning against the door as he blocks my exit.

"Well, well, well," he drawls, his Russian accent thickening each word. A slow, suggestive grin curves his lips. "I figured you would be headed this way."

Pushing off the wall, his deliberate steps land like weights in my chest, each pressing tighter as his beady eyes glint with anticipation.

"What do you want?" I snap, forcing my chin up.

I know men like him. They feed off weakness.

And I refuse to give him the satisfaction of seeing my fear.

"Ouch. So touchy," he murmurs, his grin widening. "We are just having conversation, kitten. No need for sourness."

"I don't feel much like having a conversation right now," I bite out, grateful when my voice comes out firm and unwavering.

"Oh, come now, sweet dove," he coos, taking another slow step toward me. "I just want to talk."

"Well, *I* don't."

He tuts loudly. "They really need to improve service level at hotel. I heard it is excellent, but you must not have gotten memo, kitten."

"What do you want?" I repeat, refusing to entertain his little show of dominance.

"I just want to know why you make quick exit," he replies evenly, peering at me from beneath unkempt eyebrows.

You know damn well why.

I seethe, silently cursing him with every foul word I can think of for dragging this out—for making me play along with whatever twisted game he wants to play.

"I must say, it is new experience for me," he continues, adjusting his belt loop to keep his ill-fitting suit pants from slipping down. "Women usually fall to their knees when I enter room." His lurid smirk makes my spine shiver.

I take in his thick-necked frame, his sagging jowls, and his sweaty, weathered skin.

He's utterly repulsive. And yet, I know better than to say that aloud.

I fight to keep my expression firmly blank, even as a slight, mocking lift of my eyebrow slips through.

If he notices, he doesn't react.

"With such speed of escape, someone might think you were... running from something, sweet dove."

You know I'm running from something, I scream in my head. *I'm running from you! From Viktor. From all of it!*

Defeat crashes down on me with the weight of a tidal wave.

I finally have a life. A job I love. Friends I adore. Freedom. Laughter and happiness. A life worth living.

Orlando...

The thought of never seeing him again is too painful to bear. I push it aside, swallowing against the tightness in my throat.

"Please," I whisper, failing to keep the tremor from my voice. "Just let me go."

"I cannot do that, kitten." His smile doesn't waver. "Not until you answer one little question for me."

A hundred possibilities race through my mind.

Why did you steal the blueprints? Did you really think you could escape Viktor? Did you really think we wouldn't find you?

Are you ready to die?

I brace myself. My window for escape is closing.

I bite the inside of my cheek, waiting for him to get on with it.

There's an unexpected air of curiosity in his voice when he finally asks, "Who are you?"

The question slams into me with the force of a freight train.

What?

He doesn't know who I am?

But... he *must* know if Viktor sent him here to find me.

Unless—

The confusion must be plain on my face because the man chuckles darkly. "You see, I recognised your face the moment I saw you in ballroom—and from petrified look in your eye, I think you recognise me too. But I cannot remember where I see you before. It is driving me... what is term? *Bez-úmnyy.* Crazy."

I stare blankly at him, my mind racing.

Holy shit.

He doesn't know who I am.

That means he isn't here on Viktor's orders.

He's not here to take me back.

A blinding stab of relief pulses through me, nearly taking me to my knees, but it doesn't last long. Even if he doesn't recognise me now, it would only take one phone call—one brief visit to Viktor's estate—for it all to come crashing down. And when it does, Viktor will send an army after me.

I still have to run. But now, I have a chance.

I take a cautious step back, trying to put some distance between us so I can think. But as I move, the hair clip Paige used to fasten my hair slips free and clatters to the floor, sending honeyed waves spilling over my shoulders.

The moment my hair falls free, I see it—the flash of recognition.

My heart plummets.

"It can't be..." he mutters, eyebrows narrowing as he studies me more closely. His black, beady eyes trail over my face, then my hair—so much darker and shorter than the last time he saw me. But still, undeniably similar.

I should've cut it all off. I should've dyed it all red.

"Surely, it cannot be..." His lips curl into a grotesque grin. "Ah, but yes. Yes, how could I possibly forget? Pretty face like yours usually sticks in brain, sweet dove. But now, I remember."

His voice drops into a low, almost reverent tone. "You are Viktor's little pet."

My body goes rigid, blood turning to ice.

No... No, no, no!

A chilling laugh rattles through the empty hallway. The man folds his arms over his bulging belly, taking another step closer.

He's close enough now that I can smell the stale stench of sweat and old cigarettes clinging to him. I would gag if I wasn't already so nauseated I can barely breathe.

"Ah, yes. Little Miss *Isabella.*" His smile widens, eyes gleaming. "You are exactly what I need to get back into good graces of organisation. I can already feel gratitude Viktor will show when I bring his lost *lapochka* back to him."

"No." My voice breaks as I back against the wall, panic gripping my chest like a vice. "Please. Please don't take me back to him."

His bloated hand reaches out, stubby fingers grasping at my dress—

"What's going on out here?"

The deep voice slices through the air, and a wave of relief slams into me so forcefully my knees nearly buckle.

The man's arm jerks back like he's been burned. We both swivel our heads as Orlando strides down the hallway, his glare zeroed in on the man in front of me.

He doesn't stop until he's right beside me, his presence a solid wall of protection as his hand finds the small of my back.

"Are you okay?" His voice is low and measured, but his eyes blaze with a stormy darkness, heavy with unspoken questions.

I try to answer, but my throat is too tight to speak, so I nod instead.

Orlando's back straightens immeasurably, his fingers pressing ever so lightly against my spine.

He doesn't believe me.

My near captor recovers quickly, flashing a lazy grin. "Everything is good here."

"Is that so?" Orlando's voice is flat, laced with ice.

"Yes." The man's expression doesn't waver. "Isabella and I were just having friendly conversation."

Orlando stiffens. When he looks from the man to me, his gaze is calculating. "And how do you know *Isabella* here, Mr Kuznetsov?"

My heart slams against my ribs.

Orlando knows this man?

"Ah, we go way back." Kuznetsov's grin widens. "I was very surprised to see her here this evening. It has been some time since our last meeting. I wanted to... *catch up*."

"Ah, I see." Orlando's tone is indecipherable. "Well, I'm actually glad I ran into you, Vadim. Mr de Águila asked to steal fifteen minutes of your time. He has a business proposition he wanted to discuss with you."

Intrigue sparks in Vadim's eyes. "And what is this proposition?"

Orlando doesn't so much as blink. "One he wouldn't want to discuss with other ears present." He doesn't look at me when he adds, "And I believe *Isabella* here was on her way somewhere?"

I don't hesitate.

Without another glance at either man, I bolt for the door.

I'm already sprinting when my feet hit the cobblestones outside.

Chapter Forty-Three

By the time heavy footsteps pound up the stairs outside the cabin, I'm stuffing the last of my belongings into my duffel bag.

The door flies open without so much as a knock, and Orlando fills the frame, his broad chest heaving, expression thunderous.

I barely glance at him.

Turning my attention back to my packing, I still feel the weight of his gaze as it traps the air. He shifts his focus to Tiana's bed, where my half-zipped bag lies open, clothes and belongings jumbled in a disorganised mess. The tension rolling off him deepens as I toss my toiletry bag on top of the pile.

"Why are you packing?" His voice is calm and even, suppressing the emotions simmering just beneath the surface.

I don't stop what I'm doing as I reply, "It's what people do when they intend to leave."

"And why are you leaving?"

"Because it's time."

"That's a bullshit answer and you know it," he snaps, his tone rapidly losing its edge of restraint—not that there was much to begin with.

"Says the master of deflection," I quip. Sensing his anger flare, I speak before he can cut in. "Just drop it, Orlando. I really don't have time for this." I move past him, reaching for my hairbrush on top of the small vanity table.

"You're not going anywhere."

I freeze as my fingers tighten around the brush. My back is still to him as I inject as much iciness into my voice as I can muster. "Say that again?"

"You're not going anywhere," Orlando repeats, tone unyielding.

I spin to snap at him—and nearly stumble as he storms across the cabin, movements sharp and full of purpose. In a blink, his large hands seize my duffel bag, flipping it over and shaking the contents onto the bed.

I shriek as my belongings tumble out, some scattering to the floor. "What the hell are you doing, you lumbering lunatic?!"

Lunging for the bag, I rip it from his grip before he can do any more damage. My eyes dart over the mess, stomach unclenching slightly when I don't spot the blueprints anywhere. They must still be tucked safely inside the inside pocket.

"Helping you unpack. I'm generous like that." Orlando doesn't even blink as he meets my furious glare.

My lips part, ready to curse him out, but his next words stop me cold.

"How do you know Vadim Kuznetsov, and why the fuck does the sight of him have you scuttling away into the night like a scared little mouse?"

His words are so direct, so searing, that it takes me a second to push past the chilling shock of him calling me 'little mouse'.

That is, until the anger and fear I've been fighting to suppress finally claws its way to the surface.

"One—it's none of your fucking business. And two—how dare you demand answers from me, just days after you promised we'd talk so *you* could finally open up to *me*? I guess that was just another trick to keep me pacified. Is that why you didn't come yesterday? So you could keep dodging my questions while piling on your own?"

I'm seething, my breaths coming fast, chest rising and falling with the force of my frustration.

Orlando takes a step back, some of the anger slipping from his face. "I wasn't lying when I said we would talk. I still have every intention of telling you what I can."

I scoff loudly, but he doesn't waver.

"I didn't lie to you, Elaina. But I won't have much of a chance to prove that to you if you're not even going to listen."

"Well, you can save your breath, because I don't have any interest in talking to people who're in the business of making deals with men like *that.*"

A beat of silence follows my words.

Shit. I shouldn't have said that.

Orlando's eyes narrow, understanding sharpening his expression.

"*Men like that,* huh?" he murmurs, peeling back my layers with terrifying ease. "And what would you know about 'men like that', sirena?"

"What would *you* know about them?" I fire back, fortifying my walls.

"Oh, I know a great many things about a great many men," he says smoothly. "Including Vadim Kuznetsov. It comes with the territory when you're connected to a family as powerful as the de Águilas."

"Well then, *almighty one*, it shouldn't come as a shock that a girl might want to get far away from a man like Vadim," I snap, nerves fraying by the second.

I need to get the hell out of here.

Every minute wasted is another minute granted in favour of Viktor's pursuit.

"It's not," Orlando concedes, his voice cooling again. "What I don't yet know is how you found yourself mixed up with someone like Kuznetsov in the first place."

"I could ask you the same question," I bite out. Orlando may be an expert at crawling under my skin, but this is my life hanging in the balance.

I've already revealed far too much—more than I ever thought I'd reveal to anyone.

No more.

The air between us crackles with tension, thick and unyielding. I hold his stare, expecting another battle of wills, but in the breath of a second, something in him shifts.

His shoulders loosen, his posture softening ever so slightly. When he speaks again, his voice is heavier, almost resigned.

"This is getting us nowhere." Sighing, he drops onto Tiana's bed as he rests his head in his hands.

The sudden pivot stuns me into silence. After nearly a minute of wordless tension, I sit beside him, the weight of our confrontation still hanging thick in the air.

Without lifting his head, Orlando mutters, "Kuznetsov works for Rhett Harrington."

"The billionaire?" Surprise colours my voice.

"The very same." He nods. "Harrington's company owns dozens of entertainment venues and nightclubs worldwide. He recently entered a partnership with Trident Ventures to establish a high-end bar chain on their new luxury cruise line, *Ocean Elite*. Mattia caught wind of it early and convinced Domenico to invest heavily in Trident Ventures before the deal went public."

I stay silent, sensing there's more.

"In recent years, Harrington's been trying to expand into Europe, but he's struggled to gain traction. His most successful entry point has been Eastern Europe, riding on the recent tourism boom. Vadim's one of his key contacts there.

Mattia—never one to miss an opportunity—has been using that connection to strengthen the partnership. When Harrington couldn't make it tonight, Mattia extended the invitation to Vadim and a few of Harrington's other European contacts."

Orlando's voice trails off, and silence settles between us once more.

I understand why Vadim's here tonight now, but the explanation doesn't do much to ease my concern. If anything, it raises more questions.

"So this business proposition Domenico wanted to discuss with him..." I venture, breaking the stretched silence. "Was that for Rhett Harrington?"

"There was no business proposition." Orlando's voice is flat. "That was just a ruse to get him the fuck away from you."

I gape at him.

"Vadim's a lowlife. A nobody in the grand scheme of things. While he's useful to Harrington's expansion, Domenico would never discuss business directly with him. But Vadim's a proud fucker. He thinks he's more important than he actually is. I figured, if he thought his moment had finally come, he'd take the bait."

"And why were you so intent on getting him away from me?"

Orlando's mood darkens visibly. "When I found you in the hallway with him—his body crowding you, his hands reaching for you—I nearly lost my shit, Elaina. Then, when I saw the fear in your eyes... I wanted to fucking end him."

His jaw clenches, hands curling into fists. "I would *never* let anyone hurt you, sirena."

His words settle deep inside me, healing something fragile and long buried. But they don't change the reality of my situation.

I still have to leave.

And while I can't tell Orlando everything, I know I have to tell him *something*—enough for him to understand why I can't stay.

He'll never let me go if I don't.

"It doesn't matter," I whisper, the words barely audible beneath the crushing dread suffocating my voice. "Vadim—he has a connection to my former life. A life I ran from. One phone call from him, and everything I've built here crumbles. My past will finally catch up with me."

Kuznetsov's likely already on the phone with Viktor, arranging my capture.

I need to leave. *Now.*

I've escaped before. I can do it again.

"Kuznetsov won't be calling anyone. You can trust me on that."

I draw back. "You don't know that."

"I do." Orlando's voice is steady and unwavering, penetrating me with an ironclad resolve.

"*How*? You don't even know what him finding me here means."

"I don't need to." His tone is absolute. "Vadim Kuznetsov meant to harm you tonight. That's all I needed to know. He didn't tell me much when I interrogated him, but he revealed enough to know that *someone* is looking for you, sirena. And Kuznetsov was determined to help them find you. I made sure he understands, down to the very marrow of his bones, that if he so much as breathes a word of your whereabouts, he'll regret it to his dying breath—which, as Vadim now well knows, would come shortly after."

"I—I..." My panic surges. I shoot to my feet, desperate to move—somewhere, *anywhere*—to escape these confusing, stifling thoughts.

Before I can take a single step, Orlando clasps my trembling hand, anchoring me.

"You're safe, Elaina." His voice is gentle but firm. "Kuznetsov doesn't know you work here. He thinks you were just a guests here tonight, gone by the morning. And now, he has a crystal-clear understanding of what will happen if he even *thinks* of endangering you."

A cold gleam flares in Orlando's eyes. "A subtle reminder of what Rhett Harrison would do if Kuznetsov single-handedly destroyed his *incredibly* profitable relationship with the de Águilas was more than enough to seal his mouth shut. Of course, I made sure to reinforce that lesson—with a few personal touches."

Orlando lifts my chin, his touch feather-light. His eyes search mine, probing but sincere, willing me to trust him.

"I promise you, Elaina. No matter what or who you're running from, you're safe here. With me. Kuznetsov's not a threat to you. He won't hurt you. I know you're not ready to tell me everything, and you don't have to—not yet. Just trust me when I say that I would do anything to protect you. I wouldn't ask you to stay here if I thought it would put your life in danger." His voice drops to a plea. "Please, sirena. *Trust me.*"

Desperation laces his words.

God, how I want to believe him.

I search his face, looking for deception, for any flicker of doubt.

All I find is sincerity, firm and unwavering.

"Stay with me, sirena. Please stay with me." His words are raw and unguarded. "I will always protect you."

With those words, my resolve shatters.

A sob rips from my throat as I crash into him, lips colliding in a desperate, fevered kiss. A growl rumbles through his chest as he meets every slide of my tongue with searing intensity. The heat between us ignites, consuming every coherent thought.

My legs give out beneath me, but Orlando's already shifting us, pulling me onto his lap as he guides my thighs around his torso.

My dress bunches up around my waist as his hands grip my hips, dragging me closer. His body presses into me, his growing arousal straining against my core, separated only by a few thin layers of fabric.

"*Fuck,*" Orlando groans, his fingers skimming up my bare shoulders, teasing the delicate curve of my breasts before gliding down my waist to settle at my hips. "You're all I can think about, sirena."

His words ignite a trail of flames along my skin.

His lips crash back to mine, devouring and claiming, burning with a need that matches my own. My nails claw at his suit jacket, frantic and desperate. He shifts beneath me, allowing me to peel it from his body, and I toss it blindly behind us. My hands find his shirt next, clutching at the fabric, as if it's the only thing keeping me tethered to reality.

We're still clothed, yet the heat from his every touch is unbearable.

The ache between my thighs is unbearable.

I whimper into his mouth as he moves me further onto his lap, positioning me exactly where I need him. His thick length presses against my core, teasing me with every slow, torturous roll of his hips.

Stars explode behind my eyelids as pleasure spears through me, sharp and all-consuming.

"Oh god," I gasp as his teeth scrape along my jaw, down to the hollow of my throat. My body is a live wire, igniting as I unravel."More," I plead, the word slipping from my lips without conscious thought.

Orlando stills. For a terrifying second, I think he's going to pull away.

But then—mercifully—his grip tightens, his fingers sliding beneath my dress, skimming the edge of my panties.

"Fuck, sirena." His voice is thick with lust. "I can feel your wetness through the fabric."

A strangled moan catches in my throat as I arch into him, chasing friction—chasing *him.*

His lips find my collarbone, planting soft, teasing kisses along its length as his fingers toy with the waistband of the soft silk.

The anticipation is torture.

"Patience, sirena," he murmurs when he feels me wriggle against him, his smirk pressing into my skin. "All good things come to those who wait."

"No more waiting," I gasp, my hips jolting forward, desperate to soothe the ache building inside me.

A low chuckle vibrates against my neck—and then, he finally gives me what I need.

His fingers dip beneath the silk, gliding over my slick folds.

A loud moan slips from my throat.

"Holy fuck, Elaina."

We groan in unison as his fingers stroke me—teasing, coaxing, his touch sending heat pooling low in my belly.

"Fuck, baby. You're so wet," he rasps, his voice thick with need. "So fucking hot."

"Orlando, I—I... that's—*Oh my god.*"

I can't think, can't breathe, as each slow, precise stroke of his fingers sends me spiralling higher. His gaze locks onto mine, molten silver shimmering with unrestrained hunger.

"You're so beautiful, sirena. Look at you—all flushed and needy for me. I could watch you like this for hours."

His words turn my skin on fire, making my whole body ache for more.

Sliding back on his lap, I give myself just enough room as I reach for his belt, undoing the button and zipper until his boxers come into view, his thick length straining against the fabric. Before he can protest, I grab the waistband and tug it down, my breath hitching as his cock springs free.

A guttural groan rumbles up his throat, the sound raw and visceral.

It's the hottest thing I've ever heard in my entire life.

I nearly forget my own building pleasure as I watch the way his head tips back, his lips parting on a hiss as I wrap my hand around his cock, feeling the velvety hardness beneath my fingertips. His hips jerk at the contact.

"*Fuck, fuck, fuck...*" The words spill from his lips in a ragged whisper as he thrusts into my grip, his fingers stilling for a breathless second before resuming their fevered rhythm against my core.

One finger slides through my folds before sinking inside, stretching me as he slowly fills me, inch by inch.

I yelp, my spine arching as his thumb presses softly against my clit.

"Yeah? You like that, baby?" Orlando's eyes flutter open, burning with lust as he watches me, drowning me in liquid heat.

"*Yes*. Oh god. Don't stop. Please don't stop."

"Your hand around my cock is going to be the fucking death of me, sirena. I'm not gonna last long if you keep doing that."

His words only spur me on.

Lowering my head, I watch the mesmerising slide of his long, thick shaft between my clenched fist, the tip glistening with pre-cum, his slick wetness coating every inch of him.

The wet sounds of our mutual pleasure fill the air, drowning out all other noise, all other thoughts.

Just him.

Just this.

Just *us.*

"So fucking wet," Orlando pants, the friction against my clit intensifying as uninhibited desire flares in his eyes. "Tight and ready and soaked for me. You close, baby?"

"Yes, I'm so close. Oh god, I-I'm almost there—"

"Fuck, baby," he groans, slipping another finger inside me, curling just right—and I explode.

My walls tighten around him, my body trembling as pleasure rips through me, shattering the world into a thousand tiny pieces.

Orlando watches me intently, tension fracturing into something raw and primal. As the shivers of my release ricochet through me, my thighs clench around his hand as my pussy squeezes tight around his fingers, still moving relentlessly against my clit.

Orlando's control finally snaps.

"Fuck, baby. I'm gonna come. Baby, I'm gonna come. I'm—fuck. *Fuck!*"

His head falls back, a guttural roar tearing from his throat as his release crashes through him, thick ropes of cum spilling across his stomach.

The sight alone is enough to send me over the edge again

I shatter once more, crying out his name as renewed waves of pleasure course through every limb, leaving me falling, flying, floating in a vacuum of euphoria as we fall apart together.

Slowly spiralling back to consciousness, we clutch each other tightly, breaths sharp and chests heaving.

"Holy shit." Orlando's voice is raspy with coarseness as he rests his forehead against mine, his hand slipping from my panties to rest softly against my hip.

"Yeah... Holy shit."

We say nothing for several long moments, wrapped in the haze of lingering touches and slowing breaths, hands still tracing invisible patterns over each other.

Until—

The door slams open with enough force to shake the walls as it springs off its hinges.

"What the—?" Orlando jolts upright, his sudden movement throwing me off balance. I tumble backward, landing in a spectacularly ungraceful heap on the floor.

Orlando's on his feet in an instant, one hand gripping me as he yanks me back up, while the other hurriedly shoves his dick back into his boxers.

My heart hammers as I scramble to my feet, pulling my dress down with frantic hands. I spin toward the door, my pulse slamming in my ears.

Tiana stands frozen in the doorway, eyes wide, mouth slightly open, her cheeks flushed with embarrassment. Or... amusement?

"Oh my god!"

"Oh my god!" I echo, whipping my head from her to Orlando as I smooth my palms over my dress, making sure everything that should be covered is covered.

Behind me, Orlando fumbles with his zipper, working to button his pants with slightly less grace than he usually exudes.

"I'm so sorry," Tiana shrieks, her voice an octave higher than I've ever heard it before. "I swear, I didn't mean to barge in when you guys were doing... well, *that*." A slow grin curls her lips. "But *damn*. That shit was *hot*."

Heat scorches my neck. "Tiana, we weren't—I mean, I-I—" I stammer, struggling to string together a coherent sentence.

Tiana waves a dismissive hand. "Save it. You can tell me all about *this*"—she flicks a finger between Orlando and me—"later."

She sobers, and for the first time, I notice the tension radiating off her. "Right now, we have a serious problem."

A cold weight settles in my stomach.

"What do you mean?"

Tiana flicks a glance between us, her brows knitting together. "What the hell are you doing back here, anyway? With everything going down at the castle, I figured Cindy would have the whole events crew on lock down."

My frown deepens. "What do you mean? What's happening at the castle?"

Tiana's eyes widen, and she stares at me in disbelief. "You don't know?"

Trepidation churns in my gut. "No. I left not long ago to come here."

Tiana's complexion pales, her lips pressing into a tight line. "They found a body in the castle."

The air is sucked from the room in an instant.

My heartbeat stumbles, my breaths catching painfully in my throat.

The words echo in my head, over and over, warping into meaningless sounds. A loud, rushing whoosh fills my ears, muffling everything else. The floor beneath me tilts, the room blurring in and out of focus as I try to grasp onto a single thought. To understand.

But my mind scatters, disjointed fragments slipping like sand through my fingers.

"Elaina..."

Somewhere in the distance, I catch Orlando calling my name, his voice strained. Urgent.

The sound snaps me back to reality.

And with it, everything comes crashing down on me, all at once.

Kuznetsov cornering me. Orlando pulling him away. Orlando finding me at my cabin, packed and ready to run. His plea for me to stay. His promise that I'm safe. That Kuznetsov's not a threat.

That he won't hurt me...

I whirl to stare at Orlando with wide-eyed disbelief, my pulse a frantic, erratic drum inside my ribcage.

His face is pale, his eyes round with something dangerously close to panic.

"Elaina, please listen to me—"

"Orlando." My voice is barely a whisper, yet it cuts through the space between us like a knife.

"What on earth have you done?"

TO BE CONTINUED...

AUTHOR'S NOTE

Thank you, wonderful reader, for picking up Where Shadows Whisper. Writing this book has been one of the most vulnerable and challenging journeys I've ever taken, and it means the world that you chose to step into this world with me.

This story was born from my love of romance novels that weave together slow-burn tension, a suspenseful plot, and layered character growth. I wanted to take you not only through the twists and turns of Elaina and Orlando's romance, but also into the deeper struggles they face—how life, love, and trust can be tested, broken, and slowly rebuilt. I've always gravitated toward stories where plot, romance, and character arcs are tightly intertwined, each one pushing the others forward, and I hope you were able to experience that journey with me in Where Shadows Whisper.

It wasn't always an easy book to write. Elaina's journey, in particular, weighed heavily on me at times. Her choices, her scars, and the shadows that clung to her were often challenging to explore, and there were moments where I felt the weight of her journey pressing down on me, reminding me how hard it can be to find light in the darkness. Orlando's presence, equally steady and storm-tossed, became her counterpoint—and their story often surprised me, pulling me deeper than I expected to go.

There are some heavy moments in these pages—both for me in the writing, and perhaps for you in the reading. But I felt those darker chapters deserved the weight they carry. I didn't want to gloss over the shadows, yet I also didn't want this story to be only about pain. Beneath the secrets, danger, betrayal, and darkness, this book is, at its core, about survival, the fragile rebuilding of trust, and the stubborn, unyielding hope that healing, though never simple, is always possible.

My deepest hope is that within these pages, you also found glimmers of resilience, tenderness, and the kind of love that doesn't erase the past, but helps carry it.

From the bottom of my heart, thank you for reading my debut novel, and for taking a chance on an indie author. I hope Elaina and Orlando's journey touched you as deeply as it touched me in writing it, and I cannot wait to share the rest of their story with you.

And the shadows aren't done whispering yet... Part Two of Elaina and Orlando's story is already in the works, so stay tuned.

With love & gratitude,
Amara Phoenix

ACKNOWLEDGEMENTS

I can't quite believe I'm here, writing the acknowledgements of my debut novel. To think that a story that once only existed in my head has now become a real book feels surreal. I still remember that day back in 2021, when, with my partner's encouragement, I finally sat down and began sketching out the bare bones of what would eventually become *Where Shadows Whisper*. I could never have imagined that four years later, those scattered ideas would transform into this—a finished book ready to find its way into readers' hands. It has been a journey filled with doubt, discovery, and determination, and it could never have happened without the wonderful people who encouraged me and stood by my side along the way.

Firstly, to my life-partner, other half, confidant, and best friend, Rahul. You've been my constant through every high and every low; my anchor in the storm and the steady voice reminding me to keep going when the words felt impossible. This story exists because you believed in me from the very beginning, even when I struggled to believe in myself. I will never stop being grateful for that, and for you. You are, and will forever be, my number one.

To my wonderful beta readers—Vilde, Nora, Eliana, Hedda, Anita, and Glenn. You gave my story your time, care, and honesty when it was only a rough draft of what it is now, and I couldn't be more thankful. With fresh eyes, you helped shape and strengthen these pages, and your feedback gave me the courage to carry it all the way through and the belief that this story was worth sharing with the world. I'm endlessly grateful for you all.

Thank you to my editor, Amy at Spineless Pages. Your sharp eye and careful guidance helped polish this manuscript into something much stronger, resonant, and more cohesive. Thank you for treating my words with such care and for helping me convey the heart of this book more clearly. I'm forever thankful to have found you.

To my family—my mum, dad, sister, and brother. You have always supported me with unwavering encouragement. You reminded me that storytelling has always been a part of who I am, and you were integral in giving me the courage to chase what once felt like an impossible dream. I'm so grateful for your love and belief in me.

To my ARC readers—thank you, from the bottom of my heart, for taking a chance on a debut author. You were the first to step into the finalised version of this story, and I'll be forever grateful for the way you read, shared, and championed it, helping me introduce these characters to the wider world. Your support and excitement have meant more to me than I can ever put into words.

And finally, to you, the reader holding this book in your hands: thank you. Thank you for choosing to spend your time in my fictional world, for taking a chance on a debut author, and for walking through Elaina and Orlando's shadows and secrets with me. I poured my heart and soul into this story, and my greatest hope is that it stays with you long after you've turned the final page.

I hope you'll continue with me on this wonderful and exciting journey as more of my stories find their way to the page (as there are plenty waiting impatiently in my head). I truly can't wait to share what comes next with you.

ABOUT THE AUTHOR

Amara Phoenix writes romantic suspense with fast-paced drama, heart-twisting, slow burn romance, and an irresistible dash of danger. She's always been drawn to stories that explore messy emotions, impossible choices, and the kind of love that changes everything.

Scandinavian by birth and Australian by choice, she has spent more than a decade living abroad, lending a traveller's perspective and an explorer's spirit both to her life and her stories. When she's not plotting trouble for her characters, you'll find her with a coffee in one hand, a book in the other, and a cat on her lap—most likely planning her next trip or daydreaming about far-off places while watching Formula One or the NFL.

An adventurer at heart and storyteller by nature, she believes every "what if...?" moment is just the beginning of a new chapter—on the page and in life.

Thank you for reading Where Shadows Whisper!

If you'd like to stay updated on new releases and get exclusive sneak peeks, bonus content, writing updates, behind-the-scenes glimpses, and generally enjoy lots of bookish chatter, you can follow my author journey here:

Instagram → @amaraphoenixauthor
Facebook → @amaraphoenixauthor
Goodreads → @amaraphoenixauthor
Website → www.amaraphoenixauthor.com
Newsletter → www.amaraphoenixauthor.com/newsletter/

Did you enjoy Where Shadows Whisper?

Then leave a review!

As an indie author, your support means everything. Reviews are the lifeblood of indie books and platforms like mine. They not only help spread the word, but they also give other readers the confidence to take a chance on a new author.

I would be endlessly grateful if you could take a moment to leave a review on Goodreads, Amazon and/or your preferred review platform. Even a sentence or two makes a huge difference.

And if you wish to share your thoughts on Instagram, TikTok, or another social media platform—or just share the book with a friend who loves romantic suspense, those ripples of support are priceless too.

Your words matter more than you know, and I'm deeply grateful for every single one.

—Amara Phoenix

www.ingramcontent.com/pod-product-compliance
Lightning Source LLC
Chambersburg PA
CBHW030625310726
48979CB00003B/887

9781764218023